THE
LIGHT
OF
BURNING
SHADOWS

Also by Chris Evans

A Darkness Forged in Fire

THE LIGHT OF BURNING SHADOWS

BOOK TWO OF THE IRON ELVES

Chris Evans

POCKET BOOKS

NEW YORK LONDON TORONTO SYDNEY

 Pocket Books
A Division of Simon & Schuster, Inc.
1230 Avenue of the Americas
New York, NY 10020

First Pocket Books hardcover edition July 2009

POCKET and colophon are registered trademarks of Simon & Schuster, Inc.

For information about special discounts for bulk purchases,
please contact Simon & Schuster Special Sales at
1-866-506-1949 or business@simonandschuster.com.

The Simon & Schuster Speakers Bureau can bring authors to your live event. For more information or to book an event contact the Simon & Schuster Speakers Bureau at 1-866-248-3049 or visit our website at www.simonspeakers.com.

Manufactured in the United States of America

10 9 8 7 6 5 4 3 2 1

Library of Congress Cataloging-in-Publication Data is available.

ISBN 978-1-4165-7053-0
ISBN 978-1-4391-6458-7 (ebook)

For Nat Schoen—

WWII veteran of the North African, Sicilian,

and Italian campaigns,

old New Yorker in the grandest sense,

and my friend.

You are missed.

We are the Dead. Short days ago
We lived, felt dawn, saw sunset glow.

—LT. COL. JOHN MCCRAE, MD, "IN FLANDERS FIELDS"

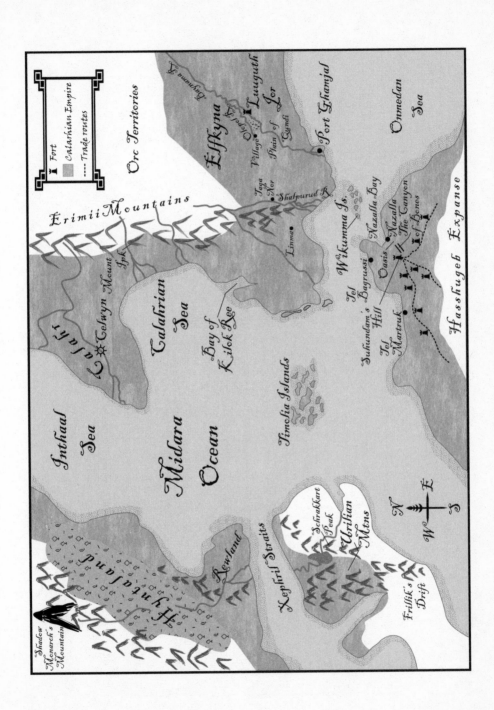

THE
LIGHT
OF
BURNING
SHADOWS

ISSUE NO. 4372

Imperial Weekly Herald

SOLISDAY, 12TH OF SEXTONTH

Is Now Published every MOONDAY, ODDAY, and SOLISDAY morning by

T. R. RAMSHIELD & CO.

79 Unicorn House, Illdar Street, Celwyn

(½ Gold Coin per annum, payable quarterly in advance)

And is distributed throughout
the Empire by the ROYAL DISPATCH CORPS *and*
the NEWS CRIER & COURIER SERVICE *of Daffold & Daffold Co.*

In This, The 47TH *Year and* 239TH *Day of Her Majesty the*

QUEEN'S BLESSED REIGN

over the

CALAHRIAN EMPIRE

A Dispatch Received from the FIELD
written by Her Majesty's Scribe, RALLIE SYNJYN

PORT GHAMJAL, ELFKYNA: The Iron Elves fight again!—Major Konowa Swift Dragon distinguishes himself on the field of battle—Elements of the Imperial Army prove victorious against forces aligned against the Empire—The fabled Red Star of the East returns!—A second Viceroy falls from grace—The Shadow Monarch casts her noxious spell—Forests most foul—Luuguth Jor is saved!—The Iron Elves sail forth in a daring gambit to stamp out evil wherever it builds a lair.

HONOR RESTORED

Through the magnificent exertions of the once more proud and honorable Iron Elves, and under the command of His Majesty, Prince Tykkin, these stalwart warriors wearing the Imperial silver-green met and defeated the most wicked of creatures controlled by the elf witch, the Shadow Monarch, in pitched battle. Most stunning of the many exceptional events that unfolded was the return to this world of the fabled Red Star, known in these parts as the Star of Sillra. In an act of supreme graciousness, Prince Tykkin allowed the Star to remain and grow in Elfkyna as a beacon of strength and purity, thwarting the works of Dark Elements.

MARCH INTO BATTLE

ajor Konowa Swift Dragon—formerly Colonel Konowa Heer Ul-Osveen—(as previously reported) has once again resumed his rightful place as an honored and respected officer in the service of the Empire. Recently restored to active duty, Major Swift Dragon wasted no time in reconstituting the regiment he once led so proudly, the Iron Elves. Though no longer composed of elves, the regiment nonetheless retains the traditions and most importantly, the battle skills of its previous incarnation, and has acquitted itself well in the field. In an act surely to go down in the annals of history, the soldiers of the Iron Elves took a Blood Oath infused with magic of unknown powers to serve their regiment and the Empire unto death and beyond. Never has such an oath been taken, but then never has such a regiment strode forth into danger against such overwhelming odds. What repercussions such an oath carries only time will tell.

INSPIRED ACTIONS

aving received his orders from the Prince, Major Swift Dragon led the brave soldiers of the reformed Iron Elves to the embattled outpost at Luuguth Jor to relieve the 35th Foot Guard. Alas, a forest of black intent had taken root there, the hand behind its design none other than the Shadow Monarch. Finding the garrison lost, the Iron Elves immediately set to the task of restoring order. Though outnumbered, the Iron Elves never faltered though the battle lasted through the day and night. With inhuman strength, creatures of shadow and darkness threw themselves against the Iron Elves' wall of bayonets. Each time Major Swift Dragon was there, his saber (a gift from his friend, Colonel of the 14th Household Cavalry and Officer Commanding Her Majesty's Cavalry in Elfkyna, the Duke of Rakestraw) whistling through the air as the enemy fell before him. Musketry crackled like dropped crystal as the soldiers fired volley after volley until their eyes were red and their throats parched from the smoke. Though they were hard pressed, these brave warriors did not break. Again and again, rakkes—yes, dear readers, the rumors you have heard are true, the great hairy beasts of fang and claw long thought hunted to extinction have returned—flung themselves on the line, but each time they were repulsed. Tales of elfkynans in league with these creatures are patently false! By the end of the battle all peoples of the Empire—elfkynan, human, elf, and dwarf—stood shoulder to shoulder as they fought the Shadow Monarch's forces.

COURAGE ABOUNDS

or his actions at Luuguth Jor, Major Swift Dragon was to be commended and awarded the Silver Sword for Bravery medal by the Queen Herself at the palace in Celwyn, a most deserved acknowledgment of his actions. However, Prince Tykkin, expressing his regrets, has ordered the Iron Elves and other elements of the Imperial Army and Navy to immediately set sail and scour the high seas for any sign of the Shadow Monarch's creatures and destroy any enemy lodgments they find. Sightings of forests of a most dark and unhealthy nature by merchant shipping suggest the Shadow Monarch is making a play for the islands in the Onmedan Sea. This cannot stand, and thus the Iron Elves, so recently bloodied in fierce contest with the enemy, will once again take up the quarrel with the foe and smite it down.

THE FALLEN ARE HONORED

Memorial Service for the 35th Foot Guard to be held in Triumph Park this coming week. The Roll will be read and family members of the deceased may place a rose or other suitable flower on the site of the future monument to be dedicated in their honor.

WANTED FOR HIGH TREASON

By Royal Proclamation be it known that Faltinald Elkhart Gwyn, former Viceroy for the Protectorate of Greater Elfkyna, is hereby stripped of all titles, honors, awards, and other distinctions, and is considered a most vile and contemptible man. His capture, prosecution, and execution is paramount and any persons aiding in his being brought to justice will be eligible for a reward of not less than 100 gold coins. Any persons known to give aid and comfort to this TRAITOR will share his decidedly dark fate.

LOTTERY OF THE STARS

The Royal Mint, in conjunction with the Soldiers' Benevolent

Fund, has launched a lottery open to all citizens of the Empire to wager a guess as to where and when the next Star will fall. The person(s) guessing both date and place correctly will receive ⅓ of the funds collected with the remaining ⅔ going to the care and treatment of wounded soldiers, or, in the case of their death, their families. In addition, the Royal Mint is proud to announce it will begin striking a collectors' series of coins commemorating each Star as it reveals itself.

ONE

There were two of him now, and neither one knew which was sane.

He stood atop the ridgeline running the length of the island and waited for the sun to drown. The ocean darkened. Shadows bled up the windward slope toward him. Bodies pierced by the trunks of obsidian trees became shrouded in the gloom. The smell of putrefying flesh fled as the heat of the day leached from the air. It was as if nothing had happened here. No horrors to relive, no nightmares to endure.

He might have believed that if not for the screams in his head. They echoed in the space between what he was, and what he was becoming.

Here, now, he stood in a world where the sun was setting and a cool ocean breeze was worrying the saw grass behind the dunes of the beach. Only the unhurried slide of waves over sand and the distant shouts and forced laughter of men from the shore party filled the air.

But he also stood here, now, where the screams of the dead

still rasped from blood-red throats. Only yesterday the trees of the Shadow Monarch had flourished in this place, feeding on all they found as Her forest continued to expand across the known world.

Frost fire burned to life in his hands. He did nothing as it arced to the steel and wood of his musket, setting it afire in cold, black flame. He brought a hand close to his face, mesmerized. This was power and curse. The union of the Iron Elves' blood oath with Her magic.

The flames climbed higher and he staggered. There was a price for this. The gulf between his polar selves widened each time he called upon this newfound power. In his mind the outstretched limbs of the Shadow Monarch's forest inched a little closer. He knew it had to stop.

The last rays of the sun vanished into the sea. Dark forms rose from the lengthening shadows, surrounding him.

Dead hands reached out. He recognized the fallen and they did not frighten him:

One-eyed Meri, killed by dog spiders.

Alik and Buuko, struck down by rakkes and the Shadow Monarch's dark elves.

Regimental Sergeant Major Lorian, sitting tall on the horse Zwindarra, both felled in the battle at Luuguth Jor.

And so many others . . .

"Join us."

He eased the hammer back on his musket. A charge and ball already rested inside. He turned the musket so that the muzzle rested firmly over his heart.

Frost fire danced along the metal in anticipation.

It would take but one squeeze of the trigger, but what would he end, and what would begin?

"Join us."

He wanted to believe that all the pain, the fear, the terrifying rage, the nightmares that stalked his sleep . . . all would sink into a cold abyss. The shades of those that had gone before beckoned him, but their voices trembled with a pain he could only guess at. Could it be worse than what he lived with now?

One final act on his part and he would find out.

His finger tightened on the trigger.

"There you are!" Sergeant Yimt Arkhorn said, trudging up the slope. The dwarf's voice boomed like a cannon in the cooling night air. "I wouldn't a thought it possible to lose someone on this wee pebble of an island, but you just about managed it. You don't want to be hanging around this sad lot," he said, casting a hand toward the blackened husks of trees and the dead. If the dwarf saw the shadows, he said nothing.

Private Alwyn Renwar lowered his musket as the frost surged briefly before guttering out. He slowly turned to face the dwarf.

"Five islands in a row," Yimt said, huffing to a stop beside him on top of the ridge. He hoisted his shatterbow up to his shoulder, hooking one of the curved arms over it so that the double-barreled weapon hung down across his broad back. He reached to his side and grabbed his wooden canteen, first offering it to Alwyn, who shook his head.

"Suit yourself, but it helps your eyeballs," he said, referring to Alwyn's need for spectacles. Yimt upended the canteen and gulped several mouthfuls of a liquid most certainly not water as the pungent vapors drifted into the night air. Wiping his mouth with the back of his sleeve, Yimt deftly stuffed a wad of crute, the rock spice the dwarf was forever chewing, between his cheek and metal-colored teeth.

"Five islands of nothing but black misery. I understand the need to weed these foul trees before they really take root, but why's it always us? I'll tell you this, Ally, if his arseness the Prince orders us to one more dust speck in the middle of the ocean, I might just risk the noose and kick the bugger right where his top and bottom halves meet. And with a running start."

A smile, Alwyn thought. *I know I should smile.*

Alwyn took a deep breath and let it out, forcing his shoulders to relax and doing his best to reassure. "I can see you're wasting no time in trying to lose those sergeant's stripes," he said.

Yimt patted his arm and traced a finger around the recently sewn-on stripes on his uniform. "These aren't what make a dwarf, Ally, though I got to admit I'm feeling a bit more protective of them this time round. Someone's got to keep their head."

"You're saying Major Swift Dragon isn't?"

Yimt rolled his eyes. "The major's spittin' musket balls. The Prince is a hairsbreadth from his last breath if he keeps sending us to these cursed islands instead of straight on to the desert wastes of the Hasshugeb Expanse. Now just between you and me, I'm starting to wonder a bit about the major. He's gettin' a bit frantic to find the first Iron Elves. 'Course, I can see his point. Be nice to have some reinforcements with all this going on," he said, again waving a hand around them. "I swear by the dew of a freshly laundered nun the major's going to do the Prince harm."

"Would that be so terrible?" Alwyn said, but the wind picked up just then and Yimt kept talking as if he hadn't heard.

"Our major is a kettle on full fire with half an ounce of water inside. We visit another island and the line of succession to the throne will be shorter by one." Yimt pointed a hand out to sea.

"Not that it'll matter a cauldron of newts if this Shadow Monarch and Stars business keeps up. Like there ain't enough pain and suffering in the world already without someone wanting to take the whole bloody thing over and make it worse. Where's the sense in that?"

Alwyn answered before he could stop himself. "Maybe She doesn't see it that way. Maybe She's in pain none of us can understand, and this is Her way of trying to deal with it. People don't think straight when they are hurting. For Her, the Red Star offered a chance to change things." He didn't add that the Red Star also offered a chance for the blood oath the Iron Elves had taken to be broken, a chance that was lost at Luuguth Jor.

Yimt spat out a stream of crute, which sizzled in the sand. "Odd way of looking at it, Ally, but even if that's true—and I don't buy it—then all the more reason to find the first Iron Elves, get a mess of axes, and go pay a visit to Her little mountain. More Stars are bound to come tumbling down and She's gonna keep trying to get her hands on every one until She's stopped. She's already brought back rakkes, heaven knows what else She'll find."

Alwyn feared and hated the rakkes. They were massive, hideous creatures with fangs and claws and milky white eyes, but what truly made them horrific was that they were brought back from extinction with only killing as their purpose. That the Shadow Monarch might bring back creatures worse than that added a whole new layer to his nightmares.

"But what of the oath we took?" Alwyn asked. "Her magic wove its way into it. We have power unlike anything else. I can do things, Yimt, that I don't want to be able to do. We weren't meant to have this kind of power. And She's behind it. Can't you feel things . . . changing?" The Shadow Monarch was ever present in Alwyn's dreams, forever calling to him. He couldn't hold out forever, none of them could.

"Changing?" Yimt lifted up the hem of his caerna and scratched at his thigh while he pondered the question. "I tried warming a cup of arr the other day between my hands, you know, calling up a bit of the frost fire. All I managed to do was light my beard on fire, and the arr was colder than when I started."

"You're making fun of me," Alwyn said. *Yimt should understand. He took the oath as well.*

"Don't get your caerna in a twist," Yimt said, smiling at him. "I just don't think it's as bad as you make out. Sure, we might be doomed to eternal service in the afterlife, but if we're still serving then we can't exactly be after life, see? I'll tell you this, Ally, having already put in a few decades in Her Majesty's employ . . . traipsing hither and yon about the Empire . . . visiting smelly little villages with nasty little people chucking all kinds of sticks and stones and spells at you . . . I have to say, it ain't that bad. Personally," Yimt said, changing his scratching to his beard, "I can see some up sides."

Alwyn looked out to sea and tried to find the view Yimt saw there.

"C'mon, Ally, we can chaw this over back at camp. Doesn't do a fellow any good to be out alone in a place like this. What were you doing up here anyway?"

Alwyn shook his head. "Nothing. I just came up here for a walk and to get some fresh air. Miss Tekoy says I need to keep in motion to get the stump used to the new leg." Just a month ago a black arrow crafted by a dark art and wielded by an even darker creature had pierced his thigh. In the effort to save his life, Alwyn lost more than his leg that night. "And Miss Red Owl says I need to keep active so that I don't dwell on . . . things. She's teaching me meditation."

Yimt cast an appraising eye at Alwyn's wooden leg. Both Visyna Tekoy and Chayii Red Owl had crafted it from a living tree, magically entwining several slender branches into an intricate and flexible design. Yimt stepped closer and looked up, locking eyes with him. "Aye, couple of witchy women there, they oughta know. Wise to heed them, Ally. They only want what's best for you."

"Yes, I suppose you're right," Alwyn said, trying to believe it. Around him, the shades still waited. The shadow of Meri moved closer, his one eye like a dark portal offering Alwyn a path far away from here, though Alwyn knew Yimt couldn't understand.

"I'm always right," Yimt said, thumping his chest. "In fact, if I was a betting man, I'd say the two of them joined us on our little sailing adventure as much for you as for the major. I figured they'd stay back in Elfkyna with the rest of those Long Watch elves to look over the tree-star thing in Luuguth Jor, but I think you've become a bit of a *project*."

"A project?"

Yimt nodded. "Aye. See, women, no matter their age or race or even how witchy they are, like to work on projects, and by projects I mean men. The more screwed up or in need of repair the man is, the happier womenfolk are. And, Ally, between you and the major, I'd say those ladies have got their hands full for a long time to come."

"You always know just what to say," Alwyn said, not sure if he should be touched or offended by the idea. Where Yimt was concerned it was always a close-run thing.

Shrugging, Alwyn began to turn around to head back down the slope. Yimt reached out and grabbed him by the elbow, stopping him. He gently took the musket from his hands and eased the hammer back into place then handed it back to Alwyn.

"A fellow wants to be careful with a loaded weapon, especially out here."

For a moment, there was only Yimt, his friend, on the ridgeline with Alwyn. He looked into the dwarf's eyes and saw the concern.

"I'll try to remember that," Alwyn said.

Yimt beamed, flashing his metal-colored teeth. "Not to worry, Ally, not to worry. As long as *Sergeant* Arkhorn's around, you'll have me to remember it for you. We've got some serious glory and gallantry ahead of us and I sure as hell ain't about to face it alone. A fellow can only wear so many medals afore folks start to think he's a bit full of himself, y'know? Now get a move on. I got a turtle roasting on the fire . . . at least I think it's a turtle, and you want to eat it while it's still warm."

Alwyn smiled this time, a real smile. "Then get down there and save me a piece. I never miss a chance to try some of your cooking. I try, but unfortunately I never miss."

Yimt raised one bushy eyebrow and wagged a thick finger at him. "Cheeky bugger," he said, turning and heading down the slope. "I'll save you some of the brains; you can never have too many."

Alwyn watched him for a while until the shadows closed in again. Meri came to stand beside him.

"Join us, Alwyn." The others joined in, each urging him on. *"Join us."*

Alwyn gripped his musket, but this time no frost fire danced along it. He started to limp down toward the campfire, the pain in his stump reminding him with each step of what he had already lost, but also of what still remained. The shadows on the ridgeline did not follow, but kept their hands outstretched.

"*Not yet*," Alwyn said back to them, "*not yet*."

TWO

Major Konowa Swift Dragon, second in command of the Calahrian Empire's Iron Elves, stood on the bow of his small boat in the predawn darkness regretting his decision to eat before setting out for Wikumma Island. His stomach roiled. Each surge and wallow of the boat acted like a punch to his gut. Sweat drenched his face and stung his eyes, making it hard to see, though in this darkness it made little difference. Someone, or more specifically, something on the island ahead of them was going to pay for his suffering. He stood up a little straighter and spat into the wind.

"Damn it!"

He wiped off his face and looked over his shoulder. Lanterns wrapped in heavy canvas and hung from iron pikes gave off a feeble orange glow, illuminating the boat and its complement of sailors and Iron Elves. Konowa cursed the need for any light at all, but the men in the boat did not have elven eyes. Looking beyond the boat he could just make out their starting point, Her Majesty's seventy-two-gun ship-of-the-line *Black Spike*. If all went well, they would be back on her decks by nightfall.

Konowa returned his gaze forward. Somewhere ahead of them lay Wikumma Island, the last and southernmost in a chain of seven islands in the Onmedan Sea stretching between Elfkyna and the Hasshugeb Expanse. The six previous islands had been—for lack of a better word—infested with the Shadow Monarch's growing forest. The small populations that had lived on the islands—mostly fishermen and their families—had been slaughtered by Her forest, leaving not a man, woman, or child alive. Each island was a sun-drenched horror, and Konowa grew angrier with every gruesome discovery.

This had to stop. He had to take the fight directly to the Shadow Monarch. For Konowa, that meant finding the original Iron Elves and marching straight to Her mountain. That She wanted the original elves for Her designs as She wanted Konowa made it all the more crucial Konowa find them first. The power he wielded was incredible, and he was the least magical elf that had ever set foot in a forest. Even some of the human soldiers showed a knack for using the frost fire, albeit with haphazard results. While the power of the blood oath bound every soldier in the regiment, its magical properties resided primarily with its only remaining elf, Konowa. Imagining what the Shadow Monarch could do with a highly trained regiment of elves completely under Her control made even Konowa shudder.

The bow of the boat dipped and took a wave over the top, spraying Konowa from head to foot.

"Damn it all to hell!"

"War is no excuse for language like that, my son," Chayii Red

Owl said. "And we are but three bowshots' distance from the island. You really should get down from there."

A snigger, a muffled giggle, even an innocent cough would have launched Konowa at the throat of the unlucky person, but not a one gave any indication that he had heard Konowa being scolded by his mother. There were five boats currently being rowed toward the island, and of course it was Konowa's luck that his vessel had his mother on board.

"Uncork your musket, unwrap the firelock, and prepare to fire," Konowa said from the bow, deliberately ignoring his mother's advice. The soldiers reacted instantly, well versed now in the drill after having stormed six islands before. They knew from experience that things would happen fast.

"Sergeant Arkhorn, ready your cannon." Each boat was equipped with a small six-pounder cannon strapped to the bow with ropes facing forward. It wasn't subtle, but then again neither were rakkes.

"Aye, sir, ready and waiting," the dwarf said, giving the barrel of the cannon a solid slap with the palm of his hand. "The beasties will know what hit 'em, but not for long." Beside him, Private Renwar peered down the length of his musket, his hands rock steady. Konowa had made it known to the sergeant that Renwar need not join them on the island assaults on account of his wooden leg. Surprisingly, Chayii had objected, though she had refused to elaborate. Konowa had also tried to bring the subject up with Visyna, but talking with her was even more frustrating. They agreed on nothing—not the use of the Shadow Monarch's power, not the role the Empire played in the world, and definitely not how to set things right again.

Naturally, Visyna agreed with Chayii about Private Renwar, but the point was moot as Renwar volunteered for every attack. Konowa was happy to have him along. Konowa had thought Renwar too fragile for soldiering, but the private was proving to be a fierce warrior, charging the beach with exceptional bravery and never once holding back despite his significant impairment.

The boat lurched and one set of oars rowed air for a moment. Konowa stumbled and grabbed hold of the cannon before righting himself. It took a greater effort to keep the contents of his stomach. He stood back up, carefully. The crew was struggling to keep the boat on course as the sea grew choppier.

"Go left, man, more left," Konowa said, brandishing his saber. The white-enameled hand guard with gold inlay was a bit showy for his tastes, but it had been a gift from his friend Jaal, the Duke of Rakestraw, and Konowa cherished it. It had taken some doing to get a new three-foot-long blade put on it after the first one had broken at Luuguth Jor, but Sergeant Arkhorn had known a dwarf who knew a blacksmith and Konowa had paid twenty silver coins and asked no questions.

"Left. We need to land on the southern tip," Konowa said.

"You mean larboard, sir," the boat's mate said.

Konowa stared at the man.

"Aye, sir, left it is! All right, boyos, you heard the officer, more left!"

Konowa turned back to face the wind, preferring the bite of the salt-tinged air and stinging spray of the water to the looks of the men he was leading. The mix of fear, anger, loathing, and resentment he saw there filled him with feelings he couldn't afford to indulge in. Chayii, for her part, simply looked sad, which only added to his pain. Something small and furry landed on Konowa's shoulder.

"Enjoying the ride, Father?"

Jurwan Leaf Talker, wizard, counselor to Imperial Army Marshal Ruwl, husband of Chayii Red Owl, and currently unwilling or unable to turn back to elf form, twitched his whiskers and said nothing. Konowa sighed. When he'd bothered to imagine his future, he'd never once allowed for the possibility that one day he'd be leading soldiers ashore to do battle against the Shadow Monarch's dark creatures with his mother and father in tow. That one now sported a very bushy tail and the other was generally disappointed with how he'd turned out did, however, seem like something he should have anticipated.

He wasn't sure which was worse.

"We could use your help, you know," Konowa said.

Jurwan scratched his nose with one small paw and said nothing. In a way, Konowa didn't blame him. Jurwan had risked his life, certainly his sanity, to get the black acorn now resting against Konowa's chest from atop Her mountain. Her dark magic must have done more damage than even a great elf wizard like his father could repair. That thought should have given Konowa pause, but he knew that where his father had failed, he would not. Perhaps, if Jurwan's *ryk faur* Black Spike, the Wolf Oak he shared a magical bond with when a member of the Elves of the Long Watch, were still alive, he would be back to his old self by now.

Konowa patted a hand against his chest and felt the familiar tingle of cold power there. A dark stain now marred Konowa's skin over his heart, but he knew he could undo it when the time was right.

"Were you able to sense anything from the ship?" Konowa asked, keeping his voice low. Jurwan, some years ago, had quietly gifted the . . . body, for lack of a better word, Konowa supposed, of his *ryk faur* to the Queen for use in building one of her ships. The gift had infuriated the elves of the Long Watch and his mother in particular. Not even the naming of the ship after the Wolf Oak could appease the elves, but Konowa doubted that anything less than the dissolution of the Empire would. Fittingly, the Queen had assigned HMS *Black Spike* to her son, Prince Tykkin, and the Iron Elves as they set sail from Elfkyna, perhaps hoping the reunion between elf and *ryk faur* would snap Jurwan out of his current state. Unfortunately, it didn't seem to be working.

A nudge against Konowa's thigh drew his attention downward. He reached out a hand to give Jir a rub between the ears, then thought better of it. For all purpose if not intent, the bengar was a large, furry, black-and-red-striped monster, not that Konowa saw him that way. The predatory beast with a stubby muzzle full of very sharp teeth and a thick mantle of fur running halfway down his back was bigger even than a tiger . . . with an appetite larger still. That they were friends spoke to an understanding between the two that Konowa shared with few others. With that understanding came the realization that Jir was now ready for battle, his demeanor one of quiet intensity.

In that regard he was the perfect mascot for the Iron Elves. Jir's eyes were fixed on the dark smudge on the horizon and his nostrils were flaring. The muscles under his fur rippled back and forth like waves trapped between two cliffs. This was definitely a time when it was best to leave him be.

Konowa returned to watching the beach. Shadows moved in and out among the trees that lined the shore. Konowa focused on the power in the black acorn. That something so small could harbor so much power, and so much danger, was a thought he pushed aside for another time. If he and the regiment were cursed by the oath that had inadvertently bonded them to Her power, then he would bloody well use that power. He let his senses flow outward. It was becoming easier to manipulate the magic. A cold clarity pulsed throughout his body in anticipation of what was to come.

Scores of rakkes roamed the island. Konowa pushed his senses further, his breath misting in the humid air. He shivered in the sudden cold and grimaced. He felt the presence of five of Her elves on the island, those born like him with a black ear tip. In the not-too-distant past, the tribes of the Hyntaland believed that to be born thus was to be forever tainted. Babies were left in the forest to die, but the Shadow Monarch gathered them to Her, and made them Her own. Konowa had been spared that, instead having his left ear tip shorn off in an act of defiance.

In his darkest thoughts Konowa wondered what his life would have been like if he, too, had been abandoned to die, then "saved" by the Shadow Monarch. Would he now be like the elves he was about to kill, a crazed and twisted thing driven by a madness he didn't understand?

The Prince had a standing order for one of the Shadow Monarch's dark elves to be taken alive, but thus far none had been. The elves chose to fight to the death. Konowa's hand strayed to his own scarred ear, then stopped. The mark alone did not determine an elf's fate. Konowa was proof enough of that . . . he hoped.

Konowa came back to himself, but not before pausing. Something else, something he could not identify, was also on the island. It felt ancient. He debated for a moment whether he should search again, then thought better of it as the boats neared the shore.

Whatever it was would soon share the same fate as the rest of Her creatures.

The first mewling cry from a rakke set off a chorus of howls on the island. The horizon turned pink as the night gave way to dawn. Konowa smiled. Black flames sparked to life in his hands.

"Fire!"

Sergeant Arkhorn reached up and slapped Konowa's boot. "You're standing over the cannon again, Major!"

"To hell with that. Fire!"

Whatever Chayii started to shout was lost as Sergeant Arkhorn touched a flaming linstock to the cannon vent. The six-pounder barked, launching a double load of canister shot.

Konowa roared his fury as two hundred musket balls ripped through the coming dawn. His ears rang with the concussion of the blast as his vision temporarily blurred and the unmistakable stench of black powder filled the air. Orange and red flame billowed from the muzzle, lighting up the sea. The small boat reared up then slammed down in the water, sending up a huge spray. Rakkes disintegrated in a thick red-black mist. Muskets crackled to life as hammers struck flint and powder flared. More rakkes fell, their cries defiant as life was once again torn from their lungs.

Farther out to sea a false dawn tore a hole in the darkness as the starboard-side guns of the *Black Spike* fired a broadside at the island. Cannonballs rumbled overhead like boulders crashing down a mountain. Konowa instinctively ducked even though the barrage was a good twenty feet above him.

The shoreline exploded in gouts of flame and smoke as sand, water, rakkes, trees, and everything else was pummeled and flung into the air. Debris thrown up by the barrage began raining down on them and splashing in the water all around their boat. Jurwan leaped from Konowa's shoulder and scampered to the back of the boat, where he jumped onto Chayii and dove into her quiver of arrows.

A dazzling white light burst above the island, elongating shadows to grotesque lengths. Konowa shook his head, opened and closed his mouth to clear the ringing in his ears, and took a quick look to his right. He was unable to see Visyna, but knew she was close by. Her magical skills in weaving the natural order in aid to his men had proven valuable on many occasions. Her light would help them now.

Cannon and musket fire erupted from the other four boats. Shouts rose up and oars bit into sand and came to rest.

The Iron Elves had landed.

THREE

The first black arrows from Her elves whistled from somewhere deeper among the trees. The Iron Elves were ready. Thick oak planks, another item borrowed from the *Black Spike*, swung up to shield the soldiers and crew. Wood and arrows splintered, sending lethal shrapnel everywhere. Men screamed. Two tumbled overboard into the water, their cries abruptly silenced under the waves.

Konowa's anger surged. Her elves had learned a new trick. Well, so had his boys.

"Cannon . . . second volley . . . fire!"

The cannon roared again, but this time Arkhorn had loaded it with chain shot. It was simple in design and lethal in use. Two cannonballs attached by a length of chain flew from the muzzle and began spinning, scything down everything in their path. Originally intended to cut through the masts of enemy ships, chain shot was equally effective at tearing through Her forest, and the creatures in it.

"Remember, we want to try to capture one of the elves!"

Konowa shouted, knowing it was likely futile. And even if they did capture one, Konowa wasn't sure what good it would do. These elves were as dark and twisted as the Shadow Monarch's trees.

Screams of rage and pain among the rakkes lifted high into the sky as the keel of the boat ground to a halt in the sand. Konowa used the momentum to leap ashore, but he was already several paces behind Private Renwar and Jir. Konowa knew his place was with the men, leading them in a methodical march across the island, but all his pent-up rage spilled forth as it had on every island before this. He knew in his heart this was about revenge. The Shadow Monarch had used his father, in a ploy to get to him, and in so doing bound Konowa and the new Iron Elves in an eternal oath. She haunted all their dreams now, calling to them. Konowa felt the pull, but he felt something else more; fury.

Frost fire burned wickedly along the blade of Konowa's saber. He grinned and charged, looking for things to kill.

Sergeant Arkhorn was yelling something about staying out of the line of fire of the cannon, but Konowa was already through the mounds of dead and dying rakkes and among the *sarka har*, the blood trees of the Shadow Monarch. Every anguish Konowa had ever experienced fell before his blade. He slashed the limbs of the trees with so much force that the tendons in his shoulder began to burn with the first few swings. Wherever his blade made contact, the wood burst into cold flame, the black fire consuming them with merciless efficiency.

Konowa smiled, a nervous habit he had in battle, and slashed again. Black, icy flames traced arcs in the air as his saber hacked and burned the *sarka har*. These trees should not exist. The Shadow Monarch's twisted mind was creating nightmarish forests that threatened every living thing. His whole life had been lived under Her tainted magic. Here, now, he could avenge that fate.

"Your power is mine, elf witch!" he roared, cleaving a tree completely in two. "And I will end you with it!"

An arrow passed so close to his cheek that the fletching brushed the skin. Konowa turned to trace the source, but Jir was faster still. The bengar leaped, his massive jaws closing on the throat of the dark elf and bearing it to the ground. Konowa didn't even bother trying to call Jir off. The elf was dead before he hit the ground.

Three rakkes burst through the trees and straight at Konowa. Their milky-white eyes bulged as they charged, drool flying from long, yellow fangs. Konowa pivoted in place to meet them. Another figure came in from Konowa's left side and crashed into the nearest rakke, knocking it off its feet and into the path of the other two.

"Renwar!" Konowa shouted, recognizing the soldier at once. Private Renwar stood above the first rakke, the bayonet of his musket lodged so deeply in the creature's rib cage that he couldn't pull it back out.

The other two rakkes were back on their feet in an instant and both now focused on the private. Six-inch-long claws swung for his head. Konowa lunged forward and brought his saber down two-handed, severing a rakke's arm at the elbow. Frost fire exploded at the wound and raced up its body, sending it whirling away.

The third rakke leaped and took Renwar to the ground. Konowa raised his saber to strike again, but a fist-sized hole suddenly appeared in the rakke's back and frost fire flew out. Konowa kicked the body to the side and reached down a hand to help Renwar up, then took it back in surprise. Black flames, darker and more intense than any Konowa himself had yet conjured, blazed in the young soldier's hands. Konowa tried to read Renwar's face, but the flame reflected in the soldier's spectacles made it appear as if his very eyes were afire.

"Behind you, Major."

The black acorn sent a cold sliver of warning into Konowa's heart as he turned to confront a group of rakkes carrying jagged shards of wood.

"Get your arse in the sand now!" bellowed a voice from the water's edge. Konowa dove forward even as the rakkes moved to within yards of him. One raised a makeshift club and began to swing it down.

A cannon boomed and the world vanished. Smoke and sand whipped over Konowa, partially lifting him off the ground. Sparks stung the back of his hands and neck as the unmistakable sound of heavy metal sawing through the air passed overhead. His nose and ears clogged with sand and something wet. Black and white and orange flashes danced across the inside of his eyelids.

Konowa blinked several times and propped himself up to his elbows. The chain shot had done its job well. What was left of the rakkes lay in a congealing puddle of blood and debris. It looked as if the dwarf was determined to keep his stripes this time.

"Renwar, are you—" Konowa started to ask, but the soldier had already gotten up and was charging off deeper into the trees. Frost fire blazed in the soldier's hands and along the length of his musket. With no time to ponder the matter, Konowa got to his feet and dusted himself off. He flexed his right hand, holding his saber, and found that it still had strength.

"Did you see where Private Renwar went, sir?" Sergeant Arkhorn asked, stepping over the bodies with little concern. He held his shatterbow at the ready, its twin muzzles sweeping the area as he walked.

"I'm fine, Sergeant," Konowa said, making a point of flicking a piece of rakke skull off his uniform.

Arkhorn nodded. "Of course you are, sir. I shouted a warning, didn't I? Have you seen Ally?"

Before Konowa could answer there was a shriek and the sound of a musket firing from up ahead. Konowa sensed frost fire burning and was staggered by the power in it.

"Never mind, sir, I know where he is," Arkhorn said. "All right laddies, we've done this before." He motioned for a section of Iron Elves to form up around him. "Make a wedge and keep your necks on swivels or it won't be Her darlings you have to worry about." Someone groaned.

"Why not let the DDs take care of this? They're dead already and we ain't. Why do we have to keep risking our necks, eh?"

Konowa couldn't see who had asked the question, but it wasn't the first time it had been voiced. It started shortly after the DDs, or Darkly Departed—the shadows of the dead—had first appeared in support of the regiment.

Sergeant Arkhorn put two fingers to his lips and whistled between his metal teeth. It sounded like twenty kettles on the boil. "One more outburst like that and you'll be swimming from here to the Hasshugeb Expanse. You bloody well know the 'Darkly Departed' don't like it when the sun's coming up. They're dead. The night is their domain and all that. Honestly, did your mum never read you any fairy tales? We're on our own. Stay smart, well, as smart as you lot can, and we'll come out of this just fine. Stay spread out and don't do anything stupid. I don't want you grouped together and making any easy target," Sergeant Arkhorn said, looking around at the soldiers and waiting until each one nodded.

"Oh, and ten gold pieces from the Prince himself for any man who captures an elf, present company excepted," he finished, touching his hand to his shako in salute.

Konowa returned it, unable to entirely hide a smile.

"By the left . . . move your arses!" The soldiers followed Arkhorn, the bayonets on the end of some of their muskets wreathed in black flame.

Konowa recognized a couple of them as they marched past, including the towering form of Private Hrem Vulhber. Konowa nodded, but the soldier only stared at him for a moment before carrying on. It was insubordination, but Konowa was letting a lot of things go these days. The sooner they were done with this island, the sooner they could finally land in the Hasshugeb Expanse and join up with the original Iron Elves. Then the Shadow Monarch would truly reap the whirlwind She had created.

FOUR

He's done it again!" Visyna shouted as the boat she was in ground to a halt on the beach. She stood near the bow weaving a pattern from the natural energy around her, creating the artificial dawn that now hung above them. Arrows zipped past her head, but a power curved their path around her. "He promised he wouldn't go charging ahead like that."

"You mean Private Renwar?" Rallie said, looking up from the sheaf of papers she was sketching on with a feather quill. The drawing of Visyna standing in the bow pulsated on the paper. Dark and light ebbed and flowed across the page as energy coursed around them.

Visyna waited for all the soldiers to jump out of the boat before she answered. "You know who I mean, Rallie."

"He's fighting demons we can't see," Rallie said, flourishing her quill as a rakke burst through the line of Iron Elves and charged the boat. The beast saw the two women alone and howled, its maw opening wider in anticipation.

"Rallie, hurry," Visyna said.

"I see it," Rallie said, her quill flying across the page. The rakke leaned forward and began loping toward the boat on all fours. Sand sprayed high into the air as its claws dug into the beach. Muskets fired, but the beast continued to close.

A wave sloshed around the boat, sending spray over its sides. Water splashed onto Rallie's page, which sent sparks of energy shooting into the sky. The air around them sizzled and crackled. Visyna continued to weave the light that gave the Iron Elves their advantage, while looking down at Rallie. The page was a mess. Rallie looked over the edge of the boat with obvious annoyance.

The rakke was almost to the bow.

"Rallie!"

Rallie set the sheaf of papers down and picked up an oar. As soon as she touched it, the wood hummed with energy. The rakke leaped, its claws fully extended as it flew toward Visyna. She closed her eyes and kept weaving.

There was a loud crack of wood splintering. The boat shook and the air smelled of burnt flesh. The howling of the rakke ended abruptly, followed by a splash. Visyna opened her eyes. Rallie stood beside her, a broken oar in her hands. Smoke wafted lazily from the wood and sparks still crackled along its length. The body of the rakke floated facedown in the water beside them, its chest impaled by the other half of the oar.

"Keep weaving, my dear—the sun isn't up just yet," Rallie said, casually putting the oar down and going back to her seat. She picked up her sheaf of papers and, wiping off the top page with the sleeve of her cloak, began to sketch again.

Visyna refocused her efforts on her weaving, pulling together more skeins of energy and infusing the light above the island with more power. Silver filigrees danced between her fingertips. She took another quick glance down at Rallie's sketching and saw that once again the boat and herself were there, the lines flowing and strong. Rallie, however, had chosen not to put herself in the drawing. Where she sat, the lines of energy curved around that space as if unable, or unwilling, to acknowledge what was there.

The sky grew lighter and fire, real fire, blazed in several locations from the sparks of musket and cannon shot. Konowa walked a short distance to stand on a jumble of rocks and look back down at the beach. Several soldiers milled about as more appeared, carrying the wounded. A makeshift first-aid station had been set up right on the beach and Konowa knew Visyna, Rallie, and his mother would be there now tending to the wounded. Farther up the beach were the still figures of several soldiers.

Konowa let his gaze drift out to sea where the *Black Spike* had dropped anchor, another full broadside ready and waiting. There were certain advantages to having the son of the Queen in command of the Iron Elves.

The ship named for his father's Wolf Oak was a towering three-masted, seventy-two-gun ship-of-the-line, one of Her Majesty's main means of projecting power around her far-flung empire. Five years ago, just the sight of her dropping anchor in the Bay of Kilok Ree had been enough to quell the rebellion there of some disgruntled natives protesting the exporting of priceless religious and magical artifacts to Celwyn, the Calahrian capital. Konowa could understand their reactions, both the rebellion and the sudden change of mind when the *Black Spike* appeared. The ship was for all intents and purposes a floating gun platform, carrying twenty of the massive sixty-eight-pounder carronades, another forty thirty-six-pounder long-range cannon, and twelve lesser guns, although six were currently strapped to the bows of her away boats. It was a pity there wasn't a way to get the *Black Spike* up the side of the Shadow Monarch's mountain. Along with the Iron Elves, the *Black Spike* could end this war, or whatever it was, in about three broadsides.

Konowa flexed his knee and followed after his men. The island was all but theirs. Everywhere he looked, rakkes lay dead on the ground and *sarka har* burned with frost fire. Now, finally, they could set sail for the Hasshugeb Expanse. Content, Konowa reached up a hand and patted the black acorn underneath his uniform tunic.

A white-hot needle of pain stabbed his heart and seared his hand.

He gasped and stumbled backward, falling to one knee. This was nothing he'd experienced before. He raised his saber in defense against the expected blow, but none fell.

He looked up. There was nothing around him. Sweat was beading on his forehead and his blood felt as if it was boiling inside his skin. The cold that normally infused him when using Her power was now replaced by a heat that took his breath away. Musket fire barked to life up ahead. Men shouted and someone started screaming and didn't stop.

Konowa forced himself to his feet and started forward. The pain was receding and he broke into a run. When he reached the soldiers on the other side of the island, his mind couldn't make sense of what he saw. Private Harkon staggered about on the beach surrounded by other soldiers.

His shadow was on fire.

White-hot flames roared wherever his shadow fell on the sand and Harkon screamed as if he himself was the one burning.

"Run into the water! Private, throw yourself in the ocean!" Konowa shouted.

Harkon looked toward Konowa, his eyes shining with madness. Harkon began tearing off his uniform. Konowa realized he would have to take matters into his own hands and charged forward.

Private Vulhber got there a step before him and roughly picked up the stricken soldier and began running for the water. As soon as he did, his own shadow caught fire. He cried out, but held on and kept running, plunging them both into the waves. Steam boiled into the air, but the flames did not go out.

Konowa reached them, but was lost as to what to do now. He spun around looking for Visyna or his mother or even Rallie, but none were in sight.

"We're still burning," Vulhber said, his voice trembling with the effort to keep calm. Blood frothed at Harkon's lips as his screams continued.

"Major, what do we do?" a soldier asked.

Konowa felt as lost and powerless as he had when his regiment had been disbanded. Now that he had command again he wasn't going to lose his regiment a second time, especially not to something he couldn't even understand.

"You!" he shouted, pointing to a soldier. "Run to the beach and get the women. Now!" The soldier sprinted off, his shako tumbling in the sand as he ran.

"Major."

Konowa turned. Sergeant Arkhorn had come up to stand beside him. He had cocked the hammers on his shatterbow. They traded a look and Konowa nodded. Arkhorn raised his weapon and aimed at the two men in the water.

"Wait," Private Renwar said, limping into the water and blocking the shot. He strode forward until his own shadow merged with theirs. It too ignited and white tongues of fire sizzled along the water's surface where his shadow lay. Renwar then closed his eyes and plunged his hands into the fire. A jolt of crystal ice from the black acorn against Konowa's chest knocked him down again. Several soldiers staggered at the same time. The white flame guttered and was overcome by the frost fire, which then hissed out.

"Help them out of there," Sergeant Arkhorn said, as Konowa climbed back to his feet. Vulhber and Renwar came out more or less on their own, but Harkon wasn't moving and had to be carried. They laid him out on the sand, then quickly stood up and backed away. It looked for the all the world as if Private Harkon was sleeping.

"He's dead," Alwyn said.

Konowa started to look away, then stopped. In the brightening dawn it looked as if the soldier no longer had a shadow at all. He cursed the tricks his eyes played on him and returned his focus to what was real.

"What new abomination is this?" a soldier asked. Konowa turned to see who it was.

"Don't you dare start up with that Creator-savior rubbish again, Inkermon," Yimt said, pointing his still-cocked shatterbow in the soldier's direction. "This isn't the place."

Inkermon held his ground. "Don't you see? It's a test, a means of measuring the man to determine the righteousness of his soul. The Stars are returning, calling up evil long banished to the depths, and we are ensnared in a dark web, tempted by a seductive power. We have sinned and must repent. Repent now and save yourselves."

"It went into the water just as we got here," Renwar said, shaking off helping hands and coming to stand in front of Konowa. Inkermon looked as if he had more to say, but Yimt's shatterbow was aimed squarely at his midsection. "Harkon was the first one here and that's when his shadow caught fire."

"What went into the water?"

Renwar shook his head. "I didn't get a good look, but it was big. I think it had been burrowed in the sand and was forced to leave when we got here." He pointed to a spot a few yards away.

Konowa was amazed he'd missed it. A large furrow perhaps six yards long and over a yard wide was indeed dug into the sand. Tracks of some kind appeared to lead away from it to the water, but the sand was so disturbed he couldn't be sure. Was this what he had sensed earlier? Konowa was about to turn away when he noticed other holes in the ground. These were smaller and ragged around the edges, and piles of ash lay at their bottoms. *Sarka har* had been burned here, but not by the Iron Elves. These appeared to have been destroyed days ago. He reached out a hand and touched the ash. It was the same temperature as the surrounding sand. A recently burned *sarka har* would still be ice cold.

"Seeing ghosts again, Renwar?" another soldier asked, drawing Konowa's attention back. The man had a weasely face and stood a bit apart from the rest of the group.

"Zwitty," Konowa said, the distaste clear in his voice. Zwitty's desire for distance now made sense—Konowa still remembered the craven indifference with which Zwitty had killed an Elfkynan warrior at Luuguth Jor.

Zwitty jumped to attention. "Yes, sir. Just commentin' on the fact that young Renwar there has a habit o' seeing things the rest of us don't."

"That's a load of shite and you know it," Arkhorn said. "Ally ain't seen nothing the rest of us haven't. He just happens to see 'em a little sooner than the rest of us. Kind of odd when you consider the lad's got the vision of a gopher, but if he says something crawled into the water, then I for one got no plans for going swimming later."

To a man, the soldiers shuffled a few more feet away from the water's edge. Konowa had instituted a tradition of allowing the Iron Elves a brief bit of relaxation after assaulting each island, including a swim and a celebratory cookout on the beach. Tradition was going to be broken tonight.

"I sensed five of Her elves on the island," Konowa said, pointedly changing the subject.

"And I counted five of them gone right back to Her," Arkhorn replied. "Those gold pieces of the Prince's are going to get stale before we ever find one of them buggers to have a talk with."

A headache named the Prince of Calahr blossomed behind Konowa's eyes. He would have to explain again, for the umpteenth time, why the Iron Elves had not managed to capture one of Her elves alive. So be it. They'd find enough of them on Her mountain once they got there and the Prince could talk to his heart's content, or until he was torn limb from limb.

Either would suit Konowa just fine.

"Clear the area and head back to the boats. We're leaving now. Bring the private's body," Konowa said, though he knew the soldiers knew the drill. His men just stood there, the shock of what they had just seen overriding everything else.

"Kester, Major," Private Renwar said. "His name was Kester Harkon."

Konowa held his tongue. What, did they think he didn't care?

A voice pitched so that it felt like needles in Konowa's ears cut through the silence.

"But begging the major's pardon, what was that? What burned them like that?" Zwitty asked.

Konowa looked around at the faces of his men. How could they despise him more? "I don't know. Whatever it was is gone, and so are we. Sergeant, get the men moving. Now."

As Arkhorn barked orders, Konowa walked closer to the place that Renwar had seen . . . something. Questions piled on top of questions.

Konowa stared a moment longer at the sand, but no answers came, only a growing sense of foreboding. He turned and began following the men back to the boats.

Out at sea, a dark shape slid quietly just underneath the surface. Silently, and without a single ripple, it lifted its head just high enough above the water to watch Konowa's retreating back. The creature never blinked as it slid back beneath the waves and was gone.

FIVE

I f life had ever been easy for Konowa, he couldn't remember it. Not during his childhood, not when he commanded the first Iron Elves, and not now when he served at the pleasure of the Prince. In fact, things had taken a decidedly downward trajectory for him since, well, always. Just how far down they could go remained to be seen.

He paused in his self-pity long enough to lean over the railing of the *Black Spike* and vomit.

Then there was this. Konowa stared at the green waves below and wondered what it would take to drain the bloody ocean and be done with it. His stomach heaved and he vomited again. For all its power and grace and family history, the *Black Spike* was still a ship, and ships had the single most unfortunate attribute of having been designed to sail on water. As much as Konowa detested traveling by horseback, riding the waves was worse. After all, you could always shoot a horse.

The ship dipped into a trough between waves, then surged upward, leaving Konowa's stomach and the last of his dinner twenty

feet below. An elf, he told himself—this elf at any rate—was designed to have his feet firmly planted on the ground. Konowa was
not—and experience had confirmed this many times over the
years—meant to be in a saddle, up a tree, or on the water. Whenever he was, the end result usually found him flat on his back on the
ground. The problem with being at sea, however, was that the
ground was a hell of a long way below the waterline.

Sailcloth snapped and rigging thrummed above his head. He
glanced up. What had been a breeze the last few days was now
turning into a steady wind. Billowing clouds on the horizon threatened a coming storm. Captain Milceal Ervod had assured Konowa
they would make safe harbor in two days at Nazalla, one of only
three cities of any size along the shoreline of the Hasshugeb Expanse, before the storm came upon them.

It couldn't come soon enough. Assaulting the seven islands
had been a bloody and costly affair. Each attack served to satiate
his blood lust, but he would have forgone even that for a quicker
passage to the deserts. Despite the number of Her creatures he had
dispatched by his hand, his anger and his frustration had only
grown. For all Konowa knew, even now Her forests were growing
again in the blood-soaked sand. The falling Star in the east had
unleashed dormant powers across the world, although Konowa was
convinced the Shadow Monarch's hand was also involved. Since
then, rumors of other Stars had rippled through the Empire and
beyond, but no sightings had yet been confirmed. In a way, Konowa
wasn't sure it mattered. The damage was done. Stars or no, the very
idea of change sped through the air. Call it unrest, call it the urge
to be free, call it fear of the unknown—the world would never be
the same again.

The Shadow Monarch haunted his sleep, though he no longer

believed they were simply dreams. Things had been set in motion that were bigger than any of them. Yes, change was coming. Knowing what he did of the world, Konowa found some small comfort in that thought . . . and a hell of a lot of trepidation.

"Sergeant Arkhorn reporting, sir!"

Konowa turned to rest his back against the railing. The dwarf stood to attention, his caerna flapping dangerously high in the wind.

"At ease, Sergeant, for all that's good and proper, at ease, and secure that hem."

"Right you are, sir," Yimt said, draping his ever-present shatterbow across his front. The back of his caerna continued to wave in the wind.

It took a moment for Konowa to realize what the dwarf had said. "Reporting, Sergeant? I don't recall asking you to report."

"Ah, no, not exactly, Major, but I reckoned you would soon enough so I anticipated your command. Sir. Besides, I can't stay too long down in the hold of a ship. Makes me feel what my great-grandparents must have gone through."

Konowa suddenly felt less sorry for himself. "So they were—"

"Slaves," Yimt said. If there was resentment in his voice he hid it well. "Last group shipped over before the royal decree abolishing slavery. Took another fifty years, mind you, before dwarves were granted the rights of full citizens, but as me mum always said, 'It's a long journey for people with short legs.' "

Konowa found himself wanting to meet the mother dwarf who had raised Sergeant Yimt Arkhorn. There were so many questions he wanted to ask her.

Yimt cast a look down at his feet before returning it to

Konowa. "I heard stories growing up, all dwarves do, about the conditions in the ships' holds. Do you know the ship owners actually threw rocks and dirt down there to make the dwarves feel more at home?"

"I didn't know that," Konowa said. "I would have thought that might have helped a little."

The dwarf's knuckles turned white as he gripped his shatterbow. "They threw the rocks in after the dwarves were already chained inside. Whoever survived and dug their way out was strong enough to work. The rest would be carted out later by the survivors."

Not for the first time Konowa questioned his service to the Empire. "I always thought my people had it the worst when the Empire brought its idea of civilization to our shores. They came primarily for the oak, looking to build more ships like this one," Konowa said, patting the railing. His rejection long ago by the Wolf Oaks in the birthing meadow still stung. *Bloody magical trees had judged him and found him unworthy of sharing their power with him.* Still, looking around a ship of this size, he found himself sympathizing, a little, with the elves of the Long Watch. "A lot of Wolf Oaks were lost in their prime. Many bonded elves took their own lives. I lost an aunt and two cousins. It was indeed a dark time."

The color in Yimt's knuckles returned. "We all had it the worst. If you aren't part of the Empire, you're probably about to be, and joining don't come easy."

Yimt took a hand off his shatterbow and began tugging at his beard, a sign Konowa knew to mean a deep and possibly deeply disturbing thought was about to be shared.

"Something on your mind, Sergeant?"

"As it happens, Major, there is. We cleared seven islands filled with all manner of terrors. We lost a few of the boys along the way, though I suppose they ain't all the way lost, but it amounts to the same thing. And now we're headed to the Hasshugeb Expanse, a land that'll cook your eyes right in their sockets, and that's just at midmorning."

"You've been there?" Konowa asked.

Yimt shrugged his shoulders. "Made port in Nazalla twenty some years ago. Never made it past the local entertainment establishments, though. Found myself in a slight disagreement with a fellow dealing cards off the bottom of the deck. One thing led to another and somehow most of his nose wound up on the floor. They've got some right nasty diseases in them parts, I told my commanding officer at the time."

"Your point, Sergeant?" Konowa said. The dwarf could peel paint from a wall just by talking to it.

"My point is, some of the men now say we have two princes leading the regiment."

Konowa stood bolt upright. "Who's saying that?"

Yimt smiled. "Ah, you see, that's exactly the sort of thing the Prince would say, now isn't it? The men are concerned, Major. A Star from myths and bedtime stories turns out to be real. So does the Shadow Monarch. Extinct monsters aren't and the lads think they're doomed to never really die. But that ain't what's really bothering them."

Konowa knew the surprise showed on his face. "It isn't? What's worse than all of that?"

"You," Yimt said, looking Konowa straight in the eyes. "They need to trust in you. They need to believe that no matter what kind of hell is out there, their commanding officer will do everything he can to bring them home."

"The Prince is—"

Yimt interrupted Konowa. "The Prince spends most of his time in his quarters with his maps and books. The lads even have a pool going on what we're really doing going to the Hasshugeb Expanse. Three to one says we're chasing another Star. Four to one has it we're going after other assorted treasure for the Prince."

"I thought you would understand," Konowa said. "When we find the first Iron Elves, we'll be whole. They're the key. We have to find them before She does. With them we'll be able to take the fight directly to the Shadow Monarch and finish this."

The dwarf didn't back off. "And just how, exactly, with all due respect, Major, is that supposed to happen? Near as I can tell, it's *us* who are bound by the oath, not them. It's *our* boys that are starting to go a bit funny in the head. Why should *your* elves want to join up for this? If Kritton, that miserable excuse for a soldier, was anything to go by, some of those lads might not be too happy to see you."

Konowa turned his face to the wind and let the salt spray sting him. The pain brought him some small measure of relief. In choosing to destroy Her forest at Luuguth Jor, Konowa had given up a chance, perhaps his only chance, to break the oath that doomed all soldiers in the Iron Elves to eternal service, and perhaps something worse. By using the Shadow Monarch's power so cunningly given to him through his father, Konowa had unwittingly done Her bidding. With every passing day, the treacherous pull She exerted grew, though whether that was Her doing or something dark and twisted within Konowa himself he did not know.

Konowa was the only one who truly saw things as they were. There was solace to be found in the fact that the soldiers currently bound by the oath were not the original Iron Elves, and Konowa clung to that thought. Even if he couldn't explain it to Arkhorn, Konowa knew finding them would mean salvation for both. He would find his original elves and return their honor to them. Combined with the soldiers he now commanded, they would overcome any foe the Shadow Monarch sent. And when Her creatures were defeated, Konowa would lead them to the very heart of Her mountain forest and break the oath for all time, setting them all free.

"We both know," Konowa said, "I can order these men to do whatever it takes, but I hope with your help they'll follow me because they know I'm right, and because they trust me."

"Well, as my dear ol' mum is wont to say, 'In for a tail, in for a dragon.' I can keep the lads focused, for now. A little rest stop in Nazalla certainly wouldn't go amiss either. After a few weeks floating around out here with only horror islands and nightmares about trees to keep them busy, they're starting to lose the polish off the old crystal ball." Yimt took a step closer to Konowa and lowered his voice an octave. "But, Major, when we do go for our stroll in the desert, I hope for all our sakes those elves of yours are there waiting."

Yimt stepped back and sniffed the air. "You know, I think I've breathed enough salt out here to never need it again at the dinner table." He stood to attention and saluted. "Evening, Major."

"Sergeant," Konowa said, watching the dwarf walk away.

Konowa turned back to watch the sea. The wind threatened to lift his shako off his head and he reached up and took it off, letting his black hair blow wild in the coming storm. A steely glint flickered in his eyes and a trace of frost fire sparkled in his hands. Soon, he would be reunited with the original Iron Elves. And with them, the regiment would be unstoppable.

Konowa held on to that thought as he heaved his guts over the side, cursing every drop of water in the ocean as he did. It almost made him long to be back in the forest.

Almost.

SIX

A ship-of-the-line on the high seas is a marvelously graceful and robust creature. Ribs of oak fully twice as thick as a man's chest, miles of rope tendons, acres of canvas muscle, teeth of brass and iron able to tear apart anything that came within their grasp, and skin of pine, copper, and tar make it the single largest collection of manmade parts ever assembled.

A ship-of-the-line is, however, an equally delicate collection of parts that is forever perched perilously in the water on a thin keel, like a walker on a rope stretched taut across a cliff. Balance is everything. Should it tip too far to either side, it would begin a downward fall into the deep abyss.

Alwyn preferred the open water. The knowledge that his life hung on the slender threads of the craftsmanship of the shipwrights, the vagaries of the weather, and the skill of the *Black Spike*'s crew filled him, perversely, with a sense of calm. Everything changed when he set foot on shore. On land his anguish was boundless, as if it grew from the very depths of the earth and flowed through him.

Out here, however, he found a certain peace, although the nightmares of Her remained.

He could almost convince himself there was still a chance things could return to the way they were before.

Someone coughed and Alwyn looked up from cleaning his musket, setting aside the rag coated in brick dust he'd been using to buff the metal to a bright sheen. The black flames of the frost fire burned away blood and other fleshy bits—a neat trick all the soldiers had quickly put to use—but rust in the salty sea air bloomed orange and red every night on any bare metal left exposed. In the army, there was always something a corporal or sergeant would give you grief about.

The surviving members of Yimt's section were grouped around one of the ship's sixty-eight-pounder carronades on the upper gun deck. It seemed appropriate to Alwyn that Sergeant Arkhorn would secure them a spot on the ship near a weapon characterized by its short, powerful, and temperamental nature. Firing a sixty-eight-pound cannon ball at a low muzzle velocity meant the projectile didn't fly all that far, but it hit with a vengeance. The slower speed resulted in the shot splintering any wood it struck instead of punching a hole straight through. The result was absolute havoc as a shower of deadly splinters sprayed forth from the impact. Unsurprisingly, the carronade had earned the nickname Smasher. No, Alwyn was not surprised at all that Yimt had chosen this as their home on the sea.

Most of the Iron Elves were quartered deeper in the ship, and it occurred to Alwyn that he rarely saw Yimt go down there. He was rarely here on the upper gun deck either, preferring instead to stay topside. Perhaps the dwarf enjoyed the waves and the wind.

Scolfelton Erinmoss, son of the Earl of Boryn, lay sleeping beside the gun, his mouth open, with drool hanging from his bottom lip. Despite his upper-class pedigree, he was simply known as Scolly. An apple-sized divot in the back of his head caused by a childhood injury had rendered him imbecilic and prone to angry outbursts. It had not, however, if the rumors were to be believed, made him ineligible to be the next Earl of Boryn.

Inkermon sat on a wooden crate, writing a never-ending letter, having gone to eleven pieces of parchment, both sides. To whom it was addressed remained a closely guarded secret and of some interest to the other soldiers. He looked up, sniffed and shook his head, and went back to his writing, mumbling about how they were all going to burn.

Beside Inkermon, Hrem Vulhber, a welcome addition to the group, reclined his massive bulk against an equally massive oak timber. He was reading an old copy of the *Imperial Weekly Herald*, his lips moving as he did so. Less welcome was the soldier leaning against the carronade and riffling through a small leather pouch. Zwitty laughed as he pulled out a small chunk of gold and put it in a hidden pocket inside his upturned shako. Alwyn thought the piece looked very much like a tooth, but said nothing.

"Out plundering again, Zwitty?" Teeter asked, pointing his unlit pipe at him. The ex-sailor with a limp that threatened to topple him over with each step had strung up a hammock from the low ceiling and was gently swaying with the motion of the ship.

"To the victors go the spoils," Zwitty said, quickly putting the leather pouch away and tucking his shako under his arm. "There's been loot on every island if you've got half a brain to look for it."

"You mean dead natives," Hrem said, looking up from his reading.

Zwitty made a long face. "That's right. They's dead, ain't they? Finders keepers, I always says."

"Robbing from the dead is one thing," Hrem said, "but these poor souls we find out here are cursed. You take from them, you take the curse."

A large vein began to throb noticeably on Zwitty's forehead. "Cursed? You want to talk about curses! We're the unlucky bastards that got cursed. The way I see it, we're owed. We're owed more than our wages and more than some stinkin' ten gold pieces the Prince is offering for finding one of them dirty black elves alive."

"Steady on, Zwitty, you're getting yourself all worked up," Teeter said. "This ain't half bad, what we got here. Grog and wine for your drink, two hot meals a day, and a hammock to keep your bones off the floor."

Zwitty spat onto the deck. "If it's so grand, why are you in the army then, and not still in your precious navy, eh?"

Alwyn found his fist clenching and made a point to fold the cleaning rag up instead.

Teeter's cheeks flushed. "I missed my ship when she set sail for the Battle of the Inthaal Sea, and they nailed me for doin' a runner. Said I was lacking in moral fiber in the face of the enemy when all I was was drunk and sleeping it off. The lads shoulda come get me before they shipped out, but the bastards didn't."

Zwitty grinned. Alwyn found himself folding the rag so tight he was creating a small red dust cloud in his hands.

"So you're not a coward then, just a drunk? Hardly seems better. Not that it matters anyway, because you're as doomed as the rest of us." He looked around at them. "Don't you get it, our holy roller there's got it right," he said, pointing to Inkermon, who began to write even faster. "We've been press-ganged into something none of us signed up for. You know what they say about curses, though . . ." Zwitty said, letting the thought hang in the air.

Alwyn actually didn't know what they said and was about to ask, but Teeter sat up straight in his hammock and pointed his pipe at Zwitty.

"You just stow that kind of talk right now."

Zwitty sneered. "I'm not saying nothing, but if a certain someone were to lose their head, I'd wager we'd be free of this curse before his pointy ear hit the—"

A large, meaty hand belonging to Private Hrem Vulhber shot across the top of the carronade and grabbed Zwitty by the collar. "When's the last time you went topside for a nice long walk? Personally, I think you're overdue."

Zwitty's face began turning purple. He dropped his shako to the deck, spilling the contents while both hands clawed at Hrem's, trying to pry himself loose. Finally, Hrem released him and Zwitty stumbled backward, drawing in great gasping breaths. "I could have you up on charges for that. There are witnesses."

Alwyn looked at the other soldiers lounging about the carronade.

"No one saw anything, Zwitty," Alwyn said, reaching down to pick up Zwitty's shako. Zwitty grabbed it out of his hand and quickly stuffed his fallen loot back inside.

"You're all fools. We can end this curse, but none of you has the guts to do it."

"Guts to do what?"

Alwyn looked up as Yimt appeared from behind another carronade and strolled up to stand beside Zwitty. Despite his significantly shorter stature, the dwarf simply exuded confidence that made him appear like a giant.

"Zwitty here was just telling us how he's going to try walking along the railing up top," Hrem said. "Says he can make it all the way round the ship without falling over. Wants us to try it with him, but we're all rather comfy here at the moment, so he's off to try it alone. Ain't that right, Zwitty?"

Zwitty glared at Hrem, but only nodded.

"Well, aren't you the daring fellow," Yimt said, patting Zwitty firmly on the arm and propelling him away from the group. "Off you go then, and watch when you get near the bow. The major's been revisiting his last couple of meals up there and the wood's a bit slick."

Zwitty muttered something none of them could hear and quickly strode away. It wasn't until Zwitty had disappeared from sight that Alwyn realized he had been holding his breath and let it out slowly.

"Now then, what are you reprobates up to?" Yimt asked, leaning against the swell of the carronade's muzzle and rubbing his back against the iron.

"Oh, discussing the whys and whats of life and love," Hrem said, flexing his hand as he got comfortable again against the oak rib. "Out getting some fresh air again, were you? If I didn't know better, I'd say you didn't like it down here."

Yimt stiffened, then smiled and laughed. "What's not to like? It smells like a dead sheep around here."

Alwyn took a cautious sniff, then immediately regretted his decision. They really did smell like dead sheep. Very old, very wet, and very dead sheep.

"Tain't our fault," Teeter offered from his hammock. "The soap they give us is made of mutton fat."

"You've used it then?" Yimt asked.

Teeter waved his unlit pipe in the affirmative. "In a manner of speaking. I traded it to one of the sailors for some chewing tobacco. Can't smoke down here, more's the pity."

"Oh, you're a clever bunch, you lot," Yimt said, bowing his head as if in great sorrow. "It's a wonder the Empire's lasted as long as it has if this is the caliber of siggers there are to defend it."

"You could always jump ship and swim for it," Hrem said. "Of course, with those metal teeth of yours, I imagine you'd go right to the bottom."

"I'll have you know I'm a first-rate swimmer. The mines fill up with water more than you'd think. If a dwarf can't swim and hold his breath, he ain't got much of a future. And speaking of futures," Yimt said, catching Alwyn's eye and giving him a wink, "yours might be shorter than you think in this elite gathering if you don't mind your manners. It's by my good graces alone that you were allowed to join such esteemed company," Yimt said, pushing himself away from the carronade to walk over and sit on a large coil of rope. "Of course, *Private* Vulhber, I could assign you to the Color Party. They're always looking for big lads that can stop a musket ball."

Hrem made a show of pondering this, though everyone knew the answer. Being a member of the Color Party was a great honor, right up until it stopped being one when you were dead. The enemy always tried to capture the Colors, making the guarding of them crucial in every battle. It also meant you were a prime target. Alwyn himself had volunteered for the Color Party three times now, but Yimt had denied his request.

"No one here's looking to be a hero," Hrem said, "well, 'cept maybe Ally there. You keep charging ahead of us like that and you're bound to come to a sticky end."

Alwyn smiled and tried to wave it off. "I just get my blood up, you know? I'm not trying to be anything."

"You'll be a Darkly Departed is what you'll be if you don't watch it," Teeter added. "You don't want to be joining our dead like Meri and the rest of those poor souls."

"I can take care of myself," Alwyn said. He could feel the color coming to his cheeks. This was nothing he wanted to talk about.

"Now, now, leave the lad alone. He's young, he's foolish, and he's got a magical tree for a leg," Yimt said. "I think it's just a matter of the wood wanting to get ashore so it can plant itself and start sprouting some leaves."

Laughter echoed off the timbers and Alwyn found himself chuckling.

"You mock his plight," Inkermon said, setting down his parchment and pointing his quill at Yimt.

"He's just kidding," Alwyn said. "There's still hope."

"Hope? You mock that, too," Inkermon said. "You all mock this . . . this *abomination* that has befallen us. Do you not see? Our curse grows with every passing day. The foul temptress haunts our dreams even as She calls forth creatures long dead, and now the very earth we walk attacks us, burning our very souls alive."

There was only the sound of the wind and the creaking of wood. Inkermon had touched on something none of them wanted to talk about. Alwyn and Hrem looked at each other, then quickly looked away. Feeling his shadow burn had been pain beyond his experience, but there had been something else as well. For a moment, before he extinguished the white fire, Alwyn had felt a clarity and sense of peace that he had not known since taking the Blood Oath. It was as if Her powers were being cleansed from his very soul.

Yimt slapped his hands on his knees and stood up. "Right. Put a big bloody cork in it, all of you," he said, turning to look each one of them in the eye. "What is or isn't the state of our eternal rest is a conversation for another day. Right now, it's time. Grab your kit and get topside. We're going to honor the poor bastards while the weather holds."

Hrem climbed to his feet and began buttoning up his tunic. He gave Scolly a gentle nudge with his boot. Scolly opened one eye and looked around.

"Are we going to bury them now?"

No one said anything. Finally, Alwyn nodded. "Yes, Scolly, we're going to bury them now."

Scolly opened the other eye and sat up, stretching and yawning as he did so. "Only, I was having a dream and the Shadow Monarch was there. She seemed . . . happy."

SEVEN

The wind began to swirl, snapping the canvas sailcloth above their heads like the musket fire they'd become all too familiar with. Alwyn kept his eyes on the four bodies laid out on the deck in front of him. Each dead soldier was sewn into an old hammock. Iron ingots from the ship's ballast had been placed inside first to ensure the bodies slid out of sight quickly, but experience had shown it wouldn't matter. The Queen's Colors draped each body, though the flags would remain as the bodies were pushed over the side. They were bound to be used again.

The regiment formed a three-sided square around the bodies, although this meant many soldiers were perched on barrels, crates, and parts of the ship in order to see. No sailors were present. Even the ship's captain, Captain Ervod, was absent. He'd insisted on presiding over the first ceremony, but after the shock of the first one, Captain Ervod left it to the regiment to handle.

Prince Tykkin stood off to one side, tapping a white-gloved hand against his sword hilt. The silvery-green of his uniform jacket looked new and was a marked exception to the dull appearance of his men. Even Major Swift Dragon's uniform looked grubby by comparison. It was only natural that the future King look the part, but Alwyn knew the main reason was that the Prince stayed on board while the Iron Elves cleared each island. It spoke volumes that no soldier ever complained about it; they all preferred the Prince out of sight.

Major Swift Dragon made a motion to Yimt, who took a step forward. "Parade . . . attention!" The soldiers came to attention as best they could. Captain Ervod was struggling to keep the ship steady, but the seas did not appear to be cooperating.

Prince Tykkin nodded to himself, then began speaking. The first few words were carried away by the wind, but Alwyn knew the speech by heart. Everyone did. The Prince went through the motions, exalting the fallen, though Alwyn doubted he would even recognize them.

". . . through their sacrifice the Empire will survive, and the light of civilization will shine in all the corners of the world . . ."

As the Prince spoke, Alwyn looked around the formation. Anticipation and apprehension filled the air. Coughs and shuffling feet were muffled by the wind, but there was no hiding the looks in men's eyes. They all shared the same thought as they looked at the four bodies. *That could be me one day. What happens next could happen to me.*

". . . in taking the fight to our foe, we stamp out disorder and chaos, bringing the order of the just throughout the known lands. Ours is a cause most worthy, and so to fall in the furtherance of that cause is an honor . . ."

Alwyn caught Yimt's eye and realized they were both sneering at the Prince's words. Alwyn coughed and looked over at the

Prince, but he continued to talk, his eyes unfocused and staring at nothing.

The ship took a wave off the port bow, sending a shudder through the timbers. The Prince stumbled, then righted himself. He looked questioningly at Major Swift Dragon, who saluted. The Prince returned the salute and without another look back, walked across the deck and into his cabin.

The roll was called for each section that had lost a man. When they got to Harkon, the entire regiment stiffened. Word of his strange death had quickly made the rounds. Soldiers understood dying in battle—they even were beginning to come to terms with the idea of a ghostly afterlife—but to have your shadow burned was something new.

Major Swift Dragon took a moment and panned his eyes along the ranks. When he came to Alwyn he paused, and Alwyn held his gaze. The major looked away and called the last name.

"Harkon."

Waves battered against the hull with dull booms.

"Private Harkon."

A clewline snapped and began whipping back and forth against a sail.

"Private *Kester* Harkon."

The ship rose on a large wave, then slid down the other side. Spray shot up from the bow and sprinkled down on the assembly, but not a person moved to wipe his face.

Major Swift Dragon pulled his saber from its scabbard and held it skyward. Four soldiers standing at the ready bent and lifted the first body and carried it to the railing.

A mournful, keening sound came from somewhere high in the

rigging of the mainmast. Alwyn knew Tyul Mountain Spring, a *diova gruss*, an elf lost to the natural order after bonding with an overpowering Silver Wolf Oak, was up there. Miss Red Owl had decided to keep him with her, perhaps as another *project*, as Yimt put it. Alwyn wasn't sure there was anything that could be done for the elf. He seemed to live in his own world. When he wasn't sitting and staring off into space, he was climbing the mainmast that had once been Jurwan's *ryk faur* Black Spike to howl whenever there was a burial at sea.

"Sends spiders crawling down the inside of me spine it does," Teeter whispered to Alwyn.

Alwyn felt something similar, but he thought it had more to do with what was about to happen than with the lost elf's sorrow.

Major Swift Dragon brought his saber down and the soldiers tipped the body over the side. As they did so the regiment began reciting the oath, a last, bitter sendoff that they had come to cherish the way you trace a finger over an old scar.

> We do not fear the flame, though it burns us,
> We do not fear the fire, though it consumes us,
> And we do not fear its light,
> Though it reveals the darkness of our souls,
> For therein lies our power.

The first body went over the side. The splash was barely heard over the wind. The regiment braced up. Spikes of frost fire shot into the air. The flames crackled with energy and spread across the water. A shade emerged from the flames and its cries of anguish reverberated inside every man. The deck became shrouded with mist as breath fogged in the suddenly cold air. The next body went over the side and the frost fire grew. It danced along the railing and surrounded the assembled soldiers in a ring of cold, black flame. Another shade appeared, adding its tortured voice to that of its comrade. Images of a dark mountain, twisted trees, and Her came unbidden to Alwyn's thoughts, and he was not alone. A few soldiers shed tears. Others laughed while a few closed their eyes tightly and prayed.

The third body went in and a third shadow was born. Its wails of terror rose even as those of the first two began to quiet. It was always this way. First the fear and the pain, then the anguish of acceptance, and then a cold, dead calm.

Hands reached out to Alwyn, beckoning him. Alwyn kept his eyes open, but kept his hands at his sides.

"Join us."

The air grew even colder, turning the mist to ice. Men began to shiver and would later tell their mates it was entirely due to the weather. All would accept the lie.

Alwyn stared at the shades and said nothing.

The last body, that of Private Harkon, was tipped over the side. Alwyn took a breath of frigid air into his lungs and waited for the last blast of frost fire, the screams, and the final call of the shades.

It did not come.

There was an audible gasp from among the troops. No frost fire rose where Harkon's body entered the water. No shade emerged. The air began to warm as the shadows thinned and then vanished. Alwyn traded looks with Yimt. *What was this?*

Voices rose and the assembly began to move.

"Steady on! No one dismissed you," Yimt bellowed, and order was restored, but only just.

Whispers raced up and down the ranks.

"Harkon was the one what got his shadow burned."

"They say he screamed for five minutes as it burned his very soul."

"Maybe, but what if it broke the oath?"

There was only the howling of the wind and the keening of a lost elf in reply.

As the ship sailed on, the mortal remains of the four soldiers sank into the lightless depths. Fish scattered as the bodies plummeted past them. The stitching came loose on the last body, revealing the face of Private Kester Harkon.

Something large and gray swam up from the depths toward the sinking corpses.

It came in close to each body in turn, but turned away each time from the first three. When it came in toward Harkon's body it paused, as if studying the face.

Harkon's eyes opened. They turned and saw the creature.

Harkon's mouth opened in a scream as water rushed into his lungs. The creature lunged forward and grabbed Harkon's body between two powerful jaws, and then swam with his corpse back toward the surface, settling just below the waves.

With the body of Private Kester Harkon firmly clutched in its mouth, the creature began following in the wake of the *Black Spike*. What remained of the man who was once Kester Harkon screamed silently as it did.

On the peak of a black mountain, a forest seethed in the cold night air. A drizzling rain fell, turning to sleet. Bolts of lightning ranged down, twisting shadows of already misshapen trees. The trees drew the lightning to them, raising their branches high as if in supplication.

Another bolt struck, splintering the pitch-black wood of one tree into needle-sharp shrapnel. Metal-colored leaves tore away in the wind to scythe the night air. Frost fire flared in the crowns of the trees and thick ichor oozed from open wounds, staining everything an oily black. The sleet hissed as it hit the ground, forming jagged bits of ice until the entire mountain peak gleamed in the night.

Underground, the roots of the trees writhed and stabbed into the rock. For every tree lost to lightning, its siblings fed on the power. Cracks on the mountain surface shuddered and ripped farther apart, creating ever-deepening chasms. Primal roars issued from the depths. The roots continued to dig.

In its need and its rage, Her forest was tearing the mountain apart.

The Shadow Monarch stood among the trees. The cloak wrapped tightly around Her made it difficult to differentiate between Her and the darkness. No lightning touched down near Her.

If She felt sympathy for the offspring of Her *ryk faur*, the Silver Wolf Oak She had bonded with all those centuries before, She did not show it. There was a price to be borne for living in such a cold, barren place—the trees sacrificed themselves to that purpose.

Far below in the great forest, Wolf Oaks grew straight and true. Down there, their limbs were protected from the lightning by the even-more-massive Silver Wolf Oaks that had grown strong and true, unpolluted by such bitter ground. Here on the mountain, however, this Silver and all its progeny were a twisted thicket of anguish. To exist like this with Her aid was pain beyond comprehension, yet the will to live remained. And so Her forest grew, a desperate union of the Shadow Monarch and Her *ryk faur* sowing the seeds of madness in ever-widening swathes of black destruction.

The Shadow Monarch stepped forward into the center of the trees. Branches interlocked in a protective shield above Her, absorbing the lightning while She remained unscathed. She looked down into a pool of ichor that shimmered and revealed the world as it was.

This world would change.

Where plains and hills now rustled with tall grass, Her forest would grow. No river, no lake, no road, and no city would remain. The very oceans would thicken with trunks until no ship could pass.

All would be Hers.

All would be forest.

Then there would be power, enough to end the pain. Though She had failed in obtaining the fallen Star in the east, Her will remained intact and the Iron Elves would be Hers. More Stars would fall, and in time She would claim them as Her own. In this, the bond between elf and tree grew stronger as each warped the other in the madness of their everlasting need.

A hunched shadow crept into the clearing, slipping over ice and rock. Lightning flashed as it neared the Shadow Monarch, revealing it to be a man clothed only in a tattered robe. Large chunks of his skin looked more like the bark of Her trees. His eyes, however, remained wholly human, showing every bit of the fear he felt. Trembling, he inched forward, finally falling on his knees in front of Her and bowing his head.

She had plans for his fear.

• • •

Faltinald Elkhart Gwyn, recipient of the Order of the Amber Chalice, holder of the Blessed Garter of St. DiWynn, Member of the Royal Society of Thaumaturgy and Science, and until recently, Her Majesty the Queen of Calahr's Viceroy for the Protectorate of Greater Elfkyna, shook as he kept his head low.

It was a position he was becoming all too accustomed to since his fortunes had changed.

Only weeks before, rulers of backward lands throughout the Calahrian Empire knew his name and feared it. He was the power of the Empire personified. When he spoke, it was not with his voice, but with the Queen's . . . and Hers. It had been a heady game, serving two thrones. Now, he was a wanted man throughout the Empire, but he doubted anyone would ever get the chance to collect on his reward.

Lightning scorched the branches just feet above him, setting his teeth chattering. His life, what was left of it, now hinged on the caprice of his only monarch.

A moment later, another figure emerged from the dark, materializing from nothing with a cold certainty. Unlike Gwyn, this one did not tremble. Its hooded cloak appeared more like that of the Shadow Monarch. There were no eyes to be seen. It, too, bowed before Her, though not as low.

Gwyn found his mind and body warring with each other as Her Emissary approached. Memories of the torture he had suffered at the cold, dead hands of this monster sent fresh currents of fear coursing through him. Even now, his training as a diplomat told him to show no emotion, but his body was not up to the task. He dug his hands into the ice until they bled, but he could not quell the shaking.

Her Emissary, an elf from the same tribe as Her, had been like

Gwyn once, Viceroy to the Queen of Calahr. And like Gwyn he, too, had chosen the path of serving two masters in the belief that he could find the balance and ride the storm that was growing between these two worlds.

Both had been brought to ruin by the same despised elf— Konowa Swift Dragon of the Iron Elves.

Anger almost overcame fear as thoughts of the elf and his friend, the Duke of Rakestraw, ran through Gwyn's mind. They were the architects of his fall. If there was justice in the world then they both would burn, and then after an agonizing period of suffering, they would be put to death. First, however, he had to survive the Shadow Monarch.

'My Emissary and my Viceroy come to me in failure.'

Gwyn gave up trying to control the shaking. He was absolutely terrified at the sound of Her voice. To hear it in person was to know fear unlike any he had ever known. He raised his head, though he did not look directly at Her, and held out his hands. "I . . . I *have* failed you, my Queen. I deserve whatever judgment you see fit."

The words galled him to say, yet at a certain level he believed them. This was indeed failure, though in it there was opportunity for power. Fear still gripped him in a steel claw, but he spied a way to use it now. He allowed his head to touch the icy ground again.

The trees crackled as branches flexed, shedding ice as they interlaced themselves above his head. It was a ceiling of dangling swords, each hanging by a thread She controlled. Only Her will kept the branches from slicing Gwyn to ribbons.

The Shadow Monarch remained silent for a long time. Sleet continued to fall. Gwyn knew if nothing else happened, he would still die from simple exposure to the elements.

After what felt like an eternity, the Shadow Monarch spoke.

'And you?'

Her Emissary radiated confidence. He had been arrogant in life and had found little humility in death. Gwyn had once marveled at such power, but now in proximity to Her, he understood its limitations. Her Emissary was a tool, a blunt, heavy weapon. There was no subtlety, no finesse. There was but one path for it to take, but if that path diverged such a weapon no longer had any use. Yes, this was a game Gwyn knew how to play. The question was, did Her Emissary?

"As you desired, Konowa Swift Dragon is bound by his oath, as are they all. Many have already succumbed and now inhabit the world between. Losing the Star was unavoidable. There was unforeseen interference."

'I am aware of her presence.'

Gwyn marshaled all of his remaining energy to not raise his head in surprise. He was trained to detect the slightest wrong note in an opposing diplomat, and he heard one now. Was that annoyance in Her voice? He refused to believe it could be something more powerful, yet if it weren't for the fact he was freezing to death, he would have sworn he detected a hint of worry.

The Silver Wolf Oak shuddered. A branch untangled itself from the forest and came to rest gently on the Shadow Monarch's shoulder.

Her Emissary continued as if it heard nothing, which Gwyn suspected was precisely the case.

"Were it not for the power of the Star, Elfkyna would be yours now. It is strong, but it can be overcome."

Gwyn felt Her Emissary's gaze upon him and knew the accusation that hung in the air. He refused to take the bait. Gwyn had already offered his life to Her, accepting whatever fate She decreed. He would play this hand to the end.

'My forest in Elfkyna was destroyed. Even now, Konowa hunts them down wherever they grow.'

"I will stop him."

'No. The elves I seek are not yet found.'

"Then I will find them."

'No, you will not.'

Gwyn felt more than heard Her command. The branch around Her shoulder lashed out. Shards of ice flew in all directions. Gwyn threw up his hands to cover his face. A single brief scream was lost to the sleet. No echo, no reverberation.

It took a moment for Gwyn to realize the scream wasn't his, that he was still alive. He lowered his arms and looked up. The body of Her Emissary hung in midair, impaled on the branch. Frost fire raged over it, the flames gouging deeply. The tree flung the body into the waiting branches of its offspring, which set about tearing what was left to shreds.

The branch slowly returned to the Shadow Monarch, curling itself around Her shoulders. Something wet now glistened on its tip and Gwyn saw that it was a blood-soaked obsidian acorn ripped from the chest of Her Emissary.

'Rise.'

Gwyn climbed to his feet, shaking, freezing, unsure of his balance. He dared to look in Her eyes, then found he could not look away.

'Will you accept my gift?'

There was but one answer, and Gwyn found voice enough to give it. "Yes, with all my heart."

The Shadow Monarch did something then that the former Viceroy of Elfkyna would remember for the rest of his life.

She smiled.

The branch of the Silver Wolf Oak uncoiled itself again from around her and snaked its way toward him.

Slowly.

'Where he failed you will succeed. You will aid my child.'

Gwyn wasn't sure he understood.

The branch inched closer, twisting in the night air.

"Your . . . child?" The branch continued to come toward him, as Gwyn's gaze tore away from Hers. Blood still dripped from the acorn.

'Look,' she said. The pool of ichor shimmered once more. A vast ocean appeared. A single ship raced ahead of a growing storm. Soldiers were grouped on the deck around four flag-draped bodies. A ceremony was taking place. Gwyn recognized it at once.

'Konowa Swift Dragon. He is the key. He seeks his brothers, the Iron Elves, and through him you will find the rest of my children and bring them home to me.'

Gwyn nodded. "I will find the Iron Elves for you. I will bring them home." As he said this, the pool of ichor flared with frost fire as the bodies of the Iron Elves were consigned to the depths. The black flame rose, then settled down, but deep in the center for one brief moment, a pure white flame burned. The Shadow Monarch said nothing, but the air around them grew colder. He gasped for breath as the freezing air bit into his lungs.

Shades now stood where only a moment ago the black of night had filled the spaces between the trees. Their forms were hazy, as if uncertain or unwilling to commit further to the darkness around them. Gwyn counted only three.

'Many have begun the journey already, but there is still a long way to go. Aid me in this, and you will have . . . my gratitude.'

Gwyn had no time to ponder what that might mean. He

wanted to ask what the white flame meant, but the branch shot forth the rest of the distance, piercing his chest. The force of the impact flung his head forward like a snapped twig. He felt the blood-soaked acorn lodge deep within his heart, and tried to scream as pain blossomed through his body. Just as quickly, the branch withdrew, leaving something new in its place.

Life as Gwyn knew it ceased. His body collapsed to the ground. Magic thick and raw coursed through him. His wounds froze over and healed as the remnants of his robe fell away in ash and frost fire consumed him.

When the flames burned out he stood, wrapped in a cloak of night.

'Bring my children home,' she said, 'and yours is the world.'

"As you wish," Her Emissary said.

EIGHT

The sky turned slate, blackening at the horizon as storm clouds formed in the distance. The cries from a flock of birds fleeing before the coming weather carried farther as the air grew colder. The wind picked up, rushing ahead of the towering clouds, churning everything in its path.

The three women ignored this, or at least gave no outward sign that they cared the weather was turning. Their attention was fixed solidly on the simmering pot before them. A gust of wind whistled between them, tearing away tendrils of steam long enough to reveal the contents therein. Each leaned closer to look. To their credit, none of them recoiled. A green, glutinous mass bubbled fiercely, giving off an odor quickly borne away by the wind.

None appeared willing to speak first. Their eyes glistened with tears as they strained to discern something knowable from the contents. The cast-iron vessel hung from a leather strap above a blazing fire attached to a tripod of three muskets. A fire burned fat and orange underneath it, oblivious to the wind, and no sign of fuel could be seen within its flames. More amazingly, the wooden deck of the *Black Spike* remained uncharred.

After several more moments of quiet contemplation, Rallie pushed back the hood of her cloak. "Perhaps the honor should go to the eldest among us." She continued to look down at the pot and so avoided the eyes of the other two women, which now turned to her.

"And that would be?" Chayii Red Owl asked, the tone in her voice not entirely lost on the wind.

Visyna looked from Rallie to Chayii and held her tongue. Chayii was elf, and they were known to live incredibly long lives. Rallie, on the other hand, was unlike any human Visyna had ever met. She spoke with a wisdom gained by much experience over a very great expanse of time. They were—by any measure Visyna could see—witches. That should have bonded them together like sisters—each a powerful wielder of magic in her own right, each using her skills to prevent the Shadow Monarch from destroying them all.

On further thought, perhaps they were too much like sisters.

"Perhaps you can decide, Visyna," Chayii said.

Visyna knew a trap when she saw it. Chayii had been more or less cordial since their first meeting, but Visyna knew Chayii was aware of the relationship between her and her son, Konowa—no matter how strained and untenable it might currently be. Chayii had yet to express her opinion on the matter, but Visyna was more than convinced she did not approve.

"Yes, child, do tell," Rallie said.

What was it, Visyna wondered, *with old witches and their need to play games?* Well, three could play as easily as two.

Without a word, Visyna took a spoon, bent over the pot and

scooped out a mouthful. She smiled at both of them as she brought the spoon to her lips, proud of avoiding a no-win situation.

Then she tasted it.

Tears welled in Visyna's eyes and trickled down her cheek, where they dried in the wind. Time ceased as her world constricted to a shining white light exploding behind her eyes. It felt as if the top of her head had been blown off.

"Well?" Yimt asked. The dwarf stood nervously across from the women. It would be his distinct honor, he had said, to cook for three such fine ladies. Apparently his fellow soldiers were not entirely appreciative of his culinary efforts. He paced a few steps one way, then back again, all the while tugging on his beard.

Rallie took her spoon and dipped it into the pot, with Chayii following suit. Each looked at Visyna, but she was no help, her nostrils flaring and her cheeks flushing pink. With a nod to each other, they both tasted Yimt's concoction.

For what seemed an eternity there was only the sound of the wind and the crashing of waves as the ship made all haste to outpace the storm. Yimt tugged so hard on his beard that he pulled several strands of hair out.

Visyna found her voice first.

"What . . . what do you call this?"

"It's me old mum's recipe for rat dragon. She got it from her mum and so on down the line." He stopped tugging his beard and started waving his hand around. "I realize it's in an iron pot and that kind of thing don't sit right with you fey folk, so maybe it doesn't taste quite the way it should . . ."

"Why is it green?" Chayii asked, her words coming out slightly slurred.

"Ah, well, as you might have guessed, we don't have any rat

dragons on board. Honestly, what kind of vessel goes to sea without a good supply of rat dragon in its stores? I checked with the cook, that one-armed fellow with the glass eye and peg leg, but while he's got barrels of salted pork, salted beef, salted goat, and I swear salted salt, not one of rat dragon. He did, however, point out that the ship had a large supply of *regular* rats."

Visyna knew the color in her face was now gone. "You mean . . ."

Yimt crossed his heart. "Regular rats in a stew? Me mum'd have me strung up by my ears. Not on your life. Nope, I hung a line off the back of the front there and caught me a few fish. At least they looked like fish, sort of. They were a bright blue when I hauled 'em on board, but looks like they go green when you put the heat to them. Oh, and I did add a little drake sweat to sort of bring out the flavors," he said, indicating a small canteen filled with the stone-eating home brew.

While he was talking, Yimt kept casting glances at Rallie, who had yet to speak. Visyna had been watching her too, worried she might topple over.

"That," Rallie began, then had to stop as she blinked and dabbed at the corners of her eyes. "That, Sergeant Arkhorn, is without a doubt the most divine stew it has ever been my good fortune to taste. You, my dear sir, are a chef of sublime talent."

Visyna looked at Chayii and saw her mouth was as agape as hers.

"You like it?" Chayii asked.

"Like it? I want to tear off my clothes and go swimming in it!" Rallie said, taking a proffered bowl from Yimt and holding it steady while he ladled out a steaming helping. If there was any doubt, she began to spoon the stew into her mouth while making soft moaning sounds. Through mouthfuls Visyna heard words like "brilliant," "exquisite," and several more she wasn't sure were ever appropriate for describing food.

Yimt beamed like a father seeing his newborn child for the first time. "You are too sweet by half, Ms. Synjyn. You honor this old warhorse. I can't tell you how it warms my heart to hear you say that."

Rallie smiled back at him and raised her spoon in salute. "My compliments to the chef. You are as enticing as your wares."

A word jumped into Visyna's mind, and no matter how hard she tried, she could not shake it loose. By all that was holy, Rallie and Yimt were flirting.

She was saved from further contemplation of the subject by the telltale thump of Private Renwar's wooden leg on the ship's deck. Alwyn limped up and stopped short when he saw the pot. His hand went to his mouth, but he quickly recovered.

"Good evening, ladies," he said, barely looking at them as he kept a wary eye on the bubbling pot. "Major Swift Dragon sends his compliments and asks that Miss Red Owl, Miss Tekoy, and Miss Synjyn join him on the quarterdeck."

"You two run along," Rallie said, waving them away as she held out her now-empty bowl for a refill. "Tell the major I'm still formulating my thoughts on the events of earlier. When I've had time to marshal them, I shall seek him out."

Visyna looked at Chayii, who nodded. "Thank you, Yimt of the Warm Breeze. In the brief time we have traveled the same path, you have never once ceased to amaze."

Yimt grinned a metallic smile, his pewter-colored teeth shining in the firelight. "One more compliment like that and I'll blush," he said, casually turning his gaze to Visyna.

"I can think of no higher one than to say it's a shame we've been called away and won't be able to stay and eat with you," she said. She stood a little straighter and smiled, pleased with another quick reaction. It was an effort to keep her smile there a moment later.

"Well, that settles it. I am officially tickled," Yimt said. He produced two more bowls and quickly ladled them full. Rallie helpfully took them and handed one each to Chayii and Visyna. Rallie's eyes positively sparkled as she bade them farewell.

"How is your leg, Alwyn of the Empire?" Chayii asked as the three of them navigated the deck toward the middle of the ship and the bridge. "Your balance appears much improved."

Alwyn nodded. He lifted the hem of his caerna slightly so that the women could see his wooden leg better. Where the magically woven wood wrapped around the stump of his leg, the flesh was bright red. A flicker of frost fire jumped from his skin to the wood, but the wood, burnished until it shone like warm brass, pulsed with a soft energy that quenched the flame before it could take hold.

"Looks like my new leg and my old one don't exactly see eye to eye."

"Is there much pain?" Visyna said, kneeling beside him and beginning to weave the air in front of her. Alwyn gently but firmly pushed her hands away. She stood back up.

"It helps me, if that makes sense. When things start to get too confusing, I can concentrate on the pain and block out everything else, at least for a while."

Chayii's expression did not change, but her hand reached out and rested on Alwyn's shoulder. A flicker of black flame met her touch, but she kept her hand still. "We will find a way. You will be free of this one day."

Alwyn smiled, though Visyna didn't find comfort in it.

"Speaking of being free of curses," Alwyn said, moving on, "we're out of sight of Sergeant Arkhorn now if you want to toss your bowls overboard."

Visyna looked down at hers and then let it fly. Chayii's followed.

"Sergeant Arkhorn's been cooking again," Konowa said, walking along the railing toward them. He wobbled slightly on his feet and his eyes had a wild look about them only partially explained by the ever-worsening seas.

Visyna fought the urge to reach out and steady him. This was his doing. Perhaps the addition of seasickness would help bring him to his senses.

"I thought we were going to talk on the quarterdeck?" Visyna asked.

The first patter of rain washed over the deck. "Bit crowded up there at the moment," said Konowa.

Visyna could tell from the expression on his face the Prince was on deck.

"I think it best we talk somewhere less . . . populated," Konowa continued.

"I'll leave you to your conversation then," Alwyn said, saluting and turning to leave.

"Actually, Private, you're the reason for our conversation. You saw something on that island, and you quenched the white fire, or whatever it was. We saw what happened at the funeral, and I've already talked with Private Vulhber, so now I'm talking to you. What was that magic back on the island?" Konowa motioned them all over to an area somewhat protected from the wind.

"White fire? I know of no such magic," Visyna said, looking at Chayii, who shook her head in agreement.

"It was white, pure white," Konowa said, "but it was burning the soldier's shadow . . . Private Kester Harkon's shadow."

Alwyn tensed slightly, then relaxed, but clearly something had happened between him and Konowa on that island.

"I don't know what I can add," Alwyn said. His voice was calm and steady, but Visyna could see in his eyes the subject was an emotionally dangerous one for him.

"Perhaps this could wait for—" was all she managed to get out before Konowa interrupted.

"Tell them, Private, tell them what happened."

Alwyn looked at Konowa. The hurt on Alwyn's face was so clear the urge to cradle him in her arms was overwhelming. He stood up straight, almost at attention, and slowly, reluctantly, began to relate what had happened. His voice never betrayed any emotion throughout the retelling, even when he himself, through his shadow, was on fire.

"But this is terrible," Visyna said when he finished. This time she did reach out and pat his arm. "It kills a person by burning his shadow. And you think this broke the oath?"

"Even if it does, it is no remedy," Chayii said, her voice grave. "Whatever happened to Private Harkon sounds a terrible fate."

"We don't know what happened," Konowa said. "And whether it truly broke the oath remains to be seen. What we do know is that it kills what She creates. It had killed many of the *sarka har* before we even arrived. It is a bane to Her." Konowa's eyes brightened. "It might mean we have an ally."

"I do not think this is a friend you want, my son," Chayii said. "There is much in this world even now we do not understand. Of what lived before, we know even less."

Konowa tapped a boot against the decking. "Before? Maybe. I sensed something incredibly ancient, but what of it? It was killing Her forest. No, this is a force that hates Her power as much as we do. If we can find it, we can use it."

"As you do with darkness pressed against your heart?" Visyna said. "How well has that worked out for you? For them?" she asked, pointing at Alwyn, then quickly lowering her hand.

"I did what had to be done," Konowa said through clenched teeth. "I saved your precious land and gave up a chance to be free and this is the thanks I get? The point is, Private Renwar proved it can be controlled. He stopped it. Imagine what women of your skills could do."

Chayii cleared her throat before Visyna could respond. The color in Chayii's face surely matched Visyna's.

"We strive to aid the natural order, to restore balance and harmony," Chayii said. "I would never use such a power even if I could, and I know Visyna wouldn't either."

Visyna nodded. "This is madness. You have chosen a dangerous path and made poor choices while on it. You sought our counsel. Will you not heed it?"

Konowa looked to Alwyn for help. "Tell them, explain to them. You felt it. You controlled it."

"I don't know what I did," Alwyn said. This time, his voice couldn't hide the wounds. "The pain of the fire was unlike anything I've ever felt. When I stepped into their shadows I started burning deep inside me in places I didn't know existed," Alwyn said. "I . . . I don't know if this is something we can use. The price might be too high."

The words were right, but something in the way Alwyn said them gave Visyna pause. *Would Konowa think the price too high, though?*

A thunderclap reverberated above them, followed by a quick slash of lightning. The rain began falling harder and the ship rose and fell with greater force, making it difficult for Visyna to keep her balance.

Konowa's voice rose above the storm. "Thank you, Private, that will be all."

Alwyn stood to attention and saluted, his face specterlike in the rain. He turned and walked and was soon out of sight. Only when he was gone did Konowa speak again.

"I want to know what it was that can kill *sarka har* and burn shadow, and I want to know where to find it," Konowa said. "Either it will help us destroy Her designs, or it will share Her fate. Private Renwar has shown we can defend against it if need be. If you wish me to heed your words, bring me ones that help me fight." With that he turned and stalked away.

Visyna looked after him for a moment before turning to Chayii for guidance. "How do I reach him? How do I make him understand?"

Chayii stared out to sea then bowed her head. "I had hoped, Visyna, that *you* could tell me. You hold a place in his heart a mother never could."

Visyna started to object, but Chayii waved her to silence. "I know, he has a strange way of showing it, but the truth of it remains. You must help him find some peace so that he sees the right path forward. He thinks he merely suffers from seasickness, but it is also more." She looked at the ship with such sadness in her eyes that Visyna reached out and held her hand.

"This ship is made of Wolf Oaks. My husband's foolish gift of his *ryk faur* stands in mockery of everything we hold dear. Even now I feel its spirit here. The pain will never go away."

Visyna understood. She had felt unsettled the moment she stepped aboard. Despite the horrors of the islands, she had welcomed the opportunities to leave the ship and go ashore, even when it meant facing the Shadow Monarch's creatures.

"The Empire has much to answer for, but for now, I will do what I can for Konowa, and for the Iron Elves," Visyna said, hoping her words were true.

"I hope you succeed," Chayii said, her face awash in rain. "I've already lost my husband to Her magic, perhaps forever. I do not want to lose my son as well."

NINE

The race against the storm was a welcome diversion. The *Black Spike* rose and fell among the waves as her sailors fought to keep her afloat and the Iron Elves simply fought to keep the contents of their stomachs.

Konowa didn't breathe easy until the vessel sailed through the gap in the breakwater that arched across Nazalla Bay. He stood against the railing on the forecastle and marveled at the captain's skills as he eased the ship between the rocks. She handled well even though the storm still raged. Perhaps some of the magic that once coursed through his father's *ryk faur* still lived on. Konowa risked a glance over the railing and saw that the waves were indeed calmer inside the breakwater, though the blowing winds were crabbing the big ship sideways as it approached the port.

It was just past midnight according to the ship's bells, and the combination of rain and cloud cover made it especially dark. Wood groaned and creaked as the sails were taken in and the anchors dropped. Konowa's stomach still roiled, but just the sight of land was enough to buoy his spirits.

Not fifty miles beyond Nazalla lay the first outpost of the original Iron Elves at a flyspeck called Suhundam's Hill. There were a series of these outposts stretching out across the desert in a sweeping arc aimed to control the flow of trade and protect the merchant caravans from raiders, but Suhundam was the closest, and the most important. The fort sat astride the meeting of three different trade routes that originated far in the interior of the Hasshugeb Expanse and wound their way to the three ports that dotted the otherwise barren coastline. Suhundam's Hill would be their first destination. Konowa knew that, unlike the situation at Luuguth Jor, here his elves would still be in full control of their outpost. He'd trained them well.

He scanned the port for a sign that the harbormaster had seen their arrival, but so far no lantern glowed. He was tempted to launch a boat at once and make for the dock, but the waves were still high enough even in here that such a trip would needlessly risk lives. He had waited a long time to get this far; he could wait a little longer.

The smell of cigar smoke made Konowa smile.

"This won't be our first talk in the rain."

Rallie walked up beside him and leaned forward, resting her elbows on the railing. Underneath her black hood, her gray hair was even more frizzled, but her gravelly voice belied a calmness that soothed Konowa's nerves.

"But perhaps our last, at least for a while. The Hasshugeb Expanse is rather on the dry side." She took a long puff on her cigar and let the smoke roll out of her mouth slowly, watching it get torn apart by the rain. "Rain or snow or something else, there is a problem."

Konowa nodded. "We cannot be afraid of this power, no matter whose it is or where we find it. A weapon is a weapon—it's all in how you use it. This 'white fire' kills Her creatures. Imagine what *we* could do with it."

"Oh, I do," Rallie said, "I do. But perhaps the better question is: What could such a power do with *you?*"

Konowa stood up a little straighter. "This isn't like the oath. We will not be beholden again."

Rallie tapped the ash from her cigar and clamped it back between her teeth. Despite the rain, the tip continued to glow orange and showed no signs of being doused. "Sage words, to be sure, and I hope they are prophetic ones. Tell me, what do you think you found on that island? What do you think happened to that soldier?"

"I was hoping you could tell me," Konowa said. His knowledge of ancient and so-called mythical creatures was not vast. Worse, what he did know too often turned out to be wrong. "Did you talk to Private Renwar? He saw it, he felt it, he quenched its fire. He obviously knows something." The image of the black frost burning in the soldier's hands remained a vivid picture in Konowa's mind.

"Indeed he does, and it's a knowledge no one should ever possess. He's gone farther, Major, farther than any of them, farther even than you," she said.

"Farther where?"

Rallie pointed out to sea. "To the other side. To the place where death reigns and this world becomes a distant memory. He's become powerful precisely because he's slipping away." She turned and looked him in the eyes. "He talks to them, you know."

Konowa felt a chill, and he knew it wasn't from the acorn. "He—why?"

Rallie shook her head. "Because they talk to him. He almost

died when he lost his leg. The power that was tapped to save his life had a price. It always does. He's connected to them in a way you aren't."

"But that doesn't make sense . . . we all took the oath, except the Prince. Surely my power is the strongest. Renwar's not even an elf."

"Is that jealousy I hear, Major?"

Konowa waved the idea away even as he wondered if, in fact, it was. "I am just trying to understand. Why would the frost fire burn so much stronger for him?"

Rallie took the cigar out of her mouth and tossed it into the water. "Because he wants to die."

It was a moment of pure clarity. Konowa had seen it before— soldiers recklessly throwing themselves into the fray. If they survived they got a medal, but few ever lived to receive it, not that they sought a medal in the first place. Konowa knew at some level that he himself risked his life more than was prudent for a commanding officer, but he was seeking to right many wrongs. Private Renwar risked his life for a wholly other reason.

Rallie nodded. "He wants the pain to end, and he's close to making the final leap. He was prepared before when all that waited for him was eternal service to the Iron Elves and perhaps the Shadow Monarch. Now that you've found something that might break that oath, he'll be even more determined. What's an agonizing death if it sets you free?"

"I'll have him put on mess detail, or assigned to assist my mother and Visyna with caring for the wounded. We just need time." This was something that had kept Konowa up at night. What if the oath *could* be broken? Would that really be in their best interest right now? They needed power to fight the Shadow Monarch's forest and Her creatures, and through the oath they had found it. So what if it was the enemy's power? Konowa had swung an orc axe in battle when his musket had been knocked from his hands. This was no different.

"Having him peel potatoes won't stop what's been set in motion," Rallie said. "Unless the oath is broken, he will end his life. Eventually, I fear that most of them will, one way or another. You know this."

Konowa took in a deep breath and let it out slowly. Resentment, anger, insubordination—these he could deal with from soldiers under his command. But this? Yes, none of the soldiers had bargained for this, but they *were* soldiers and they *would* obey. Without that single tenet no army could function, and no empire could survive. To break the oath now would be to weaken them when they needed their strength the most.

"We'll find my elves, Rallie, we'll find them and I'll set things right."

"I hope you do, Major. One of my sreex couriers found us the other day. It brought news of events in Calahr. Apparently my readers and a good many citizens of the Empire at large have been following your exploits with growing enthusiasm. The Iron Elves are the talk of Celwyn and a thousand villages and roadhouses throughout the lands. The orc drums are even reported to be carrying the story, though you are not portrayed in as flattering a light as in my accounts."

Konowa tried to imagine it and failed. Did people not have their own lives to live? "The orcs care?"

"Absolutely," Rallie said, her eyes shining at the very thought. "Everyone does. Things have gone so far that the One-Eared Donkey in the dwarf quarter of Celwyn now has a drink dubbed the

Iron Elf. The exact ingredients are a closely guarded secret, but they say it'll take you to the beyond and back . . . eventually."

The idea that people read about their exploits galled Konowa. "This is a joke to them? Men are dying out here."

"Come now, Major. When have things ever been any different? Somewhere in a distant land, elves, men, dwarves, and even orcs are always dying while back home others go to work, or the pub, and home to their wives, or at least somebody's wife. Would you really trade your life for theirs?"

The thought of trudging to a job in a mill, or a foundry, or even worse, an office with a desk and quill and ink bottle was enough to set Konowa's stomach on edge again. "No, but there are times when I wish my life could be simple like theirs. Where things are clear. You know the right course to take and your mistakes don't cost lives."

Rallie's laughter startled a couple of seagulls perched on the railing farther down. "Simple, my dear Major, is definitely not a word I would use to describe anything about you. And lives are lost every day in the 'simple world,' more, I wager, than are lost on a battlefield. But what happens out here has repercussions far greater than anything that happens back in Celwyn. And that's why you're out here, and not back there."

Konowa grunted. "I take it the same can be said about you. This isn't exactly a sightseeing expedition we're on. It's hard enough for young men let alone someone as o—" Konowa suddenly found himself staring into a pair of eyes with very little humor in them, "—oooccupied with affairs of state as you."

Rallie held his gaze a beat longer and then smiled and turned back to watch the dock. "You are a charmer, Swift Dragon. Why am I out here risking life and limb when I could be at home tucked under a nice warm shawl? The answer is simple. You. Them, the Iron Elves. The Prince. The Shadow Monarch. All of this. And of course, the Stars."

Konowa instinctively looked to the sky, but all he got for his troubles was wind-whipped rain in his face. He wiped his brow and squinted up at the clouds and tried to see a glimmer of a star in the night sky beyond, but the weather remained obstinate and he gave up.

"That's a subject I've noticed you haven't written much about in your reports back home," Konowa said. "Everywhere you go, there are legends about Stars of power. Even the orcs have them. But for all that, no one really knows anything." He shifted his position on the railing and looked again at the dock. Still no sign of the harbormaster.

"There's little to know and even less to write about," Rallie said, perhaps a bit too quickly. "The Red Star fell and Elfkyna was saved. Rumors abound, of course, but thus far only one Star has seen fit to return."

Something was nagging at the back of Konowa's mind, but he couldn't put a finger on it. "You know more about this than you're letting on, don't you? The myth of the Red Star in the east proved to be true, which means the other Stars must be real as well."

Rallie paused to look around them before speaking. "That is an assumption based on a solid supposition."

Konowa scratched his head. "I'm not sure, but I think you just agreed with me. You do know more about this. You welcomed back the Star at Luuguth Jor almost as if you knew it."

Rallie huffed. "How old do you think I am, Major? There might be a few creases in my carrying case," she said, pointing to her face, "but do you really think I am that ancient?"

Konowa held up his hands in surrender. "It's just that, well, you're a witch," he said, adding hurriedly, "in a good way. Aren't you?"

"Am I a witch, or am I good?"

Konowa decided it was best to stop talking and merely nodded.

"Yes," Rallie said.

Konowa walked his brain around that answer for a moment and concluded it was best to leave it be. He tried another tack.

"So do you know where and when the next Star will fall? Knowledge like that would be worth its weight in gold."

"A hundred times over, no doubt," Rallie said. She smiled and began pulling her cloak tight around her. The wind still whipped spray off the waves though the *Black Spike* rode at anchor with the solidity of a stone castle. "The gulf between what I know and what I think I know remains vast at this juncture, and until I can fill in some of that chasm with good, hard facts, I prefer to keep my own counsel."

"And that of my mother and Visyna," Konowa said, knowing he sounded petulant and not caring. The three women had become known, and with some affection, as "Which Witch is Which" by the soldiers.

"Not even the Prince presumes to intrude on the deliberations of three women of certain . . . abilities," Rallie said.

Konowa knew danger when it spoke softly. "My apologies. You just have no idea how frustrating it is to be kept in the dark."

Rallie tapped her upper lip with her finger and opened her mouth to speak, then closed it again. A moment later she tried again, but Konowa could tell she had changed her mind about something.

"Trust me when I say this, Major. You'll soon know more than you wish you did. Now," she said, turning to leave, "I really should retire. We're going to have a very busy morning."

Konowa was tempted to ask if that was another veiled vision of the future, but he needn't have bothered. He considered recent history and concluded that if something could go wrong for him, it most certainly would.

TEN

White sails dotted Nazalla Bay in all directions, as if a flock of geese had descended during the night seeking refuge from the storm. Konowa stopped counting ships after thirty and began hacking at a wooden beam with his saber until the splinters erupted in frost fire. It took the next couple of minutes of furious stamping to put them out.

Sheathing his saber, he went looking for the Prince. Rallie, Visyna, and his mother intercepted him on the main deck and blocked his path. Konowa wasn't in the mood. He picked up his pace to walk through them, but the looks of the three women were enough to halt his charge. As angry as he was, he wasn't prepared to challenge three women of their very specific abilities. The realization had him clenching both fists so hard that his hands shook.

"Did you know?" he asked. His jaw ached and he forcibly unclenched it. "Did you all know?"

Visyna glared back at him while his mother simply stared and Rallie looked as if she was about to burst out laughing.

"We knew, to a point at least," Rallie said. "I did say your morning would be busy."

Konowa swung his arm wildly out at the bay and the scores of ships at anchor. "There's a bloody great *fleet* out there! We're here to find the Iron Elves, not mount an expedition to conquer new territory!"

"Thirty-some ships is not exactly an armada," Rallie said, "but your point is taken. The Queen, however, sees things differently, or rather, she sees more than one opportunity here. You and your regiment are causing quite the stir back home. Your search for the original Iron Elves has captured many an imagination, including the Queen's. So while you look for your former soldiers, Her Majesty plants her flag on a few more hills and stakes out claims on any future Stars that might fall, the Prince gains experience and credibility as future King, all the while collecting for his precious repository of knowledge, the Shadow Monarch is thwarted, and the stirrings of rebellion are smothered in their cradles. She plays a very deep game, the Queen." Rallie's voice was filled with obvious admiration.

Konowa locked his hands behind his back to keep himself from grabbing Rallie by her cloak. He looked for something to kick, but nothing appropriate was in the vicinity. Giving up, he paced to the left, then back, slamming his boots down so hard his spine hurt. He brought his hands back down to his sides and forced himself to stand still.

"Why. Not. Tell. Me!"

Visyna continued to glare at him. "Look at your hands."

Konowa raised his fists, and his anger bled away as quickly as it had risen. Black frost fire wreathed his hands. Only then did he realize his breath was misting in the air and the black acorn against his chest was thrumming with cold power. He hadn't noticed any of it.

"That, my dear Major, is our point," Rallie said.

Chayii shook her head. "You are no longer in control of this, my son. Your anger clouds your judgment and She works Her will." She held up her hands to forestall his protest. "You are proud, and you are strong, and you believe you can defeat Her, but you won't. Not like this."

Konowa wasn't having it. "You're wrong. I can control this. I do control it. The Prince is still alive, isn't he?"

All three looked surprised, though it was Visyna who spoke. "And would he still be now if we hadn't found you first? I do not see eye to eye with His Highness on most things, but he is the heir to the throne, so I try. You, on the other hand, see a few ships in the harbor and immediately go looking for a confrontation. What would you have done? You have a power you shouldn't possess—the whole regiment does—but even they exercise more restraint than you."

A hangover after a three-day bender with his friend the Duke of Rakestraw didn't feel as bad as Konowa's head did now. *This really isn't happening.*

"I'm a grown elf. I lead a regiment of soldiers. I risk death and worse in service of the Empire, and yet I'm treated like a child. I'd cry, but that would only add to the agony." Konowa pinched the bridge of his nose, checking first to ensure the frost fire was out, and shrugged his shoulders. He looked up at them. "Fine . . . the three of you seem to be well informed, so you tell me. What happens now?"

For an answer, Prince Tykkin strode into their midst. He was actually whistling. He placed a boot forward and doffed his shako while bending at the waist, sweeping his other arm before him. He was positively giddy, and Konowa understood why the three women had intercepted him.

He really and truly wanted to do harm to the bastard.

· The Prince smiled as he stood up and fixed his shako back on his head. His face was browner and leaner, having lost the doughy-white complexion he'd had when they'd first met. It only added to Konowa's fury to realize the sea voyage had actually agreed with the Prince's constitution while Konowa had lost more meals than he ate.

"Ah, ladies, Major. Isn't it a grand sight? You see, Major, there was a method to all of my meticulous planning," the Prince said, his voice strong and assured. "It requires time to put together the men and material you see before you, and these are just the vanguard. To make all of this possible we needed time. Taking the seven islands gave us that time."

"That time was bought in blood," Konowa remarked.

The Prince's smile wavered, but then brightened again. "I know, Major, and every fallen soldier will be honored. I have already written to the Royal Mint and instructed that a medal be struck commemorating the island battles. Every soldier in the regiment will receive one. In addition, the families of the dead, and of any of those who may yet die, will receive a stipend as a further mark of the Empire's gratitude for their service."

"Some money, and a medal," Konowa said flatly.

"That is but the first. I am drawing up sketches now for another medal commemorating our time here in the desert. The Iron Elves will know glory and honor again," the Prince said. He half turned and smiled at the women, each of whom was keeping an eye on Konowa.

"A thoughtful gesture, your Highness," Rallie said.

Prince Tykkin brushed at the cuff of his uniform. "A necessary one, actually. I've come to know these men. We might wish to think they all serve for the greater good, but it's apparent to me now that a reward and even a good drink are equally strong motivational factors. If news of the medal doesn't lift their spirits, I know a night on the town will, eh, Major?"

Konowa kept his fingers pressed firmly against his trousers and willed himself to remain calm. The Prince's *I've come to know these men* still rang in Konowa's ears. He didn't trust himself to speak.

"I'm sure all of us will appreciate being ashore again after the last few weeks," Visyna said.

"Indeed. In fact," Prince Tykkin said, ignoring Konowa's silence, or perhaps happy to have it, "we will do things properly. The Calahrian Empire is here in force. These lands have been left relatively lawless and free of Imperial rule save for our securing of trade routes. Bandits, thieves, brigands—it's been all but ungovernable." Here the Prince's voice hardened. "That ends today. And it ends grandly. We will not simply row ashore and—how do they say it—"order a few pints." No, we will march down the main street to the city center and the message will go out that Calahr is still *the* power to be reckoned with."

Konowa avoided the eyes of the three women and spoke. "What about our true reason for being here? We must find the original Iron Elves."

The Prince smiled at Konowa and spoke to him as if he were a bit slow-witted. "And we will, Major, we will. Put your fears to bed, for I am as eager as you for this reunion to take place. Rest assured, when we are finished here, the Hasshugeb Expanse and all that inhabit it will be ours, including your precious elves. I realize you might not see it from your vantage point, but we've been presented with a glorious opportunity here."

"What opportunity is that?" Konowa asked.

"What opportunity?" The Prince looked at the women, then back to Konowa. "I've spoken at length with my very sage council here about much of this. They have come to see and appreciate my reasoning, as I trust you will, too. I must say, however, that I admire their sense of discretion. I had half expected them to have whispered enough of my designs to keep you informed."

"Apparently they chose otherwise," Konowa said.

"So it appears," the Prince said, unable to hide a smirk. "Well, no doubt they, like me, wanted you unburdened with matters of great consequence so that you could focus instead on the battles at hand. Battles, I might add, that you handled admirably. Her Majesty's Scribe has not spared the ink in writing your praises for the good people back home."

The Prince's jovial manner dissipated as he said this. Konowa had read enough of Rallie's reporting to understand why the Prince might be less than thrilled with her. While she was always careful to include something about His Highness as colonel of the regiment, it was Konowa and the soldiers themselves that got most of her attention.

"My editor has a keen nose for what sells, and the Iron Elves—these particular Iron Elves—move copy," Rallie said.

"Of course, of course," the Prince said with studied indifference. "They are a simple folk, after all." His smile quickly returned and he doffed his shako again, his flourish even more elaborate than before. "My hat off to you again, my ladies. In keeping the major in the dark, you did all womanhood everywhere proud by showing gossip is not a natural state of being for the fairer sex."

The three women were a sudden study in repressed emotion. Barely. Konowa knew that with these three, looks could indeed kill. Another time Konowa would have enjoyed this immensely, but not now.

"You were talking about an opportunity," Konowa reminded the Prince.

"Not just any opportunity, Major, the opportunity of a lifetime. It's the Stars." The Prince's voice grew soft, but his eyes burned bright.

"We only know of the one," Konowa said, "and it's now a guardian protecting the lands of the elfkynan." Something like the Wolf Oaks of the great forest of the Hyntaland, the Star had transformed itself into a majestic tree following the battle of Luuguth Jor. It had become a bridge between the sky and the earth, a channel for the elemental power of nature to spread across the land and protect it from the Shadow Monarch's encroachments.

The Prince's sunny disposition clouded over at the mention of the Star now turned into a tree. "Yes, a result I do not intend to see repeated." Prince Tykkin had very much wanted the Star for his collection. He took a deep breath and forced the smile back on his face. "Of course, the Star is much more than simply a protector, Major. It is a symbol. It is the harbinger of change. It is the return of a power long gone from this world. It's . . ." The Prince broke off and looked with wonder at Konowa. "Major, the Stars are like you. Once a force in the world, then sent away when that force became uncontrollable, and now returned and put to good use when that energy is needed the most."

Here we go again.

"You're talking about another myth, aren't you," Konowa said, looking from the Prince to the women.

"The Lost Library of Kaman Rhal is no myth. It was the finest repository of knowledge ever collected in one place in recorded history. The library of the Royal Society of Thaumaturgy and Science pales in comparison, and I've spent the better part of ten years acquiring for it."

"Is that what this is still about?" Konowa asked, motioning to the ships in the bay. "We're here to find more books?"

"Not simply books, Major, but *knowledge*. And with that knowledge we will usher in a new era. Imagine the inventions, the discoveries, and now imagine them gathered in one place."

Konowa could, and it filled him with dread. Power had a tendency to coalesce until it blew violently apart, redistributing that power over a very large area. Empires rose and fell that way. "That's been tried before, and it ended badly. Doesn't the story say Kaman Rhal was cut into a hundred pieces and scattered throughout the desert and the high seas? And that his great library was swallowed by the desert along with the town of Urjalla and all of its people?"

Konowa looked at the women, but they remained uncharacteristically silent. He couldn't tell if it was their pique at the Prince, or frustration with him.

"That was then, and this is now," the Prince said. "The Stars have unlocked the potential and it is up to the wise and the swift to harness this new wind of change and put it to use. This, Major, is politics at its finest. I will chart a new course and the Empire and all its subjects will be the better for it. Now, I want this ship unloaded before noon." The Prince took in a deep breath and surveyed the ships in the bay. "It's time for us to change the world."

ELEVEN

blighted lands. It is time to rejoice and to partake in this most Wonderful Occurrence.

For too long, you have suffered under the Tyranny of Chaos and Disunity. Without Strong and Honest governance, these lands have fallen prey to Banditry while the coastline is ravaged by the scourge of Piracy. Discredited and most foul Beliefs have flourished, poisoning the hearts and minds of good and decent people. Be it known far and wide that salvation is at hand. Rejoice!

Know that I, the Prince of Calahr, have come here not to Conquer but to Liberate. The Empire does not seek to subjugate you as you are now by these Lawless Rogues. I come to you as Your Servant, offering succor in your time of Need. Already medicinal supplies, food, and other aid are being distributed among those people who have shown themselves to be friends to the Calahrian Empire and to the cause of Enlightenment and Good Order. The path to your salvation lies in your very hands. Raise them up in praise of your Empire and you shall be saved.

-+->-<+-

CONDUCT TOWARD A

Peaceful *and* Prosperous

NEW DAY

DECREE ONE. Any person—be they human, elf, dwarf, orc, or other—taking up arms or spells against the Calahrian Army or engaging in sabotage so as to cause discomfort and worse shall be considered an enemy of all that is Good and treated without Mercy.

DECREE TWO. Any known agent of the Shadow Monarch, the orcs, or the Lawless Bands that bring only terror and woe must be reported to the nearest Calahrian representative at once. Failure to do so will be viewed as an Act of War against the Calahrian Empire.

DECREE THREE. Any act of rebellion or resistance to the Glorious and Beneficent Works of the Calahrian Empire in these Lands will be met with OVERWHELMING FORCE. Wells will be salted, houses razed to the ground, livestock slaughtered, food stores redistributed to Loyal and Law-abiding citizens, and all modes of transportation confiscated (including camels, horses, mules, and large goats; domesticated dragons any larger than a mule will be shot on sight).

DECREE FOUR. Information pertaining to the location and discovery of the Library of Kaman Rhal, a lost Star, or any other source of Knowledge and Power must be divulged immediately to a representative of the Calahrian Army. Information leading to a Find will be rewarded. Failure to disclose information will be punished (see Decree Three).

→>—<←

HIS ROYAL HIGHNESS,

Prince Tykkin

The stagnant inlet on the western outskirts of Nazalla provided the perfect backdrop for Konowa's mood. He wiped the sweat from his brow and wondered if he was ever destined to find a mode of travel that didn't want to drown him, buck him off, trample him under hoof, or possibly even eat him. He approached his latest mount keeping one hand on the hilt of his saber. The beast stood well over six feet high at its back, which was humped as if it were carrying a large supply bundle. It was covered in a light, short brown fur and was all knobby knees, huge feet, or hooves—he couldn't decide—and a long, curving neck on the end of which was a head that looked comical and unlikely to want to kill him.

Konowa was immediately suspicious.

"What did you say this thing was called, sir?"

The Prince, already mounted on his animal, laughed. "It has many names, Major. Ship of the desert, dromedary, even sand horse, though camel is the most common."

Konowa took a few steps closer, then stopped when his eyes began to water and his gag reflex stretched his jaw muscles until they ached.

"Is it supposed to smell like that?"

"They do give off a certain earthy odor, don't they," the Prince said, his smile unaffected by the pungent musk.

This was one of the many things that bothered Konowa about Prince Tykkin. He was a puffed-up piece of royalty who saw everything as some kind of adventure. It didn't matter if it was dog-spiders, the Shadow Monarch's Emissary, or a smell strong enough to rust metal—to the Prince they were all minor inconveniences that would not be allowed to interfere with his plans. And the truly galling thing was, they didn't. Even when he was thwarted, as when he lost the chance to control the Star at Luugoth Jor, the Prince simply threw a tantrum, then brushed the incident aside and found a new adventure to tackle.

The latest was preparing to lead a ceremonial parade through the streets of Nazalla just past noon under a blazing sun. Konowa squinted and looked toward the city. The cobblestone street they were to march on was bleached white by the sun and felt like the inner wall of a furnace. The effect was stifling. It was the kind of heat Konowa referred to as "stupid." Discipline melted under this kind of sun, and keeping soldiers in line became as challenging as any enemy. Flies buzzed around the assembled soldiers in black sheets. Konowa saw more than one flicker of frost fire as the flies were burned, but he chose to ignore it. He had much, much bigger problems.

The Iron Elves, along with the 5th and 12th infantry regiments, the 3rd Spears from the Timolia Islands, and two troops of artillery cobbled together from some very unhappy naval captains—who had to give up both cannon and crew to man them—were to march in formation, complete with a band, into the city center. No preparations were made at all if the welcome was anything less than joyful, and Konowa had yet to experience one of those. Normally, people started by throwing rocks at you, and it went downhill from there.

"Come now, Major, we are entering the city at the head of the Calahrian Empire. We must show the people that we are powerful, but also respectful of their customs. Regular horses don't fare well here, so we will ride these. It is fitting."

Walking on two feet is fitting, Konowa thought, *and it's highly unlikely they'll run off of their own accord, then turn around and try to stomp you.*

"I'd still like to send in a few patrols first and assess the situation, sir." A few children and some enterprising peddlers had come out to greet them, but that happened no matter what the town or what the war. "We really don't know what our reception will be like when we get into the city proper. And once we're in there, we'll be hemmed in by buildings on all sides. It could be a trap."

"Have a little faith. My proclamation was sent out by Rallie's sreexes the moment we got here and all returned safe and unharmed. The Viceroy himself will no doubt have everything ready for our arrival."

The idea of trusting to yet another Viceroy sent a shiver up

Konowa's spine that had nothing to do with the power of Her magic pressed against his chest.

"Perhaps, but it could also be the perfect way to lure us in," Konowa said, knowing he was going to lose the argument.

"Then let them lure! We are unassailable. The combined fire-power of the fleet's cannon would turn this city to dust if it comes to that, but I suspect we'll be more than a match for anything we find."

Konowa refrained from pointing out that they, too, would be in the middle of the city when the cannonballs struck, and instead tried to recall his conversations with Visyna. Despite their inability to see eye to eye on most everything, he found her words swirling around in his head often. One that stuck was "diplomatic." Konowa decided to give it a try.

"No doubt we would prevail, sir, and the men and I appreciate your confidence in our abilities. I was thinking, however, that we might consider approaching on foot. We'd show the people we are with them, you know at their level . . ."

The Prince leveled his stare at Konowa and held it for several seconds. Konowa felt dirty—if this was what diplomacy made a person do, he wanted no part of it.

"Major, you really must get over your issues with animals. Is it possible you lost the natural elvish affinity for nature's creatures when you lost your ear tip?"

Konowa's left hand was halfway up to his ruined point before he stopped it. "I get along well enough with Jir," he said, frustrated that his furry companion was currently collared and chained inside Rallie's covered wagon. He could still hear the squawking from the caged sreexes though the wagon was over a half mile back.

"A carnivore," the Prince said, his voice becoming dry. "Yes, I have noticed that. Tell me, Major, have you ever stopped to consider that when you have more in common with a four-legged predator than the people around you, it might be time to reconsider your approach to life?"

"Is that an order?" Konowa asked.

Prince Tykkin appeared to think about this for a moment, then spoke. "I dare say it wouldn't matter if it was. You, Major, are the least elflike elf I have ever met. The dwarf has more affinity with nature than you. I'm beginning to think the wars you wage are more with yourself than with anyone else . . . including me."

Konowa didn't know what to say. He realized that the Prince wasn't entirely wrong. He *was* at war, and no one understood the battles he fought. Perhaps, he reconsidered, Private Renwar might. His train of thought got no further as a great ball of a man in a Calahrian Diplomatic Corps uniform came huffing up to stand at attention by the Prince's mount.

Mostly.

The man tried to stand at attention, but kept doubling over trying to catch his breath. Each time he stood up and started to speak, his body would quiver and he'd be back down with both hands on his knees.

The Prince was clearly amused, graciously allowing the man time to catch his wind, which piqued Konowa's curiosity.

"Major Swift Dragon, meet the exalted Viceroy and Queen's representative in these parts, Pimrald Alstonfar. Pimmer, say hello to the infamous Iron Elf."

Sweat streamed off the face of the Viceroy as he stood up long enough to shake Konowa's hand, then doubled over again and heaved in a few more breaths. The Prince laughed and shook his head.

"Pimmer and I were in school together, not exactly a state secret I suppose. He was known even then as an overachiever, although sadly it was at the dinner table."

Konowa could believe that. Corpulent didn't begin to do him
justice. Swollen seemed a better description. Pimmer's jowls oozed
over the collar of his uniform so that it was impossible to see the
braiding there. The silver-plated buttons looked poised to shoot
off like musket balls as the fabric stretched taut around his frame.
His boots splayed outward to keep his considerable center of mass
in an upright position.

The first stirrings of pity rose up in Konowa, then were quickly
snuffed out. Pimmer no doubt owed his position as Viceroy to
strings pulled by the Prince. The result was a crony placed in a
position of authority while those better qualified were passed
over. This was the man who oversaw the Calahrian interests in the
Hasshugeb Expanse, which meant he was responsible for the wel-
fare of Konowa's former elves. The last vestiges of pity were swallowed up by a growing sense of outrage.

"Your Highness, I really wish you would reconsider," Pimmer
finally managed as he stood up straight and stayed there.

"The matter is settled, Pimmer."

"But, Your Grace, it is not safe for you to march through the
city. This is not Celwyn. The population is restless and there is
much talk of insurrection. News of the uprising in Elfkyna and
the return of the Star of Sillra has inflamed passions. The people
expect the Jewel of the Desert to fall next. Fortunetellers all over
the city have been predicting it for days now. The price of tea has
tripled in a week."

Konowa hadn't heard of the Jewel of the Desert, but it made
sense that the Stars would have names appropriate to their locales.

If he ever got wind of a Star of Cold Beer and Warm Women, he might just chuck it all and never look back.

"Then it is time to douse those flames, Pimmer. Really, I had expected better of you. You've had weeks to prepare for our arrival. What have you been doing with your time, besides gorging yourself?" the Prince asked, using the toe of his boot to nudge him in the stomach.

Konowa was surprised to find himself agreeing with the Prince.

"I have been negotiating with the Suljak of the Hasshugeb," Pimmer said, then continued when neither the Prince nor Konowa indicated they knew what that meant. "He's the spiritual leader for every tribe in these lands. From warlord to goatherd, they all listen to him. It is through his intervention that the trade routes remain open. It's the Suljak, and the Suljak alone, who can talk to the Gaura tribe. They make up half the population. The Suljak has brokered a deal between them and us, and because of that the other tribes are falling into line. Without him, we would be lost here, now more than ever."

The Prince waved a hand in front of his face to get rid of some flies. "Pimmer, you remain a candle without a wick. The trade routes remain open because we have outposts guarding them and soldiers patrolling them." The Prince looked down at Konowa and pointed to him. "In fact, you have among the troops at your disposal the original Iron Elves. Despite the major's past indiscretions, which we won't get into here, the regiment was, as it is again under my command, Her Majesty's finest. I am sure the elves you have are up to the task of keeping the rabble in these parts in check."

"Yes, well . . . about the elves," Pimmer began, looking between the Prince and Konowa. "The situation here is a very complicated one. There are certain subtleties that you should be aware—"

"Enough, Pimmer!" the Prince said, his voice spooking his camel. The animal reflexively kicked a front leg out and directly at Konowa. Konowa jumped out of the way, though the foot grazed his saber's scabbard. "The time for subtlety is over. Events call for action, and I can see I arrived here not a moment too soon. I thought you'd have a chance to prove yourself out here in the southern wastes and away from the pressures that gather at the center of the Empire. It appears even in this vastness you are in over your head. I will deal with you later. Now, we will march, and the people of Nazalla will know that the Empire is the only power that matters."

Alwyn took his spectacles off and rubbed them against his sleeve. He held them up to the sun and squinted. The glass was scratched in several places. Sighing, he put them back on. A moment later the order to come to attention rang out. Boots slammed down on the cobblestones, kicking up a waist-high dust storm.

The Prince rode a camel in front of the formation and looked out over the regiment with a slow, steady gaze. He paused twice, as if spying something that displeased him, then let his gaze travel on. Alwyn realized he had seen the Prince do this before. Major Swift Dragon was also astride a camel, but where the Prince was steady and at ease, the major looked like someone holding on for dear life. The major's camel took a half step, then stopped and lowered its head, nearly pitching Major Swift Dragon onto the ground. The major quickly regained his saddle and sawed back on the reins with obvious effort until the camel brought its head up.

The Prince cleared his throat. "Soldiers of the Calahrian Imperial Army! Untold centuries of history look down upon you and will judge your actions," he said, pointing theatrically out to the desert beyond the city.

A smudge on the horizon indicated a rising plateau, or perhaps just a smudge on Alwyn's spectacles, he couldn't be sure. A few soldiers turned to look, some even putting up a hand to shield their eyes. One, and it sounded an awful lot like Scolly, asked, *Where? I don't see nothing.*

"Know that I have delivered this very day a proclamation to the peoples of this land, informing them that their days of subjugation at the hands of petty tyrants and wielders of dark magics is at an end. The proclamation reads as follows . . ."

"Well, that seems a bit holier than thou if you ask me," Yimt said, dabbing a bit of white pipeclay onto his nose. Alwyn adjusted his spectacles and followed suit. He'd learned that however odd a thing might seem, if Yimt did it it was worth copying . . . except when it came to recipes . . . and crute . . . and drink . . . actually, there were a lot of exceptions, but often the dwarf got it right.

"What does?"

Yimt spat out a wad of crute, which sizzled and boiled on the sun-baked cobblestones. He immediately shoved a fresh batch between gum and cheek and continued. "Telling us brave and fearless siggers that history is looking down at us, as if we've done something wrong."

"I don't think that's what he meant," Alwyn said.

Yimt continued as if he hadn't heard. "All that untold history that came before us should by rights be looking up at us with admiration and awe. You see," he said, lowering his voice theatrically, "we're at what you call the full crumb of history."

Scolly turned his head. "What, you mean like bread?"

Alwyn started to shake his head, but Yimt nodded.

"Aye, Scolly, you're right. This heat must be good for your noggin." Yimt looked around at the soldiers near him. "The trick is, lads, to think of history as one big loaf. Slices are what you call centuries. But each slice is made up by a lot of crumbs, and in every slice there is what the peelitical types call a full crumb." A few soldiers smiled at this and Yimt wagged a finger at them. "Makes perfect sense, it does. Who among you didn't grow up savoring the smell of fresh-baked bread? Ideas is a lot like that, so it stands to reason a deep thinker would use it to explain things, knowing it's something fellows at the shallow end of the reflectin' pool like you lot could understand. See, there's this special crumb that holds the slice, or century, together. That's the full crumb, and that's where we're at right now."

Alwyn glanced toward the Prince. He'd finished reading the proclamation and was now droning on about the Empire and power and opportunities, but the soldiers around Yimt were hanging on the dwarf's every word. It made Alwyn wonder what would happen if a person could rise to power based not on his bloodline, but on his ability to captivate an audience. Then again, Yimt's nickname, "The Little Mad One," was well earned, so perhaps it was for the best he was only a sergeant.

"In fact," Yimt said, standing up a little straighter, "you could say we Iron Elves are that full crumb. We're the bit that every other bit of the slice that makes up this rigmarole with the Shadow Monarch and falling Stars and the rest of it hinge on."

Hrem leaned forward and asked the obvious question. "So, if we're this full crumb, and everything is one big slice of bread, how do we break this oath? I don't want to be a shadow for eternity doing the bidding of that elf witch and Her twisted trees. And I want Her out of my dreams."

Every head nodded at this.

"That pales in comparison to the larger issue," Inkermon said. "As vile a temptress as She is, the oath must be broken or our souls will never be free to depart to the great reward beyond. We'll be trapped."

The Prince's voice could be heard clearly in the background, but no one was paying attention now.

"So what do we do?" Alwyn asked. "How do we break the oath and free ourselves from the Shadow Monarch?"

Yimt spat another wad of crute and looked around him. He held up a hand and for the briefest moment black flames danced across his upturned palm.

"My poor, sweet, thick-as-two-fat-arsed-orcs-pressed-together. I thought it would be perfectly obvious to you by now, especially in this heat." He looked around at them with a wicked twinkle in his eye. "We make toast."

TWELVE

A regiment smells.

It's supposed to. It marches through mud and flame, washed as much by blood and filth as it is by rain. It churns the earth and rends the air as it grinds itself to a keen edge, growing thinner as it grows sharper.

It smells of sweat and urine and beer. It wears with honor the musk of old leather and the pungent sting of boot polish and the must of brick dust. The rotten-egg stink of black powder mixes with the cool tang of steel. Waves of odors steam from it in the heat, creating a distinctive blend of hewn wood, fresh manure, and maggoty bread, all filtered through the constant haze of harsh tobacco smoke.

At times, it also smells of fear, and courage—the two so inextricably entwined they are as one.

Above all, a regiment smells of life: foul, heady, and intense.

The Iron Elves, however, smelled of one more thing; the oath. It permeated everything, and though no one could describe it, it was distinct and unmistakable.

Alwyn had come to think of it as a pool of spreading blood; dark, thick, and permanent. It was a subject few of the soldiers wanted to talk about, and even when he spoke with Miss Red Owl and Miss Tekoy and even Rallie, he couldn't really explain it, and they could never fully understand.

Think staining wood, he told himself, trying to blot the image of blood from his mind. Wood could be sanded, varnished even, and painted over. Wood was malleable, natural, and retained elements of its spirit even after its death, or at least that's what Miss Red Owl and Miss Tekoy told him.

Alwyn shifted his weight from his good leg to his wooden leg and then back again as they waited for the order to march. The Prince was still talking, but Alwyn made no effort to hear what he was saying. The sun pressed its heat down on Alwyn like a thick, flat paving stone. His head was dizzy and it felt like an oven inside his shako. He ran an already sweat-stained cuff across his forehead and tried to focus on something else.

The pack on his back was digging into the fleshy bit right above his waist. He adjusted the straps and shrugged a couple of times, but failed to find a more comfortable position. It wasn't hard to figure out why. Soldiers carried their lives on their backs like two-legged pack mules, though Alwyn thought mules were probably treated better. He tried to think of what he could throw away the first chance he got. The obvious choice was the greatcoat and blanket wrapped into a roll and strapped to the top of his pack. The bundle forced his head forward at an uncomfortable angle, and in this kind of heat he couldn't see why he'd need either of them.

"Sergeant," he said as Yimt walked past checking the rows.

Yimt turned and walked over, making a show of looking Alwyn up and down. "Any chance we could lose the coat and blanket?"

"Yeah, how 'bout it, Sarge?" Zwitty added, already reaching up and undoing the straps to take his off.

Yimt grabbed the hem of his caerna and began flapping it to create a breeze. "I'd be the first to admit that this heat is frying my giblets, but it won't always be this hot. You keep that gear stowed." A few soldiers began flapping their caernas, though not with quite the dwarf's vigor.

Zwitty clicked his tongue. "Those sergeant's stripes are going to your head."

"My fist will be going upside yours if you give me any more lip, Private," Yimt said, a cheery smile on his face that suggested there would be nothing he'd like more. "Bloody babes in the woods the lot of you. Mark my words, any soldier who somehow manages to lose his coat or bedroll will be begging to buy one for twenty gold coins. This ain't like Elfkyna. This heat is quick. It fires up fast and cools off even faster."

Grumbling greeted this assessment, but they'd all learned by now that if Yimt said something was worth holding on to, you guarded it with your life. The dwarf leaned in toward Alwyn and motioned for him to bend over so they couldn't be overheard. "An enterprising young lad might just try to pick up an extra blanket if he can. You never know what the nights will bring . . ."

Alwyn pondered that as Yimt walked away, but the heat quickly pushed it out of his mind. Surely there was something he could get rid of.

On leaving the ship for the last time, a fact that had raised morale among the regiment despite the daunting prospect of fighting in an unknown desert land, they'd all been issued with four days' worth of salted beef and ship's biscuits. When Alwyn compared that with the even more daunting prospect of Yimt's cooking, he decided the food was worth holding on to. He'd never part with his housewife with its essential needles and thread, a gift from Mr. Yuimi, the little elf tailor, when Alwyn had joined up. The extra shirt, stockings, polishing kit, and coin purse were equally crucial and not to be left behind.

Alwyn looked down his front and patted the canteen filled with water and the gourd filled with *rok har*, the tree sap elixir the elves of the Long Watch drank for energy on long journeys. He wouldn't be giving those up, or the pouch carrying sixty-five rounds of musket balls and powder charges or his musket or bayonet.

He sighed and shrugged his shoulders again. Pain and suffering seemed to be the constant state of being of a soldier in the Iron Elves. He tried to remember a time when that wasn't the case, but such memories proved elusive.

Alwyn shifted his weight again and winced.

"Looks like you're due for a watering," Hrem said, pointing down toward Alwyn's wooden leg.

The twisted branches that made up the false leg did indeed look dry. Alwyn unslung his musket from his shoulder and handed it to Hrem, then grabbed the wooden gourd given to him by Miss Red Owl. He poured out a small amount of the *rok har* into his hand then bent over to rub it into the wood. It was a challenge to keep his balance, but Hrem helpfully moved closer to allow Alwyn to lean against him.

"Why don't you just take it off to do that?" Scolly asked, forever fascinated and slightly afraid of the appendage.

"It doesn't like to go back on," Alwyn said. The magic imbued in the crafted leg made for him by Miss Red Owl and Miss Tekoy was a true marvel, the woven branches flexing where the ankle and the knee would be. He had tried wearing a boot over the roots that acted as his foot, but found he had more stability without the boot and left it off except for ceremonial occasions like this one.

Alwyn lifted the hem of his caerna to show Scolly where the branches thinned and became green vines, which wrapped around the stump of his leg. Parts of the vines were blackened while the flesh of his leg was bright red and raw in a couple of places. For the moment, no frost fire sparkled along the areas where vine and skin touched.

"The magic of the oath doesn't seem to like the magic in the wood too much," Alwyn said, rubbing the area around the stump gently before lowering his caerna.

"You're a fool, you know that?" Zwitty said, staring at the leg. "Losing that leg was your ticket out of this nightmare. Why didn't you get yourself shipped back to Calahr when you had the chance, or at least stay back in Elfkyna?"

"There is no out," Teeter said. "We're all in this to the end, and maybe even beyond the end. I don't care what Sergeant Arkhorn said, I don't see how we survive this."

A sharp, disapproving snort indicated Inkermon's thoughts on the subject. "We must find a way. We just need faith."

"Or something else," Alwyn said. "We all saw what happened to Kester."

"Yeah, he burned alive with his shadow and now he's dead," Zwitty said.

"But he didn't join the others, at least, not yet," Alwyn said.

Zwitty's eyes widened. "Not yet? He's still dead, and he screamed as if the flames burning his shadow were burning him from the inside. Hrem felt it. You felt it. Are you telling us that's a pleasant way to go? And go where? There might just be worse things than serving in the afterlife, you know."

"I can't imagine them," Alwyn said. Images of ghostly hands reaching out to him remained a constant companion during his waking hours.

"Aye, I felt it," Hrem said, "and it was like being pulled apart a little bit at a time, all while burning." His voice was so soft that all the soldiers shuddered to hear him say it.

Alwyn had felt that, too, but he didn't share their reaction. "But what if we could learn to control it? What if we could use it to burn away the oath and then stop?"

"And what if you couldn't stop it and your shadow keeps burning until you're dead? Then what?" Zwitty asked for all of them.

Alwyn never got the chance to reply as bellowing broke out along the formation of troops. It was time to march.

"Right, lads, look sharp!" Yimt shouted as he strode up to them. "This is the citizenry of Nazalla's first time getting a peek at you and you'd better look aces. You're Iron Elves now and that means something to folks. We're the ones that took on the Shadow Monarch and Her beasties at Luuguth Jor and handed them their keesters in a basket."

A roar went up from the Iron Elves. Backs straightened and eyes brightened.

"We're the bloody bastards what took island after island and cleared 'em safe."

The roar was louder now. The heat suddenly didn't seem so oppressive.

"Sure, you're probably doomed for all eternity to a life of misery and woe, but oh, what woe you'll sow!"

Creases were brushed flat, spit smoothed down stray hairs, and shakos were adjusted to the perfect jaunty angle. The snap of cloth drew nods of approval as the Colors, the pair of flags that served as every regiment's badge of honor, were unfurled in the blazing sun. The Queen's Colors rose first, the royal cipher surrounded by a leafy garland on a background of silver-green offering a stark contrast to their dusty white surroundings.

The tops of boots were given a final buff on the backs of stockinged legs as the Regimental Colors were hoisted. A murmur of grudging acceptance greeted the black flag. Battle honors for Luuguth Jor and the island chain now adorned the mountain outlined in silver along with the Elvish script *Æri Mekah*; Into the Fire. What other regiment took *that* into battle?

"I'd wager my weight in gold every creepy-crawly-nasty-ugly the world over is hunting for you," Yimt said, thumping his chest with vigor. "They probably think, seeing as you ain't really elves, your poor excuse for a hide would make a nice throw rug in their cave!"

Caernas were twirled, then hitched up or down so that the hem rode right at the kneecap. Muskets were pressed just that much tighter against shoulders and jaws jutted out until they ached.

"But if anyone ever tells you lads you don't got pointy ears, by the deuce boyos, you look 'em in the eye and tell 'em you got iron balls!"

Birds startled into the air and camels bucked as the Iron Elves roared their approval. They might be doomed, damned, and buggered for all eternity, but that didn't mean they couldn't sparkle like a diamond in the sun and grin like a skull in moonlight on their way to oblivion.

A regiment smells. It's supposed to. Among all the things the Iron Elves smelled of, something new asserted itself; pride.

THIRTEEN

Visyna batted away some flies and watched the crowd lining the street as the parade marched past. Some waved, and a few brave children ran out to beg for food and tobacco, but most of the citizens of Nazalla simply stood and stared. She tried to put a word to it. The crowd was . . . careful. The people lined the streets because they were expected to. Whatever resentment they harbored they kept in check, at least while the sun was in the sky. At night, Visyna could imagine the city becoming something very different, and very ugly.

It reminded her of Elfkyna. She remembered all too well the feelings of helplessness and rage at watching the soldiers of the Empire marching across her land. And she remembered with crystalline clarity how it felt to stand up to that force and fight, in her own way, to help her people. Elfkyna wasn't free yet, but it had its guiding Star again, and the people saw that as a sign of good things to come. Visyna desperately hoped their faith would be rewarded.

Perhaps the return of a Star here would do the same for these people. *They must want to be free just as all people do.*

She shifted in her seat beside Rallie on the wagon and looked back to where the other regiments followed behind in the column.

"Not quite the same reaction, is it?" Rallie said, puffing on a cigar.

It wasn't. Once the Iron Elves had passed it was as if a cloud lifted. The once-subdued crowd became more boisterous. The mood of the people lightened. It wasn't outright joy, but the fear that they'd felt as the Iron Elves neared was reason enough to cele-brate when the regiment had passed.

"The oath is a burden the soldiers should never have had to bear. The darkness of it permeates everything around them." Flies buzzed around her face, landing in the corner of her eyes and even trying to crawl up her nose.

"It is most unfortunate, no doubt about it," Rallie said. "Still, they are handling it well, for the most part."

More people were coming out of doorways of the white-washed buildings to line the street. Shuttered windows opened and roofs teemed with the curious. A few greetings rang out, and from a couple of roofs dates and olives rained down on the soldiers. Children, fascinated by the colorful and noisy procession, scam-pered among the soldiers with unrestrained glee. Those who came close to Rallie's wagon, however, quickly retreated when they heard the noises coming from inside. Visyna wasn't sure who was more agitated by the situation, the sreex or Jir. Dandy, the massive silver-beaked falcon, was currently perched on the crow's nest of the *Black Spike*—until needed, as Rallie put it.

"How long will this last before they turn on them and a full-scale revolt breaks out?" Visyna asked. "I felt their fear as the Iron

Elves marched by. That fear is going to turn to anger. I saw it happen in Elfkyna."

"Possibly," Rallie said, "although the Viceroy in Nazalla has a decidedly lighter hand than the last two Viceroys you knew in your homeland. In the end, it probably won't matter. Between the pent-up resentment and the prospect of change, there would have been a new order here before much longer whether the Iron Elves had arrived or not. Their Star is returning," she said, pointing at the crowd, "and soon. That is what will tip the balance."

"And make for some very good reading in the *Imperial Weekly Herald*," Visyna said. She meant it as a joke, but it was hard not to notice that the more "interesting" things became, the more Rallie was interested in being there.

"I suppose I am quite like the vulture, when you put it that way," Rallie said.

"I wasn't trying to insult you," Visyna said, hoping she hadn't offended the older woman.

"You didn't, dear," Rallie said, reaching out a hand and patting her arm. "I myself have questioned the role I play on more than one occasion. I am cursed with an overpowering curiosity and thirst to know the truth of things, no matter how tawdry . . . or bloody."

"Don't you ever get tired of it?"

"Constantly, but then a new day dawns, a Star returns, and I find myself standing there in the middle of it all soaking up every morsel I can."

Visyna chose her next words carefully. "You do more than simply observe."

"I do what I can to help things along, no more. If my dispatches can aid them in any way, I would be pleased," Rallie said, pointing toward the Iron Elves.

"I wasn't referring to your writing," Visyna said. "You wield power, Rallie."

"I am not without . . . abilities," Rallie said.

Visyna decided to push the issue. "Are they any you can teach me?"

Rallie turned her head slightly to look at Visyna. "You weave magic I couldn't begin to understand. You pluck and stroke the very essence of the world around you. What I do is something very different, and not nearly as wholesome."

"Her Emissary was afraid of you, at Luuguth Jor. It said this was not your time. What did it mean by that?"

Rallie turned back to look straight ahead. The wagon rolled along the cobbles, passing more people. An open square appeared off to their left, its center adorned with a cluster of thick-trunked palms. Visyna was about to try again when Rallie spoke.

"I'm not entirely sure what Her Emissary meant. I do have a theory, but it's not one I can share with you yet," Rallie said. "Tell me, my dear, how old do you think I am?"

Visyna recalled a similar question arising on board the *Black Spike* and decided to tread carefully. "Early . . . fifties," she ventured, figuring Rallie was probably closer to seventy, possibly even eighty.

Rallie laughed and slapped a hand against a thigh. "Early fifties! Oh, you are a jar of honey, aren't you? The thing of it is," she said, lowering her voice again, "I have no idea. I can remember the last two hundred years quite clearly, but everything gets hazy after that."

Visyna sat up straight. "Two hundred years? Do you have elf blood, or is this your magic?"

Rallie gave her a quizzical look. "That's just it, I don't know. There are pieces of memory in my head clear as a bell on a cold winter morning, yet I don't recall ever being there, or doing the things I seem to remember doing. Quite fascinating, really."

"Were you bespelled? How far back do these pieces of memory go?" Visyna asked. She knew Rallie had secrets, but this was amazing . . . and a little frightening. *Who was this woman?*

"There are memories that I have no right to remember," Rallie said, brings a hand up to rub her nose. Visyna realized it also served to cover her mouth as she spoke. "Memories of when the Stars were first born."

The questions piled up in Visyna's mind until she almost couldn't speak. "How is that possible? What does it mean?"

"That, my dear, is what I am working on. At the moment, I have no good answer, but like you, many good questions. I had hoped being at Luuguth Jor would unlock more of these memories, and it has, but they are giving up their secrets rather slowly. I need to find a way to speed things up, because I have come to believe that what I remember might be very useful."

"At Luuguth Jor, you welcomed the Star back as if you knew it," Visyna said, remembering the event clearly.

Rallie looked over at her again. "The thing of it is, I think I do, but for the life of me I cannot figure out how, or why. Too many pieces of the puzzle are missing. I hope being here will fill in a few more gaps," she said, looking around at Nazalla as the wagon rolled on.

They sat in silence for some time after that. Visyna tried to imagine what it could mean. Was Rallie really over two hundred years old? And if two hundred, how much older? Could she really have been there when the Stars were born? But why would someone with such power have such a poor memory? A thought occurred to Visyna.

"Kaman Rhal's Lost Library might have some——"

"——of the answers I seek," Rallie said, finishing her sentence. "Yes, the thought did occur to me."

Visyna marveled at the realization. "All this time I thought you were here because of Konowa and the Iron Elves. You've really been following the Prince, knowing he would eventually lead you to the library."

"True, but I think I'd have followed these Iron Elves and the major at some point regardless. They are endlessly fascinating, especially Sergeant Arkhorn."

Visyna decided to leave that subject alone. A few tossed dates landed on the canvas tarp stretched over the wagon. Rallie turned around to look over her shoulder. "Be a dear and grab the one that doesn't look like the others."

Visyna turned, half expecting a joke, but she immediately saw that one was indeed very different from the others. She reached out to take it and realized immediately by its feel that it was a chunk of polished wood carved and stained to look like a date.

She leaned over to give it to Rallie, but she shook her head and kept her eyes on the street ahead.

"Open it, but in your lap so that no can see."

Visyna pulled the fake date apart. Inside was a tiny piece of rolled-up parchment. She carefully unrolled it. The script was foreign to her. She held it in the palm of her hand and tilted it so Rallie could read it.

"What does it say?" Visyna asked.

Rallie reached out a hand and gently touched the paper, which immediately turned to ash. "It says three things. The first is that we are not the only ones searching for the original elves."

Visyna batted at more flies, finally giving in and artfully weaving a touch of magic to ward them away. "We already know the Shadow Monarch is seeking them out."

Rallie continued. "It also says something other than the Shadow Monarch looks for them, but what it is and what its designs are remain unknown."

"Something else? Could it have something to do with what happened on the last island?"

Rallie passed the reins into her right hand as she rubbed her chin in thought. "As I told the major last night, I don't know, but it seems as good a guess as any at the moment."

"What is the third thing?" Visyna asked.

"The third thing it says," Rallie said, her gravelly voice growing quiet so that Visyna had to lean in to hear it, "is beware the one bearing many shadows."

Visyna sat back up and looked again at the people lining the street. "The one with many shadows? I've never heard of such a thing. Is it a riddle?" She looked at the column of marching soldiers. "The Iron Elves have many shadows."

Rallie flicked the reins and stared straight ahead. "An interesting thought. That could be it, though as we're smack in the middle of them, I suspect my informant is talking about something else."

"Why wouldn't he know?"

"*She*," Rallie said, "is in a unique position to know more than most, but not perhaps to piece it all together. Whatever this thing of many shadows is, at the moment I have no good answer."

They rode on in silence, the crowds watching with guarded expressions as the troops marched past. There were many things in this world that disturbed Visyna, but hearing Rallie say there was something she hadn't heard of suddenly shot to the top of the list. Visyna was certain that couldn't be good.

FOURTEEN

Not exactly a stroll down the Boulevard of Heroes back in Celwyn, but I'm damn proud of the lot of you all the same," Yimt said. "You kept it together and paraded like the shiny siggers that I knew you were. The major himself said seeing you march like that brought tears to his eyes."

"The major really said that?" Scolly asked.

Yimt rolled his eyes. "Sometimes I don't know if I want to pat you on the head with my hand or the butt of my shatterbow. Now listen up, lads, and you might just learn something, even you, Scolly."

They stood at the crossroads of six alleyways in a labyrinthine marketplace that made the one in Port Ghamjal in Elfkyna look positively orderly. Blind beggars lined the street with wide, flat bowls at their feet, their milky eyes staring sightlessly into the distance while their hands reached out, palms up, imploring. Market stalls were crammed in tight with little more than a hanging rug dividing them. Wares of every shape, size, and color spilled out into the alleys, and more hung from canopies restricting passage to little more than one person wide. Lanterns were flickering to life as dusk settled over the city. Everything was becoming shadow.

Alwyn pushed forward as the other soldiers gathered round. Emotions were close to the surface. Weeks of floating on the high seas with only one nightmarish island after another to break up the monotony had taken their toll. The whole regiment was ready to give the cauldron a stir and see what bubbled up.

Fortunately, they had been allowed to leave their packs and greatcoats at the temporary camp now set up on the grounds of the Viceroy's palace near the center of the city, but all had their muskets slung over their shoulders. By order of the Prince, their muskets were not supposed to be loaded. Yimt, however, had a different view on the subject, and every soldier had rammed a charge and musket ball down the barrel before they set forth, but out of view of the Prince.

Yimt looked around him and scratched his beard. Everyone leaned in a little closer.

"We've been given a night to dust off the old crystal ball and peer into the depths of our depraved and sordid souls. In a place like Nazalla, whatever you desire is most definitely available . . . for a price. After what we've been through I ain't judgin', so whatever you want, now's the time to shout it out. Now then, what sort of mayhem and mischief are you looking for?"

Roars of beer, wine, and other liquid refreshment echoed off the walls and startled a few beggars, who suddenly found their sight wasn't as bad as all that and quickly took off for other parts. Alwyn had considered staying in the temporary camp, but Yimt wouldn't hear of it, and now that Alwyn was here, he was glad he'd allowed himself to be dragged along.

"Easy, easy," Yimt said, motioning with his hands to calm down. "Let's try not to frighten them off before we get our drinks, shall we? What about you, Inkermon? They have fruit juices and arr as black as tar that they serve in tiny little cups."

"Wine is permitted on certain occasions, in moderation, of course, and with the proper rites observed," the religious farmer said. Looks of stunned surprise greeted this statement.

"Now I know the world's coming to an end," Hrem said, eliciting a few laughs. "Our holy man is going to lift a few with us heathens."

Yimt nodded his approval. "There might be hope for you yet, Inkermon. Wine, you say? If my memory serves, they make one here from watermelons that'll have you dancing the night away. Well, maybe not *dancing* exactly."

"I'm starving," Scolly interrupted, pushing his bulk forward. "All that talk about bread and crumbs earlier got my gut all worked up. I could eat just about anything right now, but no salt."

There were nods of agreement. Alwyn was convinced that if it rained now, he'd melt into one large pile of salt. How the sailors ate that food for months on end, he didn't know.

"I asked around at the palace," Yimt said. "Most of the food here will clear your pipes and set sparklers off behind your eyeballs."

"Drink and wine is, well, fine," Teeter said, "but where would a fellow go for a little . . . companionship? Doomed or not, we were on that ship a long bloody time."

This time there was some muttering and shuffling of feet. Alwyn was embarrassed to feel his face flushing. Until now, his thoughts had been so consumed with the oath and the nightmares that he hadn't even considered the possibility of anything normal.

From island to island, there had been no chance to think about a time beyond the horrors. Now that they had a whole night to just be themselves, he didn't know what to do with it. Others, but not all, appeared to be equally perplexed.

Yimt hung his head in mock shame. "I'm embarrassed to say I know you. Laddies, are you familiar with what the fine folk call reet-oracle speaking?"

Blank stares greeted Yimt.

"It's when I already know the answer to my question. Like I said, I did some asking around at the palace. The place for us is the Blue Scorpion. If the palace guard weren't lying through their teeth, whatever you're looking for tonight, and I do mean *whatever*, we'll find it there."

"I was thinking of wandering the market a bit," Hrem said, "maybe picking up a little something for the missus."

Yimt shook his head. "Forget that. You saw the crowd today. We've got to stick together, especially at night. Wasn't like this twenty years ago, I can tell you that. Nazalla's changed, and not for the better." He turned and pointed to a wall where a long scroll was pasted to the dusty-white stucco. "They can paper this entire city with the Prince's proclamation, but it ain't going to stop your purse being stolen or your throat bein' slit. There's dangerous folk here that would just as soon knife you as say hello."

"Let them try," Zwitty said. He held out his hand and frost fire burned to life. Everyone jumped back. Very few soldiers, of whom Alwyn was one, exhibited a natural skill in wielding the flame and could control it. With the rest, like Zwitty, it was like giving a loaded musket to a child.

"Douse that!" Yimt ordered, quickly looking around to see if they'd been seen. "You want a riot? Listen up, all of you. It was one thing to play with the frost when we were out on them islands and the ship, but now we're in a city where people got funny ideas about magic and curses. I don't want to see so much as a spark tonight, is that clear?"

Zwitty sneered and closed his hands. The black flame continued to burn.

"Was I not clear? Put that bloody flame out now," Yimt said.

"Quit playing around, Zwitty, and put it out," Teeter added.

"All of you stop yelling at me and I will," Zwitty said, his voice rising an octave. He squeezed his fists tighter and closed his eyes, but the frost continued to burn. The air in the immediate area began to turn cold.

Yimt blew out his cheeks and raised a fist. "Zwitty, this is your last chance. Put that blasted fire out now."

Zwitty opened his eyes and looked around at the group. Though he tried to hide it, there was terror in his eyes. Alwyn realized the problem. *He can't put it out.*

"Stay calm," Alwyn said, walking toward Zwitty.

"I am calm!" Zwitty shouted, starting to back up. "Just leave me alone. I can't concentrate with everyone yelling at me!" The frost fire was now creeping up his forearm, and mist formed with every word he said.

A few passersby stopped and stared. Hrem took a step toward them and they quickly continued on their way.

"We'd better get him out fast or all of Nazalla's going to know about it," Hrem said.

"Ally, can you put him out like you did Kester?" Yimt asked.

Alwyn nodded. "I think so. This isn't the white fire, Zwitty's just not in control of the magic."

"I know what I'm doing," Zwitty said, even as the black flames grew higher. "I just . . . it's so cold . . ." He staggered, then stood upright again.

"Ally, put him out. Now!" Yimt ordered.

Alwyn strode forward and grabbed Zwitty's wrists in his hands. Immediately the frost fire sprang to life in Alwyn's hands, and he felt the cold flow of the magic coursing through him. "Easy, Zwitty, easy."

". . . help me . . ." Zwitty said, his eyes shut tight. His lips were quivering and black frost was forming on his face.

Shadows appeared, their spectral shapes forming a ring around the group of soldiers. The air temperature dropped to freezing. Someone screamed, and running feet were heard disappearing down an alleyway.

"People are watching, Sergeant," Hrem said, pointing to a gathering crowd several yards away.

Dead hands reached out to Alwyn and Zwitty. Alwyn gritted his teeth and focused. The black flame roared higher, bathing everything in a cold, dark light, then went out without a sound. Zwitty collapsed to a knee and Alwyn blew out his breath, releasing Zwitty's wrists.

The shades wavered, then they, too, disappeared. The air immediately felt warmer.

"Nothing to see here, folks, just a little trickery by a jokester," Yimt said, his metal teeth glinting as he smiled broadly. "Get him up and get moving," Yimt whispered under his breath.

Alwyn and Scolly helped Zwitty to his feet and they all started walking down an alley.

"You okay, Zwitty?" Scolly asked.

Zwitty coughed and shook off their grip. "Course I'm okay. I just about had it when Ally here stepped in to play hero."

Yimt led them down an alley, then through a couple of turns until there didn't appear to be anyone following them. "He saved your arse is what he did," Yimt said, finally bringing them to a halt.

"I—" Zwitty started to say, but Yimt cut him off.

"You were a heartbeat away from joining the Darkly Departed is what you were," Yimt said, jabbing a finger in Zwitty's chest. "Personally, I don't give a rat-dragon's scaly little hide if you do join them, but you ain't going to ruin our night." He looked at the rest of them. "Lads, in case you hadn't noticed, we're in it up to our necks already. The last thing we need," he said, turning his gaze back to Zwitty, "is to make matters worse on our own."

Alwyn looked down at his own hands.

"Now," Yimt said, his voice sounding jovial again, "follow me, stay close, and try, *try* not to do anything stupid. Again." Yimt set off at a quick pace, motioning for Hrem to walk beside him. Alwyn was momentarily hurt by this, then realized the reason why. It sometimes took a moment for people to recognize the danger Yimt presented. Hrem's hulking frame, on the other hand, made it immediately obvious, and their route through the crowded alleyways quickly cleared.

Yimt kept up a running commentary on the joys of Nazalla as they passed by market stands. There were bolts of shimmering cloth in colors that, until that moment, Alwyn never knew existed, intricately woven wicker baskets, perfectly shaped pyramids of spices, nuts, and fruits. One sign written in several languages promised the shopper the finest in magic potions, amulets, and assorted accoutrements for the discerning witch or wizard, while another was nothing more than an oval of beaten and polished brass.

Alwyn started to make a mental note of several shops with the intent to come back and visit sometime when things were safer, but then stopped. *What did it matter? How many more times would he face death before it finally claimed him?* The pain in his stump became more noticeable and he was about to tell Yimt he was going back to the camp when the group came to a sudden halt. He worked his way to the front and found Yimt breathing deeply and smiling.

"Ahh, now this is what I'm talking about. Lads, first thing you learn in the soldiering business is you don't pick a pub on the way it looks. You pick it by the way it smells. Now all of you, take a whiff." The coming night and cooling temperature had not yet had a dampening effect on the aroma that was the Nazalla market and Alwyn took a deep breath slowly and with reservations.

At first, all he could smell was manure. Several kinds of manure. He waded through the many variations and then suddenly found a trace of something not entirely repulsive. Stale beer, harsh tobacco smoke, the charred tang of roasting meat, and sweat were clearly coming from a doorway off to their left. His mouth began to salivate and suddenly his throat was parched and his stomach rumbling. He could always go back to camp after he'd had something to eat.

He saw Yimt looking at him and smiling.

"That, my lads, is the smell of nerve-anna," Yimt said.

"She's a pungent tart," Teeter offered.

Yimt seemed to be counting under his breath for a few seconds. "Not a she, an it. Ain't you ever read a book of words? Nerve-anna—it means a place of special wonderfulness, and in this place, that's called the Blue Scorpion." He turned and motioned for them to follow, stepping through the darkened doorway and disappearing. Alwyn followed suit, watching the ground carefully so as not to trip up on his wooden leg. He passed through two sets of hanging beads after untangling them from his musket, then down a narrow hall and through another set of beads. He emerged in what up to that point he had only ever read about—a den of iniquity.

It was hard to tell where the ceiling was because a layer of dense, blue-tinged smoke hovered about six feet above the floor. Alwyn took a step and looked down. Carpets covered every inch of the floor. Each was a work of art with intricate designs of flowers and fruits that looked almost as real as paintings.

"Where do we sit?' Scolly asked.

Alwyn started to say chairs, then realized there was no furniture. Fat, wide pillows replaced chairs, and an array of silver, brass, and wood platters substituted for tables.

The patrons of the Blue Scorpion studied them closely as they entered, and though the buzz of conversation quieted, it did not stop. It took Alwyn a moment to realize there were only men here. Each brown face looked as if it had spent a lifetime in the sun, which Alwyn figured they probably had. The men wore the native garb of layered cloth wraps that flowed loosely about them. The colors were not nearly as bright as the cloth Alwyn had seen in the market, though. To a man they wore small, white cylindrical hats on their heads and everyone was clean-shaven. Yimt's beard didn't seem to bother them, or perhaps the muskets over their shoulders stopped their tongues.

A short, stocky man wearing an apron over his robes came bustling up to them and bowed. Yimt returned the bow and the two began conversing in what Alywn assumed must be the local language. At one point Yimt pointed to Hrem, then at Alwyn's leg, and finally began gesturing with his shatterbow. The hum in the pub quieted, then grew in volume as the weapon traced an arc about the room. After that there was more bowing and the conversation between Yimt and the man was clearly concluded.

"Welcome, most honored guests, to the Blue Scorpion," the man said. His smile appeared genuine and he sounded friendly, but Alwyn noticed Yimt's shatterbow was not yet slung. "Please, I have room for you in the back." They followed and found a large area partially secluded from the rest of the room by hanging curtains of fine, green-colored mesh. Dark blue pillows with gold tassels at each corner formed a circle around a large brass and glass contraption that Alywn had noticed at the center of other groups in the pub. Apparently it was for smoking, though just how it worked he couldn't yet tell.

"Grab a pillow and get comfortable. Oh," Yimt said, as they began to sit down, "and keep your muskets by your side."

"You expecting trouble?" Hrem asked, looking around the pub. He took a deep breath to swell up his chest and create an even more imposing impression. Normally, this was an impressive sight, but the effect was somewhat lessened by the fact that he immediately doubled over coughing after breathing in a lungful of the blue smoke. A few patrons looked over their way, but most were back to smoking, drinking, and talking. If it wasn't for the pillows, rugs, and funny smoking devices it could pretty much be a pub back home.

"Always," Yimt said, making a great show of sitting down with his back to the room and setting his shatterbow on a pillow beside him. There was an audible sigh in the pub and the conversation grew more relaxed. "But we should be fine here. The owner is a practical man and he knows which way the wind's blowing. At the moment, the Empire trumps all. Still, an Imperial-made musket is worth a few gold coins, so guard them like you can't afford to pay for a new one."

Alwyn checked for the exits. He couldn't relax the way Yimt

did. Wherever the dwarf went he seemed at ease. Alwyn kept an eye on the room as he eased himself down onto a pillow and let his wooden leg stretch out before him. An odd thought occurred to him as he sat down. It was strange, but he was having a hard time remembering what it had been like when he had had two normal legs. The thought became darker a moment later. He had trouble remembering what it had been like before at all. A night that included a pub, dinner, good conversation, and the prospect of nothing more frightening than the bill used to be an event for him. Now, it all seemed so foreign.

"Cheer up, Ally, the night's just starting," Yimt said, taking off his shako and unbuttoning his uniform jacket. "For tonight at least, we've left all that stuff behind us. No beasties, no dark magic, and no officers."

Alwyn nodded and gave Yimt a half-smile. "And no salted pork, I hope."

Yimt laughed. "Now that's the spirit. Ah, the first order of business," he said as a waiter arrived with a tray filled with small blue cups. "Take one, but don't drink just yet."

Each soldier took a cup, even Inkermon. Alwyn looked into his and saw an amber-colored liquid. It smelled faintly of wood and wasn't unpleasant. He sat up straighter on his pillow as Yimt addressed the group.

"Gentlemen, and I use the term recklessly, we've been to hell and back more times than a centipede has legs."

Scolly started to count the fingers on one hand, but Teeter quietly told him, "It means a lot."

Yimt continued. "We've seen things a person never should, and we've done a few things a person could come to regret."

There was quiet as each soldier contemplated the words. Even the background noise subsided. Alwyn felt his pulse quickening and forced himself to stay calm. The thoughts racing in his head were just that, thoughts. They were in a pub, not on one of the islands.

"The life of a sigger ain't an easy one, and the life of an Iron Elf is harder still." There were nods of agreement. "It'd be as easy as warm pie on a cold day to get a bit twisted up inside about it all, and who's to blame you? They don't pay us near enough for this."

There were a few forced laughs. Alwyn tried to come up with an amount that would compensate for everything that had happened, but no pile of gold coins seemed worth it.

"Still, we're here today when others aren't, and that's something. So," Yimt said, raising his cup, "to all those poor, good souls that didn't make it this far I say this."

Alwyn and all the others joined in as they raised their cups in response.

"Rest easy. Your work is done. We'll take it from here, you bloody slackers!"

They drank, and then set the cups down. For a moment, each soldier simply looked around the group. There was nothing to say. Many had fallen, but they remained. And while they did, that was, indeed, something.

"Now," Yimt said, breaking the spell, "what say we get ready for a feast. I don't know about you, but I'm feeling a mite peckish."

The dunes of the Hasshugeb Expanse disappeared over the horizon in every direction. Under the moonlight, the gentle uniformity of their shape gave the desert the appearance of an ocean frozen in time just before the waves crested and began to tumble downward. Dark, curving shadows carved great chunks out of the far side of the dunes under their peaks, creating black holes where no light shone.

Perfect hiding places, Her Emissary thought.

Her Emissary moved to the first dune, still tired from its transformation and the power required to travel the great distance from Her mountain to here. A trail of black frost twinkled in its wake.

At the first shadow, it bent and placed an acorn from the Shadow Monarch's Wolf Oak in the darkness and waited. Black flame sparked to life, but then guttered and went out.

Her Emissary stared at the sand. *Was Her power not strong enough here?* As soon as the thought entered its mind, it was banished. Something else was at work.

It reached out and touched the sand. White flame burst to life and Her Emissary's moonlit shadow caught fire. The pain was exquisite. Every fiber of its being twisted in agony. It stood up and called forth the frost fire, struggling to put out the flame. Every second Her Emissary's shadow burned, it knew it was dying. Marshaling its remaining energy, Her Emissary focused the frost fire and finally extinguished the flames. The distraction, however, had served its purpose.

Sand erupted in a geyser behind Her Emissary, hurtling it into the side of a dune. It jumped to its feet only to feel its shadow engulfed in white flame again.

Two scaly beasts crawled forth from a sandy pit, spitting fire.

Pain once again wracked Her Emissary's body. Through the roaring flame, Her Emissary saw great jaws lined with sharp teeth and eyes flickering with white fire.

"You are children of Kaman Rhal," Her Emissary said, the knowledge of its former self, Viceroy Faltinald Gwyn, coming back. It called forth more of the power of the black acorn deep in its chest. Her Emissary accepted the pain of the white fire as it marshaled icy flames like obsidian blades at its fingertips. When the frost fire was strong enough, it lanced out like a scythe, slicing into the scales of the creatures, which screamed ragged coughs of flame. The closest took the brunt of the black flame and collapsed in a writhing mass. The second climbed over the first, spitting more white flame and fusing the sand into glass underneath Her Emissary in an attempt to immobilize it. Molten glass seared Her Emissary's skin even as the white flame burned it from the inside. The creature charged, its jaws opening wider in anticipation.

Her Emissary focused the power, fashioning a long, flickering spear of pure frost fire in its hand. As the creature lunged, Her Emissary stabbed down with the spear into the creature's open mouth and down its throat. White and black flame spread across the sand, locked in a savage duel. The air steamed and shimmered, then crackled with ice.

The creature thrashed and tried to bite at the spear of flame, but its efforts slowly subsided. It then shuddered and fell to the sand, now motionless. The white flames died as the frost fire overtook them. Soon, there was nothing left of the two creatures but ash and one small piece of bone in each pile. Her Emissary bent to grab one, but before it could, a single white flame consumed each fragment and then was gone.

Standing up straight, Her Emissary looked around the dunes, the flaming spear still clutched in its hand. Nothing. No further threats. It was severely hurt, but pain was now its natural state of being. Its pain was nothing if it helped the Shadow Monarch achieve Her goals. Her Emissary flowed its senses outward, searching for more of Kaman Rhal's creatures, but detected no sign of them. Satisfied, it let the flame die out.

It moved to the next dune and placed an acorn in its shadow. This time, black frost fire sprouted from the sand, followed by an inky black tendril of a *sarka har*.

Yes, Her forest would grow here.

Her Emissary began walking the dunes. As the acorns fell, the *sarka har* took root and began to grow. Roots dug deep into the sand, searching for the rock beneath. There was a power here, bitter, thin, and old, but it was energy nonetheless and it could be used.

Branches stretched to the sky, clawing the air as if to pull the very stars from the blackness. Her Emissary knew it was not in vain—after all—the Stars were returning. The Shadow Monarch had lost the first one. She would not lose another.

Her Emissary walked south, cutting across the desert with Her forest growing and rising behind it like a black, gaping wound. A small village stood in its way, and succumbed, the screams of the dying ringing like crystal on the night air. Still Her Emissary headed south, angling the line of trees toward a point in the desert only it could see.

Her Emissary needed no map, for it was guided by something stronger. It felt it.

Another Star would soon fall.

The power long banished from the world was returning, and it was as palpable as the crunching frost under its feet. Her Emissary quickened in its task. Konowa Swift Dragon and the Iron Elves would come seeking the Star, but they would already be too late.

Her Emissary was right. Konowa would not be the first to find the fallen Star.

But neither would Her Emissary.

Alwyn shifted on the pillows serving as his seat, but couldn't get comfortable. His stomach rumbled. He had tried a bit of everything, including the roast lamb, but food had little appeal to him. It was as if his normal senses were no longer connected to his body. He scanned the room again. Any one of the patrons in the Blue Scorpion could be a spy for the Shadow Monarch, or even an assassin. He fidgeted some more and pulled his musket a little closer.

The sloshing of liquid made him turn. A waiter had quietly refilled his cup without Alwyn's even hearing him approach. He vowed not to be surprised like that again even as he raised the cup to his lips and downed the liquid in one gulp. The rumbling in his stomach subsided and a warm wave moved through his muscles. He reached forward and grabbed one of the smoking tubes from the hookah and brought it to his lips, taking a long, slow puff. Water gurgled in the apparatus with a satisfying rumble. The smoke was cool and smooth in his throat, and when he blew it out several seconds later, he had stopped fidgeting.

"My leg doesn't hurt," he said to no one in particular. He patted the wood where his knee would be and said it again. "Can't flee . . . feel, a thing." The room was gently spinning. It was a strange effect. He wondered how they did it.

"Course you can't feel it, it ain't there," Teeter said, ignoring the shared smoking device and drawing on his pipe. He pursed his lips and then blew a smoke ring across the room. An elderly man smoking a hookah had accepted the challenge and was blowing smoke rings back. Each time one got his ring to intersect the other's, a few men clapped.

"S'not what I mean," Alwyn said. "There's no pain where they meet. It's like the smoke just smoothes out the differences between the magics, you know?" He tried to show Teeter by moving his hands in the air, but his fingers just wiggled and soon he was transfixed by their movement.

"It ain't regular tobacco, see," Zwitty said, talking around a smoking tube in his mouth. Smoke curled up from his nostrils to wreathe his head in swirling gray, but what really gave him an eerie quality was the smile on his face. It looked real. "There's a place in Celwyn where you can get this, but it ain't cheap. Never knew where it came from. Might just have to see about taking some back when we ship out of here."

This drew a loud laugh from Hrem and a snort from Yimt. Both raised themselves from the progressively reclined positions they had assumed as the evening went on. Zwitty's smile disappeared, to be replaced with his more usual sneer.

"You're a businessman now, are you?" Yimt asked. "Between the souvenirs you've been collecting on our island hops and now this, you'll be able to buy a dukedom in what, another fifty years?"

"I ain't took nothing that wasn't rightfully mine," Zwitty said, reaching out to pull his shako closer. "And what's wrong with trying to make a bit of a profit? It's not like we're gonna be soldiers forever . . ."

"Found a cure for the oath, have you?" Hrem asked.

"I got one," Alwyn said, reaching out a hand to pat his musket. Yimt intercepted it with a plate of sliced fruit wedges.

"Here, eat some of these and try not to talk rot," Yimt said.

Alwyn looked down at the plate. Delicacies he'd only heard of seemed abundant here. There were oranges, lemons, and huge pink wedges called watermelon. Tasting any one of these would have filled him with glee just a few short weeks ago. He grabbed one of each so that Yimt would leave him alone.

"I think Alwyn's on to something," Zwitty said, clearly unwilling to let the subject drop. His scare in the alley was clearly still on his mind. "We've just accepted this curse and gone along and done everything we've been asked to do like good little soldiers for the Prince and the major. But what about us, eh? Who's working to see that we get out from under this thing? Where's our reward? Maybe that white fire's the cure."

"Zwitty has a . . . point," Inkermon said. He was lying flat on his back staring at the smoke swirling around the ceiling. An empty bottle of wine was tucked under his arm, while another almost empty bottle balanced on his stomach. "The more I think about it, the more I wonder if the Creator may have sent it to rid us of this cursed oath."

"By burning us and our shadows alive? Some bloody help that is," Yimt said. "We're better off with the magic we know." He quickly looked around at them. "Provided we don't use it."

"We were better off before," Alwyn said, his head clearing and visions of the islands flashing in his mind. "And the only way we'll be better again is when we're finally done with it, or it's done with us."

"Oath or not, we're fed, we're watered, and the night's still young," Teeter said, slapping his thigh and looking around at them. He reached out a boot and gave Scolly's sleeping form a nudge, waking him up after the third kick. "And all of us are awake. So, where do they keep their women?"

Teeter had every soldier's attention. Alwyn tried to laugh, but found his throat was constricted and his lips too dry to form sound. Women. It still didn't seem possible to him that they were now relaxing in a pub—talking, eating, drinking—when just a few short days ago they had been in pitched battle. And now the idea of women seemed more foreign still.

Yimt motioned for them all to lean in, a gesture completely unnecessary, because every one of them was already crowding in around him. Alwyn elbowed someone to move over and was surprised when Inkermon elbowed him back.

"I spoke with the proprietor of this establishment earlier, and explained that we've been for some time deprived of companionship of a more delicate, but not too delicate, nature. After some persuasion," Yimt said, patting his shatterbow, "he has made certain arrangements to remedy our predicament."

"Yeah, but what about the women?" Scolly asked.

"He does mean women," Alwyn said, finding his voice again.

Yimt looked to the ceiling. "Using subtlety on you lot is like a witch not wearing a hat . . . no point. Yes, women. There are women upstairs, but—" he said quickly as they all made to get up, "there is a catch."

"Our money's good here. You said yourself this guy knows which way the wind's blowing," Zwitty said.

"I did, and he does, but that's not the problem. If you all go traipsing up the stairs as a group it's going to attract attention from this crowd," Yimt said, pointing with his thumb over his shoulder, "and menfolk the world over get protective of their women, even the working girls, when outlanders show up."

"So what did you work out?" Teeter asked.

"You go up one at a time. It keeps things respectable, and we prevent a riot."

"Who goes first then?" Zwitty asked.

Alwyn suddenly found Yimt staring straight at him. A moment later the rest of the group, even Scolly, were staring at him.

"Maybe . . . maybe someone else should go first," Alwyn said, unbuttoning his jacket farther. It had gotten very hot in the pub. "We have all night, right?"

Yimt shook his head. "No one's been through more since we became Iron Elves than you, Ally, and I know I speak for every soldier here when I say if anyone deserves to go first, it's you. Right, lads?"

There were nods of agreement and a few muttered "yeahs," none of them overly enthusiastic, but no one was prepared to disagree with Yimt. At some level, Alwyn thought he did deserve to go first, but at a more fundamental level the idea scared him the way no rakke ever could.

"Well, get on with it then," Teeter said, forcing a smile. "The sooner you get up there, the sooner the rest of us get a chance."

This thought galvanized the group and the level of enthusiasm for Alwyn's looming liaison grew.

"Easy, easy," Yimt said, standing up and helping Alwyn to his feet. "He's just going to enjoy a little fun, not storm the gates of the Shadow Monarch's forest."

A waiter arrived bearing more wine and another platter full of fruit, which worked to divert the interest of the soldiers long enough for Alwyn to find himself being pushed toward a set of stairs across the room. A man nearly as large as Hrem, wearing a red vest and voluminous blue pantaloons, stood barring the entrance, his two bare arms folded across his chest like mighty oaks. Alwyn turned to Yimt.

"Listen, I appreciate this," he lied, "but I think someone else should go before me. What about you?" he asked, looking at Yimt.

Yimt smiled up at him. "I'm happily married, remember? And even if I was unhappily married, dwarfettes take marital vows seriously. Did you know they don't wear a wedding ring? Chafes their finger when swinging an axe, which, as it happens, is the traditional marriage gift a mother gives her daughter."

"Like a little silver one you mean?" Alwyn said, trying to picture it.

"Full-size and sharp enough to peel eggshells. Makes for one hell of a honeymoon, I can tell you that," Yimt said, the smile on his face suggesting it was a type of hell not entirely unpleasant.

"Okay, then what about—"

"Ally," Yimt said, holding up a hand, "there's always a first time for everything, and this is yours. Enjoy. Just be yourself and she'll find you the most fascinating man in the world." He lowered his voice an octave. "She's paid to."

Alwyn looked up the stairs past the large man, then back at Yimt. "But look at me. I'm a freak. I have tree limbs for a leg. I can conjure black flame with a thought. I . . . I talk to dead people, and they talk back to me. I'm not normal, Yimt."

"Owl droppings," Yimt said. "So you're a bit unique—just makes you that much more interesting. I'm a dwarf, Hrem's a giant, Scolly's a dullard, Teeter's former navy, Inkermon's holier than thee, thou, and they, and Zwitty is, well, Zwitty. Compared to us, you're about as normal as we got."

Alwyn wiped the sweat from his brow and took a couple of deep breaths, accidentally fogging his spectacles. "It's just that, I haven't exactly, you know . . ."

Yimt reached out a hand and placed it on his arm. "That, Ally, is the worst-kept secret in the regiment. Time to put an end to it."

Alwyn nodded and turned toward the stairs, but Yimt's hand drew him back.

"I don't think you'll be needing this where you're going," he said, gently lifting Alwyn's musket out of his hand. "Now go." Alwyn found himself spun around and facing the large man, who nodded at Yimt, then stepped out of the way. Alwyn looked up the stairs, then back at Yimt.

"They look a bit steep, and with my leg—"

"Which is no longer hurting you, remember?" Yimt said, giving him a firm push.

Alwyn stumbled up the first step then paused, said a silent prayer, and walked up.

SIXTEEN

The two men stalking the alleys of Nazalla were seasoned hunters. They'd taken down sailors, soldiers, and once even an unwary wizard. They'd never hunted an elf before, but this was their turf. There wasn't a tree in sight.

They would never be that wrong again.

Elves are very good hunters in the dark. Those bonded with the power of the Wolf Oaks are even better.

And then there are those like Tyul Mountain Spring, touched by the power of a Silver Wolf Oak.

The only sounds heard were that of two cracks as necks broke from the force of a single strike from bare hands. The two knives were caught in midair, one by a leaf-tattooed hand, the other in the mouth of a squirrel. The feel of the metal drew anguished sobs from both Tyul and Jurwan, and the knives were quickly reunited with their owners. Tyul studied the ground for several seconds, then reached out a hand as Jurwan scampered up it to perch on the elf's shoulder. With three steps, they vanished into the night.

In the morning, the bodies would be found stripped of their clothing. It would take the efforts of three men to pull the blades out of the eye sockets.

Konowa took a sip from his glass and immediately spat it back. "Tastes like horse p—" he started to say, then caught himself. Several guests in attendance at the Viceroy's palace looked his way. The din of conversation in the outdoor courtyard quieted.

"Lovely party," he muttered, raising his glass and gulping down the offending liquid to prove his point. Of course, the Viceroy would put on airs for the arrival of the Prince, and naturally the Prince would insist Konowa attend. *The bastard really does hate me.*

Konowa spotted a group of wives—at least he assumed they were wives—heading his way. They appeared just a sip away from asking him about his adventures. *Rallie!* The scribe and her damn dispatches were proving more troublesome than a roomful of drunken orcs. If Konowa had to answer one more question about his "poor" ear tip or comment on how "lonely" it must be out there, he was prepared to light the whole damn place on fire and to hell with the consequences.

The women edged closer, fans flapping and eyelashes fluttering. Already tonight, a woman had reached out to shake his hand and deposited a metal door key in his palm. She blushed and said she had only wanted to see if an elf really could hold metal, and then suggested he could return the key later . . . personally. Konowa wasn't interested.

The one woman who did interest him was, as usual, in seemingly endless discussion with Rallie and his mother. It was as if the three had become best friends. Perhaps it was for the best. As long as he was bound by the oath, Konowa saw no way he and Visyna could be together, assuming she even wanted that.

Konowa glanced at the group of women and quickly plotted his getaway. If he didn't act now it would soon be too late. Once they surrounded him, there would be no easy way to extract himself from the lace, the fawning, the laughter at everything he said, and double entendres that would make Sergeant Arkhorn blush. Konowa stood up straight and offered them a smile by way of baring his teeth. Immediately, their interest in him plummeted, and they quickly veered off, looking for easier prey. As they did, Konowa saw an opening through the crowd leading to an archway and blissful freedom.

He set his glass down on a nearby table and set out. A servant saw him and began angling toward him with a tray filled with yet more drinks. *Was there no end to this?* Konowa dodged an incoming officer from the 3rd Spears and picked up his pace. Everywhere he looked, gaggles of local officials and dignitaries, ships' captains, and Calahrian officers engaged in animated conversation drifted about the courtyard like ships cut adrift of their mooring lines. Konowa heard his name called but kept walking. He caught snippets of conversation as he passed. Talk of the fleet in the harbor, the return of the Red Star, and what it all meant filled the air and filled Konowa with loathing.

A cluster of archeologists, botanists, astronomers, and other learned types, attached to the fleet at the personal request of the Prince in his search for "antiquities of special interest," hove into view directly in Konowa's path. Konowa brushed past them without a glance, furious that the Prince still saw this as some kind of adventure expedition.

Movement off to the left indicated the servant was closing in. Konowa lengthened his stride. The noise of dozens of conversations washed over him as he passed, serving to infuriate him even more. Didn't they realize that every moment spent drinking and eating and talking was a wasted one? All their efforts should be directed toward finding the original Iron Elves. He should have set out for Suhundam's Hill the moment they landed . . . by himself, if necessary.

The archway was only yards away now, and Konowa genuinely smiled for the first time the whole evening. He would get out among the troops camped on the palace grounds. That was where he belonged, not here.

Looking through the arch, he spotted a campfire with a group of soldiers standing around it. No matter what the temperature, soldiers clustered around fires the way moths did. Konowa could already smell the harsh tobacco they smoked and the pot of arr boiling on the fire. Now that was home. That was where an elf could be an elf. He felt his shoulders relax and allowed himself a half-turn to look back at the party as he left it.

He didn't see the servant arrive one step ahead of him.

The tinkling of broken glass took several seconds to dissipate, by which time the courtyard had gone completely silent. Konowa hung his head. *So close. So bloody close.*

The servant was back on his feet in an instant. "My deepest apologies, Major. Three ladies suggested you were in dire need of a drink. They were quite insistent. They impressed upon me the matter was urgent." He leaned in a little closer, his voice shaky. "Not for me to say, but they have an air about them that suggests, well, you know . . ."

Konowa sighed. "Believe me, witches isn't a strong enough

word." He shook his head and looked down at his uniform. "Well, I'd say you completed your mission, as I most definitely have more than enough drinks to keep me busy for some time to come. Do me a favor, though, and keep open flames away until I dry."

The background noise of the party quickly swelled to its former level. The campfire still beckoned just beyond the archway, but Konowa knew it was destined to be beyond his reach even before a voice called to him.

"You almost made good your escape, Major," a man said somewhere behind Konowa, "but your strategy was flawed."

Konowa turned and had to shield his eyes as a small cart was wheeled past with yet more crystal stemwear. The light from the many lanterns hung in the courtyard reflected off the glasses, temporarily wreathing the smiling face of the Suljak of Hasshugeb. The effect created a dozen flickering shadows behind him for just a moment.

The Suljak was a wisp of a man, his robe pulled close around him despite the warmth of the night air. While his gaunt cheeks and thin gray hair suggested his desert home was a harsh one, his brown eyes twinkled with an intelligence that indicated it had honed his mind to a very sharp instrument.

"Your Grace," Konowa said, bowing slightly and reluctantly turning his back on the archway. "What strategy is that?"

The Suljak came closer and placed a hand on Konowa's arm, patting it gently as if comforting a small child. "Call me Faydarr, please. I find being called by one's title all the time rather taxing. After a while, one starts to wonder who one really is . . . don't you find, Major?"

Konowa traced the hand guard on his saber with a finger. He was determined to avoid any more philosophical discussions if he could help it. "I wouldn't know; I'm a military elf. Without the hierarchy of a rank structure, we'd be little more than rabble with muskets."

The Suljak squeezed Konowa's arm. "Few sleepless nights for you then, eh, Major, wondering about where your thread weaves into the grand tapestry of life?"

"None," Konowa lied. Dreams haunted by the Shadow Monarch were no one's business but his own. He realized his answer sounded abrupt, and made an effort to engage in small talk, at least for a minute until he could make an excuse and leave. "I sleep just fine, but then I'm probably not smart enough to know I should be worried. You mentioned something about my strategy?"

The Suljak wagged a bony finger and winked. "A diversion, of course. You really should have an adjutant for these sorts of events, a loyal fellow ready to overturn a tureen of soup, or perhaps let a rat loose in a punch bowl."

The face of Regimental Sergeant Major Lorian flashed in Konowa's mind. Their initial meeting had not been the most cordial—Lorian had tried to hack Konowa's head off with a saber—but they had come to an understanding of sorts. Konowa missed him.

"The Iron Elves are not exactly at full strength at the moment," Konowa said. "I pretty much have to fend for myself at these things."

"Ah, the lone wolf," the Suljak said, his voice sincere. "Alas, I've never actually seen a wolf, but I understand they typically hunt in packs. Only the sick or the deranged hunt alone . . . so I've been told."

Konowa blinked and looked at the Suljak again. He appeared close enough to the grave to smell the freshly dug dirt, but the timbre of the Suljak's voice bespoke a will to live that wasn't going anywhere any time soon. "Are you also a lone wolf, or do you have an adjutant to cause mischief and mayhem when events demand it?" Konowa tried to think who among the Iron Elves he would choose. Sergeant Arkhorn sprang to mind. The dwarf was a diversion all by himself.

"I have several," the Suljak said. "Though they don't always know it."

In spite of his desire to leave, Konowa found the Suljak charming. "Why do I have the feeling I am one of them?"

The Suljak shook with laughter for several seconds. Konowa worried the old man might fracture a rib.

"Another time perhaps. However, in all the commotion caused by your unfortunate accident, the three enchanting ladies escorted by the Prince took advantage of the opportunity to make good their departure. They appear to have left the party almost entirely unnoticed."

Konowa spun around and looked to where he had last seen Visyna, Rallie, and his mother. They were nowhere in sight.

"Son of a witch," Konowa said, half angry and half admiring.

The Suljak's eyes opened a little wider. "Yes, and I understand you are also the son of a wizard. Tell me, have your parents' magical abilities transferred to you?"

Konowa hadn't forgotten where he was . . . or who the Suljak was. "If getting into trouble counts, I'm certainly a wizard at that."

The Suljak tilted his head. "You are modest. Rumors swirl like dust devils about the legendary Iron Elves and Major Konowa Swift Dragon. I've been led to believe you are becoming quite adept at wielding power."

"What rumors are those?" Konowa asked. The acorn resting

against his chest gave no indication the Suljak was a threat, but it was dawning on Konowa that the Shadow Monarch's power was ill-equipped to understand the subtlety of this old man of the desert. For that matter, Konowa doubted he or the Empire were going to fare much better. *Pimmer might just know what he's talking about.*

"We get the *Imperial Weekly Herald* even here," said Suljak Faydarr, smiling broadly.

It was time to change the subject. "Pimmer . . . excuse me, Viceroy Alstonfar, tells me you hold sway over most of the desert region and the tribes living there," Konowa said, stepping out of the way as additional servants arrived to assist with cleaning up the broken glass.

The Suljak waved away the compliment. "Pimmer flatters me. I simply offer advice and leave it up to each tribe how they use it, or don't. Walk with me, won't you?"

Konowa found himself being ushered out of the courtyard and into a smaller garden no more than ten yards in each direction. The stone walls were obscured by large palm trees, creeping vines, and lush shrubbery, all of which created the illusion of jungle. It was even humid in here, no doubt because of the large gurgling water fountain set at the far end of the enclosure. Water splashed over the sides of the stone basin surrounding the fountain and drained away through cracks in the stone walkway to either side of it.

"Looking at this it's hard to imagine there's nothing but filthy, hot desert just outside the city," Konowa said, then immediately regretted the remark. "Though I'm sure the desert can be quite nice, what with all the wide-open spaces . . ."

The Suljak lowered his head for a moment, then raised it and

looked Konowa straight in the eye. "Major, should you ever be offered the position of diplomat at any time . . . don't."

Konowa accepted the rebuke with a smile. "You're not the first
to comment on that. It's been mentioned to me that getting along
with others is not exactly my forte."

"And yet you are at ease among your soldiers," the Suljak said.

"I understand them. And most of the time, they understand me."

"And what of your Empire? Does it understand you?"

Konowa felt the ground shift beneath their discussion and
wondered where it was going. His talk with Sergeant Arkhorn
about the role of the Empire in the world had stuck with him.
"The Empire is a complicated beast. For colonial subjects such as
you and I, I suppose it's even more complicated. For my part, I do
my best to keep things simple. The Queen declares someone, or
something, an enemy and I go out and kill it."

The corners of the Suljak's lips turned up in the faintest of
smiles. "And if she declared me an enemy?"

Konowa returned the smile. "We both know the answer to
that, don't we?"

"Do you see the water fountain, Major?" the Suljak said,
changing the subject. He grabbed Konowa's arm and steered him
toward it. "In many respects, this is the Empire."

Konowa uttered a silent curse. "A metaphor for the Empire's
wasteful ways with people's lives, perhaps? All the lost productivity?
The unnatural harnessing of energy put to a single use?"

The Suljak laughed, and Konowa could tell it was sincere.
"When Pimmer first arrived, the two of us talked by this fountain
for hours. It was months before he went a hundred yards from the

palace, and almost a year before he ventured out of the city. You, on the other hand, you are already out there. You stand here with me, yet in your heart you are roaming the desert now, no?"

He made as if to pat Konowa's chest, but Konowa caught his arm and casually lowered it. The Suljak continued talking as if nothing had happened.

"You are a man of action, but tonight, well, tonight you stand among those who talk, and it is like pulling teeth, yes? Here you are, staring at a water fountain, talking to an old man, and wondering how long you have to humor him before you can make your excuses and get back among your soldiers. Or am I wrong?"

Konowa started to object, then saw no good reason to. "You aren't wrong. However, I am sure I would enjoy our conversation more after I've done what we came here to do."

The Suljak waved a hand to the sky. "There won't be an after, I'm afraid."

Something in his tone made Konowa turn. "What do you mean?"

"The fountain. See how the water gushes forth, forever filling the basin? That is the Empire, surging forth into uncharted—or at least little explored—lands in order to shine the light of civilization among the heathen and lift them up from their ignorance."

"I'm not unfamiliar with this line of reasoning," Konowa said.

The Suljak smiled. "I am sure you are not. I was most fortunate in that I had a lovely conversation with your mother and the delightful Miss Tekoy and Miss Synjyn earlier. I had hoped to engage them again, but it appears they had other business."

Konowa groaned. "They always do. I'm also sure they informed you of my feelings about discussing the affairs of the Empire in general."

"Indeed," the Suljak said, his voice light with laughter, "but it is actually not the Empire I wish to speak to you about, but rather what comes next."

Konowa gave a quick snort. "Despite what you've heard, I don't think Calahr plans on going anywhere."

Suljak Faydarr patted Konowa's arm again. "I'm sure it doesn't, but despite the Prince's utmost faith in himself and your regiment, the wind of change he so boldly claims to harness is even now being hitched to other wagons."

Konowa suddenly wished for another drink, no matter how foul. If he was going to have a headache, he'd rather it was from a hangover. "With all due respect, Your Grace, I have had my fill of riddles. You spoke with the three . . . women, so please, if you have something to tell me, just say it."

The Suljak nodded. "I knew from the moment I saw you that you were an honest elf. Perhaps *too* honest for your own good, but I can see that Her Majesty's faith in you is entirely justified."

Konowa couldn't keep his voice from rising. "You've spoken with the Queen?"

"Not directly, no, but through . . . intermediaries. She is an astute women. Her thirst for knowledge is insatiable."

"Like her son's," Konowa said, looking over his shoulder and relaxing. There was no sign of the Prince.

The Suljak gave Konowa a sad smile. "No, not really. The Prince seeks knowledge—is quite fascinated by it—and dreams that the simple act of accumulating it will stimulate change. Her Majesty is more practical. Her accumulation of knowledge is always in service of an end."

"And what is that end?"

"The peaceful dissolution of the Empire," the Suljak said.

Konowa almost smiled, then realized the Suljak was serious. "She said this?"

"She is not stupid—far from it. This world is in flux, Major, the return of the Stars only exacerbates what lies underneath all these years. Tell me, are the elves of the Long Watch happy with Calahrian rule? Are the dwarves, the elfkynan, and all the other peoples? The Stars' returning gives focus to something that already existed."

"You're talking about rebellion," Konowa said. "Hundreds upon hundreds of elfkynan died when that Star fell. They died believing a lie. And the Empire still rules their land."

"True, but thousands upon thousands did not perish. Elfkyna has already begun to change. The Red Star returned, and now *it*, not the Empire, is seen as the true guardian and ruler of Elfkyna. That one, simple notion is more powerful than a thousand cannons. The Star seed you planted there has given rise to much more than a magical tree. It has given birth to the idea of freedom."

Konowa paced a few steps, looking about the garden and feeling as if he was back in the Elfkynan wilderness. It wasn't a pleasant feeling. "Even if you're right, and the next Star—the Jewel of the Desert—returns here to the desert, then what? There are still grave dangers out there only the Empire can truly oppose . . . or do you think the Shadow Monarch will not venture so far south?"

"I have every confidence that She will. In this regard She is less astute than Her Majesty. The Queen knows the days of empires and one rule are coming to an end. The Shadow Monarch does not."

Konowa shook his head. "I've seen what the Shadow Monarch is capable of. If She gains a foothold in your desert, it will take the Empire to dig Her out again."

"How fortunate you are here then," the Suljak said. There was no trace of sarcasm in his voice. "Alas, the Shadow Monarch's coming to these lands is thousands of years too late. A deadly power already exists here that threatens all."

"You mean Kaman Rhal?" Konowa asked, walking back to stand close to the Suljak. He debated mentioning what had happened on the island, but decided against it. "I know the story, at least some of it. Are you saying he has returned?"

"I don't know. There are stirrings in the desert. Rumors abound. It is a fact that his body and that of his reported wife, the she-drake, were never recovered, but buried along with his library and the city of Urjalla. How much is real and how much is superstition I cannot say, but enough darkness has risen as of late to suggest that what was once thought impossible is now only improbable."

"My fight is against the Shadow Monarch . . . and all enemies of the Empire," Konowa added. "If Kaman Rhal or any remnant of his power attempts to interfere with us, it will be dealt with. More ships are coming. The Prince is keen to find Kaman Rhal's resting place."

"I hope he does," the Suljak said.

"Really? You aren't concerned with the Empire looting the accumulated knowledge and treasure of your people?"

"I harbor many concerns. I am concerned about the return of Kaman Rhal and the encroachment of the Shadow Monarch, but these worries pale in comparison to my greatest concern."

"And what is that?"

"You."

"Me?"

The Suljak nodded. "Earlier, you mentioned you slept well.

Alas, I do not. My dreams have been haunted lately. Do you know what I see in them? You, Major. You with the Jewel of the Desert in your hands, just as you held the fate of the Red Star in Elfkyna. You gave up that power once in order to preserve the lands of the elfkynans. A very selfless act, Major. Tell me, could you do so again?"

"My duty is to defend the Empire, and that is what I intend to do."

The Suljak bowed his head for a moment, then raised it and looked straight at Konowa. There was no longer any mirth in the Suljak's eyes.

"And my duty is to defend my people and their land. I will do so, no matter what the cost."

Konowa understood. "My quarrel is not with you, Faydarr. I'm here for my elves. Once I have them, I have my own enemy to defeat, and She isn't you."

For a long moment, neither one spoke. The water in the fountain gurgled and splashed as the excess sloshed over the sides and ran down the stone and onto the cobbles. *What a waste,* Konowa thought, *all this water for a fountain in a land as dry as bone.* As the water seeped between the cracks, an image of spilled blood came unbidden to him. The fountain *was* like the Empire. *All those dead, and for what? If the Empire really was breaking up, what had it all been for?* Konowa looked at the Suljak. "The Queen isn't the only one who plays a deep game around here."

The Suljak of the Hasshugeb winked at Konowa and patted his arm. "I'm sure I don't know what you're talking about." He let go and turned to leave. "Oh, if a person were looking for a quiet way to leave the festivities, he might want to take a walk around behind the fountain. He'd find a path that leads him to a side gate and back to the main grounds without having to walk through the courtyard."

Back at the party, the guests were momentarily startled by a loud whoop from somewhere off the main courtyard. Conversation quickly resumed, as there was clearly no need for alarm; the shout had been one of pure joy.

SEVENTEEN

Having marshaled enough of his courage to make it up the stairs of the Blue Scorpion, Alwyn pushed aside a silk curtain and stepped into a room unlike any he had ever been in before, or smelled before. He had no idea what scents were floating on the air, but everything was soft and inviting. He blinked and looked around. There was nothing remarkable about the furniture, just more pillows, but it was who was sitting on the pillows that put a wobble in his one remaining knee.

Women. As in several. As in more than Alwyn had ever seen in one place at one time. He wasn't sure how many, however, because he'd closed his eyes almost as soon as he realized they were wearing sheer robes. *You could see their bodies underneath, and they weren't wearing anything at all!* The first time he heard the mewling cry of a rakke hadn't terrified him as much as this.

With his eyes still closed, he took off his spectacles and cleaned them on his jacket before putting them back on. He risked opening an eye. They were still there, still staring at him. One giggled behind a jeweled hand and Alwyn riveted his gaze on her face. She looked magical. Everything about her was perfect. Her skin, her long dark hair, her bright green eyes . . . the graceful line of her arm as it rested near her—Alwyn brought his eyes back up to hers.

"I think, that is, um, I think I'm supposed to . . . choose. One of you, I mean. Uh, if that's okay?" He was certain that wasn't okay. *Why hadn't Yimt told him there would be so many!* "Oh, I'm Private Renwar, I mean, Alwyn . . . hi."

Now several of the women laughed and Alwyn could have sworn his wooden leg began to shake. *This had been a terrible idea.*

"You do not choose us, Private Renwar Alwyn," one of the women said, rising to stand. His eyes traced her outline from her feet to her head while his heart roared in his ears. Curves. All he could think of was curves. "It is we that choose you, and I can see that Nafeesah has already chosen."

The woman who had giggled earlier now stood, and Alwyn found his hand clenching air, remembering Yimt had taken his musket from him. Not that he thought he needed it, but not having it at hand made him feel naked, which only compounded his nervousness. He hadn't been without his musket since joining the Iron Elves.

"Come with me," Nafeesah said, holding out a hand.

Alwyn gulped, took a look over his shoulder at the exit, then reached out to take her hand. It was soft and warm. To Alwyn's amazement, not even the hint of frost fire sparked at her touch. She smiled and led him past the other women and into another, much smaller room through three sets of beaded curtains.

Nafeesah motioned Alwyn to sit on yet more pillows, and he

did so, carefully easing himself to the floor so that his caerna didn't reveal more than he wanted. It was a courtesy Yimt was utterly incapable of mastering.

Candles burned merrily in several small alcoves notched into the plaster walls, giving off a warm light and a scent of pine trees. A long, flat pillow lay in one corner, which Alwyn assumed was the bed. He immediately felt his cheeks grow hot.

"You are an Elf of Iron, yes?" Nafeesah said, tucking her legs underneath her as she sat down in front of him. A sizable chunk of her thigh was revealed, the skin smooth and unmarred.

"Yes!" Alwyn said, surprised at the loudness of his own voice. "Uh, yes, Iron Elf actually, although we're not really elves, but I guess you knew that. Well, except the major really *is* an elf. Then there's his mother, Miss Red Owl, and Tyul Mountain Spring, and the major's father, the wizard, only he's not exactly himself right now. Oh, and there was Corporal Kritton, but he ran off back in Elfkyna and we haven't seen—"

Nafeesah's finger rested against his lips. "And you are nervous, yes."

This wasn't a question.

"What, no. I mean, maybe a little. Is it hot in here? It feels hot in here. Have you tried a hookah before? I just did, earlier I mean, and that smoke really gets to you." *Did his voice really sound that high? And why was he talking so fast?*

Nafeesah smiled. "So you've done this before then."

Alwyn nodded several times. "Yes, of course, I mean lots of times . . . well, no, not yet, not with a woman."

Nafeesah raised an eyebrow.

"Or a man, or anything else either, I mean!"

Her smile widened. "Then I am honored I will be your first, Renwar." She reached out her hands and began unbuttoning his tunic.

"That's my last name," Alwyn said, not sure what to do with his hands. "My first name is Alwyn, not that it . . . matters . . . doesn't my leg bother you?"

Nafeesah sat back and looked at him, tilting her head to one side. Curly locks of black hair fell across her face and Alwyn wondered if this was what falling in love felt like. He felt as if he was going to be sick, faint, and break out in hysterical laughter all at the same time.

"You are a soldier. These things happen in battle. You survived, and you are now here with me. Is this not a good thing?"

She leaned forward again, but Alwyn caught her hands in his. "I guess, I mean yes, yes it is," he quickly said as a glint of steel flared in her eyes. "It's just that so much has happened and I don't . . . I don't know who I am anymore."

What's wrong with me? Alwyn released his grip and started to get back up. Nafeesah pushed him hard in the chest, pinning his back to the wall. Alwyn half-smiled and tried to sit forward, then stopped. Her green eyes blazed with something that stilled his tongue.

"Who you are is someone who needs to relax." She sat back and then reached for a small wooden box that had been between the large pillow and the wall. The wood of the box was very worn and its brass furnishings polished smooth with much use. She set it down between them.

"I'm not sure I feel like smoking or drinking anything else right now," Alwyn said, hoping he didn't offend her. "It's just that my head's a bit fuzzy at the moment."

Nafeesah smiled at him. "Then we will fix that." She waved a hand over the box and the lid popped open on its own.

"Neat trick," Alwyn said, trying to peer inside.

Nafeesah said nothing, but reached into the box and pulled out a cloth-covered orb. Alwyn tried to keep the disappointment off his face. He wasn't sure what she might have in the box, but it looked as if it was just a plain old crystal ball, and that didn't seem all that . . . exciting.

She held the cloth-covered object in one hand while she waved the other over the box. Again, the lid operated on its own and closed without a sound. She then placed the orb above the lid and removed her hand. The ball, with its cloth covering over it, floated a few inches above the box.

"Okay, really neat trick," Alwyn said, still not that impressed.

Nafeesah looked at him with an expression Alwyn couldn't read. Finally, she smiled. "These are not . . . tricks." She brought both her hands forward and began weaving them over the ball much in the way Miss Tekoy did when she practiced magic. The realization surprised Alwyn.

"Are you a witch?"

Nafeesah continued to weave the air. After a few more moments she spoke. "Remove the cloth, please."

Alwyn reached out, grabbed the cloth in one hand, and pulled. A perfectly round ball of sand particles floated above the box. Alwyn looked closer. He could see grains of sand shifting and moving in every direction. He gently reached out a finger and touched the surface, expecting to find a thin glass shell, but his finger passed right through and into the ball itself. The sand swirled around his finger with a warm, ticklish sensation. "How are you doing this?"

"Put both your hands out, palms up," she said, ignoring his question.

Alwyn complied. The orb of sand fell into his open hands and formed a thin sheet that wrapped around his hands as it continued to swirl. "That tickles," Alwyn said, lifting his hands up to take a closer look.

"Keep your hands flat," Nafeesah said, her voice stern. "If you move too much, you will break the spell."

Alwyn brought his hands back down. "Sorry. So, this is magic, which means you are a witch of some kind, right?"

"I have some skills. Now, let's see if we can find a way to relax you. I am going to slowly remove your worries and your pain until you are completely at ease, Alwyn."

Alwyn started to object, but Nafeesah made a pushing motion with her hand. A small portion of the sand broke away from the mass and flowed up the sleeve of his jacket and formed a small circle on his chest. Pressure built at that spot until Alwyn was pinned against the wall. "Wait, you—"

Nafeesah made another gesture and another small amount of sand flew up his arm and stopped at his throat. He could still breathe, but he could no longer speak.

Alwyn struggled to free himself, but now his hands were immobile as well. He looked at Nafeesah, trying to make her understand, but she only smiled and concentrated on the swirling sand.

"Now, we will banish this pain you carry." She stared intently at the sand as her fingers traced increasingly complicated designs above it. Frost fire sparkled among the sand. "Ah, you are a wielder of the black flame," she said. "You are one of the oath takers. I have heard rumors about this, but did not think it true."

Alwyn tried to shake his head, but the pressure against his chest and neck made it impossible.

Nafeesah smiled and leaned in close. The smell of her perfume washed over Alwyn and he felt the heat of her skin on his. Her lips brushed his right ear. "There is more here than meets the eye, but I will set things right." She pulled back and held out her hands.

Two perfectly round orbs of white flame danced in her palms. She gently blew on one and it tumbled from her hand and floated down to land on the burning sand covering his hands.

White fire! Alwyn tensed, expecting the pain he'd felt on the island. The black and white flame danced across the sand, intertwining but never becoming one. The sensation was as if Nafeesah herself were massaging his hands in hers.

"Stop fighting it," Nafeesah said, directing her focus to the flames in his hands. She made a quick motion with one finger and the sand on his throat flew back to his hands.

"You have to stop . . . you don't know what you're dealing with!"

Nafeesah pouted, but continued to weave, tightening her pattern as she did so. The white flame grew, clearly trying to overwhelm the frost fire. "I have never seen anything like this, but do not worry, I can help you. Mine is a subtle power, but potent nonetheless."

Alwyn banged his head against the wall and let out his breath with a huff. Mist formed in the air. "You need to stop, now, before it's too late."

Sweat beaded on Nafeesah's forehead, but she refused. "Just a little bit . . . longer . . ."

"Please, stop. I can't control this much longer."

". . . I can help you . . ."

"*No,*" Alwyn said. The room grew frigid. Shadows stretched out on the walls looming over them. Alwyn recognized Meri, and saw the black blade in his dead hand. The other shadows moved closer. Alwyn knew he had to stop Nafeesah now or the shades would. He willed the power to him and black flames surged in his hands, consuming the white fire in a flash. The sand on his chest froze with black frost and shattered, as did the sand covering his hands.

"What are you?" Nafeesah asked, looking between Alwyn and the shadows around her.

Alwyn closed his eyes and the frost fire died and went out. The shades lingered, but Alwyn shook his head and they, too, vanished. When he opened his eyes again, Nafessah was still looking at him. She had not backed away.

"I am bound by an oath," he said, the enormity of it coming back to him in a rush. "I wish I'd never . . . I just . . ." Tears filled his eyes and began to run down his cheeks, which only added to his misery. Faces of the dead swam in and out of his vision, and he couldn't tell if it was memory or hallucination. *So much death. So much pain. And for what?*

Alwyn expected Nafeesah to run, or call for help, or yell at him to leave, but she did the most unexpected thing: She leaned forward and kissed him.

"I don't understand," Alwyn said, wiping the tears from his eyes.

"You didn't ask for this, and that is why I am still here," she said.

Alwyn nodded. He felt thin, as if the only thing keeping him together was the sound of Nafeesah's voice.

"What . . . what is your power?" he asked. He had to keep talking to her. Her voice was the last anchor keeping him here, keeping him sane.

Nafeesah dipped her head, then brushed the hair from her face. "Nothing like yours. We use it to cure small injuries and to soothe troubled spirits. We call it *KamRha,* after the ancient Kaman Rhal, ruler of the Expanse."

Alwyn's heart beat a little faster. "Wait, wasn't he the one who built that library? Our Prince talks about stuff like that all the time."

Nafeesah brightened. "Yes, one and the same. Kaman Rhal was a sorcerer and pursued knowledge wherever he found it, no matter what the cost."

Alwyn closed his eyes. "Seems everything old is new again."

"I hope not," Nafeesah said. "Rhal was a great king, but also a terrible one. It was said that in his day he could command the power of the sun to burn his enemy's shadows to ash, capturing their souls for all eternity."

Alwyn opened his eyes and sat forward. "He had this power?"

Nafeesah nodded, her eyes wide as she looked into Alwyn's. "He was most feared for this, but that was hundreds, perhaps thousands of years ago. Then a great sandstorm is said to have raged for a hundred days and a hundred nights, and when it was over Kaman Rhal, his great library, and even the town of Urjalla were gone. His power, however, is said to have been carried on the wind of that storm, and those of us who practice the art today are said to possess a little bit of it, but it is nothing to what he once wielded."

Alwyn pressed his left fist into the side of his stump, using the pain to help him focus. "Are there any wizards or witches with more of this power, enough to be able to kill someone? Could enough users band together to do it?"

"No, no one. Not by themselves and not in a group. It doesn't work that way. What few of us there are only use it for good. I told you, it's a subtle power. It gently burns away that which troubles a spirit, no more. What you speak of is impossible. Only Kaman Rhal commanded power that great." Nafeesah's eyes narrowed. "Why? Why do you ask this?"

"No reason," Alwyn lied, looking down at his hands. "I just was curious."

Nafeesah reached out and touched his face and forced his head up to look at her. "Why do you ask me this, Alwyn?"

Alwyn knew they were not supposed to talk about it, but the idea of following one more order when it was orders that had put him—put all of them—in this situation churned up an anger he couldn't ignore.

"We . . . we met someone, or something, using Kaman Rhal's power. It was on an island off the coast. There was white flame, not a little like you use, but a lot. Enough to . . . burn the shadow of a soldier and kill him."

Nafeesah's eyes widened. "What? This cannot be! Rhal is . . . dead. His magic is lost to the ages, save the small spark a few of us carry. Surely you are mistaken."

Alwyn shook his head. "I felt it. I felt it deep inside me, burning, scouring away the oath that binds me to . . . that I took when I joined the Iron Elves."

"Gossip travels fast in a city like Nazalla, especially in a place like this. We have many pillows for such talk," she said, nudging him and smiling.

Alwyn didn't smile back. "You said the flame burns away troubles. If there was enough of it, could it burn away more?"

Nafeesah stopped smiling. "No. A magical bond is a complex thing. It ties the living to the natural world in ways we cannot understand. The weave would be too entwined with your spirit. To burn one would be to burn both."

Alwyn shook his head. "I know, but with enough power, it could be controlled. Just enough . . ."

Nafeesah shook her head violently. "No! If this is Rhal's magic, then nothing but pain and suffering would await you. You have had your power how long, months? You are no wizard, Alwyn; you are not even an apprentice. Kaman Rhal's power is old, as old as the sand."

"Then I need to learn more," Alwyn said. *There must be a way to use it.* "The soldier that was burned did die, but his bond to the regiment was cut."

"Yet he is still dead," Nafeesah said, softening her voice. She started to weave her hands together above the scattered sand, reforming it into an orb. "Did you cremate his body?"

Alwyn hadn't expected that. "No, we gave him a burial at sea."

"How far away were you from here?"

"I don't know, not that far. It was the last island before here. Why? What does it matter. He's dead."

Nafeesah muttered a curse. She quickly gathered up the last of the sand, and waving a hand over the box lid, put the sand back. "There are worse fates than death in this world."

"I know," Alwyn said.

"No, not everything you don't. Rhal was said to be able to hold sway over creatures that could move between land and water.

Great beasts gifted with his fire. Some say they were his children by a she-drake, but as four-legged creatures they were not suitable for his designs, so he sent them out to kill and bring him back the bodies."

Alwyn remembered the shallow trench on the island. "Why? Why would he want bodies?"

Nafeesah shuddered. "Before he was wiped out by the storm, Kaman Rhal was building an army."

"Why? Who was he going to war with?"

"All those from whom he had stolen knowledge." Nafeesah sat up and turned to look at Alwyn. "Don't you see, his library was so vast and his power so great because he took knowledge from wherever he could. It became an obsession. All that mattered was acquiring more."

"Believe me, I understand that kind of thinking, but I still don't understand the bodies."

"Kaman Rhal couldn't trust anyone. The more knowledge and power he acquired, the more he came to view it as his own. In the end, he trusted no one, save the she-drake, and their offspring, but they were not an army. So he collected bodies."

"And did what with them?"

"He made an army he could trust, because he controlled them completely. Kaman Rhal created an army of the dead."

EIGHTEEN

Tyul, now garbed in black, followed from a distance as the body of Kester Harkon was carried through the maze of back streets and alleyways of Nazalla. Several times the figures he pursued would pause and turn, looking back the way they had come. Each time they saw nothing out of the ordinary and continued. Had they looked up to the flat rooftops they still would have seen nothing, but they would have at least been looking in the right direction.

Tyul jumped lightly from roof to roof, his movements little more than a wisp of shadow. It was an odd sensation to be this high and not be surrounded by trees. Tears came to his eyes at the thought of the forest. In some part of his mind, he knew that following Chayii Red Owl had been the right thing to do, though that part receded deeper into the darkness with each passing day. As an elf in the Long Watch bonded with a Wolf Oak, he willingly took the solemn oath to protect the great forest from the Shadow Monarch. That the oath would take him so far from home had never occurred to him.

He leaped across an alley, then crouched low, as the figures below stopped and looked back again. Tyul remained motionless, waiting for the group to continue. Images of Black Spike came to his mind. To see the body of a Wolf Oak so desecrated pained him deeply. That Jurwan offered up his *ryk faur* to be used as a ship's mast mystified Tyul, but then so much of the world made no sense to him. More tears welled up in his eyes. The pain enveloped him and it took all his concentration to block it out. The Wolf Oak was dead, yet something of it remained. Tyul felt it with every breath.

He knew, as all elves knew, that to have a Silver Wolf Oak as *ryk faur* was to risk your very sanity. Now, though, he saw it differently. His bonding with Rising Dawn had opened his mind to a plane of existence few elves would ever experience. He was closer to the natural order than most living things, and it was intoxicating and at times overwhelming. He knew, as few others ever would, that the spirit of the Wolf Oak really felt sorrow in its death as its limbs were slashed, its roots cut, its crown shorn, and its body desecrated with iron and made to serve on a sailing vessel, instead of being returned to the *mukta ull*, Mother Earth, to be reborn.

Tyul understood pain. He sensed it in Jurwan, too. They shared a bond, each affected by a Silver Wolf Oak, though Jurwan's experience was very different. Tyul wondered again why they followed these men. He sensed nothing of the Shadow Monarch. But Jurwan had told him it was important, so for now he would track them as only he could, and when necessary, he would return them to the *mukta ull*.

The small group with the body moved on again, crossing an open space where several alleys met and disappearing around a corner. There were no buildings near enough to jump on. Jurwan chittered in his ear and Tyul leaped to the ground, landing softly on the hard-packed dirt. Instinctively he reached down to grab some earth, but came up with a handful of sand. It was cold and strange to the touch. There was power here, but different from the warm, vibrant energy of the great forest of the Hyntaland, different even from the force in Elfkyna. The grains of sand stung and he flung the handful away. He stood and ran silently across the open square and into a pitch-black alley, though with his elven eyes he was able to see enough to guide his way.

That saved both his and Jurwan's life.

A dull, white sword swung out of the darkness aimed directly at his head. Tyul easily ducked the stroke and stepped forward, a wooden dagger, a bond weapon given to him by Rising Dawn, now gripped firmly in his left hand. The wood gleamed with energy, and a voice as if from a great distance filled the air as he plunged it into the heart of his attacker, the sound of wood scraping bone echoing off the walls around them.

The feeling of a thousand bee stings attacked Tyul's hand. He let go of the dagger and withdrew his hand. As he did a rasping scream sprang from his assailant as the hood of its dark cloak fell back. Tyul looked with wonder into the eyes of the man he had just killed.

A grinning skull with black runes carved into it stared back at him. Each eye socket was aglow with a small, white flame.

Tyul stepped backward, clutching his hand to his chest. The skeletal man in front of him reached up with one hand and grabbed the hilt of Tyul's dagger, still stuck in its chest. White fire burst to life and burned with an intensity that made Tyul shield his eyes. Soon the figure's cloak was aflame and then burned away, revealing a skeleton in the shape of a man. But this had been no man.

The skeleton that stood before him was made of what appeared to be several different creatures. Tyul had seen enough animal carcasses to recognize several horse bones among others he did not. Most of the bones were cracked and ill-used. Many bore teeth marks. Where muscle and tissue had once held bones together, a wet, black tar now kept them in place.

A sane elf would have known to be afraid. Tyul was fascinated. What stood before him were elements of the natural order, but assembled and animated in a way that perverted that order. This close he felt the magic that kept the collection of bones together. Like the sand, it was old and bitter.

"I want to help you," Tyul said, his voice soft with caring.

White flames still burned where his oath weapon remained stuck between two ribs of the skeleton. The spirit of Tyul's *ryk faurre*, Rising Dawn, struggled against the flame. Jurwan peeked out from Tyul's quiver and started pawing at the back of his neck. Tyul turned. Three more skeletons were closing in on him.

Tyul smiled. "I will help you, too."

He lunged forward at the first skeleton, grabbing the hilt of his dagger and twisting, knowing the pain would be intense. At the same time he brought his right elbow up and across, smashing it into the skull. There was a snap and the skull went toppling to the ground. Tyul pulled his dagger from its chest, though the skeleton did not fall. It remained standing in place, but now showed no signs of movement. Tyul turned to face the other three.

Each held a long, curved sword made of bone in a skeletal hand. Death whispered on the air as the blades arced toward him, but Tyul jumped gracefully to the side and out of their path. His left hand throbbed, but he kept it clenched on his dagger while with his right hand he reached behind his back for his quiver and grabbed Jurwan by the scruff of the neck. With one fluid motion, he threw the squirrel at the nearest skeleton while he pivoted to attack the other two.

Jurwan flew through the air and landed flat on the front of a skull. He scampered out of the way as the skeleton brought its sword up to cleave him in two. The sword missed Jurwan, but hit above the skeleton's left eye socket, fracturing a large opening in the skull. Jurwan dove into the opening, his bushy tail disappearing a moment later. White flame flared in the skull's eye sockets and its lower jaw dropped open in a silent scream. The skeleton crumpled to the ground.

Tyul sidestepped a sword cut and reached down for a large clay pot sitting by a wall. He scooped it up one-handed and swung it like a club against the skull of the nearest skeleton. Both skull and pot smashed, leaving Tyul with just a pottery shard in his right hand. The white fire in the skull's eye sockets went out immediately as the skeleton wobbled and fell to the ground.

The last intact skeleton lifted its sword high above its head, prepared to strike. Tyul saw his opening and took it, running forward and jamming the dagger and the shard into its eye sockets. The impact shattered the skull in a burst of white fire. Tyul fell backward, both hands numb and twitching. His dagger and the pottery shard slipped from his grasp.

Tyul looked over at the first skeleton. It still stood in place. Jurwan emerged from the wreckage of his opponent and leaped over to the skull with fire still burning inside. He sniffed at it, then turned and chirped to Tyul.

Tyul looked around and gingerly picked up another clay pot in his throbbing hands, wincing as he did so. He calmly walked over to the skull. The white flame grew brighter as he neared and the jaws began to open as if to speak, tipping the skull backward so that the light shone toward the sky. Tyul brought the pot down onto the skull, smashing both. A spear of white flame shot skyward and was gone. A clattering noise marked the collapse of its skeleton as it fell to the ground and disintegrated into a pile of dust.

Voices called out from a nearby building. The sound of running feet echoed off the walls. Tyul bent and picked up his dagger as Jurwan climbed onto his back. He sifted the sand through the fingers of his right hand, then cast it in an arc over the ground.

"You're welcome," he remarked, and ran after his quarry.

NINETEEN

I've lost sight of Rallie," Visyna said, holding the hem of her gown as she hurried to follow along. Chayii led her to the far end of the palace grounds, to which Rallie's wagon and menagerie of animals had been relegated. They passed by several soldiers, who seemed unsure if they should bow or salute or both.

"She knows where we're going. Hurry, we must hurry," Chayii said as she darted between some flowering cactuses.

Visyna hoisted her dress up even higher and broke into a run, hoping no one would see her like this. "What is it you think you heard?"

"I heard the voice of Rising Dawn, no matter how faint," Chayii said, not slowing her pace. "Tyul has used his oath weapon, and not without cost. Another magic is at work here."

"The Shadow Monarch," Visyna said.

"I have no doubt Her forces are here, but no, this felt different." Now she did stop and turned to Visyna. "Did you not hear or feel anything?"

Visyna shook her head. "I'm not sure. Earlier I thought I did sense something, but all the noise at the party made it difficult to understand, and then it was gone."

Chayii gave her a brief smile. "You are more attuned to the natural order than I thought."

Visyna blushed slightly at the compliment. Chayii turned and they both ran the rest of the way to Rallie's wagon. The glow of a cigar tip revealed that the old woman was already there.

"How did you do that?" Visyna asked. "You were behind us when we left the party."

Rallie blew out a mouthful of smoke and smiled. "I know how to get around. Speaking of which, mind your step, dear. This is definitely a well-attended party."

Visyna looked down and saw what Rallie meant. Piles of horse and camel manure dotted the lane. The more manure there was to clean up in the morning, the more horses and carriages had been there the night before.

"An odd way to measure the success of a party," Chayii said.

"Think of it in terms of tracking quarry," Rallie said. "If this were a forest, you could glean much from what's scattered on the ground around us, no?"

Chayii made a small bow. "Your city-craft is impressive. I have always had difficulty navigating through large, populated areas such as this. The desecration of the natural order is so violent here."

Visyna felt it as well. A city oozed pollution like an open wound. The land became sick and the natural power tainted. For weavers of magic such as herself it took great effort to sift through the energy to find clean, usable threads. She sighed. She could spend her whole life purging the polluted energy in Nazalla and still never be done.

The sreexes, Rallie's batlike courier birds, squawked from inside the covered wagon and a moment later Jir jumped out of the back, his collar and chain no longer attached. He stuck his head high in the air and sniffed.

"Feels good, doesn't it, boy?" Rallie said, leaning down to scratch the bengar on top of his head.

Jir's purr grew so loud in volume that the hair on the back of Visyna's neck began to rise. She gave herself a shake. The bengar was a powerful force even when it was contented.

Visyna quickly changed out of her gown and into travel clothes. She threw the gown into the back of the wagon. Chayii had no need to change, as she'd refused to put on a gown and kept her elven clothing, while Rallie had merely adorned her black cloak with a pink bow, which she now removed and put in an inside pocket.

"There, back to informal. Now, shall we go?" Rallie asked, sitting down on the wagon seat and grabbing up the reins.

Visyna and Chayii climbed up after her while Jir hopped into the back, seemingly content now that he wasn't collared.

"We must find Tyul," Chayii said. "In his state, he is very unpredictable. I thought he would be safe if left on the ship. I thought they would both be safe."

Visyna reached out and placed a hand on Chayii's shoulder. The elf bore more heartache than most. Tyul was *diova gruss*, lost in the power of a Silver Wolf Oak. Her husband, Jurwan, was equally enthralled and remained locked in squirrel form.

And then there was her son.

"At least we know where Konowa will be for the next several hours," Visyna said.

Rallie clicked her tongue and flicked the reins. The brindos tossed their heads, then settled down and began to walk. Looking for all the world like horses wearing dark gray armor, the plates of their tough hides slid over their bodies in an unsettling fashion, while the animals' floppy ears bounced up and down as they moved forward. Their stubby tails wagged furiously—whether in joy to be on the move, or in a vain attempt to keep away flies, it wasn't clear.

Chayii smiled. "His childhood was not easy. He was one of the first elves not banished at birth. I was the one who docked his ear. His father had wanted to leave it, to show the Hynta-elves and the world that no son of his would bow to a fate not of his choosing." Chayii's voice grew soft. "I knew he would have a difficult enough path to travel without adding that."

"But why is he so . . ." Visyna wasn't sure how to finish the question.

"He would never admit it, but his rejection in the birthing meadow hurt him deeply. In our culture, there is no higher honor than to be bonded to a Wolf Oak. It is said that until that day, no elf is ever truly complete. Konowa believed that on the day he bonded, everything would change for him. He would be the first elf marked by the Shadow Monarch to take a *ryk faur* and join the Long Watch."

"And when he was rejected?" Visyna asked.

"He turned his back on us, on his people, and on himself. He joined the Imperial Army shortly thereafter. His father encouraged him." The bitterness in Chayii's voice was clear, but so was the regret.

"It's not too late for him," Visyna said, hoping her words were true. "It's not too late for any of them. We restored the Red Star to my people and saved Elfkyna. We destroyed the Shadow Monarch's forest on the islands. We will prevail here, too."

Chayii's head turned and she studied Visyna carefully. "Your land and your people were indeed saved, yet here you are."

Visyna blushed, but did not look away. "Konowa is still in peril, and I will save him, too . . . if I can."

Chayii said nothing, but reached out a hand and held Visyna's in hers. Rallie looked up to the sky and pointed at the stars. "Best keep your eyes open then, because we are going to need every bit of help we can find."

The wagon rolled through the grounds and approached a palace gate. Several sentries stood watching, but made no effort to stop them, simply tipping their shakos at the ladies as they passed. Visyna looked at Chayii and Rallie and considered the contents of the wagon, and realized the soldiers had made a very wise choice.

"Shouldn't we tell someone?" Visyna asked, watching the lights of the palace disappear as they turned a corner.

"Best that we keep this quiet for now," Rallie said. "Besides, we have my sreex. When we need to get a message to the Prince and the major, we'll do so. In the meantime, the less attention we attract the better."

"Head south, out of the city," Chayii said. "Rising Dawn's voice came from over there."

"South leads us to the desert. Interesting," Rallie said. She clicked her tongue against her cheek and the brindos broke into a trot.

Shouting erupted downstairs. Alwyn tried to make out what was being said, but it was too garbled. He reached for his musket and remembered he'd left it with Yimt. The shouting rose in volume, and one voice was louder than the others.

Yimt.

"I've got to go," Alwyn said, scrambling to stand up.

Nafeesah grabbed his arm. "It is nothing. Stay. We have yet to explore the reason you came up here in the first place."

Alwyn looked at her, his mouth dropping open. "I can't, not now. Don't you see, Kaman Rhal's power is here. Somebody or something is wielding the white fire. I don't even want to think about the idea of an army of the dead." In fact, Alwyn had spent the last few weeks thinking of nothing but, as the shadows of his fallen comrades never left him.

"What do you think you can do? Why must men always rush about yelling at the top of their lungs threatening to do something?" Nafeesah asked.

The sound of breaking furniture came up through the floor, which briefly intrigued Alwyn, because all he could remember seeing were pillows.

"I really need to go," Alwyn said, buttoning up his jacket. "I don't know what's going on, but whatever it is I need to find out, and I need to tell my sergeant." He began to part the curtains, then turned and came back to kneel beside Nafeesah. He felt as if he needed to say something reassuring, though whether it was for her or himself he wasn't certain. "Maybe, when all this is over, I'll be able to come back here . . . and see you." He leaned in to kiss her. Their lips touched and Alwyn forgot everything. For a blissful moment, there was no pain, no oath, no death.

"You're smiling," Nafeesah said, her lips still pressed to his.

"Thank you," Alwyn said, not wanting the kiss to end.

Nafeesah pulled back and looked him in the eye. "You can thank me properly on your return."

Alwyn's smile faltered. "I'd like that, but I—"

She put a finger to his lips. "You will return, Alwyn Oath Taker, Elf of Iron. I know it."

Alwyn held her gaze, then a thought struck him. He gently grabbed her hand and held it. "What do I tell the others, about this? Us? I mean, what was supposed to happen up here?"

Nafeesah shook her head, brushing her curls in Alwyn's face. "You tell them you were so exceptional, I refused to take your money."

More shouting shook the walls. "I really should get down there."

She nodded. "Be safe."

Alwyn let go of her hand and turned to leave. Nafeesah grabbed his arm and pulled him back. They shared one more kiss. Alwyn had begun to wonder if he really did need to rush downstairs when the sound of shattering glass came up from the stairwell. "I've got to go!" he said, turning and hobbling to the stairs. He took one last look back at Nafeesah and then went through the curtains and down the stairs.

At the bottom he found himself in the middle of a full-fledged brawl.

It seemed Yimt's attempts to prevent a riot hadn't succeeded. As Alwyn's eyes grew accustomed to the gloom he realized it wasn't Iron Elves against locals, but rather Iron Elves against a group of soldiers from the 12th Regiment. The locals were running for cover.

Yimt was pummeling a sergeant from the 12th while Hrem, Scolly, and Teeter were surrounded by at least seven soldiers. Inkermon had a broken bottle in one hand and a glass of wine in the other and was holding three more soldiers at bay. Zwitty was nowhere in sight.

"Duck!"

Alwyn crouched, unsure if the warning had been directed at him. The woosh of a bottle passing over his head suggested it had. He stood back up as two soldiers of the 12th charged toward him.

"There's another one of the buggers."

Alwyn reached for the first weapon he could find and came up with a pillow. He ripped the covering and tossed it into the air, scattering feathers everywhere. In the ensuing confusion, he ran through the white cloud and met the soldiers on the other side. His fist struck first. The nose of one soldier made a wet, crunching sound and he dropped straight to the floor. The second soldier hit Alwyn in the jaw, sending him reeling backward. Alwyn reached up and put his spectacles back in place, amazed they hadn't broken. The soldier came on, his fist poised to punch again, when he stopped, staring at Alwyn's wooden leg.

"Aw, hell, I didn't realize you was a cripple."

Another wet, crunching sound came as the soldier's teeth flew out of his mouth. Lightning exploded in Alwyn's hand, but he only smiled and looked around for more.

Whistles and shouting sounded from outside, and there was a mad rush toward the rear of the pub. Hrem grabbed Alwyn up under one arm and carried him. There were more beaded curtains and then they were in an alley.

"Put me down, Hrem, I can barely breathe," Alwyn said.

"What, oh, sorry," Hrem said, setting him onto the ground.

"Everyone accounted for?" Yimt said, rearranging his shako on his head. He was puffing and his face was red, but for all of that he was smiling. "Where's Zwitty?"

"Right here," Zwitty said, emerging from the back door of the pub. He was carrying two muskets, one of which he threw to Alwyn. "Don't want to lose that."

Alwyn caught it and nodded his thanks. The others were catching their breath and buttoning up their jackets. Teeter had a nasty gash on his forehead and both of Hrem's hands were bloodied, but otherwise they looked as if they'd fared well. Inkermon was still clutching his now-empty wine glass.

"What was that all about?" Alwyn asked as Yimt started to lead them down the alley. Without a word the soldiers spread out, their muskets ready in their hands.

"That," Yimt said, "was about regimental pride. Those cheeky buggers thought they'd make a few disparaging remarks about the Prince and the major, so we had to tune them up proper. A rather energetic discussion ensued, which I think you caught the tail end of."

"But we've complained about them ourselves," Alwyn said.

"Aye, we have, and that's our right. They're our colonel and second-in-command and we have the right, nay, the *duty* to complain about 'em. Them other duffers don't. Just the way it works."

Alwyn tried to get his head around that. "Even so, now none of you get to go upstairs"

Yimt turned to look at him, the smile still on his face. "True, but *you* did. So how did it go?"

Alwyn felt all their eyes on him.

"Not the way it was supposed to," Alwyn said, remembering too late what Nafeesah had told him to say. Before the hooting could start up, he quickly related everything else about Kaman Rhal and the white fire.

Teeter shook his head. "You sure you didn't dream all that? You were hitting the hookah pretty hard."

Alwyn shook his head. "I was wide awake, believe me. Look, if what she said is true, even some of it, then we know what we're dealing with."

"He's right," Hrem said. "It's about time we knew what we were up against."

"Or we could just leave well enough alone and not say nothing to no one," Zwitty added. "We got no way of knowing if anything she told Alwyn was true."

"It fits, though, don't it?" Yimt said. He turned to Alwyn. "You sure about this, lad?"

"Go back and ask her," Alwyn said, then quickly added, "Sergeant."

Yimt ran a hand through his beard and pulled out a piece of orange. He popped it in his mouth rind and all. "All right, I believe you, but you sure do have some of the strangest encounters."

"So what do we do now?" Hrem asked.

Shouting echoed off the alley walls. "For starters," Yimt said, grabbing Alwyn by the arm and pulling him toward the end of the alley, "we get our arses out of here. The Viceroy's got all kinds of constabulary just waiting to lock up innocent soldiers like us."

Alwyn looked down at the dwarf as they hurried away. "Innocent?"

"Figure of speech, Ally, figure of speech," Yimt said, huffing as he pumped his short legs. "Stands to reason that we're always innocent of something, even if we're guilty of something else."

Alwyn couldn't argue with that logic, but then with Yimt it was usually because you didn't understand it.

"This isn't the way back to the palace," Alwyn said as they rounded a corner and headed off down another alley. He looked behind them and was relieved to see the rest of the section was keeping up.

"No point going back there now anyway," Yimt said. "The streets will be swimming with people, including a herd of lads from the twelfth looking for some payback. Our best bet is to head away from all the hubbub and lie low for a while."

"But we need to tell the major. This is important," Alwyn said, shaking loose Yimt's grip and coming to a stop. "If even some of what Nafeesah said is true we have to act."

The other soldiers came to a halt and promptly bent over or slumped against a wall. It sounded like a pack of race horses after a mile and a quarter.

"And we will, lad, we will, but you have to trust your sergeant. There's a time to go running off half-cocked, and there's a time you want to be fully cocked." More shouting erupted from somewhere nearby. Yimt motioned with his thumb toward another dark alleyway. "And this is definitely one of those times."

Alwyn pushed his spectacles back up his nose and set off after Yimt. They were rounding another corner when a thought occurred to Alwyn. "Sergeant? Which one of those times is it?"

TWENTY

After another five minutes, Yimt led them to a dead-end alley with a tarp for a roof and several lanterns hung from rusting iron hooks set in the walls of the surrounding buildings. Wicker baskets, some as large as a man and others smaller than a rabbit, filled the space. A leathery-faced dwarf wearing local robes with a gray beard tucked into his belt sat on one of the baskets chewing crute and spitting into an earthenware pot on the ground. Frowning, he got up when they approached, a drukar appearing in his right hand.

Yimt took a moment to catch his breath, then walked forward. His shatterbow remained slung on his back. "Well met this fine evening," he said, holding out his bag of crute.

"Don't got drink or women here, and I don't keep more than a few copper coins in my purse," the dwarf replied, taking a pinch of the offered crute and placing it between his gums and cheek. His metal-colored teeth flashed in the light as he smiled, then quickly went back to a frown.

"Both more trouble than they're worth," Yimt said, smiling

broadly. He sat down on another wicker basket and pointed toward Alwyn and the group to come closer. He looked around the stall.

The dwarf snorted. "Quite a commotion going on at the Blue Scorpion tonight by the sounds of it. You wouldn't know anything about that, would you?"

Yimt held out both arms wide. "We're innocent."

The other dwarf grinned. "I don't doubt it, but what are you guilty of?"

"Nothing they'll get us for if we keep our wits about us," Yimt said, scowling briefly as he looked at Scolly. "Now, we got a bit of time to kill and could use a diversion for perhaps an hour or two, one that would remove us from these fair streets, and away from prying eyes."

"We could get tattoos," Teeter suggested. He had pulled a bottle out from somewhere in his uniform and was mid-drink. "I always get a tattoo when I land in a new port. Sort of a tradition in the navy, you know."

"You ain't in the bloody navy no more," Zwitty said, grabbing the bottle out of Teeter's hand and taking a drink. "Besides, where are we going to find an inker around here, anyways?"

"Tattooing is considered immoral in these parts," the dwarf merchant said, lowering his voice. "Folks round here figure you're desecrating your body if you get ink done. A fellow could lose a hand that way if he got caught . . . if you catch my meaning."

Yimt held out his hand until Zwitty walked over and put the bottle in it. "Times are changing," Yimt said. "In case you hadn't noticed, the Empire is now in town."

The other dwarf spat and laughed, a harsh sound that was not at all comforting. "Sure, you're here now. But where will you be a week from now? A month from now? Times are changing all right. Stars are falling, the Shadow Monarch is rising, and the Empire is scrambling to hold on to what it can. I was here the first time the Empire waded ashore. Less than a year later, they were gone save for a token trading delegation and a few siggers to keep up appearances. That was decades ago. Only thing different since you boys arrived is the price of just about everything has gone up."

"Oh, I hear there's at least one more difference," Yimt said, pointing a thumb over his shoulder toward the desert outside Nazalla. "Way we hear it, sounds like the Shadow Monarch ain't the only one stirring things up."

The dwarf shrugged. "The Suljak keeps the tribes in check. In return for a cut, the trade caravans pass through the Hasshugeb Expanse and come in to Nazalla, then on to Calahr. Nothing new."

Yimt took a pull on the bottle, then offered it to the dwarf. He shook his head.

Alwyn stepped forward. "Uh, Sergeant, maybe we should be moving on. We have to get back to camp, remember?"

"Ally, I told you, we got time. You know, Teeter ain't got a half-bad idea. Maybe a little something to remember our night here in the big city is just the ticket."

The dwarf stood up from his basket. "I might be able to help you," he said. He pulled up a sleeve on his left arm, revealing a large tattoo of a stake with several orc heads skewered on it. Alwyn looked closer and counted eight.

Yimt stood up and looked around at the other soldiers. "Lads, we're in the presence of greatness. There's only one regiment in the whole Calahrian Army that wears a tattoo like that, and that's the Queen's Own Shields."

Alwyn whistled. The QOS were famous the world over for their stand against the orcs at Frillik's Drift in the Second Border War over fifty years ago. Six hundred dwarves held off ten thousand orcs for over a week. When it was over, thirty-four dwarves made it back.

"You're one of the thirty-four," Alwyn whispered.

"Well, if I wasn't you'd be talking to a ghost," the dwarf said. He held out his hand to Yimt. "Sergeant Griz Jahrfel, retired."

Yimt grabbed his hand and shook it vigorously. "Sergeant Yimt Arkhorn, Iron Elves. I know, I know, takes too long to explain. And this motley bunch is my old section. I was showing them the sights of Nazalla when we ran into a few lads from the twelfth."

Griz nodded. "Ignorant buggers with hard heads and soft kneecaps."

"Especially if you hit it just right," Yimt said. Both dwarves started laughing.

"So are we getting tattoos or what?" Teeter asked. He'd found yet another bottle and was drinking from it. "We want to get a move on if we are, 'cause you know damn well they'll be sending us out to that desert to chase down that Kama Wall fellow soon enough."

Alwyn waved at Teeter to be quiet.

"Wait, you're serious?" Griz said. "You lads really here to go after Kaman Rhal's ghost?"

"Wasn't no ghost that burned ol' Harkon," Teeter said, swinging the bottle to make his point. "That white fire fried his shadow like an egg getting . . . fried."

"Teeter, why don't you do us all a favor and pass out already," Yimt said.

Griz whistled and stepped back. "I've heard some tall tales in my time . . . told most of them, so I ought to know, but you don't want to be talking about white fire and shadows around here. People get upset at that kind of talk."

"It's true," Alwyn said. "We fought it just a few days ago."

The dwarf looked from Yimt to Alwyn then around the group. "You're having me on. Kaman Rhal is as dead as dead gets. His power was lost when his library was. It's just local myth handed down through the generations."

Yimt shook his head. "Myths aren't what they used to be. These days, everything old is new again."

"I heard something over here!" a voice shouted from down the alley.

Griz peered into the distance. "Might be some of those weak-kneed knuckle draggers from the twelfth. Quick, lads, follow me," Griz said, "we can continue this conversation in private."

Griz hurried over to a large wicker basket the size of a grown man and stepped behind it. When no one followed, he reappeared and waved his hand. "Well, come on then."

Alwyn was the first to walk around the basket. He discovered that the back half of the basket was in fact a secret door that opened onto a hidden entrance. Closer inspection revealed a set of stairs. The light from a candle or lantern somewhere below illuminated the steps enough for him to see. Unslinging his musket, he crouched and descended the stairs. They twisted around several times before finally emptying out into a small tunnel with a curved roof about six feet high lined with hardened mud bricks.

"This way," Griz said, holding a small lantern. Alwyn looked behind him and was reassured to hear the others thumping down the stairs. He set out after the dwarf, who walked quickly for someone with such short legs, forcing Alwyn to almost hop along behind him. Alwyn was about to ask how much farther when Griz stopped and knocked on the left side of the tunnel.

The muffled sound of knocking came in reply from the other side, and then a hidden door opened up in the tunnel wall. Griz motioned Alwyn inside. Alwyn looked back down the tunnel the way he came. Yimt appeared a moment later, with the others following along behind.

Alwyn stepped inside, and for the second time that evening found himself in a room unlike any he had ever been in before. "It's, uh, cozy," he said, removing his shako and standing up. His hair just brushed the ceiling. Another dwarf stood just inside, but instead of robes, this one wore heavy leather boots, dark leggings, and a leather and chainmail overcoat. His red beard was shorn so that it only reached the top of his chest. A drukar hung from a leather belt around his waist.

This was a dwarf you didn't mess with, which got Alwyn thinking he hadn't actually met a dwarf yet whom you did want to mess with. He nodded at the dwarf, who only stared at him in reply. Alwyn looked around the room. Lanterns hung from iron hooks set in the ceiling. The room itself was a perfect cylinder, with curved walls of ordinary field stone so perfectly laid that Alwyn had to squint to make out the joint lines.

"Not a drop of mortar in the entire place," Griz said, hooking his thumbs in his belt and beaming. The younger dwarf snorted, or perhaps sneezed.

Alwyn ran a hand along a section of wall. It was as smooth as a polished slab of marble. Fittingly, instead of pillows and hanging curtains of fine cloth and beads, the dwarf had furnished his underground home—if that's what it was—simply. There were several low, wide stools and benches of slate. There were no wicker baskets in sight.

"Do you have a large family?" Alwyn asked, noticing several dirty mugs and plates sitting on a long, low table on the far side of the room.

Griz looked over at the table, then at the younger dwarf, and cursed under his breath. "Uh, just the hired help."

The rest of the group now entered the room. Hrem came in almost bent double. He looked around, then sat down and leaned his back against the wall. The younger dwarf's hand came to rest on the hilt of his drukar, but he otherwise remained still.

"Trij, make yourself useful and get these boys a drink," Griz said when everyone was in the room. Behind them the door to the tunnel slid shut silently.

Trij stood still a moment longer, studying every soldier in turn. On spying Yimt, Trij squinted and focused on the shatterbow that was now slung under Yimt's arm and ready to use. Finally, the dwarf slowly took his hand off his drukar and turned and walked toward a section of the wall. He reached out a hand and lightly punched one of the stones. There was a click as the stone sank into the wall an inch. A moment later, another secret door swung open and Trij walked through it. Alwyn kept expecting to hear grinding stone, but there was barely a speck of dust set floating on the air as stone glided over stone. These dwarves knew masonry.

"You're first," Griz said, grabbing Alwyn by the arm and leading him to one of the stone stools. "The rest of you lads can grab a seat and get comfortable." He sat Alwyn down, then pulled a stool up beside him. Griz stared at Alwyn's ears until Alwyn pulled back a bit.

"Something wrong?" Alwyn asked.

Griz shook his head and smiled. "What, no, just thinking it's a bit funny you lot being Iron Elves when the real ones is out in the desert."

"No," Alwyn said, "it's really not that funny at all."

Griz's smile wavered, then he winked at Alwyn. "No, I suppose it isn't. Now, sonny, lose the jacket and roll up your sleeve. You want the right or left arm?"

"Right," Yimt said, looking around the room as he walked over to watch. Trij returned through the secret opening carrying two fistfuls of pewter mugs with beer froth dripping down the sides. He handed them out quickly, saving Yimt's for last.

"Good weapon," Trij remarked.

Yimt took a drink from his mug, then set it down on a bench. Foam covered his beard. "Yours, too," he said, looking at Trij's drukar.

"Forged in the Maiden Works under Schrakkart Peak." Trij unsheathed it and held it up to the light.

Yimt peered at it and nodded. "Those gals do good work."

Trij sheathed the blade. "You do not carry one?"

Yimt scowled. "I did, and I will again."

Trij nodded, walked away, and began clearing the plates and mugs from the table.

"Nice enough fellow, bit on the talky side, though," Yimt said, picking up his mug and taking another swig.

Griz chuckled. "That's the most he's said in three days."

Alwyn looked from Griz to Yimt. "How can you be so calm? Evil is—"

"Easy, lad, easy," Griz said, patting Alwyn on the arm. "You'll rupture yourself if you keep gettin' all excited like this." He looked over to Yimt. "You'd think this was the first time the world hung in the balance."

"Kids these days," Yimt said, taking another drink from his mug and winking at Alwyn. "I tell them you gotta take a breath once in a while and stop and smell the nuns, but do they listen?"

"The thing you have to remember," Griz said, reaching underneath a stool and pulling out a small, black leather valise, "is that there's always trouble brewing somewhere. An elf-witch on a mountain. A dead wizard in a desert. Stars tumbling to earth. It's the way of the world." He opened the valise and brought out a quill with a metal tip and a jar of black ink.

Alwyn gulped. "But if Kaman Rhal's magic really is back, we need to find it. This is important."

Griz nodded. "Aye, I can see that. Trij is off looking for a map now. I'm pretty sure I got an old survey map from a hundred years ago or so. Should help you a bit if the cartographer knew what he was doing."

Alwyn looked over to where Trij was busing the table, but the dwarf was gone. "Where'd he go?"

"Quiet, that one. Don't tell him I said so, but I'd wager there's a little elf in his blood. Never met a dwarf that could move as quiet as him." Griz grabbed a small bottle out of the valise and uncorked it. "This might sting a bit."

"Wait, what are you going to tattoo on me?" Alwyn asked. He felt like screaming that this wasn't the time, but he was clearly outnumbered.

Griz sat back and looked at him. "Mercy me, your first one? Lad, I have no idea. It ain't me that decides, it's *you*. I just wait to see what appears." He sprinkled a few drops of the liquid onto Alwyn's arm, then sat back. "See, a good artist lets the canvas—in this case, *you*—speak to him."

"But I haven't told you what I want," Alwyn said, watching the skin on his upper arm. The area where the liquid touched tingled. "I'm not really sure I want anything, to be honest. I just—ow!"

Alwyn stopped talking as tiny tongues of black flame flared up, then quickly vanished on his arm. Griz stroked his beard a couple of times and looked over at Yimt. "That's new. Still, the potion never lies." The dwarf picked up his quill and dipped it into the ink. "Odd though, I figured you for crossed muskets like the other—" Griz caught himself, then smiled. "Like the other soldiers that have been through here. Now, let's get you inked," he said, jabbing the quill into Alwyn's arm as he began to trace the faint outline of a black acorn that appeared just underneath the skin.

Visyna lightly descended from Rallie's wagon and walked to the center of the open space between the buildings and alleyways. Between the moonlight and flickering lanterns, she was able to see well enough. Jir padded alongside her, providing additional comfort that no one, or no thing, was going to surprise her. Visyna raised her hands and began to gently tease at the fabrics of natural energy around her. Light shone from between her hands as she sorted through the many threads, searching for traces that would tell her what had happened. Clearly, a fight had taken place here, and recently. Old, bitter threads marked the three piles of ash that dotted the ground, but just what those piles had been, she couldn't tell. She concentrated harder, searching for telltale signs of the Shadow Monarch's power.

"I don't think you'll find it here," Rallie said, still sitting in the wagon and looking down. "This is something else entirely."

Chayii knelt a few yards away, thoughtfully sifting sand through her hands. She grimaced and stood up, throwing the dirt away. "The magic used here was ancient. Much older than Hers. Tyul was here, and my husband," she added.

Visyna wasn't sure if it was annoyance or concern in her voice. *Probably both.* "Then is this Kaman Rhal's doing?" she asked. She stretched her senses a little further, worrying at a thread so thin she couldn't quite grasp it with her mind. She let out a deep sigh and lowered her hands.

"That," Rallie said, "is what we're going to find out. We still have a few hours of darkness, so let's make the most of it and get out of Nazalla with as few eyes watching us as possible. I assume we're still heading south?"

Chayii nodded. "Tyul is all but untrackable, but Rising Dawn is not. They are definitely heading for the desert."

"Why, though? Why would Tyul and Jurwan leave the ship and come here?" Visyna asked, climbing back onto the wagon and turning to help Chayii up. The elf smiled her thanks and sat down beside her.

"Tyul sees things differently than us. To him, the world is simple, or should be simple. Things are either in their natural state or they are not. That is why he is still with me. He understands the threat the Shadow Monarch poses and seeks to restore Her mountain to its pure form. If he detected something equally wrong, he would have sought it out. In his mind he would be helping it, even if that meant killing it."

"And Jurwan?"

Chayii shook her head. "My husband is a fool. Brave, intelligent, loving, but a fool. No one else could have survived Her mountain, and I'm not entirely sure he did. What he wants, what he knows, I can no longer say."

The brindos lurched forward and the wagon began rolling again. Visyna continued to weave the air around her, puzzling through the various energies and trying to make sense of them. Being tricked by Her Emissary in Elfkyna had been deeply humiliating to her, and she wasn't about to let it happen again.

It wasn't easy to weave magic this late at night on a moving wagon in a large city. Visyna yawned and had begun to let the threads go when something caught her attention. She tried to pinpoint it, but it was too difficult to grasp.

"Do you—" she started to ask the other two women, but had gotten no further when she turned toward them. Both were looking to the southern sky. A thin blue light glimmered among the stars.

"I feel it, too," Chayii said, her eyes unblinking as they watched the night sky. "The Jewel of the Desert is returning."

Rallie snapped at the reins and the brindos picked up their pace. "That's not the only thing that's coming. There's a change in the weather, masking a power out in the desert."

No longer feeling sleepy, Visyna focused her energy on her weaving, following threads deep into the desert.

After a distance of some miles, the threads frayed and became lost in a swath of bitter cold darkness. Visyna was all too familiar with its taint. "The Shadow Monarch's forest has crossed the sea and is out there in the desert," she said. She lowered her hands and rubbed them on the tops of her thighs.

Chayii cursed in Elvish. "Tyul and Jurwan are heading straight into it," Chayii said. "They won't have the sense to turn back.

Neither's mind is clear enough. We must get out there and save them from themselves."

"We'll need help, Chayii," Visyna said. "Rallie, we must get a message to Konowa at once. The regiment needs to move. The Star will fall and the only powers out there will be Hers and Kaman Rhal's. We three alone won't be enough. We need help."

Rallie pulled up hard on the reins as the wagon shuddered to a halt.

"Rallie, what are you doing?" Chayii asked.

Rallie pulled a cigar out of her cloak and lit it, drawing in a huge breath until the end of the cigar was bright red. "I think we just found some help," she said, as shadowy figures emerged from an alleyway to block their path.

TWENTY-ONE

I t stings," Scolly said, rubbing his right arm.

"Then quit worrying it, and keep your voice down," Yimt said, scratching at his upper arm, too. They stood among the dwarf's wicker baskets in the alley, waiting for Hrem to appear. A moment later, Hrem struggled his way out of the secret opening behind the large wicker basket and put his shako on his head.

Alwyn flexed his bicep and found that his tattoo didn't bother him at all. It was his first one. He'd always imagined that if he ever got the courage up to get a tattoo, it would be something manly like a sword or the name of a special woman or even crossed muskets like Griz had mentioned. A black acorn had never entered his mind.

"What do you think, Sergeant? Could we head back to the Blue Scorpion for a bit?" Teeter asked.

Yimt stood still for a moment in deep thought. Finally, he slapped the stock of his shatterbow. "I hate to break it to you, but we've got to get back to camp and let the major know what's going on," Yimt said.

Teeter kicked at the dirt and looked at Yimt, his eyes pleading. "We don't really know all that much, do we?"

"There's nothing for it, we have to report," Yimt said, looking around the section as if waiting for more objections.

Alwyn wasn't surprised the group remained quiet. No one wanted to go out to the desert, but the sooner they got out there, the sooner they might find a way to break the oath. Alwyn flexed his wooden leg and got a twinge of pain for his efforts. The effects of the drink and the tobacco were wearing off. So, too, was the high he'd felt with Nafeesah. Once again they were about to go off into the unknown and battle forces bent on trying to kill them, and worse. He looked around the darkened alley and gripped his musket a little tighter. Alwyn tried to recall a time when he didn't know there was something more dreadful than being killed.

"I thought you said it got cold here at night," Zwitty said, casually opening the lids on some of the wicker baskets and peering inside. "Feels all right to me."

"You're three sheets to the wind for starters," Yimt said, walking over and slamming a lid out of Zwitty's hand with his shatterbow, "and we're in a city on the coast. Wait till we get out in the open desert, and see if you think it's still warm at night."

"What time is it?" Teeter asked, looking up at the sky.

"Midnight, maybe later," Hrem said. "Sergeant, you have a pocket watch?"

Yimt laughed. "Do I look like I've got gold bullion tucked up under this caerna? Those devices cost a pretty penny. Besides, I don't need one to tell me the time." He looked up at the sky as well. "It's late."

"Very helpful," Inkermon said, leaning unsteadily against a wicker basket and looking up at the sky as well.

"Why's everyone looking up?" Scolly asked.

Alwyn looked up. "The sky looks a bit blue, don't you think? And it feels different, too."

"Different how?" Yimt asked, pointing a warning finger at Zwitty, then walking over to Alwyn.

"I don't know, but it doesn't feel the same from when we went down the tunnel to now," Alwyn said. A general unease settled in Alwyn's blood. "You don't suppose it's the Star, do you? I can't explain it, but something is different. You're right, I think we need to get back to camp."

Inkermon lurched away from his resting place and strode out into the alley. "It doesn't matter. You know what this means, don't you?" he said. His jacket was off and his undershirt sleeve rolled up and he was gently tracing the outline of the acorn with his finger. "It means we are truly marked by Her. Our souls are unredeemable. That's what you're feeling. Our souls are gone . . ." Inkermon gasped and began sobbing.

Yimt walked out to where Inkermon was and put a hand on his shoulder. With the other hand, he reached out and punched Inkermon's new tattoo. Inkermon quit crying and started yowling.

"Hush your drunken self, you want half of Nazalla to hear you wailing on like a baby?"

Inkermon quieted down. Alwyn expected a fiery retort, but the farmer-turned-soldier simply walked over to a wall and slid down it to sit with his head on his knees.

Yimt took off his shako and scratched his head a couple of times, then put the hat back on. "Look, nobody's soul has gone anywhere," Yimt said. "We got these tattoos of our own free will.

Fine, I'll admit it's a bit creepy to know the acorn mark was already there, but that's magic for you. We are oath-bound, after all. It'd have been a bigger surprise if that dwarf's magic quill had called up a puppy or a bouquet of bloody flowers now, wouldn't it? And let's not forget we made a few modifications of our own. I don't think the Shadow Monarch would approve."

Alwyn looked closer at Inkermon's bare arm. It was highly unlikely the Shadow Monarch would be thrilled to see a bayonet stuck through the heart of the acorn with the words *Æri Mekah*—"Into the Fire"—inscribed above it, and *And Right the Hell Back Out!* underneath it.

Yimt motioned up to the sky, then snapped his fingers to get their attention. His face showed fierce determination. "What I'm trying to say is, don't you ever let *this* own you. Not the oath, the afterlife, not any of it. We've been in tough spots before and got out of 'em. We'll figure out a way to make it through this, too."

"So what's Ally feeling then?" Zwitty asked. "'Cause if he's getting twitchy, then you know something is going on."

Yimt shrugged. "Maybe there's a big sandstorm brewing. They get them here, absolute monsters. Winds strong enough to scour the flesh off your bones."

"Lovely," Hrem said. "Well, my appetite for the pleasures of Nazalla is pretty much spent. If we're supposed to be heading back to camp, we might as well get going. The longer we stand around here, the more likely trouble's going to find us. If it's the desert for us, at least we can get a few hours' sleep before we go."

"Spoken like a man with his head on straight," Yimt said. "Right, Hrem, get Inkermon up and let's go set a few more of those wheels of history in motion."

"I hear something," Scolly said, unslinging his musket and pointing toward the other end of the alley.

Alwyn turned his head and tried to listen. "Sounds like a carriage. Going awfully fast, too."

Yimt hefted his shatterbow and cocked the hammers. "That doesn't sound normal, not at this time of night. Wake up, sober up, but stay calm. Follow me and be ready."

"Ready for what?" Alwyn asked. He wiped a palm against his caerna to dry the sweat.

"Anything," Yimt said, as he walked to the end of the alley with the section close behind. Without pausing, Yimt strode out into the middle of the road. Alwyn recognized Miss Synjyn's brindos at once and started to relax. "Well, that's a relief, Sergeant."

Yimt lowered his shatterbow and sighed. "Somehow, Ally, I don't think it is." He waved to Miss Synjyn. The wagon wheels juddered across the cobbles as the brindos halted. A wash of dust swept over the soldiers and Alwyn turned his head and coughed. When he looked back, Miss Tekoy and Miss Red Owl were off the wagon.

"Alwyn of the Empire, what are you doing out here so late? This is not suitable behavior, young man. You need to rest your leg if it is to have any hope of truly grafting," Miss Red Owl said.

Light laughter echoed off the surrounding buildings behind Alwyn, but he refused to turn to see who it was. He felt his face flush. *I'm not a kid anymore.* "I'm fine." He spat the words out with force. He saw the surprised looks on the faces around him, but he couldn't hold it in. "In fact, *I* figured out what attacked Kester on the last island, and *I* got us a map of the desert and an idea where to find it. I really wouldn't know what's appropriate for a young man anymore, but for an Iron Elf, this is."

Silence reigned for several seconds. Finally, Rallie coughed and leaned over the side of the front bench of her wagon. "May I see it?" she asked, holding out her hand. "The map you so forcefully procured."

Yimt looked over at Alwyn, then at Rallie. "I'm still the sergeant around here," he said, pulling the map from his jacket and handing it to her. "Leaving in a bit of a rush, aren't you? Going somewhere or just taking the brindos out for a late-night trot?"

Rallie took a drag on her cigar until the end became bright red and ignored Yimt's question. She bent over the map and studied it in the glow. "Tell me, Sergeant, how did you—I'm sorry—how did Private Renwar acquire this map?"

Yimt looked over at Alwyn again before answering Rallie. "Met a dwarf, one of the thirty-four survivors of Frillik's Drift, no less. When he found out we were heading out to the desert he dug this up. Damn nice of him, I'll say."

Rallie continued to study the map. "Really? Whatever is he doing here?"

"Retired," Yimt said. "Guess he came down here for the heat. The mountains get mighty cold in winter."

"That they do," Rallie said. "Well, this *was* very nice of him indeed. This is far more detailed than any map of the Hasshugeb that the Prince has in his possession. I'd guess this dwarf is a bit of an explorer, too."

"Griz? Naw, he runs a basket place off the market. Well, probably does a little black market on the side if I had to guess looking at his setup, but solid as a ton of lead," Yimt said.

Rallie sat up and took the cigar out of her mouth. "Griz Jahrfel?"

Yimt nodded. "Aye, that's him," he said slowly. "You know him, then?"

Alwyn wondered if there was a hint of jealousy in Yimt's voice. Up until now he'd been the only dwarf in Rallie's life, not counting her editor back in Celwyn, a fact Alwyn knew Yimt didn't know.

"Must have bumped into him somewhere or other years ago and oceans from here," she said, rather quickly, Alwyn thought. "Now then, judging by this, it appears were both heading in the same direction. I can't imagine that's a coincidence."

"That's where you're headed? Out into the desert, just the three of you?" Yimt said.

"Sergeant, events are once again moving rather rapidly. Tyul and Jurwan left the ship sometime earlier this evening and are tracking something into the desert." She looked up to the sky before she continued. "With the imminent prospect of a Star returning, this has most definitely piqued our curiosity. More curious, though, is that all paths appear to be leading straight for *this*." Her finger stabbed down on an area just to the southeast of Suhundam's Hill. Alwyn peered over Yimt's shoulder for a better view.

"The Canyon of Bones, lovely," Yimt said. "Probably a scenic little picnic spot. I'm sure nothing unpleasant or remotely horrifying has ever happened there."

Alwyn looked over at Scolly, waiting for the inevitable question about picnics, but Scolly just scratched his arm and said nothing. It was just possible even Scolly got the gist of Yimt's sarcasm. *Would wonders never cease?*

The rest of the soldiers clustered around. "I don't like the sound of that one bit," Teeter said. "Who names a canyon that? Why not just call it 'Bloody Terrible Place Where Monsters Live.' "

"Nobody said anything about monsters," Yimt said.

"Don't have to, they just seem to show up unannounced these days," Teeter said.

"All the more reason to keep your eyes peeled, then," Yimt said, shooing them all back from the wagon. Alwyn turned to go, but Yimt motioned for him to stay. A light flickered to life in a window down the street. "See what I mean? Spread out and stay sharp." Yimt jumped up onto the wagon for a closer look, then reached out a hand and helped Alwyn up. "Teeter does have a point. Things are getting a mite peculiar. Ally felt something earlier. You know, I think I even did, too," he said, looking skyward. "That blue light up there means something, doesn't it?"

Rallie cocked her head to one side. "Interesting. We three felt it as well. I dare say before too long most of Nazalla will have a sense of it. Another Star is indeed returning."

Yimt whistled. "Here we go again. Okay, I'll get the lads moving, and the rest of us will stay put here with you until they return, then we can head out."

Rallie was shaking her head before he finished. "No. There isn't time to waste. The Star is coming *now*. We have to get out there. The regiment will have to catch up as best it can."

Now Yimt was shaking his head. "Oh, no, I'm not letting you go out there on your own. It's too dangerous. We all saw what happens when a Star returns."

Movement down the street behind the wagon caught Alwyn's attention. More lights were flickering on in windows, and several people had now stepped outside. A few were even standing on their roofs. Everyone was looking up.

"We've got company," Alwyn said, tugging on Yimt's sleeve.

The dwarf cursed under his breath. He looked to Rallie. "You live and breathe this political stuff—what's about to happen here?"

Rallie looked over her shoulder. "Simply, the Empire arrives in force and that very night the Jewel of the Desert—the guiding Star of the Hasshugeb Expanse—returns. Who here wouldn't see that as a repudiation of Imperial intent?"

Repudiation was a new one for Alwyn, but he caught the meaning. "People are going to be upset, aren't they?"

Rallie offered a sad smile. "Change never comes easy. Some will be overjoyed, but most will be scared, then upset, and then angry. You saw what it was like in Elfkyna. This time it will be worse. The world as people have known it is shifting under their feet and over their heads. Were it a simple matter of the Empire protecting its citizens from an ancient power like Kaman Rhal or the Shadow Monarch, things might remain more or less stable . . . but the Stars change everything."

"How can they have such power?" Alwyn asked. He understood the power of magic in the way he understood the power of a cannon. "How can they affect people's minds that much?"

Rallie took the cigar out of her mouth and waved it. "They don't, not directly. It's what the Stars *represent* that is so potent. Think of that uniform you wear. Under it, you're a man like any other man . . . well, most of you is. But when you put it on, you become the shiny, sharp point of a very long bayonet wielded all the way back in Calahr. And you've been that point at a lot of people's throats for hundreds of years. Now a Star returns, one that you, as symbol of the Empire, have given little credence to. This Star promises nothing but possibilities."

"That's all well and good," Yimt said, "but I'm not letting you go out there alone."

"I don't think we could go back even if we wanted to," Miss Red Owl said. An artificial daylight was rising up from Nazalla, as now thousands of people were simultaneously lighting lanterns and coming out into the streets. Raised voices could be heard in the distance. Alwyn strained to hear what was being said.

"I don't understand the language, but that really doesn't sound good," he said. Anger, an emotion he was all too familiar with, drove the voices through the streets with growing force. The people of Nazalla were not going to let the Empire take their Star.

"I do," Rallie said, "and you're right, it isn't good."

"All right, let's get this little band on the road. Get your arses on the wagon, now," Yimt said, "we're moving out."

A small group of people had formed a line in the street twenty yards away in front of the wagon. They were talking quietly amongst themselves while keeping a watchful eye on the soldiers. Alwyn didn't see any weapons, but with the loose robes they wore, they could have all manner of them tucked away. More people kept arriving as the crowd built. As they did their whispers became louder. With numbers came courage. This wasn't going to end well. Before long, the street would be so jammed with people they would never be able to get the wagon through.

"Listen up," Yimt said, "no one do anything stupid and fire a shot. They aren't prepared to openly attack the Empire . . . yet. Let's see if we can't ease our way out of here and not give them an excuse. Stay calm, no shouting, no sudden movements, and for the love of whatever creator you pray to, *no frost fire.*"

Inkermon began to pull out his bayonet, but Yimt motioned for him to stop. "No bayonets either. Accidentally stabbing someone won't help our cause one bit. Right now we're outnumbered about thirty thousand to ten, so let's keep our heads on straight and we'll get through this just fine."

"You cannot take our Star!"

Alwyn tried to see who had shouted that, but it was impossible to tell. He saw people nod. A few even raised their fists. It felt like the first drop of rain. The air hummed. A storm was about to break.

"Go back to Calahr and leave us alone!"

"We can't, we're going into the desert to—"

Yimt slapped Scolly on the back. "Did you hear anything I said? We're trying to prevent a riot," he hissed.

"It's true!" someone shouted. "They are here to take the Star! They must be stopped!"

"Time to go," Rallie said. "I'd suggest everyone hold on tight. Visyna, be a dear and give us a little light?"

The surge of voices around them grew, as did the size of the crowd. Nothing had been thrown, yet, but Alwyn could see clenched fists. The anger of an entire people was boiling to the surface in Nazalla, and they were right in the middle of it.

Visyna climbed up to stand on top of the canvas-covered cages in the back of the wagon and began weaving the air with her hands. "I'll steady you," Alwyn said, climbing back to help.

"Thank you, Alwyn, but you can't. The power in you is . . . not compatible with mine. Chayii will steady me." Alwyn started to object, but realized she was right. He doubted there was anything in the world that was compatible with the power the Iron Elves had acquired. He crouched on top of the wagon and brought his musket around to face forward.

The crowd grew even louder as more shouts rose up. They

were no longer simply directing them to go home. Alwyn saw more than one man make a cutting motion across his neck, then point at him. The meaning was clear.

A brilliant, white light suddenly appeared a few hundred yards to the west. It hovered a hundred feet or so above the ground, the light so strong it was impossible to look straight at it. Joyous cries of "The Star, the Jewel of the Desert!" rose from the crowd, and the Nazalla citizenry turned and stampeded toward it.

"And that would be my cue," Rallie said, snapping the reins. The wagon lurched forward as the brindos responded. People still lined the street in front of them, but now their attention was riveted on the appearance of the "Star." A charging wagon with fearsome-looking creatures pulling it was something interesting only insofar as they were concerned about getting out of its way.

Rallie never let up as they thundered through the narrow streets of Nazalla. The breeze felt wonderful on Alwyn's face, but it was hard to enjoy as he fought to keep his shako on his head and himself on the wagon as it bumped and swayed over the cobbles.

"I can't do this much longer!" Visyna shouted.

Alwyn turned and looked up at her. She was still weaving the air, but every time the wagon jolted, the pattern would falter and the "Star" she had created would flicker. Rumblings from the crowd in the street suggested they were beginning to have their doubts as well.

"Just a little bit more!" Rallie shouted, slapping the reins hard as the brindos broke into a full gallop.

Alwyn gave up any pretense of trying to watch for trouble and clung to the canvas with everything he had. Buildings and clusters of people flashed by in a blur. The light from Visyna's "Star" fluttered, then went out. A roar went up from the crowd.

All eyes became firmly fixed on the wagon and its occupants. Suddenly, like a boulder perched on the side of a mountain, all the repressed rage and resentment of a people ruled by a foreign sovereignty tumbled forth.

As new voices were added, the anger grew. This land belonged to the people, not the outlanders from across the sea. The soldiers in the wagon were the force behind the Prince's insulting and threatening proclamation. If they couldn't attack the Prince, they would avenge themselves on the soldiers in their midst.

A brick, or perhaps a cobblestone, bounced off the side of the wagon. The sreexes squawked and shrieked and Jir growled. Alwyn risked lifting his head and saw several people pointing at them. In the light of the lanterns many were carrying, he saw others tearing up the cobblestone street behind them.

"We're still not clear!" Rallie shouted, urging her brindos on. "We need one more diversion to get us through."

"Ally, can you do anything?" Yimt asked, pointing up ahead where another crowd barred their path. Beyond them, Alwyn could see open desert.

"Like what?" Alwyn asked. "I don't want to hurt anyone!"

"Just do like Miss Tekoy and give 'em a light show."

Alwyn shook his head, then realized Yimt couldn't see him. "I've never used the magic that way. I don't know how!"

More and more citizens were running to block their escape. A flaming torch bounced off the side of the wagon, showering the crowd in sparks. People screamed. Up ahead another group was dragging and pushing a wooden cart toward the street. If they got that in place, there was no way the brindos would be able to get through.

"None of us can control it the way you can. You saw what

happened to Zwitty. Do something or we'll have to shoot!" Yimt shouted.

Alwyn saw Yimt start to wrestle his shatterbow into position as the wagon careened around a broken pot in the middle of the street. The side of a building loomed toward Alwyn, then retreated.

"I'll try!" he shouted, and got to his hands and knees. Hrem reached out a hand to steady him. "Thanks." Alwyn raised himself up off his hands and held them out before him. Frost fire burst to flame in his palms, but he already knew he couldn't throw it.

And then he remembered Nafeesah's room.

"Meri, I need your help," Alwyn called out.

The shades of the dead instantly appeared as shadows projected on the walls of the buildings, keeping pace with the wagon as it raced toward the growing crowd. Alwyn focused on the power. The brindos' breath turned to white clouds and frost sparkled wherever their hooves hit the ground. Jir roared from inside the wagon while the sreexes shrieked in terror. Miss Tekoy and Miss Red Owl cried out, but Alwyn couldn't stop.

Shards of black ice trailed the wagon wheels and began spreading up the walls of the buildings they passed. Alwyn shivered and pointed forward. The shadows flitted ahead of the wagon and appeared in a line in front of the crowd blocking their path. Swords writhed in icy flames appeared poised to attack. The shadows began to advance.

Some in the crowd shrieked and ran. Those pushing the cart abandoned their effort and scurried away. A few, however, stood their ground.

"No!"

The swords of the dead slashed into the crowd, cutting down

any who stood in their path. Frost fire leaped in the air until a wall of shimmering black flame stretched across the entire street.

The brindos screamed as they reached the line of shadows and flame and thundered on through. The whole wagon screeched as if a thousand nails were scraping a chalkboard. Alwyn's spectacles froze over, his lungs burning with the cold. From somewhere in the wagon, a grown man wailed like a child.

The shadows exploded as if they'd just driven through a black mirror.

Alwyn fell backward and would have tumbled from the wagon if not for Hrem holding on to him.

The wagon continued on its path. Alwyn could just make out that they were free and clear; there were no more buildings beside them.

They had made it through, but at what cost?

TWENTY-TWO

What do you mean, gone?"

Konowa raised his voice at the corporal standing at attention before him. The sound of a city in turmoil reverberated around the Viceroy's palace, and the first rays of the sun were only just beginning to spread out over Nazalla. Konowa had hoped the oncoming heat would quell whatever it was that had stirred up the population, but the dawn of a new day seemed to be doing the opposite. He needed information, now.

The corporal blanched. "It was close to midnight, sir. Just before the people started coming out into the streets. Apparently the men on duty at the southern gate saw the three ladies ride out in Her Majesty's Scribe's wagon."

"Why didn't you try to stop them?" Konowa asked, then immediately waved the soldier to silence. No sentry was going to stop those three. *Hell, I'm a major and I can't.* "This should have been reported earlier."

"I know, sir, and I take full responsibility," the corporal said.

"It's just that once we had people in the streets, the talk of uprising started making the rounds and I suddenly had a lot to deal with. It's looking like a absolute riot out there."

Konowa knew the soldier was being honest. "Very well. Get back to your men and keep them calm. Something's stirred up the citizenry of Nazalla, but we still have the upper hand. The last thing we need right now is some of our men firing off a volley into a crowd of people. This is only our second day in Nazalla—I was hoping to avoid a full-scale rebellion for at least a week."

The corporal didn't laugh.

"Go, and keep the lads in check. We're not on an island anymore," Konowa said, surprised to find himself wishing they were. The islands—as horrific as they had been—had also been simple. Everything there had been enemy. Here in Nazalla, it was all a gray area.

The corporal saluted and quickly hurried off.

"How dare they!" the Prince shouted, marching up to Konowa and waving away his salute. The Prince's eyes were red and his usually immaculate uniform was less than pristine. Apparently it had been a long night for everyone.

"Your jacket is buttoned up wrong, Your Highness," Konowa said.

The Prince looked down at his jacket and stomped his boot on the ground. He began ripping at the buttons to undo them. "I trusted them!"

Konowa kept the surprise from his face as he realized it was up to *him* to calm the Prince down. "We saw this in Elfkyna, too, your Highness. I'm confident we can control the situation and get the city back to calm before too long."

The Prince looked up from his buttons. "Are you daft?

Of course we can control Nazalla. I'm talking about the women. I took . . . *rip* those three . . . *rip* into my confidence. I listened to their advice *rip*. I've allowed them to travel with us, and I've let Rallie . . . *rip* write whatever she wanted!" A button went sailing through the air like a cannonball launched from the *Black Spike*.

Konowa almost reached out a hand of sympathy to rest it on the Prince's shoulder. Instead he nodded and waited for the Prince to continue. Color Sergeant Salia Aguom—known as "Sally" by absolutely no one wishing to retain what teeth they had in their head—marched up and saluted. The battle scars covering the sergeant's face looked fearsome even when he smiled, which wasn't now. Konowa turned to him and returned the salute. The Prince was still working at a final button.

"Beg to report, sir, seven men are absent."

Konowa quickly ushered Sergeant Aguom a few steps away from the Prince to keep their conversation private. "Let's keep this between us right now," he said, motioning with his head to the Prince. "You've searched the grounds? Looked in bushes and under carriages? The bordellos?"

Aguom nodded. "Not a sign of them, sir. Last sighting was in a pub called the Blue Scorpion, then all hell broke loose and they ain't been seen since. The rest of the regiment is accounted for, except for them."

Konowa thought out loud. "Normally I'd figure they were sleeping it off somewhere, but with all this racket, I hope they've done the smart thing and holed up in a safe place. Has there been any word of fighting in the city between our troops and the locals?"

"That's the thing," the sergeant said, scratching at the side of his head. "It's chaos out there. There's no end to rumors, and trying to make sense out of any of them while we're bottled up here is next to impossible."

"Try me," Konowa said.

Sergeant Aguom looked over at the Prince, who had now flung his jacket to the ground and was shouting for another one to be brought at once. "I don't know what to make of it, but we got reports of some kind of skirmish in a back alley. Bodies burned to nothing but ash and bits of bone. They say magic was used, Kaman Rhal's magic . . ."

The screams of Private Kester Harkon echoed in Konowa's ears.

"And?"

"More than one person said they saw a small furry creature with a man dressed in black. This man killed several others and turned them into ash. Oh, and he had a big bushy tail . . . the furry animal, not the man. Sort of sounds like a . . . well, like—"

"My father," Konowa murmured, finishing his sentence. *Parents. One takes off without a word, while the other embarks on a killing spree with a crazy elf.*

"That's not the worst of it," Sergeant Aguom continued.

"No, why would it be."

Sergeant Aguom ignored Konowa's sarcasm. "There's a rumor that several people saw a Star appear over the city, and that when it disappeared a wagon was seen racing out of the city and into the desert."

"They think the Empire loaded the Star onto a wagon . . . ? "

"Yes, sir. The other rumors say the Star hasn't arrived yet, and most people seem to believe that, but everyone is certain about this wagon."

"Why?"

"Well, sir, it's not often you see a wagon burning with black fire while being pulled by monsters and guarded by creatures of shadow."

"No, I suppose not," Konowa said. "Still, if that's the worst of it, we might be able to calm the waters. The other colonels are no doubt moving their regiments into the city to restore calm."

Sergeant Aguom shook his head. "They say twenty people were killed trying to stop the wagon."

The ground spun beneath Konowa's boots and it took all his strength to stay upright. This nightmare just kept growing. "How certain are you about this?"

"I can't verify any of it other than the fact that there's an angry mob now surrounding the palace grounds shouting for the Empire to leave or die. I need to get out into the streets to find out for sure."

"Careful what you wish for, Color Sergeant," Konowa said. He paused and ran through scenarios in his head. "Spread the word. I want every soldier ready to march inside the hour. Full packs, great-coats, rations—everything." It occurred to Konowa that Sergeant Arkhorn had unofficially taken over the duties of regimental sergeant major since Lorian's death. *Why wasn't he here giving Konowa the report?* "And have Sergeant Arkhorn report to me at once."

Aguom grimaced. "Sir. Sergeant Arkhorn is one of the ones not here. It's him and his old section that's missing."

Konowa gripped the hilt of his saber and let out a slow breath. "When were you planning to tell me this?"

"Honestly, sir, I wasn't. Old Arkhorn is the best in the business. I figured he'd show up, probably at the head of a parade," he said, the admiration clear in his voice. "Permission to speak candidly, sir?"

"Granted."

"He don't deserve to be flogged, sir, none of the boys do. Those islands were hell. If a man, or dwarf, wants to blow off some steam, I figure that's his right after something like what we went through. If they aren't back, it's because Arkhorn found them a safe place to lie low."

"No one's being flogged," Konowa said, frustrated that he hadn't stopped the Prince from flogging several soldiers back in Elfkyna. It was the wrong way to discipline a soldier. *Be firm. Be fair. And don't ask them to do anything you wouldn't do, and they'd follow you anywhere.* Konowa wished he could have proven that to the troops, but the true ramifications of the Blood Oath had since become apparent, and the Prince had ordered no corporal punishment since.

"The men will appreciate that, sir," Sergeant Aguom said.

"Just have them ready to march, Sergeant," Konowa said. He saluted, dismissed the color sergeant, and turned to address the Prince. A violent roar went up from the crowd outside the gates. The number of voices sounded like thousands. Getting out of the palace wasn't going to be easy.

"Major, I want the regiment on the march as quickly as possible," the Prince said, buttoning up his new jacket.

Konowa noted that the Prince had no need to switch his medals and ribbons over from one jacket to another, as each tunic came fully decorated. "Sir, about last night—"

"I've heard enough to know we need to get out of here now and into the desert. I want the regiment ready. Now. That rabble will not stand in our way."

"Very good, sir," Konowa said, relieved to not have to answer questions. "I'll see to it right away. But how are we going to get out? That crowd is ready to explode."

The Prince quit fussing with his uniform and strolled over to stand beside Konowa. Konowa instinctively breathed out, hoping to avoid any more of the Prince's cologne, but was surprised at not smelling any. He realized the Prince was also no longer wearing his personalized shako, the one several inches taller than standard issue. "Perhaps I inadvertently inspired them more than intended," the Prince remarked.

"Inspired who, sir?"

Prince Tykkin turned to look at Konowa as if it were obvious. "The women, of course, Major. All my talk of a new order and changing the world must have gotten their blood up. Don't you see? They divined that the next Star was returning and raced out to find it first. No doubt they intend to beat both of us to the punch."

Konowa had trouble following the Prince's logic at the best of times, and this was definitely not one of them. "You think they went out . . . to get the Star for themselves?"

The Prince smiled in that way that made Konowa daily reconsider his oath to serve and protect the Empire and its royal house. "Oh, no, not them. Don't misunderstand—I hold all three ladies in the highest regard. Their intentions are pure, I am certain. They will find the Star and allow it to serve its function as guardian of these lands and peoples. After all, they wouldn't want me getting hold of it and taking it back to Calahr. And they most definitely wouldn't want you getting it and using its power to break the oath."

"Sir?"

The Prince turned and looked Konowa straight in the eye. "Let's be frank, Major. Things have changed. I've come to realize that capturing a Star for myself is not in my best interest. In fact, I'm better off letting the Star fulfill its apparent destiny. It's the *ap-*

pearance of the Star that matters. That's what unlocks the power. Think of it, Major. What's a Star but a path to a treasure a thousandfold more rewarding? I'm after Kaman Rhal's library. This new Star is going to lead me right to it. That's the real prize."

Konowa found himself staring at the Prince with something close to admiration. The feeling was as odd as it was unsettling. "Very clever, sir, but what of the elves stationed in the desert? You aren't suggesting we forsake them out there?"

"On the contrary, Major, I want you to find your elves more than ever. You see, it occurs to me that I'm not the only one who has come to reassess things," the Prince said. He smoothed out a nonexistent crease in his uniform jacket before continuing. "What would have happened if you had used the Red Star in Elfkyna to break the oath? You and the regiment would have been freed, but at the cost of losing this power you now wield. And without this power, how will you ever take the battle to the Shadow Monarch and finish Her off once and for all?"

"We would find a way, oath or no oath," Konowa said, the conviction in his voice strong. "But as it stands, this regiment is the most powerful in the entire Calahrian Imperial Army with the oath in place. For the time being, I think it would be foolish to throw that advantage away."

"I don't suppose the troops see it that way," the Prince said, watching as soldiers hurried past in preparation for their departure.

"No, they wouldn't," Konowa said. "But they don't understand things the way we do." Even as the words left his lips, Konowa felt a twinge of shock at saying them. "And it's the same with Kaman Rhal's power. If we find it, we should attempt to use it or forge an alliance with it to defeat the Shadow Monarch. The oath will be broken when the Shadow Monarch is dead, and the quickest way to do that is to employ any and all means we find."

Prince Tykkin looked at Konowa for several seconds as if seeing him for the first time. "A thought worth considering, Major."

"Sir, we still have to get out of the palace. The city is seething. We might have to fight our way out," Konowa said, hoping that wouldn't be the case.

"You get the regiment ready and let me worry about that." The Prince saluted and turned and walked away, looking over his shoulder once at Konowa.

Konowa had no time to reflect on that. A group of fifty soldiers from the 3rd Spears, the regiment of dark-skinned warriors from the Timolia Island chain, stood off to one side of the courtyard. As soon as they saw Konowa was free, they stood to attention. It was a magnificent sight. No man looked to be under six feet tall. Unlike the Iron Elves, they wore the traditional uniform of the Calahrian infantry, including the standard dark gray trousers, but they went without boots. The bottom of each pant leg was bound tight around their calves by a long, thin strip of black cloth called a puttee. Konowa marveled that they could march into battle in bare feet, let alone over the hot cobbles of Nazalla.

Each soldier carried a musket slung over one shoulder, but in keeping with their native tradition, instead of regulation bayonets, their muskets sported ones twice as long. Five of them only wore pistols, as they carried the eight-foot-long spears from which the 3rd Spears derived their name. Konowa had seen those spears in combat—spear points filed to create sawlike edges, inflicting truly horrific damage on flesh.

Konowa spotted Color Sergeant Aguom nearby talking with other soldiers and motioned for him to come over. The sergeant did so at once.

"From your homeland?" Konowa asked, pointing to the soldiers of the 3rd Spears.

"They are from an island nearby mine, but our tribes are friendly," Sergeant Aguom said.

"Why aren't they with their regiment?"

"They came here last night escorting carriages. They were supposed to return to their camp down by the docks this morning, but with this crowd, they can't get through without a fight."

"Just as well. Fine, tell them to stay here and wait for orders. I'm sure things will calm down. They can wait it out here when we leave for the desert."

"They want to come with us."

Konowa waved his hand. "Their colonel would not be thrilled to know we'd absconded with fifty of his men."

Sergeant Aguom wasn't to be deterred. "The want to see the Star, Major. They want to be there when it returns. They heard the stories about Luuguth Jor and they want to see this one."

"At potential risk to their lives? Why?"

"Our legends talk of a Star of Knowledge guiding the elders of our islands many centuries ago. They want to see with their own eyes if this one is real. If it is, then there is hope for my people, too," Sergeant Aguom said, his voice dropping away as the full meaning of the words registered.

"Would your people rebel?" Konowa asked. The world kept shifting under his feet. He was finally starting to comprehend just how widespread the desire to be rid of the Empire really was.

"They simply want to chart their own course in the world. The Stars offer that chance. What people would refuse such a gift?"

Konowa shook his head. "You know it's real. You were at Luuguth Jor. Tell them."

"I did," the sergeant said, "and it has only made them more determined to come with us." He paused for a moment as if considering how to say the next sentence. "They are willing to take the Blood Oath to join us."

Konowa wasn't sure he'd heard that right. "They what?"

"They'll take the oath. They are brave warriors. For them, there is great honor in sacrifice. They see that the Iron Elves are losing soldiers, and no new recruits are coming. And they know that where you are, the Star will fall."

"I admire their spirit, but this isn't the time. Thank them for the offer, but tell them no." Konowa saluted and waited for the sergeant to do the same.

Color Sergeant Aguom stood his ground. "If this costs me my stripes, then so be it. Sir, if they are refused, they will desert their regiment and follow us anyway. They see it as . . . their destiny."

"Their destiny? How in blazes did they come to that conclusion? If they hadn't noticed, this regiment is called the Iron Elves. *Elves!* This is my regiment, and when I find my elves everything will be right again." Blood pounded in Konowa's ears. "How dare they presume to claim this as their destiny."

"Your *elves* stand all around you, sir. An Iron Elf stands in front of you now . . . or am I less a soldier in your eyes because my ears do not have points?"

A cold, black anger welled up in Konowa. In the back of his

mind, he heard his mother and Visyna pleading with him. This was not the way.

But in an even deeper place inside himself he heard Her voice. She understood.

The Shadow Monarch knew the importance of the elves. She fully realized the bond Konowa felt with them.

With an effort that caused him to grit his teeth, Konowa pushed the anger back down. Lightheaded, he swayed on his feet. Wiping some sweat from his eyes, he looked again at Color Sergeant Aguom. "Sergeant, you have my apologies. *Every* soldier matters to me. Every single one. If these men want to join us and see the return of a Star, I will not stand in their way. I'll handle it with the Prince that there are no repercussions. But understand this: I will *not* administer the oath to them. They can come with us, fight alongside us, and chase whatever glory and honor they desire, but I will not subject them to the oath. Is that clear?"

Sergeant Aguom beamed. "I thank you, on behalf of all of them. They will not let you down, sir." He saluted, and without waiting for Konowa to return it, turned and ran over to the waiting soldiers. A loud cheer broke out a moment later.

Konowa shook his head. The Prince approached, looking at maps held by two corporals who were walking backward so the Prince could study the terrain as he walked. He looked up when he heard the commotion and, dismissing the map carriers, came back over to Konowa.

"I shouldn't think there's much to cheer about," the Prince said, tapping his sword scabbard against the top of his leather riding boot.

"I didn't think so either, but apparently they're eager to get out of the city," Konowa said, choosing not to reveal the real reason. "They've volunteered to come with us into the desert."

Konowa waited, wondering if the Prince would see this as an affront to his authority or a boost to his ego.

"They volunteered to serve directly under me, knowing we're almost certainly going into battle?"

"Yes, sir, that's exactly what they did."

Prince Tykkin drew in a breath and stood up a little straighter. He drew his sword from its scabbard, lifted it into the air, and turned to the soldiers of the 3rd Spears. *"Well done, lads!"*

The soldiers cheered in response, breaking out in a war chant in their native tongue. Spears and muskets were raised in the air. Several soldiers of the Iron Elves standing nearby looked at them with varying degrees of confusion and annoyance.

Konowa noticed that at the sound of raised voices from the 3rd Spears, the growing crowd outside the palace grew silent. He looked through the palace gate and was amazed to see the citizens of Nazalla leaving in a hurry. The reputation of the warriors of the Timolia Islands was clearly known even here.

"Best we get moving, sir, while we can," Konowa said.

The Prince lowered his sword and resheathed it, his face aglow. "Yes, I suppose you're right. Still, I think we'll let them enjoy this moment a little longer. Who knows what the day brings? We'll be hard-pressed to make it out of Nazalla in one piece, let alone get through the desert."

The tone in the Prince's voice suggested otherwise, which meant he must have worked something out. "Sir? Do you have a plan to get us out of the city without having to go to war with the civilians in it?"

"My proclamation was clear enough," the Prince said.

Konowa's heart raced. "Sir, they're civilians. It'd be a slaughter. There has to be another way."

The Prince looked at Konowa as a mother would, comforting her child. Konowa's stomach churned.

"There is, Major, there is. Come now, you don't think I'd really send the regiment out to murder innocents, now do you?"

Konowa didn't trust himself to answer. Luckily, the Prince made the question rhetorical as he kept talking.

"Not to fret, Major," the Prince said, "I've already negotiated our safe passage. Get the regiment formed up, we're moving out in ten minutes." Then the Prince did the most unexpected thing. He smiled at Konowa, reached out, and punched Konowa good-naturedly in the shoulder before turning and walking away.

Konowa stood rooted to the spot for several seconds. "What the devil was that all about?"

"The devil, you say?" said the Suljak of the Hasshugeb Expanse, appearing at Konowa's side. "Perhaps, perhaps not."

Konowa looked down at the old man. "You're helping us?"

The Suljak looked surprised. "I've been presented with a golden opportunity to escort the Iron Elves out of Nazalla and deep into the heart of the desert, and all without further risk to the lives of the local populace. Why wouldn't I help?"

Konowa wasn't as gullible as the Prince . . . he hoped. "Because you'll have ensured that we have a force ready to sweep in and claim the Star, that's why."

With the U formed by finger and thumb the Suljak stroked either side of his mouth as if in deep thought. "A conundrum, to be sure. Still, better to throw the viper from your home and then worry about it outside your door, no?"

Konowa started to nod, then stopped. "Wait, you said escort the Iron Elves. What about the other regiments?"

"There are limits to my powers of suggestion," the Suljak said. "I can ensure the safe passage of the Iron Elves, as I ride with them, but I cannot do so for the others, spread out as they are around the city and by the docks. It will take some time for them to swing round the city to follow us, and time," the Suljak said, looking up to the sky, "is most definitely not going to wait for man or elf."

"Or Star," Konowa added, looking up as well.

The Suljak patted Konowa on the arm. "Indeed, my dear Major, I believe it should be a most interesting trip."

TWENTY-THREE

Alwyn sat on top of the canvas-covered rear of Rallie's wagon along with the rest of the section. Each man looked out in a different direction, muskets loaded and at the ready. Alwyn faced the rear, watching the lights of Nazalla dwindle in the distance.

Events of the last few hours played through his mind in a never-ending loop. He had called forth the shades and they had followed his orders.

But then they had killed those innocent people. He hadn't wanted that. The shades had to know he hadn't meant for that to happen, but they did it anyway.

"You should put your head down for a bit," Yimt said, turning around from the front bench to look back at Alwyn.

"I'm fine—I just can't get what happened out of my head."

"It wasn't your fault, Ally. Those people were balancing all day twixt giving us a kiss on the cheek versus a pitchfork in the arse, and the pitchfork mentality won. Once a mob starts doing your thinking, it's all over but the killing. The Darkly Departed were doing what soldiers are trained to do. If they hadn't, we probably wouldn't be here now."

"Do you really believe that? Do you really think they were just being soldiers . . . like us?" Alwyn asked.

Yimt looked at him for a long time before replying. "I hope so," he said. "Now, get some shut-eye."

Alwyn yawned, surprised that he could feel so tired even being this unsettled, but then he realized he hadn't slept at all last night. The rocking motion of the wheels over the roadway they followed was lulling him to sleep. He shook his head and stretched his arms. He set his musket down on the canvas and twisted his wooden leg to a more comfortable angle. It still hurt. He knew Zwitty had some of that tobacco from the hookah back at the Blue Scorpion, but decided to wait to ask him for some later. So far it was the one thing that eased the pain of his stump.

The wagon groaned in protest as its wheels hit a pothole, jostling everyone and everything on board. Alwyn yawned again and peered back along their path. A misty veil of dust hung behind them, obscuring Nazalla even more. He turned and looked out over the desert. Dawn was infusing the grays and blacks of the dunes with deep red. He felt his mood lift slightly as shadow gave way to shape, despite the fact that they were heading into the unknown.

He twisted around farther to see if he could actually make out anything ahead of them. Miss Red Owl and Miss Tekoy were riding the lead brindos. They had said they were doing so to better follow Tyul's path into the desert, but he suspected it was in part to get farther away from him. He didn't blame them—the other soldiers had given him as wide a berth since their escape into the desert.

Alwyn wondered again if this was the right thing to do, and was happy the decision hadn't been up to him. Chasing after Tyul and Jurwan without the regiment seemed foolhardy, especially when both elves were not right in the head. Zwitty muttered something about how the two elves were probably out gathering nuts, but a look from Yimt had shut him up. In the end, it hadn't really mattered, because they would have been torn apart by the citizens of Nazalla if they'd tried to get back to the Viceroy's palace . . . or the shades would have slaughtered the crowd.

Even if they could have made it through the crowds unscathed and back to the palace—and without having to murder innocents to do it—Sergeant Arkhorn was not about to let the three ladies head out into the desert unescorted. So here they were, once again the shiny tip of the Calahrian Empire's bayonet leading the way into trouble.

Sighing and yawning at the same time, Alwyn finally raised his head and looked up at the lightening sky. Every time he did, he dreaded what he might see. The path to the Red Star in Luuguth Jor had been—at some level—something hopeful. There had been a chance to break the oath and free themselves of the Shadow Monarch's pull. But then the fighting began, the endless carnage. Now another Star would fall, and everyone—the Empire, the Shadow Monarch, maybe even Kaman Rhal himself—would butcher each other to claim it.

Alwyn lowered his head and turned again toward the front of the wagon as he caught bits of conversation between Yimt and Rallie. They were discussing old family recipes that Alwyn did his best not to overhear. Merely the sound of some of the ingredients made his stomach roil.

"I think I'll try to catch up on some of that sleep now, Sergeant," Alwyn said. He reached out with the butt of his musket to nudge Yimt.

"What? Sure, Ally," Yimt said, reaching out a hand and patting his hand. "Rest those peepers. You've had a busy night." He raised his voice as he addressed the other soldiers. "Same goes for the lot of you. Get your heads down while you can. I imagine we won't be getting much sleep when we get where we're going."

"Thanks," Alwyn said, as Yimt went back to chatting with Rallie. The rest of the section tried to get comfortable on top of the wagon as best they could. Not surprisingly, no one had tried to venture inside where Jir and the sreexes were.

Alwyn lay his head down and closed his eyes.

The first rays of the sun beat down upon his face as the vision of a Star filled his dreams.

He opened his eyes a moment later to find he was standing on top of a mountain.

His natural reaction was to bring his musket to the ready, even though he knew this was still a dream. He'd been to the Shadow Monarch's domain before in this state, but this was different. The Wolf Oaks here grew tall and proud, their limbs gently curved as they lifted great leafy crowns skyward in a brilliant, blue sky. An elf walked among the trees, her hand gently brushing the trunks as she passed. She wore a long, flowing dress of red. She looked as young as Alwyn, and she was beautiful, her blond hair draping over her shoulders. And she looked familiar.

He walked toward her, aware that he was still dressed in his uniform. He started to sling his musket over his shoulder, but something made him keep it in both hands, though he couldn't see why. Birds chirped gaily among the leaves and the air was warm and inviting.

"Hello," he said, still at some distance, lest he frighten her.

The elf turned and smiled at him. Alwyn smiled back. "I know you, don't I? I haven't met many elves, but for the life of me, I can't place you."

'You know me, Alywn Renwar, and I know you.'

Alwyn almost fired his musket at the sound of Her voice. He looked around wildly, expecting rakkes to come charging at him from between the trees. Instead, a gentle breeze ruffled the tops of mountain flowers and a butterfly wobbled through the air to land on the end of his musket.

'Do not be afraid. I only wished you to see my realm as it will be,' the Shadow Monarch said.

She continued to smile at Alwyn, tossing her long blonde tresses in a way that reminded him of Nafeesah. "No, you want to destroy everything."

Her face darkened, and in an instant, so did the sky. The breeze grew into a cold wind, tearing the wings from the butterfly perched on his musket, which fell to the ground to flop helplessly in the dirt. A moment later She smiled, bringing the warm, sunny day again to the mountaintop. 'I want to set things right. Do you not see? There is much that is wrong with the world. Its people make war against each other. They kill, they desecrate nature. I want peace, Alwyn. I want things to be the way they were meant . . . to be.'

"What about the rakkes, and the dark elves? The blood trees?" He kept looking around, still expecting an attack at any moment. "What about us? *Why us?*"

'I mean you no harm, truly,' She said. 'My desire has only

ever been to right the wrongs that have been done. I want to heal that which is wounded and return that which was lost.' As She spoke, black ichor bubbled to the surface of the small clearing, forming a pool. She waved a hand across it and the surface changed, showing Alwyn scene after scene of death and destruction. None of them were by Her hand.

"I was at Luuguth Jor. I've been to the islands. You can't fool me," Alwyn said.

'Change is painful, Alwyn, but it is necessary. Look at what you hold in your hands. Is a death by your weapon any less a death?'

Alwyn shook his head, trying to clear it. This wasn't what he had expected. Her arguments had a logic to them Alwyn couldn't deny. "Please, I just want to be left alone. I want this to be over."

The Shadow Monarch smiled. The mountaintop grew cold and darkness fell. Color bled from the world, leaving shades of gray pierced through with black. Freezing rain began to fall, each drop a crystal shard of ice. The wind scoured the ground, ripping away the grass and flowers and exposing the rock beneath. The Wolf Oaks twisted into *sarka har*, and shadows of dark creatures ringed the forest. 'Come, Alwyn, and let me show you how.' She reached out a hand.

Alwyn stared at it for what felt like an eternity, then reached out his hand. Shadow enveloped them both and Alwyn saw a way for the pain to end.

Despite every instinct in his body screaming this was a mistake, Konowa slung his musket over his shoulder and climbed into the saddle strapped to the camel. The smell of the beast almost had him vaulting right back off. Nothing alive and healthy should smell this bad, yet the beast did not appear to be at death's door. *Not yet, anyway.*

Suppressing his urge to vomit, Konowa gripped the saddle until his hand and arm muscles burned with pain as the beast jerked its way to a standing position. Konowa looked down at the ground and wished he hadn't. He knew he was only ten feet up, but from the saddle it felt and looked like a thousand. One small slip and he'd plummet to his death.

"Breathe, Major. It's actually quite enjoyable once you become used to the height," the Suljak said, walking his camel up to halt beside Konowa's. He sat perched on the saddle on the beast's hump with one leg tucked underneath his body, looking as comfortable as if he were lounging on pillows safely set on the ground.

"I have no intention of being up here long enough to find out," Konowa said. Now upright, his camel stood stock still, showing no inclination to move. Konowa wasn't sure if he should kick the beast with the heel of his boot, smack it with the flat side of his saber, snap the reins, or simply shoot it and walk. He knew his preference would be frowned upon. "Any advice on how to ride this thing?"

"Remember that the animal is both emotional and intelligent. It has feelings, and it knows when a rider is afraid."

"I'm not afraid," Konowa said, "I'm concerned."

"Of course," the Suljak said. "Firm grip on the reins, not too tight and not too loose, and enjoy the ride. The camel has done this many times before. All you have to do is sit on top and look majestic."

Konowa snorted. "I'd rather look tired and dusty down there," he said, pointing at the ground. The camel suddenly moved a few feet to the right, almost granting Konowa his wish.

The Suljak smiled. "Elves never cease to amaze me. Do you know the ones stationed in the desert outposts are not overly fond of riding either? Some of the tribes thought to take advantage of that fact and raid a few caravans some miles from the nearest outpost, thinking the elves would never patrol that far into the desert. The raiders found to their chagrin that the elves could move rather quickly on two feet."

Talk of his elves brightened Konowa's spirits immensely. Pride welled in his chest to hear of their exploits. "You've met with them, then? I've had a hell of a time trying to get any information about them. Viceroy Alstonfar has been less than forthcoming. He said they prefer the isolation of the desert to the city. I was hoping to talk to him more about them, but he's been busy all morning with this," Konowa said, waving around them at the city.

The Suljak grew quiet. "It's been some time since I've been to an outpost. Much of my work of late has been here in Nazalla dealing with the Viceroy. These elves of yours, they are interesting fellows." The Suljak spoke hesitantly, as if the subject was one he would prefer to not discuss.

"They're good soldiers," Konowa said, knowing he sounded defensive and not caring. "In fact, they're the best there are."

"Better than the latest crop of Iron Elves?"

Konowa carefully sat up in the saddle and looked around. No troops were within earshot. "I'm proud of the regiment as it is, but when my brethren are reinstated in the Iron Elves and their honor restored, the regiment will truly be whole again."

"And are you that certain that these elves will rejoin? Do you expect them to take the Blood Oath that now binds you—if the rumors be true—in life and death?"

It was a sticky point. Konowa had envisioned a thousand times his reunion with the elves of his homeland, and he'd never gotten past the initial greeting. He knew what he hoped—that the elves would welcome him as a long-lost brother and pledge their loyalty to him and his fight to overthrow the Shadow Monarch and forever erase Her taint. But would they? Kritton had wanted to kill him all the way through their journey to Luuguth Jor, and he had remained in the relatively civilized land of Elfkyna. What would elves banished to the desert be like, especially when they had committed no crime other than to follow him? Would they see Konowa as their savior, or as the elf who had condemned them to suffer because Konowa, as their commanding officer, murdered the Viceroy of Elfkyna in cold blood for that elf's suspected ties to the Shadow Monarch? By not bringing the Viceroy up on charges, Konowa's rash act cast a pall of suspicion on the trustworthiness of all the elves and led to his and, by extension, their downfall.

"Things will work themselves out," Konowa said, his voice sounding far more confident than he felt.

"I do hope so, but I should warn you, Major—even a short length of time in the desert will change a man, or elf. I would suggest caution in your optimistic approach."

As Konowa thought about that, Viceroy Alstonfar rode up on his camel, his rotund form at ease on the saddle. "The Prince requests both your presences at the front of the column. We are moving out."

"The city is still seething, Viceroy," Konowa said. "Do you really think we can just waltz on out of here?"

Viceroy Alstonfar and the Suljak shared a look before the Viceroy spoke. "Concessions have been made. *Significant* financial concessions to the families of those who lost members last night."

"You bought them off with gold?" Konowa asked. He turned in the saddle, despite the risk, to look more closely at the Suljak. "A few gold coins is enough to grant us free passage?"

"No, but that and my assurances about the fate of the Star are. Politics is a messy business, Major, and it requires setting a price on things that should never be valued in that way. Still, it is a necessary evil."

Another look was shared between the Viceroy and the Suljak that Konowa didn't like. Another time he would have pressed for more answers, but time—as so often happened—was not on his side.

The three snapped their reins and their camels began walking. There was still a sizable crowd outside the palace, but they were subdued as the gates swung open. Anger still emanated from them, but it was held in check. The Suljak waved to the crowd, and they began to back slowly away from the gate.

The Iron Elves stood shoulder to shoulder six men wide. Bayonets were fixed at the end of their muskets, which they held against their left shoulders as they awaited the order to march. The rising sun now glinted off the sharpened, bare steel with unmistakable menace.

The soldiers wore looks of grim determination, but Konowa knew much of their fierceness was anger felt at being sent out to the desert after just one night in Nazalla. It was a bitter blow after weeks on the high seas assaulting islands held by Her creatures, but it had to be; there was no choice. Staying in Nazalla was the equivalent of keeping a lit match in a powder magazine. There would be time enough to rest when they found the elves.

And the next Star.

Konowa caught himself. He wasn't sure even he believed that about the Star, for after this Star there would be another, and another. Stars would keep falling and they would keep fighting, until when? How long could this go on?

Konowa reached the Prince at the head of the column and saluted. The Prince returned his salute, then turned his camel to face the assembled troops. Konowa expected a speech, but the Prince merely drew his sword, held it in the air, then brought it down. A drum took up a beat and the regiment marched in step out through the gate and into the city.

It was a somber procession, save for the still-grinning volunteers of the 3rd Spears. Konowa placed them at the rear of the column, hoping their presence there would discourage any kind of last-minute attack by a few rogues in the crowd. Though they appeared calm, the city seethed under the sweltering heat. The rumors of last night seemed to grow as the temperature rose. Konowa wondered if they could make it out of Nazalla before the citizens believed he had murdered babes in their cribs.

The Suljak rode serenely at the front, and when the citizenry saw him, they quickly stepped aside, bowing deferentially as he passed. Konowa recognized power when he saw it. He had no doubt that it would take but a flick of the Suljak's hand to have these same people throwing stones and worse.

The column moved through the streets, silent but for the sound of their boots echoing off the walls. For now at any rate, the bargain had been made. Konowa suspected there were ramifications neither the Prince, nor the Viceroy, nor the Suljak saw, but what they were was anyone's guess.

What Konowa was certain of was that if a price was to be paid, it would likely be exacted in blood from the Iron Elves.

TWENTY-FOUR

Tyul rested near an outcropping of rock. He took the chance to take a drink from the waterskin that Jurwan had found for him before they left the city in pursuit of the remaining skeletal creatures. Tyul poured out some water into his palm for Jurwan. The squirrel drank slowly, pausing to look up periodically before lowering his head to drink again.

The sun approached its zenith, as did the heat. Tyul had removed the black clothing early in the morning, though the aberrations of nature he followed had kept theirs on. Tracking them was proving difficult. Despite moving on foot, they covered ground faster than should have been possible. Tyul found himself running in order to keep them in sight, which in itself was a challenge.

He peered around the rock. The three remaining skeletal creatures and the body they carried disappeared in the shimmering haze like true apparitions. He continued to watch until they reappeared several seconds later. They had covered much ground in the interval.

Tyul knew a power was at work aiding their journey. The farther they traveled into the desert the faster and more elusive the creatures became. As good a tracker as Tyul was, he realized he would not likely be able to keep up this pace for more than another day and night. He considered attacking them and killing them all while he still had the strength to do so, but then he would not have any answers—not know where they were going—and Jurwan had conveyed to him that that was the most important thing of all.

Jurwan finished drinking and scrambled up Tyul's arm to rest on his shoulder. Understanding it was time, Tyul took another glance around the rock. The shimmering air stilled for a few seconds and he noticed something far in the distance. He squinted and tried to bring it into focus. Yes, there was something enticingly green up ahead. He blinked and looked again. He was certain there was a tiny smudge of green in a sea of brown. Tyul could track them to that.

He crossed over the rocks without disturbing the dust and renewed his chase. The creatures either did not see him or no longer cared that he followed them. Where the forest was Tyul's home, this was clearly theirs. Tyul picked up his pace and kept them in sight.

Those were trees in the distance.

Tyul knew how to hunt among trees.

Alwyn crested a dune and paused, using the vantage point to scan the horizon. The sand dunes rippled in every direction, interspersed with rocky outcroppings that with time would be worn away as well. The heat slid over him like molten metal. He ran his tongue across his lips and winced. They were cracked and sore, and his eyes smarted as sweat stung them with every blink. Despite this, he found it was actually a pleasure to be off the wagon and walking.

The movement gave his body something to do besides enduring the jarring of the ride. Although his stump was giving him trouble, the marching also helped him clear his head, and more important, it meant no more dreams.

The one of just a short time ago had faded to the point that he wondered how much was his, and how much was Her.

He remembered the Shadow Monarch reaching out Her hand . . . and he remembered reaching to Her . . . but then everything blurred. His memory went blank after that.

A brindo brayed and Alwyn turned to watch the wagon slowly creak past. As tough as they were, even the brindos needed a respite from pulling the extra weight. The three women remained on the wagon, talking quietly among themselves. Every once in a while, Miss Tekoy or Miss Red Owl would get off and sift the sand and weave the air, then they would set off again, always heading south.

Like Alwyn, the rest of the section walked along behind the wagon in single file. Even Jir had come out from his resting place to stretch his legs, though he seemed disoriented by the lack of trees. It was hard to mark territory when there was nothing to mark. Alwyn had already had to shoo him away from his wooden leg twice. Jir now slunk underneath the wagon, keeping pace and walking there in the shade.

Alwyn preferred the sun right now, no matter how hot. The limbs that made up his new leg creaked in the dry heat, and sand began to wear the burnished sheen of the wood. He didn't want to use any more of the special tree sap until it was absolutely necessary, but if he didn't find a way to protect the leg, it would eventually grind itself apart in the sand.

He looked around and then found a solution.

"Hey, Jir, come here, boy," Alwyn said, beckoning to the bengar.

Jir looked out from underneath the wagon, his head tilting one way, then the other.

Alwyn clicked his tongue and motioned for the animal to come to him. "It's all right, I just need you to mark a little territory."

Teeter marched past, his chin resting on his chest as he limped through the sand. "That's genius, and disgusting," he said.

Jir came out and padded over to Alwyn, who pointed at the wooden leg and smiled hopefully. "You know you want to," Alwyn said.

Jir sniffed at Alwyn's wooden leg, then walked around him a couple of times. He stopped, sniffed again, then took care of business. Magic sparked briefly throughout the leg. The limbs became supple once again. Alwyn had to quickly shake his leg to keep it from trying to take root in the sand. Without earth to delve into, the magic channeled its power up the leg, reviving the wood as it went. Alwyn felt new shoots wrap around his stump and knew the leg would be good to walk on again for some time to come.

"Remind me," Yimt said, trudging up to stand a few feet away, "to never borrow a toothpick from your leg again."

"Great that your leg's watered, but what about us?" Zwitty complained. "Shouldn't we be coming up to that oh-way-seas place you were talking about, Sergeant?"

Yimt glared at Zwitty, then pointed forward. They continued walking. "We'll get there when we get there, and no, Scolly," he said, looking over his shoulder as the soldier came near, "we are *not* there yet."

Scolly's opened mouth closed into a pout.

They walked on in silence, each coping with the heat and the sun as best he could. Yimt flapped his caerna a few times to create a breeze before moving back to take his place walking beside the wagon and chatting with Miss Synjyn.

"You had to go and talk to the girl at the Blue Scorpion instead of just getting on with business," Zwitty said, breaking the silence. He came close to Alwyn and poked a finger in his back. "Why couldn't you have left well enough alone? We would have lived like kings in Nazalla. Now look at us. We're right back out in the middle of bloody nowhere looking for more monsters. Who gives a damn if this Kaman Rhal character is out here? He can have his desert. There's nothing here any sane person would want."

"This is important, Zwitty," Alwyn said. "We couldn't just sit and wait in Nazalla hoping things would work out. And those people wanted to kill us. For all we know the Iron Elves and the other regiments are fighting them now," he said, though he suspected that if that were really the case he would have sensed it. "We don't have a choice."

"We don't have a choice?" Zwitty asked, holding his hands up in disbelief. "Ever since we took that damned oath we've had nothing but eternity staring us in the face. I figure we might as well enjoy the time we got here and now while we can."

"What are you saying?" Alwyn asked, looking behind him.

"Yeah," Hrem said, moving in closer as they marched, "what are you getting at?"

Zwitty looked around at them, then shrugged. "If we only got a short amount of time as men, and forever as shadows, why waste our time here plodding around deserts and jungles and the like? Why not go off on our own?"

"You're talking about desertion," Alwyn said. "They'd have you shot for that." The rest of the soldiers bunched up around them to listen.

Zwitty snorted. "Don't be a fool. What do you think's going to happen to us if we stay here? Eventually we'll be shot anyway, or cut down by a sword, torn in half by a cannonball, or something worse. I think I'd rather take my chances out there," he said, waving his arm at the desert.

Yimt suddenly appeared beside them, the wings of his shako flapping as he stomped along to keep pace. He stuffed a pinch of crute between his gums and cheek, then stuffed a pipe into the corner of his mouth and lit it. "There's more noise from you lot than a bag full of dragons and one virgin. I'd say you lads was gettin' sun-crazy if I didn't already know you. What are you jawing about anyway?"

"Zwitty was talking about having dessert," Scolly said.

Zwitty snarled something under his breath.

Yimt puffed on his pipe, sending clouds of acrid smoke skyward. "Is that so, Zwitty?"

"The halfwit is talking through his shako. I didn't say nothing about dessert."

Yimt looked Zwitty up and down. "No, I'm sure you didn't. But you know, seeing as we're on the subject, I thought I'd relate a little story to you all. The sun and the heat out here can fry a man's brain pan quicker than an egg on a skillet if he ain't careful. Scrambles his thinking, it does. Before he knows it, he's thinking the army life ain't for him, and maybe he'd be better off out on his own."

"Kritton got away with it," Zwitty remarked.

The bowl of Yimt's pipe sparked violently for a moment then

subsided. "Aye, he did, but that was in Elfkyna. No shortage of water and food in that place if you know how to get by in a forest—and whatever else Kritton was, that elf knew how to take care of himself. But in case you haven't noticed, this ain't Elfkyna. Have a look around." He took a few more puffs on his pipe as that sank in.

Alwyn did. Everywhere was shades of beige. Heat shimmered above the sand like sheets of glass wherever he turned his gaze. Rocks and great curving sand dunes provided the only change in an otherwise flat vastness of desolation. How anyone could live out here was beyond him.

"Not exactly paradise, is it?" Yimt continued. "Now if we was in Calahr or some other civilized place, a man might make a run for it, but then you have to ask yourself why? If you're in a good place with food and drink and things is relatively calm, what's the point of doin' a runner? On the other hand, in a place like this there's even less point. Where would a fellow go to out here? There's nothing but sand, sun, and dying of thirst if something worse don't get you first. You're safer off with the army than not."

Alwyn wasn't so sure. It was being in the army that had brought them all to this point—oath-bound by the Shadow Monarch's magic and doomed to eternal hell if they couldn't find a way to break the oath. He looked around. Eyes betrayed fear and uncertainty.

"Now, it's not for me to judge a man, elf, or dwarf who's reached his breaking point," Yimt continued. "The army will do that, and with a rope or a musket ball. Thing is, we all got 'em. Every sigger that ever put on the uniform has a breaking point. The major does. The Prince does. Even I do."

"So what's your point?" Zwitty asked. "We're all going to snap like twigs in this heat and go stark raving mad?"

Yimt pulled his pipe out of his mouth and pointed it at them. "My *point* is that when a fellow reaches that breaking point, if he's got buddies around who don't entirely hate his guts, they'll probably help him keep his head until he gets back to himself again. It's the only way armies work. Going off to war and killing will crack anyone's crystal ball. That's why they keep soldiers together in regiments. You get to know the other fellow and maybe even become friends." Yimt turned to look directly at Zwitty. "A friend, Zwitty, is a person who will do something for you without expecting anything in return."

Zwitty only sneered and said nothing.

"I hate to interrupt your little chat, gentlemen, but I believe the oasis in question is just ahead," Rallie said from the front seat of the wagon.

Alwyn and the others turned and climbed up the gentle slope to where she was pointing. At first, all Alwyn saw was shimmering sand and sky. Blurred images swam in and out of focus. He took off his spectacles and rubbed his eyes and immediately regretted it, then put them back on and tried again.

"Wait, I think I see it," he said. A cluster of low, white-walled buildings appeared beside several palm trees. He looked away and then back. The palm trees were now smudged and fragmented, but now that he'd seen them he could keep some of it in focus.

"Load your men, Sergeant," Rallie said, "I think it best we get there as quickly as possible."

"You heard the lady," Yimt said, "get your arses on the wagon. Move."

Alwyn walked over to the wagon and began to climb on, not

an easy feat with a wooden leg—no matter how magical—then paused and looked around. "Where's Jir?"

The bengar was sniffing in the sand a few yards away. "Jir, let's go," Alwyn said, motioning with his hand. The bengar ignored him and continued to worry at a spot in the sand. He began pawing at it.

"Ally, get your butt on the wagon—the beastie can catch us up," Yimt said.

"Just a minute," Alwyn said, walking over to Jir. Alwyn gently nudged Jir out of the way with his musket, then looked down. It was only some cloth. Alwyn started to turn away when something about the fabric made him reach down and grab it.

"We're getting baked to a crisp out here, Renwar," Zwitty shouted. There were a few grumbles of agreement.

Alwyn ignored them and shook the cloth a few times to rid it of sand and dust. It was an unremarkable black save for a small section of embroidery just visible at one tattered end. Stitched on the cloth was a green vine. Alwyn looked down at his caerna and placed the cloth beside it.

The color and the vine were a perfect match.

This was part of the uniform of an Iron Elf. *But how?*

"I've half a mind to take off your leg and beat you about the head and shoulders with it," Yimt said, huffing as he stomped toward Alwyn. "What are you doing?"

Instead of answering, Alwyn called forth the frost fire. It sparkled in his palm and ignited the cloth. There, for just a moment, a tiny white flame burned before being consumed. The pain told him everything.

"Tell me that wasn't a piece of a caerna . . . and that I didn't just see white flame." Yimt said slowly.

Alywn turned and looked again toward the oasis. "We have to save him."

"Save who?"

Alwyn lowered his head and shook it slowly. "I don't know how, but Kester Harkon is here. That's who we have to save."

TWENTY-FIVE

Why are we risking our live bodies to try and save a dead one?" Zwitty asked. "If something really has Harkon's body, which makes no sense at all if you ask me, I say let him keep it. Harkon's got no more use for it."

Alwyn was tired of arguing the point and kept his mouth shut. Zwitty was far too concerned with his own well-being to understand that it was much more than simply the body—this was a battle for Kester's soul. Alwyn flexed his fingers around his musket and scanned the ground ahead of him.

The section was spread out in a line moving slowly toward the oasis. Palm trees and some figs grew up around a green area that Alwyn hoped contained a well or even a pond. His head pounded with the relentless heat, his eyes were on fire from the punishing sun. Then there was the sand, which was in everything and everywhere; all over his uniform, boots, and pack; in his eyes, up his nose, in his ears and mouth so that all he tasted was grit. It felt like being simultaneously slow-roasted and ground between scouring pads.

Alwyn narrowed his eyes and pulled his shako a little farther down over his forehead. A cluster of five single-story buildings sat off to one side of the oasis, indicating there might be inhabitants here . . . though there was no smoke from a fire and no sign of movement. A ridge of sand ran behind the oasis, blocking the view beyond, but until they searched the buildings and the oasis itself, whatever was beyond could wait.

The sun was now scorching the right side of Alwyn's neck, and he twisted his head and hunched his shoulder to compensate. Alwyn tried to relax his grip on his musket and stay calm. The hammer was cocked, a musket ball and charge were loaded, and the bayonet was fixed. The same thought kept racing through his mind—*they had Kester's body.*

"I cannot tell what, if anything, is in there," Miss Tekoy said, indicating the oasis while walking a few paces to the left of Alwyn. Miss Red Owl was on the other side of Yimt and Miss Synjyn was standing on top of her wagon holding on to Jir. The bengar stared straight ahead, the fur on the back of his neck standing up. Definitely not a good sign.

It bothered Alwyn that the women were there—not that he didn't appreciate their abilities, but it seemed wrong somehow for them to be putting themselves in such grave danger.

"There is no safe place out here, Alwyn of the Empire," Miss Red Owl said, displaying her uncanny ability to respond to Alwyn's thoughts.

"Maybe Jir's just excited to see all those trees," Hrem said, attempting some levity. He pointed with his musket toward the palms that lined the small watering hole. "Be a nice change of pace for him after only having Ally's leg to water."

They kept walking. Alwyn shivered and stomped his one good leg on the ground. Cold, as if he'd just taken a breath on a snowy night, filled his chest and then was gone.

"But how did they get his body all the way out here?" Scolly asked. "We buried him at sea, just like all the rest of them."

"He didn't become a shadow, did he?" Inkermon said. "His soul is lost. It is as I feared."

"Do we have to talk about this?" Teeter asked, holding his head with one hand. "I'm hot, tired, and hung over, and talking about something out there waiting to steal our bodies and souls is not helping."

"So stick your head in the sand if you don't want to listen," Zwitty said, pointing his musket toward Teeter. "See, this is exactly the kind of thing I was talking about. Bet leavin' the army don't seem so crazy now, does it?"

For a while there was only the muffled sound of their footsteps as they plodded through the sand. The silence built until Alwyn felt the need to cough just to hear something, but Yimt spoke first.

"Ever notice wherever you go you can always find a mud hut? It's true. You know, I've lost count of the number of countries I've been to," he said, keeping his shatterbow ready at his hip. "But it doesn't matter if it's so far north you sneeze ice, or so far west you find yourself east, you can always find mud huts."

"How's that, Sergeant?" Hrem asked.

"Like those ahead," Yimt said. "Clearly made out of mud bricks. Same with most of Nazalla, too."

"I'd say they were more buildings than huts," Teeter said, apparently deciding this was a conversation he approved of. "See how that one there has a window opening? Clearly a building."

Alwyn looked to where Teeter was pointing. There was a window opening in the wall of one of the structures. He didn't care, if it offered shade from this sun.

Yimt stared at Teeter for a moment before turning his head back to scan the buildings up ahead. "It's just that it's mud. Water and dirt mashed together. Oh, sure, sometimes they mix in some straw, or cattle manure, but in the end a mud hut is a mud hut is a mud hut. I don't know, I guess I just *was* hoping we'd go someplace and be surprised for once."

"I see something!" Scolly shouted, followed by the crack of his musket firing. The sreexes in Rallie's wagon started screeching. Jir growled and leaped from the wagon, bounding across the sand and into the short vegetation growing around the oasis.

"I think we just got our surprise!" Alwyn shouted, as they all broke into a run.

Scolly crashed through the vegetation first, his caerna flying. Jir let out a piercing roar.

The air vibrated with an energy. Alwyn was sure he could hear a voice carried on it.

"An oath weapon!" Miss Red Owl shouted, running after Scolly. "Tyul is in there! Be careful!" Behind Alwyn, reins snapped and brindos brayed.

"Keep spread out! Inkermon, Hrem, watch the buildings!" Yimt ordered as he plunged through the brush with Alwyn right behind him.

As the entered the clearing, they saw three black-cloaked figures standing near a watering hole, a small rock-lined pond ten feet across. Each held a long, curved sword in its hand. A body lay face-down on the ground behind them. It was still sewn up in canvas sailcloth, but Alwyn knew it was Kester. A few feet away, Tyul Mountain Spring faced the figures with his dagger drawn. The voice Alwyn had heard was coming from Tyul's weapon. Jurwan sat perched on Tyul's shoulder, his tail bushed.

"Drop your weapons," Yimt shouted, pointing his shatterbow at the nearest figure.

It motioned to the other two, which bent down and picked up the body. The first turned toward Yimt and raised its sword.

Scolly was furiously reloading his musket. "Kill them, kill them!"

"We've got this under control, everyone take a breath. Now," Yimt said, taking a step closer to the mysterious figures, "drop your weapons and that body."

Scolly slammed his ramrod down the barrel, cutting his hand on the bayonet. "Kill them! They don't got no shadows!"

Alwyn glanced at the ground and realized Scolly was right.

Scolly paid Yimt's orders no mind; he simply raised his musket, aimed, and fired with the ramrod still in the barrel. The ramrod and musket ball flew across the water and hit the first figure in the side of the head, tearing away the hood of its cloak.

A grinning skull with eyes of white fire stared back at them.

Yimt's shatterbow fired at the same time as several muskets. A hail of musket balls pulverized the creature's skull and two shatterbow darts blew the rest of it to pieces.

Alwyn didn't join the attack. Bitter cold gripped his chest and his breath misted before him. He spun around to face the water as several beasts now surged out of the pond, their jaws of razor-sharp teeth snapping loudly. Water steamed off their scaly hides as they clambered onto the sand. Each appeared fifteen feet long, with a hide of scales gray-green in color. Their heads were long and pointed, like hinged wedges filled with flesh-rending teeth. They stayed just a few inches above the ground, scrabbling forward with four short, but very powerful legs splayed out to the sides. Great slashing scars covered their scales, as if they fought amongst themselves when there wasn't something meatier to eat. Their eyes burned with white fire and their open maws held it like a foundry furnace.

Alwyn squeezed the trigger, his musket bucking in his hands. The musket ball punched a neat hole in the head of the closest creature, which sank back into the furiously bubbling water. A few of the pond monsters immediately began tearing chunks off the dead creature while the rest crawled forward. They opened their jaws wide, hide around their throats expanded, and they began convulsing. A moment later they spewed out pure white flame.

Shouts and screams echoed off the walls of the nearby buildings. With no time to reload, Alwyn called forth the frost fire, setting his bayonet aflame. He lunged forward to the water's edge, skewering one of the beasts. White fire washed over Alwyn, the burning sensation he'd experienced on the island wracking him again.

His shadow was on fire.

"Get out of there, Ally!" Yimt shouted.

Alwyn ignored the order and waded into the water, stabbing down with his bayonet as more creatures emerged. He thrust again with his musket, piercing the jaws of one creature closed as it was about to spew more white fire. It tried to pull its jaws free, but Alwyn kept them pinned even as the white fire grew inside it. Finally, its neck tore apart violently as gouts of flame ripped through its scales and shot out across the water.

Black flame rose in response to the white, as each powerful fire roared higher and higher. The surface of the water began to alternate between boiling and freezing. Alwyn ignored everything except the creatures. He stabbed and burned until his mind went blank and all he was, all he would ever be, was a dispenser of death.

A third power tried to weave its way around Alwyn. He recognized Miss Tekoy's magic and realized she was trying to protect him, but he didn't need protection, not for this. He called up more of the frost fire and brushed her efforts aside.

A musket fired nearby, followed by the distinctive double blast of Yimt's shatterbow. Water frothed around Alwyn until he could barely see, but he didn't need to. He sensed where every creature was as his bayonet slashed down again and again, each time finding its mark. Still the white flame burned his shadow, and he felt the first threads of the Shadow Monarch's grip part even as he burned. *Yes. He could master this.*

Another beast came at him. Alwyn threw aside his musket and dove forward, thrusting his right arm down the creature's throat. Its teeth sank into his shoulder, but Alwyn didn't care. He felt around with his hand until he grabbed something small and hard. It was bone, and it burned like the surface of the sun.

Alwyn squeezed as his whole body spasmed in pain, his vision going completely white. Somewhere impossibly deep inside Alwyn, the white fire seared through the black threads of the oath, burning away strands of it like cutting taut strings. More of the oath that bound Alwyn to the Iron Elves and the Shadow Monarch frayed and parted. The creature reared up in the water and tried to use the claws on its feet to tear at Alwyn, but its stubby legs made it impossible.

"He's gone into the tunnel!"

Alwyn's focus was broken and he looked up. Tyul was disappearing down the tunnel after the skeletons carrying Kester's body. Miss Tekoy and several soldiers raced after the elf, though Alwyn couldn't see who it was. More of the fire creatures lunged for the tunnel entrance, followed by the sound of Yimt's shatterbow firing. There was a huge explosion and the tunnel entrance disappeared in a cloud of smoke, dust, and a blinding ball of white flame.

Alwyn stumbled and only barely kept himself upright. He brought his attention back to the creature he fought, and drew even more of the white fire into himself. The creature gave up trying to claw him and let itself fall back into the water, taking Alwyn down with it. As soon as they were submerged it began rolling about and thrashing, trying to twist Alwyn's arm from his body.

The sound of the fighting grew muffled as Alwyn and the creature twisted and rolled under the water. Alwyn drew in a breath and water filled his lungs, only to vaporize in a flash. Muscles tore in Alwyn's shoulder and a new, more understandable pain tried to render him unconscious, but still he held on.

The oath was breaking. The power of the white fire was cleansing him from the inside. That it also burned him until every nerve in his body quivered in pain was a price he was prepared to pay. Every twisted piece of the Shadow Monarch's magic that was severed felt like claws raking his flesh from the inside. He knew he was close. One more squeeze would do it. Alwyn focused all his energy on his right hand and began to crush the bone in it. He was going to finally be fr——

Something hard and heavy hit him in the back of the head and color burst before his eyes as the muscles in his hands relaxed. He tried to regain his grip, but already he was being pulled up out of the water. Another musket fired and there was unintelligible shouting as he took a breath. He opened his eyes and realized his spectacles were gone. Water gurgled in his ears.

"—most idiotic th . . . ever seen!" Yimt shouted at Alwyn as he leaned over him. "—let that thing eat you . . . were you thinking?"

Alwyn closed his eyes and turned away. He had been so close.

Next time, he vowed, as the pain in his shoulder spread and the nerves in his body reacted to the violence of the last two minutes. He opened his mouth to scream as a new wave of pain washed over him, but he blacked out before he could.

TWENTY-SIX

A coldness came over Konowa that defied the heat of the desert sun.

He knew somewhere ahead of them the missing soldiers and the three women were in trouble. He pounded his fist against his thigh in frustration and turned to look back over the column.

Midway back, the Prince and the Viceroy chatted amiably on their camels. Affixed to the saddle furniture on their camels were two large, green parasols trimmed with silver brocade, which swayed above their heads while providing ample shade. The rocking motion of the green canvas brought to mind ocean waves, and Konowa's stomach gurgled in distress. He quickly looked past the parasols to see the sun glinting off spear tips marking the position of the Timolian soldiers of the 3rd Spears.

Bringing up the rear now that they were safely out of Nazalla were two supply wagons pulled by mules and three cannons pulled by donkeys. Konowa was unclear on the distinction between the animals and didn't care, as both had a tendency to bite and kick.

The cannons, two nine-pounders and one six-pounder, were naval equipment left in the palace grounds for show after the parade through Nazalla. Unfortunately, there was only enough powder and shot for fifteen rounds each. Konowa doubted it would be enough if they ran into trouble, but then that seemed to be the constant state of things. Marching sullenly alongside the cannons were their naval gun crews, no doubt cursing the sea of sand they now found themselves in.

Konowa felt for every marching soldier. The Iron Elves trudged with their heads bent forward and a silence that spoke volumes about their general mood. The oppressive heat from the sun above and the broiling sand below produced a scorching environment not even magically bound soldiers like the Iron Elves could ignore. It was past noon, but that still meant hours of energy-sapping heat before the brief cool of the evening brought any relief, followed by a freezing cold—if the Suljak was to be believed—that would create a whole new set of problems. The smart thing to do would be to wait for nightfall and march then, but time, as was so often the case, was not on their side.

The Jewel of the Desert was indeed returning, and though Konowa couldn't point to a single piece of concrete evidence to prove it to himself or anyone else, he knew it was tonight. Maybe he was finding a way to finally make sense of his elven heritage, and this both intrigued him and concerned him. He had tried in the past to understand the natural order, and usually got kicked in the arse for his efforts. This time, however, he could feel it. He was seeing what Visyna and his mother saw, although he suspected not in the same way. The Star was going to fall somewhere in the Canyon of Bones near Suhundam's Hill and his original Iron Elves . . . and if they didn't pick up the pace he wouldn't be there when it did.

"I believe the expression is a watched pot never boils, though I've never quite understood that, because of course the pot will indeed boil whether it's observed or not," the Suljak said, talking matter-of-factly as he rode alongside Konowa. The camels kept pace and moved across the sand with ease, if not with grace. Konowa's back and neck ached from the constant jostling, and he was unable to find the rhythm of the animal. He suspected it kept changing it on purpose.

"We're going to be too late," Konowa replied. "Why aren't you upset? The Star means more to you than any of us."

The Suljak nodded. "True, but worrying about things we cannot change is not the most productive use of one's time. Besides, I have something you apparently do not."

Konowa rolled his eyes. "I really don't want to discuss faith right now."

"I was referring to patience, Major. If the legends are true, the Stars have been gone for thousands of years. A few hours more is but a grain of sand in, well, this," he said, waving a hand in an arc.

"Take it from me, a few hours can make all the difference in the world," Konowa said, turning to look back again at the column. A lingering dust cloud hung in the still air behind them, marking their passage through the desert. It could be seen for miles. The feeling in Konowa grew colder. "Damn. We're not going to make it to the Star, are we?"

The Suljak twisted slightly in his saddle and observed the cloud of dust following the column. He stroked the wisps of hair that made up his beard and gave Konowa an enigmatic look. "As I told you, Major, politics is a messy business."

"You've made another deal with the Prince," Konowa said. It wasn't a question.

"A force of several thousand tribesman is coming up from the south. Their intent is peaceful."

The Suljak emphasized the word, as if somehow saying it clearly made it more likely. Konowa sincerely doubted it.

"They will welcome the Jewel of the Desert and prevent any interference with its rightful resurrection. It is as it should be, Major. No doubt the Prince will show his displeasure publicly, as is expected."

"No doubt," Konowa said dryly. "But what of the Shadow Monarch, and whatever is out here stirring things up? They certainly have different views on the matter. Your tribesmen aren't equipped to handle powers like this."

"They'll have help, of course."

The Suljak's demeanor did not change, a fact that irritated Konowa no end. The man had no idea what horrors his people were about to face. The thought gave Konowa pause. He really didn't know, either. As terrible as Elfkyna had been, the islands had been worse in their own way. Who was to say the desert wouldn't find new ways to increase the horrors they all faced. "What help?"

"Major, I really do admire your single-mindedness. For you this is all quite simple, isn't it?" His tone of voice suggested a gentle mocking. "Alas, the path to my aims is far more indirect. There will be fighting, Major, of that I am certain, but I see no reason that it should be the Empire against the peoples of the Hasshugeb. Rather, we will come together as one—allies of equal stature—and together we will defeat our enemies."

"You expect the Prince to help you after your maneuvering to take the Star and usurp his authority? Pimmer is one thing, but the Prince is the future King. I doubt he'll be as agreeable to your vision as you seem to think. We're still in the Calahrian Empire, even out here."

Now the Suljak sounded genuinely surprised. "Major, don't you see, everyone gets what they really want. The Star is returned to my people. The Prince finds the Lost Library, the Shadow Monarch and the necromancer Kaman Rhal are destroyed . . . assuming he has returned. And if not destroyed, they will most definitely be thwarted in their endeavors, at which point you are reunited with your brethren. Beautiful, is it not? Machinations within intrigues woven with finesse and finished off with just the right amount of controlled violence." The Suljak beamed, his voice taking on an almost childlike glee.

"Somehow I doubt that's what will happen at all," Konowa said.

"Patience, Major, patience. Tonight, all will be revealed. You will see. All will come to pass as I have foreseen it."

"And what of my mother, and Rallie and Visyna? They got a head start on us. What if they get to the Star first?"

For the first time in their conversation the Suljak lost his annoying calm. His fists clenched for just a moment before he saw Konowa watching him. The Suljak relaxed and smiled. "A not entirely unanticipated event, displeasing as that might be. Still, they understand the way of things, Her Majesty's Scribe especially. My brief discussion with her was most . . . fascinating."

Konowa took some pleasure in noting that it didn't sound as if the Suljak believed his own words for a second. It was small consolation. Konowa knew the Suljak was wrong. Whatever the night revealed, it was bound to be more than anyone had bargained for.

• • •

Alwyn opened his eyes and instantly knew some time had passed. The sun was low in the sky and already the air was cooling. He blinked several times and began to make out figures moving around him. He recognized Yimt and relaxed. Someone had removed Alwyn's jacket, as he saw it lying on the sand beside him. The right sleeve was completely shredded. Gritting his teeth, he propped himself up on his elbows, expecting pain as he did so. Surprisingly, he felt none except for a throbbing at the back of his head. Miss Red Owl appeared before him and handed Alwyn his spectacles, somehow recovered, which he took with his left hand and put on his face. His vision blurred.

He took them off, buffed them on his sleeve, and had begun to put them back on when he realized that he could see fine without them.

He slowly raised the spectacles to his eyes, and as before his vision blurred. As he lowered them, it returned. He could see perfectly without them. Maybe the knock in the back of the head had fixed his vision?

Miss Red Owl came over and gently laid a hand on his wounded shoulder.

"You are fortunate to still be with us, Alwyn of the Empire," she said.

Alwyn looked at his shoulder and at first didn't understand what he was seeing. Ugly, black scars criss-crossed the entire shoulder, each emanating from where the pond creature's teeth had dug into his flesh. Instead of open wounds, however, frost fire had healed them with barklike grafts. The skin around the wounds was gray. He flexed his fingers. No pain. In fact, there was no feeling at all. He looked down at his hand. More black scars, but the fingers were still there and moving.

"I can't feel anything in my right arm," he said.

"I'm worried about what's between your ears," Yimt said, walking over to join them. He kneeled in the sand and looked Alwyn in the eye. "What in blazes were you thinking?"

Alwyn looked at his arm again. There was no point in keeping up pretenses. "I almost had it. The white flame was burning away the oath. I could feel it. Just a little more, and I would have been free."

Yimt raised his hand as if he wanted to slap Alwyn, and then placed it on his good shoulder. "Free? Laddie, don't you understand? One more foolhardy stunt like that and you'll be dead."

"No, it's you that doesn't understand. I can't explain it, but I know." He sat up a little straighter. "I felt a powerful magic hit me, just before I was going to break the oath."

"Yes, well, it wasn't so much magic as it was a three-pound rock," Rallie said from behind Alwyn.

He turned and saw she had brought the wagon up to the edge of the oasis. The canvas cover was off and Rallie was opening the sreex cages. The large birds with their leathery, batlike wings squawked and flew into the air, wheeling overhead in a tight circle.

"You threw a rock at my head?" Alwyn asked, reaching up with his left hand to rub it. Sure enough, there was a large bump and the whole area was tender to the touch.

"I wasn't about to wade into that water with those *drakarri* splashing around spitting fire, now was I?" she said.

"*Drakarri?*"

"Ancient creatures," Rallie said, pointing at the ash piles around the oasis, "although these days, that term has come in for some abuse. Drake spawn, you'd call them, though they are unique even for that. These fellows are—if one believes legends, and it seems we'd be well advised to heed them—the most unfortunate offspring of Kaman Rhal and his damnable mating with a she-drake."

Alwyn's head tried to navigate around that image and failed completely. "He . . . mated with a dragon?"

"Apparently it gets rather lonely out here in the desert," Rallie said. She looked around, but no one seemed inclined to laugh. "Ah, tough oasis. Again, legend has it that it was more a magical mating, a weaving of two powers that should never have been joined."

A twinge of pain in the back of Alwyn's head brought him back to the here and now. "And so that's why you threw a rock at my head?"

Rallie brushed some dust from her cloak, making the cloth snap. "There was nothing else for it. Visyna tried to weave around you, but that didn't take, so I had to employ a more . . . direct approach."

If Zwitty had thrown the rock, Alwyn might have called forth the frost fire and burned him then and there, but looking at Rallie, Alwyn's anger stayed in check. "How could you? You ruined *everything.*"

This time, Yimt did smack him on the side of the head. "You watch your manners, lad, that's a lady you're talking to. You clearly don't see it, but she saved your life."

Alwyn started to say something, then changed his mind. "How's everyone else?"

Yimt sat back and looked at the sand. "Fine, I hope. Two of those skeleton things grabbed Harkon's body and ducked down a tunnel entrance on the other side of the oasis before we could get to them. Tyul, Jurwan, and Jir went tearing after them, and Miss Tekoy went chasing after *them.* I sent Hrem, Teeter, and Zwitty to go bring them back. The rest of our little group is still here, and more or less in one piece."

"We have to get going then," Alwyn said, starting to get up.

Yimt held him down. "In the fighting, a couple of those *drakarri* things tried to get into the tunnel after the lads. We got the beasties, but their thrashing brought down the entrance. It'd take a day to dig it out."

"Then why aren't you digging?"

Yimt let go of Alwyn's shoulder and pointed a finger at him. "We've got other problems, but right this second, we're going to deal with yours."

Alwyn shook his head. "I'm fine."

"Really?" Yimt asked, his voice growing gruff. "Right, Rallie, show him."

"No," Miss Red Owl said. "He's suffered enough for now."

Yimt stood up. "Then he'll suffer a little more. Private Renwar, on your feet."

Scolly held out a hand and Alwyn took it. His wooden leg creaked ominously and he saw several of the limbs were cracked and broken.

"Rallie, your looking glass, please," Yimt said, holding out his hand.

Rallie stepped forth and silently gave Yimt a small square mirror. He held it out to Alwyn.

Alwyn peered into it and then recoiled. Scolly kept a grip on him. Alwyn wiped his left hand across his mouth and then leaned forward and looked again. He didn't recognize the face staring back at him.

One of his eyes was liquid black, the other white flame.

"I . . . I don't understand. What's happened to me?"

"You have both magics in you now," Rallie said. "In trying to harness the white flame, you brought it into you. Think of it as if you took a second oath."

Alwyn held out his hands and called on the frost fire. Black flames burst to life in his right hand, but in his left a pure white flame flickered and burned.

Alwyn screamed. Immediately, the two magics warred inside him, tearing and burning, twisting and ripping every fiber of his being. His lungs froze while his head burned.

Scolly yelped and let go of Alwyn.

The flames went out. Alwyn staggered but did not fall. He smelled smoke and looked down to witness his wooden leg smoldering. Terrified, he turned to see if he had accidentally lit Scolly's shadow on fire. Alwyn was relieved to see that he hadn't.

That's when he noticed his own shadow. It was still there, but instead of the black denseness of everyone else's, his was gray and insubstantial.

"This can't be, I—I didn't mean for this . . ." Alwyn was at a loss for words. *What had he done?*

"No time to worry about that now, because we've got bigger problems," Yimt said.

Alwyn raised his head and followed Yimt's gaze. A dust cloud to the south smudged the horizon, and it was moving fast.

"That's the regiment," Alwyn said, "isn't it?" His head felt light and heavy at the same time. His right knee started to buckle, but he caught himself and stood up straight. He noticed no one came close to steady him.

"No, that ain't the Iron Elves," Yimt replied. "They'll be coming down from the north following the same route we took. Whoever that is is heading northwest. My guess is that's the tribes of the Expanse. If the people in Nazalla know a Star is returning, you can bet their desert kin will, too."

"Our quarrel is not with them," Miss Red Owl said. "Surely they will see we share their desire to restore the natural order."

"Chayii, you forget we're part and parcel of the Iron Elves now," Rallie said, "and that means we're seen as agents of the Empire."

Miss Red Owl looked as if she'd been slapped. "But that's absurd! I oppose the Empire and its wanton acts of destruction. I side with it now only because we share a common enemy in the Shadow Monarch that threatens all our existence. Surely these people can be made to see reason."

"Another time, perhaps," Yimt said, "but I wouldn't bet my life on it today."

Rallie brought out the map. "The Canyon of Bones is just ahead. We should head for it now while we still can."

"We'd be exposed if we got caught out there. Here we have defensible positions," Yimt said. "Those huts are sturdy and give us a good line of fire."

"We can't stay here," Alwyn said, "we have to go after Kester. Wherever they're taking him is where we have to be as well."

"We still have Hrem and Visyna and the others in that tunnel. I don't know about just leaving them behind," Yimt said.

"But the Star isn't coming here. Can't you feel it?" Alwyn said. "I don't know how to explain this, but . . ."

"He's right," Rallie said. "Power fills the air, Sergeant, power from a time long past. When that power arrives, we need to be there. Private Renwar needs to be there."

"You're probably right," Yimt said, "but it don't do us any good if we're killed before we get there."

"Sergeant," Scolly said, coming up to stand near Yimt.

"Not now, Scolly, we're busy. If you're hungry go check the wagon. Now," Yimt said, turning back to them, "I don't see that we have a ch———"

"Sergeant," Scolly said again, this time tugging on Yimt's sleeve.

Yimt spun around and looked up at Scolly. "What?"

"I don't want to go into the forest," Scolly said. His voice was quiet with fear.

Yimt kneaded his forehead with his fingers. "Other than four bloody palm trees and a couple of fig trees, there ain't a forest for a thousand miles around here."

"Yes, there is," Scolly said, pointing northwest toward the distant coast.

Alwyn almost reached for his spectacles, but there was no longer any need. He felt the forest before he saw it. Twenty, perhaps thirty, miles away a cold, obsidian stain was spreading out across the desert floor. It was a mass of black *sarka har* crawling across the sand. Frost fire sparkled in its depth. It spread out as far as the eye could see. Miles upon miles of *sarka har*. This was nothing like the small forest that had ringed Luuguth Jor. This was enormous.

"Oh, hell . . ." Yimt said.

It was like watching an incoming tide. "It'll be here by nightfall."

"It's the end," Inkermon said, closing his eyes and praying.

Yimt stomped the dirt. "You might not be too far off, Inkermon, but let's see if we can't postpone that for a bit, if it's all the same to you."

Rallie walked briskly to the wagon and mounted it in one leap.

She picked up the reins in her hands and looked down at the soldiers. "We need to get moving. My team can make the canyon before either the Hasshugeb or the *sarka har*. We'll find a place to hole up once we're inside, but we need to go, now."

"Rallie's right, we must go forward," Miss Red Owl said. "The risk is great, but to do nothing is to risk so much more. You know this, Yimt of the Warm Breeze. The others in the tunnel are capable of fending for themselves. Visyna is with them, and her power is strong. We must trust to things greater than ourselves now."

Yimt got a firmer grip on his shatterbow and looked toward the forest of *sarka har* spreading toward them, then to the dust cloud rapidly closing from the other direction. "Are you sure your brindos can outrun that forest? If we get caught in that there's no amount of frost fire that's going to pull us through."

Rallie pulled a cigar from her cloak and stuck it in her mouth. The cigar lit itself. She took a puff and then cracked her neck, first to the left, then to the right. She looked up to the whirling sreexes and whistled. The birds squawked once in return and wheeled and headed north. "Every second we delay casts the possibility in further doubt, so we had better move now."

"Mount up!" Yimt ordered.

Alwyn limped to the wagon and climbed into the back with the empty cages. Scolly and Inkermon came in after him, while Yimt and Miss Red Owl sat up front. The wagon was already moving while Alwyn was still looking for a place to get comfortable, a search that he quickly realized was pointless. "Hang on to whatever jiggles because this ride is going to be a tad bumpier than last night!" Rallie shouted back to them.

The wagon flew over a small crest and plunged down the other side. Dust flew into the air and the wind whistled past Alwyn's ears.

At another time this would have been exhilarating if terrifying. Now, it felt too slow. He looked over the side and watched the approaching forest. It crawled like a broken-legged spider, the trunks and limbs of the *sarka har* thrusting out of the sand and clawing forward with ragged, uneven lunges.

Dark clouds grew taller above it. A single bolt of lightning slashed down among the trees, setting off a cascade of frost fire. This forest was a sick and angry thing. Alwyn felt the pain radiate out from the trees.

And the hunger.

He turned away, casting his glance to the oncoming tribes of the Hasshugeb. He could just make out dark shapes at the base of the towering dust cloud above them.

The wagon was now between closing pincers. He looked forward.

Wind buffeted Alwyn's face and grit got into his nose, ears, and mouth, but not his eyes. Whatever grit touched his eyes burned with either white flame or black. It was an odd sensation, but it helped to take his mind off the roiling forces inside him. *Was he like those creatures he'd killed just a few hours ago? Two magics joined that should never have existed in the first place?*

Finally, there in the distance the land sloped upward and became two rocky shoulders overlooking a narrow passage between them—the Canyon of Bones.

Alwyn slumped in the wagon and held on as best he could. The sun continued to sink and shadows lengthened as they raced for the opening and whatever waited for them there.

Alwyn silently urged the brindos on. Another bout of pain racked his body. The new Star was coming. It pulled at his senses as if tied to his very soul. The world was about to change again.

He studied his hands as they held his musket and knew he could not go on like this.

Tentatively, he tried to call up the frost fire, just a little. Immediately, the white flame responded as well, and the magics scissored through him. He tried to extinguish the flames as he gasped for breath, but he couldn't put them out. He focused harder. The flames came under control, but they would not die.

"What are you doing?" Inkermon asked, looking at him with horror. "Put those flames out! You'll burn us all."

Alwyn tried to speak, but the effort to keep the fires under control made it too difficult. He grimaced and closed his eyes.

A bright, blue Star beckoned him. It hung motionless in a silk-black sky.

It was almost here. He just had to hang on a little longer.

He opened his eyes and looked at Inkermon. Inkermon still crouched before him, but all Alwyn saw was a dark outline of a man with a core of smoldering frost fire. He turned to Scolly and saw the same thing. Then he looked down at himself. Frost fire and white flame twisted and burned within him, pulsating with an energy he couldn't control much longer.

"*Hurry*," Alwyn said to no one in particular. "*Please hurry.*"

TWENTY-SEVEN

Visyna ran as fast as she could, trying to keep up with Tyul and Jir, but the elf and bengar were much too swift for her.

With her breath coming in gasps and blood pounding in her ears, she stopped and bent over, clutching her sides. She leaned against the tunnel wall and stayed there for a minute.

Finally able to breathe normally, she straightened up and noticed the construction of the tunnel for the first time. The stones were placed so precisely that no mortar had been used. More curious, however, was its size and condition. Once she had traveled a hundred yards or so from the opening at the oasis, it opened up to the width of a small cart, and a fascinating moss grew on the ceiling that gave off a soft glow, allowing her enough light to see where she was going.

The image of the skull with flaming eyes was seared into her memory. She well knew of necromancy, but thought it a relic of a dark past. *Could it be true,* she wondered, *was it possible that Kaman Rhal had returned?* The thought chilled her. Her Emissary had fooled her once by pretending to be the power of the Star of Sillra. Perhaps something—or someone—was using Kaman Rhal's power. Whatever the case, she had been so focused on keeping the Shadow Monarch from obtaining a Star that she had given little thought that there might be other ancient powers out there waiting for just such an opportunity to rise again.

"Miss Tekoy!"

Visyna turned as Private Hrem Vulhber appeared out of the dark. Frost fire tinged his bayonet, and he, too, was panting heavily. A moment later Zwitty appeared. Visyna loathed the weasely faced soldier, but under the circumstances she knew he could kill, and that was a skill they would almost certainly need. Teeter hobbled into view a few seconds later.

"Where are the others?" Visyna asked, looking back down the tunnel.

Teeter shook his head. "We're it. Sergeant Arkhorn sent us in after you, then the entrance caved in."

Visyna had faith that Chayii and Rallie could fend for themselves, knowing their powers and Sergeant Arkhorn's skills were a match for most anything, including those fire-spitting monsters. For many reasons, she worried more about Private Renwar.

"Then we must press on. Tyul is already well ahead of us. He still needs our help," she said.

"Who's going to help us?" Zwitty muttered from behind.

A good question, Visyna thought.

As the sun began to slide down the sky, the shadows of the marching column stretched and flowed out across the sand. Konowa found the image disturbing. It made the regiment's shadows look twenty feet tall. He focused on the path ahead.

Wagon tracks cut neat furrows in the dirt, heading more or less straight south. Konowa knew the tracks had to be Rallie's—enough reports had already reached the regiment of a wagon ablaze in black fire being pulled by armor-plated beasts that it could be no other.

The Suljak confirmed that the track's course aimed directly toward a place called the Canyon of Bones, which lay somewhat to the south and west of Nazalla.

"Why do they call it that?" Konowa asked, adjusting himself in the saddle to spread the pain around. He winced as he found a particularly tender spot on his backside. He vowed never to ride another beast again—the Prince could have him shot if he wanted, as long as it wasn't done in a saddle.

"It is a blighted place. Centuries ago, there was once a forest there, but Kaman Rhal's she-drake is said to have burned it all because it *offended* her." The Suljak looked apologetic as he said this. "I can't imagine why."

Konowa shifted in the saddle again. "I can. Trees have a way of doing that."

The Suljak was momentarily nonplussed, then seemed to gather his wits and continued. "Yes, so I've heard. Whatever the cause, all that remains today are withered tree trunks bleached white by the sun and scoured by the sand—giving the land the appearance of an unearthed mass grave."

"Charming," Konowa said.

"It's actually rather fascinating," the Prince said, trotting his camel into line with theirs. He no longer had the parasol up, and looked surprisingly fresh.

A knot formed in Konowa's stomach. He wondered if all his bottled-up anger was slowly, inexorably eating him up from the inside. Repressing a sigh, Konowa tried to look interested. "Really, Your Highness, how's that?"

The Prince smiled, obviously pleased to impart some newly attained knowledge. "The legend surrounding the canyon fits perfectly with the level of sophistication of the tribes out here, but a new theory in archeology argues that given the right conditions, a tree can absorb enough minerals to essentially become hard as rock. They actually *transform.* So you see, it seems far more likely that these trunks weren't burned by some legendary dragon at all, but simply succumbed to the natural effects of the desert."

"But how could a forest grow out here in the first place?" Konowa asked, deciding it might be best to put some space between the Prince's comments about the tribes. "How does *anything* grow out here?" He wasn't disappointed that no trees blocked his path. The unimpeded sight lines meant a leader could manipulate and direct his troops in a battle while being able to keep an eye on his forces. The frustration of a communication's not making it to an officer some distance away and out of direct sight would not be as challenging in this place.

"You'd be surprised at the amount of life teeming around us," the Suljak said. "For instance, there is an oasis ahead where your soldiers and our mounts can drink. All manner of plants and animals thrive in such areas." His voice rang with pride.

"What's that?" the Prince asked, pointing toward the north and the coast.

Konowa turned and squinted. "Storm clouds. I wouldn't have thought you get much rain here, Suljak," Konowa said.

The Suljak sat up straighter in his saddle. He appeared visibly nervous for the first time Konowa could remember.

"We don't. I have never seen clouds like that before." He turned to look at the Prince. "Have you lied to me? Is that part of your army out there?"

"It most certainly is not," the Prince said. He seemed equally ill at ease as he stared at the clouds.

"They're moving awfully fast, even for storm clouds," Konowa offered. "Much too fast."

The Suljak worried at his beard. "Perhaps . . . perhaps it would be best if we increase our pace."

"A good idea," the Prince said. Konowa turned in his saddle and motioned to the drummer to pick up the beat. The man did so at once and the column lurched forward, the soldiers' steps kicking up even more dust.

"Is that another storm *ahead* of us?" the Prince asked. He pulled out a brass telescope and held it up to his eye. After a minute, he passed it to Konowa, who took a quick look, already knowing what he would see.

"That, Your Highness, is the warrior tribes of the Hasshugeb Expanse moving to block our path," Konowa said without emotion. He refrained from saying more, but it annoyed him no end to be caught in the middle of yet another diplomatic dance.

The Prince looked to the Suljak and then back to the dust cloud. "A moment ago you accused me of subterfuge and now you blatantly break our agreement. How dare you, sir. Do you truly wish to go to war with the Empire?"

The Suljak seemed genuinely shocked at the Prince's response, though Konowa wasn't. The Prince always expected things to go his way.

The Suljak waved away the question. "I assure you, as I have assured the Viceroy for months, the people of the Hasshugeb want only to be left alone to conduct their lives as they see fit. What you see on the horizon is merely our expression of that intent, to ensure the Star remains where it belongs."

"And should other . . . things be uncovered?" the Prince asked, his voice casual.

Konowa marveled at how quickly the Prince could change emotion. One moment he was building into a fury and the next he was coolly calculating odds.

The Suljak was equally matter-of-fact. "The people of the Hasshugeb lay no claim to artifacts discovered that are not cultur-ally tied to this land. I have no doubt arrangements can be made that satisfy all parties."

Konowa thought the Suljak was giving away Kaman Rhal's purported library rather easily, but as he pondered it more, he saw the genius in it. Were the Hasshugeb to lay a claim to the li-brary and its holdings, they risked not just the Empire's avarice, but that of every other nation and people from whom Rhal had stolen. The re-emergence of the library with its fabled treasure would draw thieves—both individuals and armies. By allowing the Empire to take away much of what resided in it, the Suljak was al-lowing the Empire to accept much of the burden. *Oh, that's really clever.*

"I believe that's the oasis up ahead," the Prince said, choosing to change the subject.

Konowa's eyes drifted back to the dark clouds coming in from the coast and felt another chill. That was no storm. He turned to the oasis and caught the slightest tinge of lingering magic from a battle that had taken place there only a short time ago. He flowed his senses outward to the oasis.

"What is it?" the Prince asked.

Konowa said nothing as he tried to concentrate. Power was everywhere in the air—so roiled that he could understand very little of it, but what he did comprehend filled him with dread.

"There's no time to stop at the oasis. We have to push on now and reach the Canyon of Bones." Konowa looked back at the column. It was spread out over several hundred yards and plodding along. They were going to have to move much, much faster than this.

The Suljak coughed. "Major, the Prince and I have an agreement. The Hasshugeb and the Empire are not enemies this day. This regiment has but to enjoy the hospitality of the oasis this evening and then proceed in the morning. By then, the Star will have arrived and much will be revealed."

A cold jolt against his heart told Konowa exactly what he didn't want to know. He smiled, and it wasn't meant to give comfort. "There's more than two moving pieces on this board, and She isn't about to follow any gentleman's agreement." He pointed to the looming dark clouds. "That's Her forest, and it will be here by nightfall."

The Prince brought his brass telescope up to his eye. "What?"

He turned to look at Konowa and the Suljak, the telescope still pressed to his eye, before he blinked and lowered it. "This makes no sense. We cleared the islands. I have more of the fleet landing along the coast from Nazalla all the way west to Tel Martruk. There's no way Her forest should have gotten through."

The Suljak lost some of his calm. "Another fleet! You did not tell me your fleet was traveling so far west, Your Highness. An oversight, no doubt? And yet even with this fleet the Empire has proven unable to defend its people, laying them bare without defenses to this coming monstrosity." He paused and regained his composure. "No matter, the Shadow Monarch is known here, as are Her failed attempts to gain the Red Star in Elfkyna. You both defeated Her with this very regiment. This night, the warriors of the deep desert stand guard, and they are twenty thousand strong. Bring what She may, we will prevail."

The Prince was back to looking at the looming ebony forest and the storm, mumbling about how huge the storm was. Konowa was certain the number of desert warriors the Suljak referred to was inflated, but something else was bothering him. "By the looks of that storm, Her forest could be hundreds of thousands strong. And where there are blood trees, there are the creatures it pulls from the depths. That's a lot of faith to place in your warriors, Suljak. And what of Kaman Rhal? You don't seem overly concerned about that possibility."

The Suljak smiled. "You forget, Major, that whatever else Kaman Rhal is, he is first and foremost of the Hasshugeb. If he has returned, he will no more let the Shadow Monarch take the Jewel of the Desert than will you."

Konowa leaned back in his saddle. He looked to the Prince, expecting him to jump in, but he'd let his camel stray several yards away. Prince Tykkin was absolutely fixated by what he saw through his telescope. "You think you can use the power of Kaman Rhal?" Konowa asked.

The Suljak leaned forward. "A question equally pertinent to you, yes? The Shadow Monarch is an enemy to us both. Kaman

Rhal's power can be harnessed." The Suljak's eyes gleamed. "Major, I should know . . ."

The truth hit Konowa hard. "You . . . called him back. You called back the power of Kaman Rhal."

The Suljak bowed slightly. "Power is power, Major. I knew the Empire would come when the first Star returned. I had to prepare for any contingency. Our warriors are brave, but they are no match for the Empire, not yet. So I dug deep . . . and I found the threads of something long lost . . . and I began to pull them back."

Konowa raised a fist covered in frost fire. The urge to reach out and kill the Suljak raced through his veins. *The fool! Did he not see how dangerous it was to play with power you didn't understand?* "I lost a soldier because of you. He died in agony on that island." With an extreme effort Konowa unclenched his fist and let the frost fire die.

The Suljak held out his hands, his eyes wide. "I will defend my people. I have done my best to keep power contained, but it is challenging even for me. But do not worry—the creature that killed your soldier was the only one that escaped my grasp. Even then, it only ventured across the water because it sensed the coming of Her forest. Now that Her forest has invaded this land, the creatures will destroy it, no matter how large it grows."

"You mean there are more than one?"

"Hundreds, perhaps thousands by now," the Suljak said.

The casualness with which the Suljak said it made Konowa wonder how much control he really exerted over these monsters. "And Kaman Rhal? Where does he fit in all of this?"

"He doesn't. Major, Kaman Rhal is dead. His power is that of the desert. He only harnessed it and became lost in his avarice— and it cost him his life and everything he possessed. I have not made the same mistake. I simply used enough power to secure the Star and my land. When this is done, the creatures of his power will be returned from whence they came."

"And what if they don't want to go back?"

"Ah, but you see, Major, you have already proven the argument. With the Red Star, you destroyed Her forest. With the Jewel of the Desert, I will do the same to everything not of this time and place."

"The Prince won't stand for this," Konowa said, looking over at Prince Tykkin and realizing he wasn't sure at all what the Prince would think. In a truly horrifying way, this changed absolutely nothing.

The Suljak shrugged. "Perhaps, but it is more likely he will. Why needlessly complicate matters that are already decided? I *will* get the Star, he *will* get his library, and you *will* be reunited with your elves."

Konowa hated the logic of it. "It never works out that way. You should know that by now."

"Oh, but, Major, I do. There are always variables that cannot be foreseen. The Queen is not the only one who plays things deep. You will be a good soldier and follow orders."

"Why would I do that?" Konowa asked.

"Because as long as you do, your world makes sense. Without rules and orders there is only chaos. You broke the rules once, and look where it got you. I do not think you will do so again."

The frost fire came unbidden to Konowa's hands again. "Are you really that certain?"

"Come now, Major, you must understand how affairs of state are conducted. Agreements have already been made. You have but to wait a little longer and you will get what you want."

The fire in Konowa's hands burned colder. The temptation to lash out at the Suljak filled him until he couldn't breathe. He'd been lied to and played for a fool again. A voice somewhere deep within him told him this is what happens when you rush blindly forward without thinking, but that voice got little attention from Konowa.

Slowly, agonizingly slowly, Konowa let the fire die. For now.

"Now you see, Major, that wasn't so hard, was it?"

"No," Konowa lied, "that wasn't hard at all."

TWENTY-EIGHT

Visyna pushed herself as she led the soldiers through the tunnel under the oasis. Twice she thought she caught a glimpse of someone up ahead, but she could never get close enough to determine who or what it was.

"I . . . I need to rest," Teeter said, slowing to a walk. "I'm sorry, but I can't keep this up. We're never going to catch that damned elf anyway, no matter how fast we go."

Visyna slowed as well. She wanted to yell at the soldier, but she knew he was right. She wiped the sweat from her brow and then brought her hands in front of her, beginning to weave the air.

She hissed and stopped. The tips of her fingers burned—the natural order here was toxic. She flexed her fingers for another attempt, but had to stop as the magic stung her again.

"I feel it, too," Hrem said, coming up to stand beside her. His face was red and he was breathing heavily. "Everything is wrong. It's like something's crawling on my skin and I can't get it off."

Zwitty stayed off to one side. "Then why keep going? Where

is it written that we have to risk our necks and play hero? If we stay here, we're safe," Zwitty said, looking around at the tunnel.

"Do what you want," Visyna said, "but I'm going on."

Hrem stood up straight and looked over at Zwitty. "We're all going."

"Wait, did you hear something?" Visyna asked. She held up her hand for silence. Yes, there was definitely something up ahead.

The sound of hammers on muskets being pulled back echoed off the tunnel walls.

Visyna drew her dagger. Hrem and Teeter moved ahead of her, crouching low.

An indistinct shape cast a shadow on the wall up ahead. Something was coming toward them. Visyna gripped her dagger tighter and cursed the air around them. Without being able to weave the natural order, she was useless. In this instance, the soldiers' muskets were far more powerful, despite the perversion of combining wood and metal. Her thoughts immediately turned to Konowa and she almost smiled, but then frowned. He was so full of rage that it was impossible to talk with him. If he couldn't learn to control it she saw no future for him, or them.

"I hear it," Hrem whispered. It was a noise like bone scraping against stone.

Visyna strained to see more. The shape took on more definition, but it made no sense to her. It was too low to the ground to be Tyul. She rotated her wrists and flexed the fingers in her left hand. She would weave if all else failed, no matter how much it hurt.

The scraping noise grew louder.

Visyna let her breath out slowly, aware that she had been holding it. The creature came on as the light from the moss finally revealed Jir dragging part of a skeleton in his mouth.

"It's only J——" Visyna said as Zwitty fired.

The musket blast filled the tunnel. Orange and black flashed before Visyna's eyes, followed by white-hot sparks. She cried out and ducked her head as the sound beat against her ears.

"—old your fire!" Hrem shouted.

Visyna shook her head and looked up.

Jir was lying on the ground. She ran to him, kicking pieces of bone out of the way.

"Oh, Jir."

Tyul's head was screaming in pain. Everything inside the tunnel was wrong. The power coursing through the rock felt like black tar in his lungs. He tried to keep track of Jir, but the bengar seemed unaffected by the magic, and was soon lost from sight. Jurwan chittered in Tyul's ear and the elf reluctantly slowed to a walk. He pressed his hands against the side of his head, but the pressure didn't help.

The floor in front of him showed just the faintest scuff marks arcing out in a curve from the right side of the tunnel wall. Tyul knew little of masonry, but he was an expert tracker, and this was a sign. Jurwan leaped from his shoulder and landed on the wall, clinging to the stones with his tiny claws. He sniffed at the minute cracks between the stones as he crawled over them, until he stopped and bushed his tail.

Tyul stood up and placed a hand on the stone Jurwan was gripping. It depressed a quarter of an inch, and a section of the wall slid open like a door. A new tunnel was exposed, leading away, going deeper into the canyon.

Jurwan jumped off the wall and took a few steps into the opening, then paused and looked back at Tyul. The elf shook his head and pointed down the main tunnel where Jir had gone.

Jurwan squeaked and took a few more steps into the side tunnel. Tyul knew he should follow the bengar and the skeleton, but Jurwan was a wizard.

Tyul took one last look down the main tunnel, then stepped in through the entrance and began following Jurwan.

There wasn't as much glowing moss here, but there was enough. Behind him, the tunnel wall closed back up without a sound.

"Hang on, Ally, hang on," Yimt was saying. Alwyn nodded and tried to keep his focus.

The flames would not go out.

The wagon flew over the sand. The sound of the wheels changed and Alwyn felt shadow. He opened his eyes. They were passing through the opening of the Canyon of Bones. The pain increased. He saw clearer out of his left eye as his right fogged over.

The wagon shook to a stop as the brindos suddenly dug in their hooves. Rallie snapped the reins several times, but the brindos refused to go any farther.

They were stopped among what looked like a pile of bones sticking out of the canyon floor. Huge, curving chunks of the white material rose up at odd angles, some towering more than thirty feet in the air. More lay scattered all about the canyon floor, as if a giant predator had fed here, leaving behind the remains of its kill.

Rallie tied off the reins, stepped down from the wagon, and immediately began to unhitch the brindos.

"What are you doing?" An alarmed Inkermon was jumping down from the wagon. "We'll be stranded here without them."

Rallie kept working at the harnesses. "They aren't going to take us any farther, so this is as far as they go. Baby has a nose for danger, and he's clearly smelled his fill."

Miss Red Owl went to help her. Once they had the animals unhitched, the women took off the brindos' harnesses and Rallie slapped them on the rear. "Take them to safety, Baby, get them out of here."

Baby raised his head and brayed and the other brindos tossed their heads and took off back out of the canyon at full gallop. In moments they were gone, although the sound of their thudding hooves continued to echo off the canyon walls for several seconds after.

"We need to find some cover," Yimt said, reaching out a hand to help Alwyn out of the wagon.

"You'd better not touch me, Sergeant—I don't know what will happen." Alwyn slowly got to his feet, each movement sending new ribbons of pain twisting through his body. He climbed down and steadied himself against the wagon. He shivered with chills as a wave of frost fire surged inside him, then swayed as the heat of the white flame pushed back.

"Hang on, Ally, hang on," Yimt said, reaching out to him, then stopping. "Aw, lad, I wish I knew what to do."

Alwyn tried to smile, but all he could manage was a small nod of his head. He realized Yimt was now more father to him than the stepfather he had grown up with. He was going to miss him.

"Where are we going to hide?" Inkermon asked. He was alternating between peering around rocks and looking back toward the canyon opening. "At least at the oasis we might have held the forest off . . . for a bit."

"Inkermon . . . just keep looking and keep your observations to yourself," Yimt said. "No one said this was going to be easy, but—"

"There's an opening in the rocks over there," Miss Red Owl shouted. Alwyn turned to see where she was pointing. At first all he saw was a thin fissure in the rock, but as he examined it more closely he noticed that a trick of the light made it appear smaller than it really was. A person could easily fit through that gap.

Miss Red Owl started to walk toward it, but Yimt held out his hand.

"Easy. The others chased those skeleton things into a tunnel." He looked around the canyon floor. "This Canyon of Bones seems like just the sort of place a bunch of walking skeletons would be heading to. Scolly, Inkermon, get in there and see if it's clear."

Inkermon took a step back. "Are you mad? You bring us to a canyon filled with bones and now you tell me those hellish skeleton creatures are probably coming here, too? So what, you want us to just stroll in there and poke around?" Inkermon asked.

Yimt stomped the few yards separating him from Inkermon and grabbed the soldier by the front of his tunic, yanking him down until they were eye to eye.

"You can deal with whatever is in that tunnel, or you can deal with me."

Inkermon's mouth opened and closed. He nodded. Yimt released his grasp.

"Hey, there's lights in here," Scolly said from a few feet inside. I can see just fine."

Yimt pointed at Inkermon, then at the opening. Inkermon

kicked at the dirt, but followed after Scolly. Yimt turned to the women. "Let's get you inside. Ally and I will bring up the rear."

Miss Red Owl ducked into the tunnel. Miss Synjyn started to, then stopped and turned. "Yimt, I heard shouting, I think there's something in there!"

"If Inkermon's acting the fool again I'll have his hide."

"It sounds like Scolly," Rallie said.

Yimt looked from the tunnel entrance back to Alwyn, then to Rallie. "Okay, I'm going in. Help Alwyn inside," he said, and ran into the tunnel with his shatterbow at the ready.

Alwyn began to stumble toward the opening when Rallie pulled out a quill and small sheaf of papers from her cloak. She began to draw. Alwyn felt a new power in the air. It was different from the two that were slowly tearing him apart. This was subtle and controlled, like a sculptor precisely chipping away at a block of marble one little piece at a time.

The walls of the canyon shook, and a moment later rocks and dirt tumbled down to bury the entrance. Alwyn expected the entire rock face to come crashing down on top of them, but the slide was focused on just the one small area above the tunnel entrance.

Alwyn turned to Rallie, then looked down at what she had drawn. The canyon wall and rock slide were perfectly illustrated on the page. The lines pulsed with energy. "You . . . you just drew that rockslide."

Rallie lifted the quill from the paper and the power that was in the air vanished. "In my duties as Her Majesty's Scribe, I pride myself on being on the scene as interesting things happen."

Alwyn shook his head. "No, I mean you *drew* it. You *made* it happen."

Rallie took a fresh sheet of paper and placed it on top,

then held the quill above the page. "Let's just say the timing was . . . impeccable."

More pain wracked Alwyn's body. The power of the oath struggled against the white fire. Glimpses of the Shadow Monarch's mountain flashed in Alwyn's mind, interspersed with an endless sea of burning sand. It felt like being immersed in ice, then flame. There was no longer any haven in Alwyn, no place where he could simply be himself. The two warring magics were going to destroy him in their quest to dominate him. Only one could win, but Alwyn knew either way he was going to lose. "Get out of here, Miss Synjyn. I can't hold on."

"Please, dear, call me Rallie." Her quill touched the page and she began drawing. She winced, but then smiled and kept going. "They say knowledge is power, did you know that? Well of course, power is power. A punch in the gut still hurts even if you know it's coming, but if you know it's coming then you can avoid it or at least prepare for it. Do you understand?"

Alwyn shook his head no. The fire in his left eye flared as the black one sparkled with frost. His stump bled as the magic in the wood thrashed and tightened around it as it fought to survive. The power of the white fire was killing the magic in his leg.

"What I'm trying to say is we know the Star is coming, so we need to get ready. I will do what I can to help you until it arrives, but after that I'm afraid it will be up to you."

Alwyn still didn't understand. "Rallie . . . I—" he paused. The pain in his body subsided. He took a shuddering breath and stood up a little straighter. "What did you do?"

Rallie's quill was moving slowly across the page, her hand trembling with the effort. Sweat beaded on her forehead. Alwyn looked down at the page. It was him, but nothing like how he looked now. In the drawing he looked younger, happier. His eyes were normal and he still had both legs.

"I'm simply using my powers of observation to assist you. You are a good man, Alwyn Renwar, and that is what I'm drawing. I want you to remember that. *You are a good man.*"

Alwyn wasn't sure what to say. "I don't know, Rallie. I don't know what I am anymore." He walked over to a rock and sat down as she continued to draw. Every muscle ached, and his vision kept going in and out of focus, but the pain was manageable.

"If life was easy, everyone would be doing it," Rallie said, trying to chuckle. The effort clearly hurt her. She bent over the paper and pressed even harder with her quill.

"I can't ask you to do this for me," he said, taking a breath and standing back up. He wobbled and a few of the limbs in his wooden leg snapped. "This is my burden. I want this to end, Rallie, I just want it all to end."

Rallie pressed so hard that the paper tore. Alwyn felt a sharp stab of pain. "I'm sorry, dear, I slipped." She lifted her head briefly to look at him, then looked to the sky. "It won't be much longer now. You're going to need your strength soon, and that I can give you." With her other hand she reached into her cloak and pulled out a cigar. She placed it in her mouth and took in a breath as the cigar lit itself. She smiled and looked back at her drawing. "I really should give these up one of these days."

The ground beneath their feet vibrated. Alwyn used his musket to balance himself. "What was that?"

The canyon floor continued to shake. The bleached-white trunks trembled and began to work themselves loose. Cracks opened in the canyon walls all around them. Cloaked figures began emerging from the cracks.

"Rallie," Alwyn hissed. He clenched his fists in preparation. A skeleton turned to look at them, then walked farther down the canyon floor, where it disappeared from view behind a rocky outcropping. More figures emerged, and many of them carried bodies, or parts of bodies, and all headed in the same direction. None came toward them.

"Why aren't they attacking us?" Alwyn asked, slowly unclenching his fists.

Rallie pushed her hood all the way off her head and took another quick look to the sky. A deep blue tinge was forming above the canyon. She turned back to her drawing. "They no longer have any need. The Star is almost here, and their work is almost done."

"Work, what work?"

Rallie flipped the page and began a new sketch. Alwyn lost his breath for a moment as the page turned over. He looked down at her drawing. He recognized the arrival of a Star in the night sky, but there was something below that forming on the canyon floor that he couldn't make out. The lines Rallie drew kept shattering and reforming in an erratic pattern. "What is that thing?"

Her Majesty's Scribe's quill never stopped moving as she looked up at Alwyn. "That, my dear boy, is my next big story."

TWENTY-NINE

Konowa fumed as they came upon the oasis. The sun had almost dipped below the horizon and a cold wind was blowing in from the north. The Suljak's lies and gambits made his head spin. He tried to marshal an argument in his mind that would sway the Suljak to reconsider, then tried to think of a way to convince the Prince to ignore the agreement—he even considered using brute force to beat the old man into submission—but he knew with every second that it no longer mattered.

Her forest was huge. *Sarka har* stretched as far as the eye could see, and his elven eyes could see far. Everything to the north was a sea of seething black death. For centuries the elves of the Long Watch had kept this horror confined to a mountain peak. Even in Elfkyna it had amounted to only a few thousand at most, but now, it covered hundreds of miles. Konowa looked to the sky and found himself wishing he believed in a god so that he could pray. He tried anyway. "If anyone's listening, it's about bloody time you got off your damn cloud and did something useful."

Just a few thousand yards away the lead elements of the Hasshugeb warrior army stood and waited. They looked impressive on top of their camels and seemed calm, despite the wall of black death approaching. The Prince and the Suljak rode around the oasis and toward the Suljak's army. Konowa chose to stay back with the Iron Elves. He looked around, and on spying Color Sergeant Aguom motioned for him to come over. The sergeant jogged over and saluted. Konowa leaned over the side of the camel while trying to keep his balance.

"Get the men into the oasis, but I want them pushed right to the far edge and ready to march out the other side. We will not be staying here tonight."

Sergeant Aguom looked over his shoulder at the approaching forest, then back to Konowa. "I hope it's a bigger Star this time."

Konowa could only nod. He dismissed him and guided his camel through the oasis. Signs of battle littered the ground. There were no bodies, but he wasn't certain that was a good thing. He got to the other side of the oasis and then watched as the regiment marched through. Satisfied, he urged his camel forward.

The Shadow Monarch's forest had come to the very edge of the right shoulder of the Canyon of Bones while the massed riders of the desert tribes had reached the left. Neither had yet engaged the other, but the gap between them would close within the hour. If Konowa was going to get the Iron Elves in the canyon it had to be now.

The Prince and the Suljak were talking with some of the Hasshugeb warriors. Konowa tried to urge his camel forward, but the animal jerked to a halt and refused to budge. He cursed and gave it a whack with the flat of his hand, but the animal would not move. The other camels began to act oddly as their riders fought to keep them under control. A moment later the sand around them geysered into the air and scaly beasts emerged, their jaws alight with white fire.

"My *drakarri*," the Suljak said. He dismounted from his camel and walked toward the creatures.

The *drakarri* followed his movements, their heads moving in perfect time with his steps. White flame dribbled from their jaws and spilled onto the sand, where it fused the grains into blackened glass.

The Suljak turned and looked at Konowa. The acorn against Konowa's chest crackled with frost as the two locked eyes.

"I told you, Major, that politics is a messy business! But in the end, power is what rules the day. And this," he said, sweeping his hands to encompass the *drakarri* arrayed before him, "is my power! This is the power of the desert!"

The Suljak turned back to the creatures and began to speak. The wind picked up, and sand particles swirled into the air. The voice the Suljak spoke with was in a tongue that grated on Konowa's ears. He knew without understanding that it was an ancient language. Hundreds more of the creatures clawed their way out of the sand. As each breached the surface it turned to look at the Suljak. His voice rose higher, and with it the wind began to howl. Konowa raised an arm to protect his face from the wind-whipped sand.

As one, the creatures turned and began to move toward the forest. They scrabbled forward on their stubby legs, their jaws snapping in anticipation. Frost fire engulfed the leading *sarka har* as the sand around them froze over.

It was nightmare against nightmare.

Then the *drakarri* stopped.

The Suljak's voice rose above the howl of the wind, his arms high as he commanded the creatures. The *drakarri* started to move against Her forest again, then turned around and began crawling back toward the Hasshugeb warriors.

Ice crystals of warning seared Konowa's senses as a new voice carried on the wind. It was coming from the Canyon of Bones. This voice rasped the very air, and Konowa shuddered. He sensed commotion in the ranks and turned. "Steady! Steady, lads."

The Suljak shouted again, but the creatures were no longer listening. Their heads were cocked as the voice from the canyon called to them. Their jaws snapped open and closed as more white flame dripped down to splatter on the sand.

Then the voice from the canyon ripped through the air like a cannon volley.

The *drakarri* shrieked, and half of them wheeled and charged toward Her forest. The others charged at the Hasshugeb warriors.

"No!" the Suljak screamed, as white fire began to arc among the assembled warriors. The Hasshugeb muskets crackled to life. Konowa called up the frost fire and smacked the camel again. This time it moved.

He held on as it galloped across the sand toward the Prince. When they got close, Konowa pulled back on the reins and shut his eyes. Miraculously, the camel stopped, perhaps finding some small comfort in being around others of its kind.

The Suljak was slowly walking backward, shaking his head. "No, this cannot be. I command the power! The Shadow Monarch cannot be this strong so far from Her mountain." He used the ancient language again, but the *drakarri* paid him no heed. They were listening to a voice much, much older.

Konowa looked around them. Men screamed and *sarka har*

flailed as the white fire scorched the sand and everything on it. "Isn't it obvious? You didn't just call back Kaman Rhal's power— you got *him* back as well!"

"No, that's not possible. The power flows through me, I command it," the Suljak said, looking down at his own hands. He raised his eyes and pointed at Konowa. "You! You've done this. It's your corrupting influence that has caused this to happen."

"The major is a loyal officer, and I will not have him slandered," the Prince said, striding forward to come between the Suljak and Konowa. "Get those abominations under control."

The Suljak glared at Konowa. "You conspire with the Shadow Monarch. Before your arrival my control was complete. I underestimated you and the power you wield, but I will not make that mistake again." He brought both hands together and closed his eyes. Wind roared around the three of them as the sand beneath their feet began to shift.

Konowa reached inside himself for the frost fire, but the power of the Suljak's magic made it difficult to bring it forth. He tried again, but all he could manage was a small flicker.

Prince Tykkin glanced over at Konowa, then at the Suljak. Without a word, the Prince cocked his right fist back and slammed it into the Suljak's face. The old man flew backward and landed on his back. The wind died down.

"In light of current circumstances, our agreement," the Prince said, "is null and void."

The voice from the canyon grew louder. The white fire on the desert floor burned brighter. The sound of screaming intensified.

Konowa looked at the Prince, and for a moment couldn't find the words. Finally, he turned back to the Suljak, who was slowly climbing to his feet. He was no longer a powerful manipulator, but a scared old man. "It looks as if your game wasn't deep enough," Konowa said. He spat the words, unable to keep his disgust in check. He turned back to the Prince. "Once that gap closes we have no chance of breaking through, sir. We need to move now while there's enough chaos out there."

The Prince studied the gap. "Can we get them through?"

Konowa nodded. He'd get them through if he had to kill every living and dead thing in his path. *The time for gambits was over.* "Yes, but we have to go now."

The Suljak looked at them both, a mad light in his eyes. "We are still part of the Empire. It is your duty to save my people. I . . . I command you to save my people! Call forth your soldiers and rid the desert of these defilers! You brought all of this upon us. You must fix it!" His calm demeanor was gone. In its place was something Konowa recognized all too clearly.

"Your people's only hope is if we get to the Star before anything else," Konowa said. "They can't get to the canyon now, and Her forest is held at bay, but that won't last for long."

The Suljak watched the battle and wrung his hands. "The Jewel of the Desert is returning. It must be protected. It cannot fall into the wrong . . . hands."

"It won't, if you get your men out of here," Konowa said. "If they stay on the field of battle, they die." He grabbed the Suljak by his robes and spun him around. "Look at what's happening. I don't give a damn about how messy politics might be. This is a battle now. The time for the finer points of manipulation are over. This is slaughter!"

White fire burned in patches all over the sand, marking the

bodies of fallen Hasshugeb warriors. Riderless camels galloped past in fear, some on fire. They left ghostly images of flame and terror on Konowa's mind as they disappeared into the night. A few *sarka har* snaked forward until their branches were able to stab down at the *drakarri* spitting fire at them. White and black flame exploded wherever the two powers met. The space between became an inferno of swirling tremendous magics. Men screamed, animals shrieked and howled, and over it all a voice of ancient power drove the fire creatures to ever greater frenzy.

"You are still the Suljak of the Hasshugeb," the Prince said, his face white as he watched the destruction unfold. "Do *your* duty and save your men. I will determine the fate of the Star later."

Konowa shook the Suljak. "Tell your men to fall back from the canyon opening. If they keep dying where they are we're going to have a hard time walking over all the bodies," Konowa said, knowing it was cruel and not giving a damn.

The Suljak began to shake. "This is not how it was supposed to happen. It was planned so well. It was . . . beautiful."

The musket fire of the Hasshugeb warriors grew more controlled, but Konowa doubted that would last for long. The voice from the canyon directing the *drakarri* kept growing louder. Thoughts of controlling that voice vanished from Konowa's mind.

They'd be lucky to survive.

"And this is now!" Konowa shouted. "Order your warriors to fall back. You can worry about your precious plans later."

The Suljak looked up, his eyes glazed over. "The Star, the Star is all that matters."

"Do as the major says, Suljak! Get your men away from here

and the Star will be saved," the Prince shouted. His fist was clenched again for another punch. Konowa did not reach out to hold his arm.

"I . . . I will order my men back," the Suljak said. "We will regroup in the desert."

"Go to hell," Konowa said.

The Suljak climbed back onto his camel, snapped the reins, and began to trot toward the battle. Several tribal leaders rode out to meet him. The conference was quick. The leaders galloped their camels back to their men and began shouting orders.

"Major, we have our opening," the Prince said. "Let's go get that Star."

The bengar lay crouched on the tunnel floor. There was a long gash on his right shoulder where the musket ball had torn across his fur and skin. Visyna put away her dagger and moved closer. Jir's ears were pressed back on his head and his jaw was open in a snarl. Visyna reached out a hand toward the bengar, but Jir uttered a low, rumbling growl from deep within his chest.

"Easy, Miss Tekoy," Hrem said, now standing beside her. She hadn't heard him approach, but her ears were still ringing from the musket shot. "He might be the major's pet and our mascot, but Jir's still a wild animal."

"Is he okay?" Zwitty shouted from way back in the tunnel. Visyna turned and saw he was frantically reloading his musket.

"It's just a scratch, but you could have killed him."

"I saw the skeleton so I took the shot," Zwitty said. He finished reloading and walked slowly toward them. Teeter and Hrem both glared at him.

Jir's growl grew louder when he spied Zwitty. Visyna turned

back to the bengar and tried to calm him. "It's all right, Jir, it was only an accident. Zwitty's sorry, aren't you?"

"Trying to save our lives is what I was doing," Zwitty muttered. "How was I supposed to know he'd be coming back with half a skeleton?"

"Tell Jir you're sorry," Hrem said, pointing at Zwitty.

"What, why? He's just a stupid animal."

Jir showed more teeth and the fur on his back rippled as his muscles tensed.

"You want to be his dinner?" Teeter asked. "Just apologize already."

"Okay, okay," Zwitty said. He held his musket across his body as he looked at Jir. "I'm sorry I tried to save us all by shooting at the skeleton and you got in the way."

Hrem shook his head. "Were you ever human?"

Zwitty looked as if he wanted to shout something, but he just turned and walked a few paces away, muttering under his breath. Jir relaxed and his ears slowly came up as his fur went down. Visyna reached out a hand and this time he didn't growl. She gently rubbed his head then smoothed his fur down to the wound. Blood matted the fur, but it would heal on its own. She would have woven some magic to help it heal, but not here.

"Anything in this tunnel heard that shot," Hrem said. "We'd best keep moving. Tyul might be just ahead."

"At least there's one less skeleton to worry about," Teeter said, trying to sound jovial.

Visyna hoped he was right. She followed Hrem as he led off. Jir stayed beside her. The bengar licked at his shoulder a few times and favored his right front paw, but for having been inches from death he was in remarkably good shape.

Hrem stopped and held up his hand. Jir tilted his head to one side as if listening. Visyna shook her head and strained to hear what had gotten their attention.

"I can't hear anything, but I smell fresh air, as if a door just opened," Visyna said. She smelled something else, something familiar. Pipe clay. Gunpowder. *There were more soldiers in the tunnel!*

"Hrem, there are so———" she started to say, but the rest of the sentence caught in her throat. Soldiers lined the tunnel ahead of them. They were still cast in shadow so that Visyna could not make out their faces, but their outline was unmistakable.

One of the soldiers stepped forward until he was visible in the dim glow. He held a musket in his hands and had it leveled at his hip ready to fire. Visyna's eyes widened. "You!"

Private Takoli Kritton smiled. He was still dressed in the uniform of an Iron Elf. A large, black blade with a distinctive kink in it hung from a leather thong on his cartridge belt. Visyna recognized it as Sergeant Arkhorn's drukar.

"Imagine finding you all here," Kritton said, his voice smooth and calculating. "I'm afraid I'm going to have to ask you to come with me. The way ahead is blocked."

"Tyul is up there, Kritton," Hrem said, looking past the elf at the soldiers behind him. He was squinting, trying to make them out. "Some skeleton demons have the body of one our men. They're trying to take his soul! We have to go after him."

Kritton went pale. "Be thankful they only have the one. The creatures you speak of are the long-dead remains of Kaman Rhal's army. They started gathering up the dead again shortly after the first Star reappeared in Luuguth Jor, but that is none of our concern."

"How can you say that?" asked Visyna.

"Because for too long the Empire dictated what was right and wrong, but no longer." Kritton leered at her. "Don't look so surprised, isn't that what you're always saying? Just like Elfkyna, there's a power growing in this desert, and it is welcome to this wasteland."

"You sound well informed for someone who's been on the run," Visyna said, glaring at the elf.

"I've had my eyes opened to a lot of things," Kritton said. "Knowledge is a powerful tool, especially if you know how to use it."

"What are you talking about?" Visyna asked. "You ran away in Elfkyna when these men stayed and fought. And now you stand here as if nothing has happened."

Anger flashed in Kritton's eyes, but he kept his voice calm. "Much has happened. Come with me and I'll show you."

"You're in no position to be giving orders anymore," Hrem said, taking a step forward. "You're a deserter, or have you forgotten the forest in Elfkyna when you saved your own miserable skin and left the rest of us to die?"

"We're all dead anyway if something isn't done," Kritton said, his lips white with anger. "I ran because I saw a chance to get away and make a difference. I wasn't trying to save my life, I was trying to save all of us from this abomination," he said, taking a hand off his musket and grabbing at his uniform above his heart.

"You had the right idea," Zwitty said, inching forward. "See, I told the lot of you desertin' was the smart move."

If Zwitty had expected a sign of approval from Kritton he didn't get it. "I did not desert!" Kritton shouted. "We are here to set things right. We will no longer follow the orders of those who deceive and dishonor us!"

Visyna stepped forward before anyone else could speak. "Who is 'we'?"

Kritton looked over his shoulder and whispered something. The soldiers behind him came forward, their muskets pointing at Visyna and Hrem. Visyna gasped. Every soldier had a shorn left ear tip while the right still had its point.

"We," Kritton said, a look of fierce pride on his face, "are the *true* Iron Elves."

No one said a word. A tear came to Visyna's eye. These were Konowa's men, his brothers. She looked at them all, seeking to understand who they now were. All still wore the uniform of the Calahrian Imperial Army. The cloth was tattered and worn, but their muskets gleamed with care. Each stood at least six feet tall, their frames thinner than Konowa's, not as broad across the shoulders. Gaunt faces looked back at her. None sneered, none smiled. She looked into their eyes and understood why.

These elves were in pain. Enormous pain. She sensed it without needing to weave the air. They had been abandoned and dishonored, and none of it had been their fault.

"Listen to me, all of you. Whatever Kritton has told you is a lie. Konowa did not desert you. The reason we are here now is you! He has come back for you. We've all come here for you," she said, pointing around her at the other soldiers. "Even now your regiment goes to battle. Go to Konowa and help him. He needs you."

Kritton's laugh echoed off the tunnel walls. "He needs us? What about when we needed him? Where was he then? No, Miss Tekoy, we will not be fooled again. Our honor will be restored, but it will not be by him."

Visyna cast her gaze across the elves in front of her, searching for a sign that some of them, or even one, would listen to her. Each elf met her gaze, their eyes revealing what they would not say. She refused to give up.

"You know this is wrong! I can see it. This isn't who you are. No one can take away your honor. Being banished here was terrible, I understand that, but only you hold your fate in your hands. Only you—"

"Enough!" Kritton roared. "You will not lecture us again. We have already regained our honor, and you're going to see how. Now move," he ordered, motioning her toward the tunnel entrance.

Visyna started to make one more plea, but Hrem reached out a hand and touched her arm.

"Forget it, Miss Tekoy. They aren't the elves we thought they were."

Visyna could only nod. As she stepped into the side tunnel the only consolation she could muster was that she was glad Konowa wasn't here to witness what his elves had become.

THIRTY

Konowa turned and looked at the regiment. Already they had edged out onto the sand. Death stood just a short distance away yet still the sergeants had to restrain the men from lunging forward. They knew battle was upon them, and they were ready. Frost fire limned them as darkness grew.

It was time.

Konowa and the Prince trotted their camels back to the oasis and brought them to a halt in front of the column. Konowa looked to the Prince, who nodded. Konowa cleared his throat. "Iron Elves . . . shoulder arms!" As one, they picked up their muskets in their right hands and threw them across their chests. Frost fire arced from bayonet to bayonet as they moved through the air. Each soldier caught it with his left, cradling the butt of the musket in his palm and pressing the musket against his left shoulder.

"Color Party will keep the Colors low until we are through the gap." Konowa knew that without the order the Color Party would hoist the flags high, their pride overcoming their instinct for survival. They would all be targets soon enough, but Konowa didn't want to lose the Color Party through sheer foolhardy bravery.

"The regiment will march in column . . . by the center . . . march!" A drummer with the 3rd Spears immediately set up a rhythm to keep everyone in time. Konowa steered his camel toward the young boy. "When you see me raise my saber, then drop it, I want you to pick it up to double time."

The drummer nodded and kept up his pace. Konowa trotted his camel back to the front of the column and then out past it to where the Prince and Viceroy Alstonfar waited. "I suggest you both get to the middle of the column. It'll be safest there."

The Prince looked toward the battle, then at Konowa. "You're right, but I won't. These are my men, and the only way to lead is from the front."

"Your Highness, Major Swift Dragon is right," the Viceroy said. "You are the future King of the Calahrian Empire. You must be protected."

Prince Tykkin smiled and slapped the side of his camel with his scabbard. The animal brayed and went down to its knees and the Prince dismounted. Konowa and the Viceroy followed suit. "I shall lead them on foot," the Prince said, adjusting his tunic and reaching up to push his shako a little tighter onto his head.

Konowa knew he should object, but a part of him admired the Prince for this. It was foolish, needlessly reckless, and the men would see it and their chests would swell and their eyes would glint and woe be to the enemy that stood astride their path.

"Go, Pimmer," the Prince said, reaching out and placing a hand on the Viceroy's shoulder. "Get yourself back there and try not to be too big a target."

The Viceroy licked his lips nervously and then shook his head.

"Respectfully, no. I am the Viceroy of this territory, and whatever else people might think of me, it will not be said that this day I added coward to the list. My place is here, and if you don't like it, I suggest you take it up with the Queen next time you see her."

The Prince stood with an ever-widening grin on his face, looking at the Viceroy before turning to Konowa. "I do believe, Major, that I have just been told to go stuff myself."

Konowa smiled. "Actually, sir, I think it's a bit more accurate to say Pimmer has instructed you to get stuffed, but close enough."

The sound of marching boots heralded the front of the column. "Well then, gentlemen, we shall lead this regiment into the gap and let nothing stand in our way. To the Star!"

Konowa and the Viceroy drew their sabers, and all three raised them in the air. "To the Star!" Boots crunched over sand and rock with an inexorable beat. The entire regiment took on a slight lean as it anticipated the fall of the saber. Konowa let his saber fall.

The drumbeat sped up and the regiment shouted. The men began to march faster, keeping time with the drum. The cannons wheeled to the fore, the mule drivers cracking their whips to keep the animals in check.

Ahead of them, the battle raged. To the left, the warriors of the Hasshugeb were slowly falling back. They had formed a ragged line several hundred yards wide, firing their muskets in sporadic volleys at the rampaging *drakarri* spitting their deadly fire. Several of the creatures rushed forward, breaking the line and wreaking absolute havoc among the panicked Hasshugeb. White flames spiked twenty feet into the air as warriors were consumed in the supernatural furnace.

The sound of the Suljak's voice cut through the din and the fire died down. More musket fire ripped the night air and several *drakarri* fell. It was just enough of a respite to allow the Hasshugeb to reform their line and continue in as orderly a retreat as they could manage.

Over on the right flank it was a different story. The *sarka har* slashed and shrieked as they pushed forward against the white fire. The trees were actually tearing themselves apart in an effort to kill the *drakarri* by whipping their branches around with such force that the limbs broke free and sailed through the air like spears.

Konowa had hoped Her forest would be contained by Kaman Rhal's creatures, but the blood trees were still gaining ground. A shadowy figure at the edge of Her forest wielded a lance of pure frost fire that none of the fire creatures could withstand. Wherever it moved, frost fire overwhelmed the *drakarri* and left them gutted husks.

"Her Emissary," Konowa spat.

The Prince and the Viceroy said nothing. It occurred to Konowa then just how remarkable it was that both men were marching beside him. Neither the Prince nor the Viceroy were bound by the Blood Oath of the Iron Elves. They did not have the power of the frost fire burning within them, yet they did not flinch as the Iron Elves marched closer to the fray.

They approached to within five hundred yards of the canyon opening. The Prince raised his saber again and waved it back and forth, then brought it down. The regiment halted. The drummer ceased his drumming as boots thudded to a halt in the sand. The sounds of battle washed over the regiment as it stood, waiting.

The Prince and the Viceroy walked back toward the column while Konowa strode several paces away on its right flank. He then turned and faced the regiment. "Colors to the center, 3rd Spears to the right and left flanks . . . the regiment will form two rows in

line . . . now!" Despite the horror taking place in front of the column, it spread out with smooth precision, each soldier taking measured steps as he found his place. In moments, the Iron Elves
stretched out across the sand in two neat rows facing the canyon.

"Nine-pounder cannons to the right flank, six-pounder to the
left . . . deploy!" Whips cracked and wheels creaked as the gun
crews brought their guns up to the line. The cannons were quickly
unhitched and the mule teams taken back behind the line while the
gun crews rushed to get their guns set for firing. Cannonballs and
powder charges were unloaded from limbers as the gun commander
of each cannon began sighting down the barrel and adjusting the
elevating screw.

Konowa glanced toward the canyon. A blue light was beginning to fill the sky just inside the opening between the two rocky
shoulders. The way forward was littered with burning bodies. Fire
creatures dashed back and forth spitting white flame while musket
fire popped. The *sarka har* continued to grow, pushing the boundary
of the forest ever closer to the canyon opening. The Iron Elves were
going to have to move fast.

"Cannons . . . on my command . . . fire!"

Round shot hurtled out of the three cannon barrels and arced
across the night sky toward the mayhem ahead. The shots fell short,
but this was not a bad thing. The iron balls bounced low over the
sand, smashing through anything that stood in their way. A *drakarri*
exploded in a flash of white that temporarily turned night into day.
Sarka har were cut down by the dozen, their trunks shorn in two by
the shot.

Round after round roared from the cannons and the troops
watching cheered as the path ahead was cleared. All too soon, however, the last shot left the barrels and silence reigned across the line

of Iron Elves. The smoke from the cannons drifted lazily up into the sky and once more the voice of battle swept over them.

"Regiment . . . make ready!"

The muskets of the front-row men dropped from their shoulders and came to rest at their hips. Those in the back rank brought their muskets across their chest to port.

Konowa stayed to the side, raising his musket again. Frost fire flared along the length of the blade.

"By the left . . . march!"

Every soldier stepped forward and the Iron Elves began the march toward the canyon. The drummer picked up the beat again.

Fire creatures turned to face the regiment, their jaws opening to reveal the furnaces that burned inside.

"Steady!"

Konowa sensed a cold fury from the *sarka har* and saw Her Emissary begin to angle the forest toward the Iron Elves. The regiment continued its steady pace, closing the distance with measured steps. Whatever fear the soldiers felt was suppressed by the proximity of the soldier to either side of him. They were one, and they would live or die as one.

He took a quick look to where the 3rd Spears were lined up, wondering too late if the terror of this night was too much for men not bound by an oath such as that of the Iron Elves. He could see immediately that he needn't have worried. The soldiers of the 3rd Spears were inching their way forward by taking longer strides, so that they were making a mess of the line. More than one sergeant was yelling at them to hold to the pace. The soldiers' eyes were wide and intent on the battle ahead of them. While the tips of their swordlike bayonets did not sparkle with frost fire, there was a fierceness in their stance that imbued them with a power no magic could ever fully replicate. These were warriors, and they would taste blood this night.

Already, the gap cleared by the cannon fire was beginning to close up again. Konowa knew it was now or never.

"Regiment . . . halt!" Again boots crashed down on the ground and dust swirled up around them. The rear rank took one extra half step forward and to the right, interlocking the two rows so that every soldier had a clear shot to the front. "Front rank . . . prepare to volley . . . fire!"

The front row of the Iron Elves vanished in a cloud of smoke as musket balls spat forth. They tore through the creatures with satisfying violence, but more surged from the sand to take the place of the fallen.

"Second rank . . . prepare to volley . . . fire!"

Before the smoke had cleared, Konowa was racing forward. The Prince and the Viceroy, breaking all tradition and ignoring common sense, came through the double line to join Konowa out front. Viceroy Alstonfar's breath whistled like a kettle on the boil, but he did not slow down.

"By column . . . the regiment will march . . . now!"

Color Sergeant Salia Aguom strode forward with the Colors as the two lines fell into place behind them. Screams burst from the forest as the Iron Elves began to enter the gap. The fire creatures spat fire in front of their advance, but Konowa had expected this.

The acorn against his chest grew frigid and then the frost fire roared to life in his hands. Shadows emerged from the darkness and kept pace with the regiment, shielding it in a black wall of flame as white fire lanced and arced across the sky. The opening into the canyon was clear. Only a hundred yards to go. The sky above the canyon grew to a deep, pulsing blue. Konowa knew it was time.

He raised his saber in the air. The Prince did the same. "Regiment . . ."

The Iron Elves roared. The Colors shot proudly into the air, unfurling and blowing full.

"Charge!"

Tyul followed Jurwan as the wizard scampered along the stone floor. He kept looking over his shoulder to see if Tyul was following. Tyul kept pace, though the pain from the power flowing through the rock weighed him down until it felt like walking through water.

The floor became easier to see, and Tyul realized they were approaching an opening. Jurwan continued without slowing and disappeared into the light. Tyul hurried as fast as he could, drawing his oath dagger and shielding his eyes as he stepped out from the tunnel. He heard the language of his tribe called out to him and he relaxed. Tyul lowered his arm and tried to understand what he saw. Dozens of elves stood before him, all wearing the uniform of the Calahrian Empire. Their shorn left ears identified them immediately, but that wasn't what left Tyul stunned as they gathered around him and escorted him away.

He hadn't entered a room at all—he had set foot in the deep forest in the Hyntaland.

He was home.

THIRTY-ONE

Visyna grabbed hold of Jir's neck as she and the soldiers were escorted by Kritton and the elves through the side tunnel. With every step Visyna felt the ancient power that resided here. They walked in silence, and Visyna lost track of time as they went. No one talked. The air was heavy with power, and worked to stifle any conversation. Finally, the way ahead lightened, and the group was led out into a room so large Visyna could not see its far end.

She gaped at what she saw. Pillars carved from the very rock rose to the ceiling hundreds of feet above. Hundreds upon hundreds of alcoves dotted the walls. In them Visyna could see endless rows of books, scrolls, parchments, and more lining the shelves. The main floor was a sea of artifacts. Brass, ivory, marble, glassware, rich brocades, bundles of tapestries, gems, gold coins and jewelry, and treasures Visyna couldn't begin to comprehend. Yet that wasn't the most startling find. In the distance, she saw a huge cluster of trees.

There was a forest growing within the edifice.

Farther on there appeared to be a lake. The water rippled as if a light breeze were playing upon it. Visyna's hair fluttered across her eyes and she realized there really was a breeze.

It made absolutely no sense, yet there they were.

"Welcome," Kritton said, "to the Lost Library of Kaman Rhal."

"It's really true," Visyna said, looking around her as the others did the same. Now she noticed more of the elven soldiers of the original Iron Elves. They moved among the alcoves carrying large bundles. They were in a hurry, grabbing up armfuls of books and scrolls, running them out to large tables set up in the middle of the library, and placing them there, where a group of dwarves were sorting them into different piles. Wagons pulled by camels were neatly lined along one side of the tables. *They were loading a caravan inside the library.*

A dwarf overseeing the operation looked their way and came over.

"Griz Jahrfel!" Hrem said, recognizing the dwarf.

"We meet again," Griz said, bowing when he saw Visyna. "My lady, gentleman. I see you've discovered our little hideaway." There was genuine pride in his voice.

"But how, how did you find this?" Visyna asked.

Griz winked at her. "Legends and myths aren't what they used to be, or so I've been told. The Lost Library was never really all that lost. The sandstorm that buried Kaman Rhal and the town of Urjalla was the real tragedy. This library has always been here, it's just that everyone who knew about it died. Well, almost everyone. A few so-called descendants of Kaman Rhal knew of its existence and passed the information down generation to generation until such time that the library would be revealed again." He looked up to the ceiling. "A time like now, with the imminent return of the Jewel of the Desert. The Suljak decided it was well past time to move more of the . . . precious items, knowing the Prince and the Empire were sure to come."

"The Suljak knows? But you're looting the library," Visyna said, still not believing what she was seeing.

Griz nodded. "Aye, you could call it that, but pretty much everything in here was looted from somewhere else at one time or another. You know the old saying: 'You never really own anything—you just loot it until the next bugger comes along and takes it.'"

Visyna turned on Kritton. "This is how you break the oath, by working with thieves? Where is your honor?" *How could these be Konowa's elves?* She looked around her and raised her voice at the other elves. "Konowa is still out there fighting for you! He leads men like these," she said, pointing to Hrem, Zwitty, and Teeter, "against all enemies, including the forces of the Shadow Monarch. And here you skulk like petty criminals. How dare—"

Kritton lunged forward and grabbed her by the throat. His fingers were ice cold as frost fire singed her flesh. "Don't you ever question our honor, wench!"

Jir's fangs and the three muskets of the human soldiers found themselves facing dozens of muskets held by the elves. "Let her go!" Hrem yelled. Black frost coated his bayonet, but it did not flame.

"The magic here is too old and too strong for that to work," Kritton said, still holding Visyna's throat. She could breathe, but each time she did a frigid gale enveloped her lungs in pain. "This is our leverage. The Prince wants the library. It's all he ever talks about. His search for knowledge while the world slowly goes insane. Fine, if he wants knowledge, we have it, and for a price, we'll sell it to him."

"You want to cut a deal?" Hrem asked, his voice incredulous.

"We want our honor restored. We want the stain of our disgrace removed once and forever. It's a simple enough deal. These elves know we were deceived and dishonored by Swift Dragon and the Empire. They had a lot of time to dwell on it. When I told them how the Iron Elves had been reformed without them, well, they saw things as they really are."

"I doubt that, traitor," a booming voice shouted from another tunnel entrance.

Everyone turned as Sergeant Yimt Arkhorn stepped into the library followed by Chayii and the other soldiers. Visyna tried to speak, but Kritton's grip remained firm.

"Let Visyna go, Kritton—you're in enough trouble as it is," Yimt said. His shatterbow was held steady at his hip, both barrels pointing directly at the elf.

Kritton laughed. "Or what? You'll shoot me? We both know you'd kill her, too, if you tried, and there are hundreds of elves here who'll shoot down every one of you a moment later."

"Sergeant, lower the shatterbow and let's talk dwarf to dwarf," Griz said, raising his hands for calm. "This is a complicated situation that requires time to fully understand."

Yimt nodded as if in agreement, then turned and pointed his shatterbow at the wagons being loaded. All work immediately ceased. "Looks like a lot of valuable, and, if I'm not mistaken, flammable things you got there."

"Don't be a fool, Arkhorn," Griz shouted, backing away from

Yimt. "Kritton, let her go. This is insanity. There's enough treasure here for everyone to get whatever they want a thousand times over."

"Not their honor," Yimt said, looking at the elves. "You're still soldiers. Act like it."

Visyna watched even as her vision began to go gray around the edges. The elves looked to Kritton. For the first time she saw doubt enter their eyes. They knew this was wrong. Whatever Kritton had said to them couldn't be stronger than what they knew in their hearts.

"You've lost, Arkhorn," Kritton said. "The rest of you, drop your weapons, now."

He squeezed Visyna's throat even tighter and she convulsed. The room began to swim.

Muskets clattered to the floor. The pressure on her throat lessened and then he released her. She gulped warm air and sank to her knees as Chayii ran over to hold her.

Kritton grabbed his musket in both hands again and pointed it at Yimt. "They know who they are, and they know what's been stolen from them. This," he said, swiveling his head to indicate the library, "is our way of setting things right."

"This," Yimt said, looking at the elves, "is looting. How in blue blazes do you think this restores your honor? Do you think you can buy it back? How much?" he asked, pointing his shatterbow at one of the elves. "How much does it cost to buy an elf these days?"

"You . . . don't . . . understand!" Kritton shouted. "Our honor—"

"Stuff your bloody honor!" Yimt bellowed. "There's more important things to worry about now than your damn hurt feelings!"

Kritton trembled with rage. The elves looked between him and Yimt, but still none made a move.

Yimt stood there for a moment longer, looking as many elves in the eye as would meet his gaze. Finally, he glanced over at Visyna and smiled. "Tell Rallie the secret ingredient in all my stews is love." He pulled the trigger on his shatterbow and sent two explosive darts hurtling across the room. They hit a wagon and exploded, sending flaming debris twenty feet into the air. The camel team startled and broke into a gallop, pulling the burning wagon with them. Fire broke out in a trail behind the runaway camel team as elves and dwarves ran for cover.

"No!" Kritton shouted.

Visyna felt Chayii tense, and they both acted at the same time. Chayii's dagger was already flying through the air as Visyna brought her hands in front of her and began to weave, but they were already too late.

Kritton fired.

Chayii's blade caught Kritton in the shoulder, knocking his musket from his grasp. Visyna tried to create a barrier in the air in front of the musket, but the energy she tried to weave burned her too severely. She cried out and had to stop.

Kritton's shot hit Yimt in the center of his chest. His mouth opened in surprise as the shatterbow slid from his hand and clattered to the floor. He brought his right hand up to his chest and placed it over the wound.

"Bugger," he remarked, then fell face-forward, motionless.

"Yimt!" Scolly cried, running forward toward the dwarf. The elves blocked his path.

Griz strode forward, pulling at his beard. "Damn it all to hell! All right, we're out of here now. This place is going to become a funeral pyre. You," he said, pointing at Kritton. "You get your elves to get this lot out of here. We'll meet at the rendezvous point in three days' time as agreed." With that he took one last look at Yimt's body and turned and hurried off. Flames were climbing the walls around them as thick black smoke billowed from the alcoves.

Kritton motioned to the elves to get them moving.

Tears filled Visyna's eyes, but it wasn't from the smoke. She took one last look at where Yimt lay and then was pushed along toward the far side of the library. The last thing she saw was smoke rolling over the dwarf's body and then a shadowy figure standing where the dwarf had fallen.

THIRTY-TWO

Alwyn grabbed his chest. *Yimt!* Something terrible had just happened to his sergeant and his friend. He tried to focus on the feeling, but it was impossible. The magics continued to war inside him, and now the sounds of battle echoed off the canyon walls as Rallie continued to draw.

Alwyn took in a few deep breaths and began walking toward the outcropping of rock. Above him, the air thrummed with blue light while underneath something ancient and dry clawed to be heard. It was the thing in Rallie's sketch. It was the source of the white fire. He felt that magic in him flaring as the voice grew louder and more insistent. He was being drawn to it, as were the skeletons that continued to flow from cracks in the mountains, carrying their grisly cargo.

"Alwyn."

He turned, expecting Rallie to try to stop him, but she smiled at him instead. "Remember what I said. *You are a good man.*"

Alwyn said nothing. He turned and walked toward the outcropping. It was all going to end. One way or the other, it was all going to end tonight. The white fire burned hotter inside him and the frost fire flared in response. The pain staggered him, but he kept walking. His body was now a pyre of white and black flame, but still he walked. He rounded the outcropping and stood face to face with the heart of the white flame that would break the oath, or kill him.

Above him, the Jewel of the Desert burst into being, its light casting everything in brilliant, blue shadow. The white flame flared in response and clawed into the sky after the Star. Alwyn smiled, opened his arms wide, and ran headlong into the fire.

The Iron Elves tore through everything before them, bayoneting, shooting, clubbing, and burning. The shades of the dead slashed with swords of black frost fire, cleaving fire creatures and *sarka har* with grim precision.

Black ice flowed through Konowa's veins and all the weeks of pent up frustration poured out through his saber. Nothing stood before him. He ran faster, letting loose his anger on anything he found. White flame washed over him in sheets and he grinned and cut the *drakarri* in two, never pausing. A hollow carapace of a scorpion the size of a camel lumbered forth, its pincers clacking. Konowa simply ran between its outstretched claws and drove his saber into its head to the hilt. The beast shuddered and blew apart as frost fire burned it to nothing.

Two more scorpion shells scuttled across the sand, each with a huge stinger four feet long hanging above its head. Before Konowa could attack, soldiers of the 3rd Spears charged the creatures, their sword bayonets flashing as they thrust and hacked at the scorpion bodies.

One soldier was caught between pincers and shorn in two, but the others only redoubled their efforts, as several began climbing up onto the scorpions' backs to hack at them from above. Soon both stingers had been cut from their tails, and the scorpions collapsed under the assault.

Every emotion inside Konowa poured out of him in a flurry of saber strikes. Limbs from *sarka har* snaked toward him. He turned and cut them with vicious strokes of his blade. The trees screamed and writhed. Konowa slashed and burned until no memory and no feeling was left.

For a time, he was only death.

His shoulder muscles screamed as he hacked through more *sarka har*, but it only drove him harder. All the lies and deceptions were vanquished with every slash of the blade and every burst of frost fire. Mountains would have crumbled and seas parted in the face of his fury.

More skeletons marched toward him, and Konowa leaped forward, grabbing the closest grinning skull. White flame brightened in the skull's eyes, then was blown out as black frost shattered it into hundreds of pieces. The rest of the bones clattered to the ground. All around him the shades of the dead scythed through the skeletons, extinguishing their unholy light with cold efficiency.

Konowa ran forward and almost stopped when he saw Rallie with her sketchbook, but he felt the power that surrounded her and knew she was in no immediate danger, so he kept going.

Everything before Konowa became a blur, and he cut things down he barely saw or understood. Nothing was going to stop him. Nothing.

And then no more creatures stood before him. Konowa knew without looking that the regiment was behind him, and he slowed to a walk, his eyes bulging and his lips twisted into a sneer. Frost fire licked between the fingers of his left hand and bathed the saber in his right.

At that moment, Konowa was a god.

His was the only power. Nothing could stop him.

Blue light from the Jewel of the Desert bathed him—he knew he had won. He walked around the outcropping of rock and looked up into the burning eyes of a dragon.

"Oh, sh—"

The flame in Konowa went out. He stared with his mouth wide open.

It was a dragon made of bones.

The dragon opened its jaws wide. Instead of teeth, white flames arced between its upper and lower jaw. More flame burned in the eye sockets of its skull. Deep within its chest a fire of white and black flame twisted and burned, but Konowa had no time to puzzle about that as the dragon stretched out its wings, then stumbled and righted itself as it moved toward him. The bones that made up its body twisted, and several clattered to the ground. Sand swirled around its frame as if helping to keep its hideous form together.

Its jaws opened wider and a blistering torch of white flame issued forth. Konowa rolled out of the way, but some of the soldiers behind him were not so lucky. Konowa turned and saw only ash where several Iron Elves had once stood.

He looked at the drake again and saw that the wings were not yet complete. As Konowa got over his shock he realized that much of the skeleton was incomplete. He looked closer. He recognized partial skeletons of camels and even humans, elves, dwarves, and orcs. But that wasn't the worst of it—the skulls of the dead had flickering white flames in their eye sockets, and their jaws were open.

They were screaming.

Konowa recoiled from the sight. Were some of his elves part of this monstrosity? It then dawned on him that this wasn't Kaman Rhal's work at all. This was the she-drake married to Kaman Rhal. *She* had always been the power behind the throne. The Suljak hadn't called back Kaman Rhal's power at all—he had called back *hers*.

And now it was rebuilding itself as best it could, with the bones of the dead.

As Konowa watched, more skeletons scrambled over the dragon. They were tearing themselves and other bodies apart to construct her wings. Konowa looked up where the Star hovered in the sky above the canyon. If the dragon was able to fly, it would easily seize the Star.

Konowa called on the frost fire and let it course through him. He still had no idea how to attack a creature such as this.

The regiment grouped around him, the staccato fire of muskets chipping away at its bones, but it would take a thousand muskets days before they could whittle it down to nothing. Without cannons they could never shoot it apart.

The night sky blazed with the light of the Star. The metal of the muskets gleamed with it as they fired. Smoke gushed forth from the muzzles, adding red and orange flame to the night. Musket balls flew forth, scything through the bones of the dragon. It made no difference.

There had to be another way.

The dragon lurched forward, the fire in its chest turning whiter as it came on. Konowa felt something, but the air was awash in energy and there was no way to pinpoint anything.

The shades of the dead moved toward the dragon, tearing through its skeleton army. The dragon shook its skull and opened its jaws even wider. Flame poured out like a molten river. Frost fire burst like sparks wherever the river of flame touched a shade. Screaming filled Konowa's head. The shades could not go forward. They began to retreat.

"Attack!" Konowa shouted. Black flame climbed higher around the shades and they moved forward again, but again the white flame pushed them back.

"I command you to kill it!"

The shades of the dead hesitated, even as white flame scoured their ranks. Konowa felt their pain, but there was no choice. *They were already dead.*

A black fissure opened up in the chest bone of the drake, and out stumbled the figure of a man. Before Konowa could determine if this was indeed Kaman Rhal, the figure raised its hands and pointed them at the drake. Black frost fire of a magnitude to rival the white fire of the drake blasted every skeleton crawling over the bone dragon to dust.

The drake staggered on her claws, then righted herself and directed her massive head down at the figure standing below it. It opened its maw wide and white flame gushed forth. The figure disappeared within the column of flame.

When the flame subsided, the dark figure no longer stood before the drake alone. Now there were two. Konowa recognized Her Emissary at once.

"Gwyn?!"

Her Emissary and the figure both raised their hands and throbbing, twisting coils of black flame began to build around them. The air in the canyon reeked with its energy.

Konowa was driven to his knees as the power grew. It pulsed deep inside him until he thought his ribs would surely break. The acorn against his chest became pure, black frost, drawing the last vestiges of heat from his body. His vision began to gray, and he had opened his mouth to speak when the world tore apart in front of his eyes.

The drake reared up on its legs and flapped its now-rebuilt wings once in preparation to seize the Star that hung in the sky, waiting.

Her Emissary and the figure thrust their hands forward, sending a maelstrom of frost fire at the creature.

It blew apart into thousands of shards as the roiling jet of black frost fire seared it to the core.

Konowa was knocked to his back as the blast rolled over him. For a moment he lost all sense of sight and sound. Images flashed before his eyes.

His mother. Yimt. Visyna. The Shadow Monarch. The Star.

His elves.

Sound roared back into his ears, and he realized it was screaming. His vision cleared. The wall of approaching *sarka har* was incinerated by a sheet of obsidian flame. *Drakarri* and the drake's skeleton army of the dead burned with the same black flame. Frost fire was cleansing everything in and around the canyon. Konowa got to his feet. Only the regiment remained, surrounded by frost fire. Among them Konowa spied the survivors of the 3rd Spears. Nearby, the Prince and the Viceroy stood looking in the same direction, their eyes wide. The shades of the dead were gone.

Konowa looked back to where the dragon had stood. Two pillars of frost fire now occupied the space. They reached up into the sky and enveloped the Star, and brought it back down to earth. The flame guttered and went out, revealing the figure of a soldier wearing a caerna and Her Emissary both holding the Star in their hands.

"Renwar!" Konowa said.

"I hope so," Rallie said, emerging from around the rocks and walking toward Alwyn. She stopped a few paces away from him and smiled. She ignored Her Emissary. She was looking at the Star. "You've been away a long time, haven't you?"

The Star gleamed in Renwar's hands.

"Away with you!" Her Emissary shouted. *"The Star is Hers!"*

"Rallie, what's going on?" Konowa asked, taking a few steps forward.

She raised her hand to stop him. "This is no longer our fight, Major."

Konowa took another step. "Renwar! Free the Star! Her Emissary only wants it for Her designs. You must know that."

Private Renwar looked at Konowa with eyes shining blue starlight.

"I . . . I know," he said.

"Then do as I command. We can defeat Her Emissary." Muskets grounded as soldiers began to load another round.

Alwyn raised one hand while keeping the other on the burning Star. "No, you can't defeat him. I . . . I have struck a deal."

Her Emissary laughed. *"You see, Swift Dragon, you were defeated before you began."*

The import of what Renwar was about to do struck home. *Renwar was going to break the oath.* "Wait! Her forest is still out there, and it's growing. And my elves! We came here for them. I have to save them. *We* have to save them. The Star must stay here."

Renwar looked down at the Star. "And who saves us, Major . . . ? Who saves us?"

Konowa's heart ached. He felt the eyes of every soldier on his back. *Why was the answer never simple? Why did it always have to hurt this much?* Tears flowed freely down Konowa's face. Anguish filled every part of him until he couldn't breathe. "I will. I swear it. One day the oath will be broken, but not here, not this way. You know that. A deal with Her Emissary is a fool's deal." He turned to look at the Iron Elves behind him. "You all know that. We can't break the oath, not this way."

"They deserve better," Alwyn said. "We all do. Would it be so wrong to end the suffering? Why not us, Major? Why not end this?"

Konowa wiped the tears from his face. "Because we're soldiers. And before this oath we took another one. We swore to defend the Empire . . . to protect the people we love. That's an oath that we can never break. No matter what the cost. We give our lives so that others may live. It's not fair, but it was never supposed to be."

"That oath is for fools!" Her Emissary said. *"The deal is done."*

Konowa suddenly realized something. "Renwar, you cannot trust him. Why would he allow you to break the oath for all the Iron Elves? Think about it. It's a trick."

Alwyn looked at Her Emissary, then at Konowa. "You misunderstand . . . you both do."

The shades of the Darkly Departed reappeared to stand around Alwyn. Konowa recognized the soldier Meri, and Regimental Sergeant Major Lorian. More and more shades appeared. Their hands reached out to Alwyn, and Konowa heard their cries in his head. *"Save us . . . save us."*

"You're a good man, Alwyn Renwar," Rallie said, her voice radiating calm. "You know what you have to do."

Every soldier in the Iron Elves watched the Star in Alwyn's hand. Their fate rested in a ball of blue light none of them understood, just as it had before with another Star.

"You struck a deal with Her," Her Emissary said.

Alwyn turned and looked at Her Emissary. *"Yes, with Her . . . not with you."* Black frost fire shot from his hands and enveloped Her Emissary in a sheet of twisting black flame. Her Emissary screamed and tried to grab for the Star, but its body was torn away in a gale of flame until nothing remained.

Alwyn calmly looked up, his eyes staring at something only he could see. He lifted the Star up to the sky and let it go. Blue light cascaded outward in waves. Konowa raised his arm to protect his eyes as the light flared like a million suns, then vanished.

When Konowa lowered his arm, a massive tree stretched skyward, its limbs wide and strong. Energy pure and clean radiated from it, washing away the remnants of the ancient power that had poisoned this land for centuries. From deep within the *sarka har,* Her Emissary screamed as the Jewel of the Desert began to push back against Her power. Her Emissary's vice broke with inconsolable rage at Private Renwar's deception, and Konowa wondered, perhaps fear at the rise of a new force.

Konowa wanted to find a way to feel glad, to feel something, but nothing came to him.

"Renwar? What have you done?"

The soldier lifted his head and walked forward. When he emerged, the shades of the dead clustered around. His eyes no longer reflected the blue Starlight, but were now gray. The acorn against Konowa's chest flared in recognition of a power it understood.

"*Alwyn's dead,*" Renwar said, his voice now an eerie match to the former Emissary's.

Konowa shook his head. "I made a vow, and I will keep it. The oath will be broken and one day you will all be free."

"*I know that,*" Renwar said. The shadows continued to hover around him.

Dread filled Konowa. *What had Renwar done?* He looked around him at the Iron Elves. Konowa looked down at his own hands and called forth the frost fire. It sparked to life as it always had. "You didn't break the oath," Konowa said.

"*Yes, Major, I did,*" Renwar said.

"I don't understand," Konowa said. "What oath did you break?"

"Don't you see, Major," Rallie said, smiling sadly as she looked at Alwyn. "He *did* break the oath, only not yours, and not those of the living. He's freed the dead."

Konowa looked at the shades. He tried to call them forward, but they ignored him. "Why?"

"*She must be destroyed if the oath is to be broken. I could not save you as you live, but I could save those already gone. Now it is up to you to finish the fight.*"

The Iron Elves stood in stunned silence. Konowa realized that in a way he never expected he had achieved what he wanted. The power of the oath's magic remained.

"But what of my elves?" he asked.

"*She searches for them still, though she has not found them . . . yet.*"

It was small comfort, but it was something.

"Renwar, I—"

"*Alwyn's dead,*" Renwar said.

Rallie held up her hand before Konowa could reply. "Then who are you?" Rallie asked.

Renwar turned to look at her. "*I'm all that remains.*"

"Who are you?!" Konowa shouted. "Tell me who the hell you are!"

Renwar closed his eyes for a moment. A cold clarity gripped Konowa. The shades pressed closer around Renwar, their hands resting on his shoulders. When Renwar's eyes opened again, Konowa already knew the answer.

"*I am Their Emissary now.*"

GLOSSARY

Arr An aromatic, if bitter, bean grown in hot climates that when dried and then boiled in water creates a drink that awakens and revives.

Bayonet Typically a ten-inch piece of steel shaped like a dagger and attached to the end of a musket. Used primarily for close-in fighting as a stabbing weapon.

Bengar A large, carnivorous predator weighing up to eight hundred pounds and usually sporting black fur with dull red stripes, large fangs, and a short tail. The full extent of its range is unknown. One male of the species, Jir, has been adopted as mascot of the Iron Elves.

Black powder Also known as gunpowder, it is a mixture of coal, sulfur, and saltpeter that when ignited by a spark creates an explosive reaction. Used in muskets and cannons.

Blood Oath Oath taken by the Iron Elves pledging loyalty to the regiment. Due to Major Konowa Swift Dragon's possession of an obsidian acorn from the Shadow Monarch's Silver Wolf

Oak at the time of the oath, all the soldiers are now bonded to the regiment and increasingly under Her sway, in death and beyond.

Brindo A rare deer species native to Elfkyna known for its distinctive dull black hide of interlocking plates and floppy ears.

Cannon A large length of metal tube with a smooth bore that fires projectiles such as iron cannonballs over long distances. Gunpowder is used as the explosive force. Typically made of brass for smaller sizes and iron for larger ones.

Caerna Traditional Hyntaland elf garb of cloth worn around the waist and reaching to the knee. Soldiers in the Iron Elves wear caernas though the officers do not as they are often mounted on horses.

Carronade A very large, short-barreled cannon capable of firing a heavy projectile over short distances.

Colors Every regiment in the Calahrian Imperial Army carries two large flags known as the Colors into battle. Usually made of cotton with fine wool stitching, one flag bears the Queen's Royal cypher while the other the regimental crest.

Crute Rock spice chewed by dwarves. The powder is rich in mineral ores and has the side effect of turning the users teeth metallic in color.

Darkly Departed The nickname given to the shades of the dead of the Iron Elves.

Dïova Gruss Elvish, meaning a lost one, referring to an elf that has bonded with a Silver Wolf Oak and been overwhelmed by the purity of its magical powers.

Drakarri Name for drake spawn that legend suggests were the offspring of the mating between the wizard Kaman Rhal and a she-drake (dragon). The creatures walk on four legs, have large jaws filled with sharp teeth, and spit pure white fire.

Drukar A heavy, angular blade favored by many dwarves over the battle-axe for its ease of use and durability in battle.

Faeraug Also known as dog spiders, these eight-legged creatures attack their prey with a pair of curving pincers at the front of their heads.

Halberd A long pole of perhaps eight feet or more, often topped with a metal spear point and/or axe blade. Carried by N.C.O.s as an easy way to identify them on the field of battle.

Housewife Small cloth or leather pouch containing such items as a needle and thread used by soldiers to mend their uniforms.

Jewel of the Desert Name of the Star believed to be returning to the Hasshugeb Expanse.

Korwird A long and thin multi-legged creature with needle-sharp teeth much like a centipede, except *Korwirds* can grow more than twenty feet in length. Previously thought extinct.

Linstock A wooden staff that holds a length of lit cord used to ignite the gunpowder in a cannon.

Maiden Works Dwarf metal foundry specializing in weapons manufacture, especially the *drukar.*

Muraphant Standing more than fifteen feet tall with huge ears, a long trunk, and a pair of curving tusks of black ivory, the animal is used in Elfkyna to carry supplies.

Musket A muzzle-loading, smooth-bore firearm that fires lead balls by way of a gunpowder charge placed at the base of the barrel by a ramrod.

Puttee A long strip of cloth used to wrap around a soldier's leg from the ankle to below the knee.

Rakke A large, bipedal carnivore growing up to eight feet tall and known for its ferocity and willingness to attack any living thing. Once thought to have been hunted to extinction, its return is credited to the magic of the Shadow Monarch.

Ramrod A thin metal rod used to press a lead ball and powder charge down the barrel of a musket.

Red Star Also known as the Star of the East and the Star of Sillra, this Star of Knowledge and Power returned to Elfkyna during the Battle for Luuguth Jor.

Regiment The standard military unit of the Calahrian Imperial Army, comprising several hundred men armed with muskets and usually lead by an officer holding the rank of colonel.

Rok har Elvish for tree's blood, meaning tree sap. As prepared by the Elves of the Long Watch, the liquid acts to give the drinker renewed vitality.

Ryk faur/faurre Elvish for bond brother/sister referring to the magical bond that is created between an elf and a Wolf Oak.

Saber A long, curved sword used primarily by the cavalry.

Sarka har Elvish for blood tree, one of the sapling offspring of the Shadow Monarch's Silver Wolf Oak. These trees thrive on the blood of the living.

Shabraque A covering placed over a saddle to protect it from wear. This covering is typically colored and embroidered to signify the regiment the rider belongs to.

Shatterbow Double-barreled crossbow that fires explosive darts. This is Sergeant Yimt Arkhorn's main weapon.

Shako A tall, cylindrical hat with a leather peak worn by soldiers in the Calahrian Imperial Army. It is typically adorned with a metal badge, plumage, or other devices to identify a particular regiment.

Siggers Nickname given to soldiers in the Calahrian Army derived from the silver-green color of their uniform jackets.

Sreex A bird with large, leathery wings and a whiskered muzzle instead of a beak. It was once thought to be extinct.

Wolf Oak Ancient tree species able to channel the natural power of the world. They were brought to a state of sentience by the first elves, and since then form a magical bond with elves. Silver Wolf Oaks are rare and channel the purest energy. Elves bonding with a Silver Wolf Oak typically are unable to cope with the energy and become *dïova gruss* as they lose themselves in the natural order of the world.

ACKNOWLEDGMENTS

At the writing of this I don't have children, or pets, or even plants—living ones anyway—plants I mean, but I do have family and friends, and my gratitude for their continuing support only grows. The act of writing might be a solitary pursuit, but being a writer doesn't have to be.

There are two intrepid souls who step fearlessly into the breach time and again as my first readers: my brother Michael and my great friend and artist/writer, Deb Christerson, both of whom read the manuscript multiple times and still profess to like it . . . and me. Now, that's friendship.

Equally important in providing encouragement and advice are three exceptional people I met early on in my publishing career. Shelly Shapiro, Chris Schluep, and Bill Takes are great counselors in all things publishing, but even better friends, and I am a better writer, and person, for knowing them.

There's an ever-expanding group of friends who worked especially hard to keep me sane, healthy, and focused, and to them my debt is high. Whether it was a well-timed joke, a swift kick in the creative process, or simply being there, they made the writing of this book both possible and enjoyable: my aunts, Nancy Whitson and Brenda Sandusky; Col. Robert Black and his wife, Carolyn; Edith Dunker; Peter Ferk; Karen Traviss; Natalie Wessel; and Jeff Young all deserve my sincerest thanks, and they have it.

I want to make special mention of my editor at Pocket Books, Ed Schlesinger. Ed patiently and skillfully talked me through the sophomore issues of a second novel, a task made all the more challenging as, being an editor myself, I know just enough to be really dangerous to the whole process. Ed's expert guidance made sure everything was smooth sailing.

Thanks, too, to Pocket Books Deputy Publisher Anthony Ziccardi and my agent, Don Maass, for their strong and unwavering support in building my career. I couldn't have asked for two brighter, or more dedicated, publishing professionals in this regard.

I drew support and encouragement from many others in many different quarters—Mike Bechthold, Charles Coleman Finlay, Rome Quezada, Peter Rossi, Shawn Speakman, Jessica Strider, Mark Zug, the superlative staff at the New York Society Library, and the Gracie Mews diner for helping to feed my mind and body; at S&S UK, Sally Partington; at Pocket Books, publisher Louise Burke, Barry Porter, Melissa Gramstad, Lisa Keim, Amre Klimchak, Kerrie Loyd, Jean Anne Rose, and Alan Dingman; and at Stackpole Books, president and fellow author David Detweiler, Janelle Bender, Cathy Craley, Anne Lodge-Smith, David Reisch, web designer Tessa Sweigert, and my other publisher and supporter, Judith Schnell.

And finally—and always—my parents. Without them, I would not be where I am, or who I am, today.

Chris Evans
New York City, March 2009

आय १२ १०/११ ५ २/११